Books by

STAR FORCE SERIES
Swarm
Extinction
Rebellion
Conquest
Battle Station
Empire
Annihilation

IMPERIUM SERIES
Mech Zero: The Dominant
Mech 1: The Parent
Mech 2: The Savant
Mech 3: The Empress
Five By Five (Mech Novella)

OTHER SF BOOKS
Technomancer
The Bone Triangle
Z-World
Velocity

Visit BVLarson.com for more information.

BATTLE STATION

(Star Force Series #5)
by
B. V. Larson

STAR FORCE SERIES

Copyright © 2012 by the author.

ISBN-13: 978-1477637142
ISBN-10: 1477637141
BISAC: Fiction / Science Fiction / Adventure

-1-

My scattered fleet looked like broken shards of glass, glinting in the wan light of a distant star. Counting my own ship, the surviving task force consisted of twenty-three destroyers and seventeen frigates. I'd arranged them in a circular pattern around an alien artifact of unknown origin. This artifact was known to us as a *ring*, a vast loop of dark material, similar in nature to rock, but closer in density to the collapsed matter found at the core of dead suns.

The ring orbited a small world which was the last in a long line of planets, the furthest from the system's single yellow star. While unusual, it was not unprecedented to find a ring associated with a planet. We'd found other cases that were similar. The Venus ring was buried in the planet's crust, and a small ring back on Helios had been located at the center of one of the termite-mound cities of the native population.

The icy world below was composed primarily of nickel, iron and frozen ammonia. It orbited a yellow star I'd named Eden. The planet's surface was heavily frosted by cyrovolcanoes that periodically spewed out unpleasant liquids. These events were dramatic spectacles. Ammonia and methane bubbled up from the planet's guts when tidal forces heated up the interior. Once these liquids reached the surface, they quickly froze into vast crystalline plains.

The ring sailed around this inhospitable planet with us, as cold and dark as the world below. I'd spent a long week staring at this ancient alien structure which connected the Eden system to—somewhere else. It was galling, not knowing what undiscovered star system was on the far side. I'd thought about sending scouts through a dozen times, but had always vetoed the idea. I knew the Macros might be waiting to blast us on the far side. They often seemed to operate on the basis of a triggering event, and I didn't want to give them the opportunity to come at us again with renewed vigor. We just weren't ready yet. My current plan was simple: if the Macros poked their snout out of that hole, we planned to blow it off for them. Otherwise, we'd wait.

The waiting was not easy. The ring was like a siren's call. To be instantly transported to another system was exhilarating enough, but not to know what was on the far side of a structure that was only a few miles distant was positively maddening. The ring was ten miles in diameter, and there was plenty of room to fly all our ships through it— but we didn't dare.

After spending a long hour in my ship's observatory, staring at the ring and the cold, dark world below, I decided I didn't really like the name Eden-21. The name was only temporary, of course. I decided to allow my marines to name this dismal rock. I set up a pool to give the place a more suitable title.

My troops were bored, and bored people tend to become overly concerned with small things. There were arguments and lotteries. After putting it to a vote, the winning name was "Hel" the Norse name for a frozen version of an unpleasant afterlife.

I had to smile. It was a fitting name for this unforgiving rock, and those stationed here would at least have the pleasure of reveling in jokes that would never get old: *At our duty-station, Hel has frozen over—permanently.*

* * *

Two weeks passed, during which I conversed with Crow at Star Force headquarters twice. The round trip time for a message all the way to Earth and back was roughly three days. I was overdue for Crow's next response.

The first message had been initiated by me, and had contained the welcome news of victory. I'd chased the Macros out of the Eden system, thus liberating the Centaurs as we'd promised to do months ago. Three days later, I'd gotten Crow's reply:

Congratulations, Colonel! Fantastic work! Please return as soon as you secure the Eden system. Earth needs every vessel we have to defend our home skies. Again, congratulations, superlative work!
—Admiral Jack Crow

I'd waited a number of hours before sending my response. Somehow, I didn't think he'd like my next note, so why rush things?

Admiral Crow: all remains quiet here on the far front, but it is not yet secure. First, we'll have to clean enemy forces off the local worlds to free them for the Centaurs. Next, I plan to build a permanent fortification here at the ring orbiting Hel to seal off enemy access to our systems from this direction. We need heavy production facilities to build the new fortifications. Please send eight factories. Do not worry about providing raw materials, we have plenty of those in close proximity.
—Colonel Kyle Riggs

After sending off that note, I knew somehow I wasn't going to be congratulated again when the next message arrived. Crow and I rarely saw eye-to-eye on strategy. His take on things was usually very defensive and, in my opinion, self-serving. He didn't care much if we left Eden and the Macros came rolling back to enslave the Centaurs again. What he cared about was the number of ships defending Earth and his own personal posterior.

I couldn't condemn him entirely for his conservative ideas, of course. In the end, maybe he would turn out to be right. Maybe trying to take four systems and hold them was too much for Earth right now. I would freely admit that I might turn out to be the fool today. But I couldn't give up on all these territorial gains without a fight. We had the advantage, at least momentarily, and I wanted to seize it and milk it for all it was worth.

When Crow's response did finally come in, it was as I expected:

Colonel Riggs, perhaps I did not make myself clear. You are hereby ordered to return all Star Force Fleet units to the Solar System. Feel free to leave a few ships behind, including one at each ring for purposes of communication and surveillance.

Kyle, I know you have big ideas, and I appreciate that. But I can't spare factories or ships. We must rebuild, mate! You won by a thread out there, don't push it!
—*Admiral Crow*

I sat in my command chair, brooding. There were three other officers aboard *Barbarossa*, and they were all avoiding eye contact. I heaved a sigh, read the message again, and then deleted it with gloved fingers tapping hard on the screen.

I had to make a decision. Was I going to obey what seemed like a reasonable order from headquarters, or was I going to ignore the recall and possibly shake up our command structure?

I sat there for several more long minutes in my contoured chair. Growing bored with that, I stood up and paced around the bridge. There wasn't a lot of room for this, so it wasn't terribly satisfying. No one aboard the destroyer spoke to me. Even Marvin, who tracked me with two of his cameras as I paced, said nothing. They had to have some clue as to what I was thinking. They may not know what the message from Crow said, but they could guess what it was about.

I thought about the men around me. They were loyal. Probably, most of them were more personally loyal to me rather than to Star Force itself. Throughout history, when a charismatic leader led troops into grim campaigns and won through, his troops tended to trust him more than their own governments. Julius Caesar had marched home with his own loyal legion from Gaul one day and crossed the Rubicon River. At that point, he'd become a rebel. Unlike most rebels, his rebellion was successful.

I wasn't ready for that kind of thing—not yet at least, and probably never. I did feel some sympathy for old Julius, however. He must have gotten orders he didn't like from distant Rome. He must have felt he was the unappreciated hero in the field, tired of the fat gray-beards back home who sought to micromanage him from afar. Interstellar distances had taken us backward in time as far as military communications went. It now took days for messages to be transmitted to headquarters and back. There was no instant, live-feed video, connecting us firmly to Earth.

"I'm ordering a staff meeting," I announced over the command channel. "Commodore Decker, Captain Miklos, Marvin and Kwon, I want all of you in on this. We'll meet in the troop pod on *Barbarossa* in thirty minutes."

Commodore Decker was the last to arrive at the meeting. He paused at the entrance, staring at the assembled group. Captain Miklos was missing large sections of hair and his exposed scalp was covered in purplish-red weals. He'd been pretty badly banged-up in the recent fleet battles with the Macros. It was only due to the miracle-working nanites in his system he was able to sit at the conference table I'd shaped from the floor of the ship for the occasion. Kwon sat across from Miklos, a hulking noncom that looked out of place at any formal meeting. He barely fit into his battle suit, even though it was the largest size we made. Last, and certainly not least, was the freak Marvin had become.

Marvin had given himself another makeover in recent days. To the uninitiated—which definitely included the gaping Commodore—he was horrifying to gaze upon. Formed of a mass of nanite-streams and struts with random pieces of equipment poking out here and there, he was vaguely humanoid in shape. The most disconcerting thing about him had to be the whipping arms. There were seven of them, all of varied lengths. He used these snake-like independent tentacles to drag himself around, slithering like an octopus out of water. In order to keep his mass upright, several of these tentacles tended to grasp the backs of other people's chairs for support. A dozen camera eyes poked out of his body-mass from his knee-joints and the tips of extra tentacles. Every camera simultaneously moved and tracked something different, adding to the distraction.

"What the hell is that?" Decker asked.

"That's Marvin," I said, as if the robot were the most natural thing in the world to encounter. "Don't be rude, Commodore. I'm considering him for a commission in Star Force."

"You want to make that contraption into an officer?"

"Excuse me, Commodore," Marvin interrupted. "Is my appearance somehow disturbing?"

"Positively nightmarish."

"I apologize. I'd thought by taking on a body mass that approximates human configurations, I would be more acceptable."

I nodded. "Ignore the Commodore's bigotry, Marvin. It's only natural. Once people get to know you, they will be less frightened."

The Commodore snorted at this. He straightened his spine and took one of the chairs. The entrance vanished behind him, turning into a smooth nanite wall again. I suppressed a smile. Off-handedly referring to him as a cowardly bigot had gotten him to move his butt to the table where I wanted it. In truth, I had sympathy for Decker's reaction—Marvin was a metal terror. But I didn't like Decker, and I needed to get him past worrying about Marvin.

"May I make a suggestion, Marvin," Kwon said, leaning toward the robot.

Several cameras swung toward Kwon, who sat at Marvin's side. "Of course."

Of all the people who'd met Marvin, only Kwon seemed undaunted by his current configuration. He hadn't even made a remark up until this point regarding the robot's appearance.

"You do look vaguely human in shape, but with extra—things here and there," Kwon said. "Humans often find large people intimidating. I'm a big man, so I know all about that. Perhaps you could reduce your physical size if you want to put people more at ease."

I nodded, thinking it was good advice. I listened to Marvin's response with interest.

"I will consider your suggestion at my next point of reconfiguration. The process of choosing my non-ship form is not yet complete. I must weigh many considerations when redesigning myself. This form has excellent sensory input, but it has poor locomotion capabilities under the influence of gravity. I'd originally designed it for a zero-G environment."

"The thing designs *itself*?" asked Commodore Decker.

"Absolutely," I said. "He rebuilds his body when it suits him, much as a man might select a new outfit for dinner.'"

Decker's eyes flicked back to me. "You brought a sumo sergeant and a renegade robot to this meeting? Is this some kind of attempt to intimidate me, Colonel?"

He had figured it out faster than I'd expected. I waved my hand at the group and denied everything. "These are my confidants. The veterans of Star Force. I'm sorry if they don't meet with your approval."

Decker heaved a sigh and put his elbows on the table. "Okay, I'm over worrying about your crew, Riggs. Let's get down to business."

We all looked at him.

"I'm assuming you received the recall message from headquarters," Decker said. "In fact, I know you did, and I know exactly what it said."

My face tightened. I reminded myself to ask Marvin if he'd finished the new secure command messaging system. This business of publicly emailing orders from star system to star system wasn't going to be acceptable any longer. I'd put up with it so far because the system was only a few weeks old. But now we needed to be able to keep messages private. Especially orders I didn't like.

My first thought was to yell at the Commodore, delivering a new, perfectly clear message regarding what I thought of his reading everything that came in from Fleet. But I held back, telling myself the situation was better out in the open. He'd come forward and put his cards on the table. I could appreciate that.

"Commodore, you'll be glad to hear that I've decided to comply with the orders."

Decker looked honestly surprised. I found this amusing. Did I really have that bad of a rep? I supposed that I did.

"Well, I—that's excellent, Colonel. When do we fly?"

"Immediately," I said.

Decker demeanor changed from surprised to enthusiastic. I could tell he relished the idea of getting back home to Earth. I couldn't say I blamed him for that.

"I recommend a column formation," he gushed. "That way, we will limit our exposure to mines. There are a lot of them out there, most of them undocumented. We can put the destroyers in the vanguard, as they possess our best point-defense weaponry. If—"

I interrupted him with a gauntleted hand, which I raised into the air. "The destroyers won't be going home, Commodore. At least, not most of them."

His mouth opened, closed, and then opened again. "What?" he demanded when he managed to absorb my statement.

"Just as I said. Most of the destroyers will be staying. I'm posting one at each ring. Each vessel will contain a full complement of marines in their troop pods. They will provide security and serve to relay messages back to Earth. Then there is this destroyer, *Barbarossa*—I'll keep it as a command ship. My own personal ship, *Socorro*, will be staying as well. Most of the rest of them will be remaining behind as my core task force. I need the ships to mop up the system and defend against any future attempt to reconquer it."

"You can't do that! Our orders are clear, Colonel."

"Indeed they are," I said. "Let's review the orders, shall we?"

I read Crow's words out loud, emphasizing the line: *Please return as soon as you secure the Eden system.* Followed by: *Feel free to leave a few ships behind, including one at each ring for purposes of communication and surveillance.*

"He didn't mean you could keep the destroyers!" Decker sputtered. "This will not stand, sir. Mark my words, this will not stand!"

"You can mark them all you want from the deck of your command ship—which will be an empty frigate on the way home, I'm afraid. Dismissed."

Decker stormed out, leaving me with the rest of them.

"You seem to have upset the Commodore," Marvin said.

"The Colonel does that all the time," Kwon said, laughing in his unique, hitching way.

"Kwon, have you secured the ship's armories?" I asked.

"Yes sir, already done."

"Marvin, have you rerouted the ship's messaging system yet?"

"Yes Colonel," Marvin said. "All communications will go through me now—literally. I've automated the system and the processor load should be quite low. I've set up a series of key phrases and conditions to flag questionable messages for your personal approval before they are allowed to be transmitted or received."

I turned to Captain Miklos next, who had listened throughout the meeting without making any comments. "Captain, are the new ship rosters ready? I want those crews remixed before Decker pulls out."

"Yes sir," Miklos said. "You're longstanding veterans are all moving onto the destroyers. May I say something, Colonel?"

I nodded.

"I find the entire process of commandeering these ships disturbing. Is it absolutely necessary?"

"I feel that it is."

"Very good, sir."

The meeting broke up. Everyone left quickly, as they all had something urgent to do. I watched them go with mixed feelings. I hadn't crossed the Rubicon yet, but I'd certainly given Crow a good look at my middle finger. I wondered how it would all turn out in the end.

-2-

When avoiding the intent of your orders, but not completely blowing them off, it is important to maintain appearances. Therefore, I decided to "clean up the system" as my first action. There were plenty of Macros running around on the local planets, and I meant to eradicate them.

I had ulterior motives to choosing this course of action. One was to appear to be following orders—but there were other reasons. I wanted the Macros dead, of course. And I wanted to help the Centaurs regain their lands as I'd promised them I would. But more than that, I wanted factories. I couldn't run a campaign on what we had with us this time, which was a single factory. *Socorro* had the sole production unit. As my command staff split up and went to perform their various duties, I crossed over to *Socorro*. I quickly reassigned the two-man crew to Decker's group, bidding them a fond farewell. They exited with bitter glances back at me. *Good riddance,* I thought, even as I beamed and waved at them.

Once aboard *Socorro*, I ceremoniously changed the locks. This amounted to altering all the passwords and resetting the rules as to who was allowed to board and command her. Essentially, I reduced the list to a single person: me.

I stretched out on my command chair and heaved a sigh. "It's good to be home, Socorro."

"We are in the Eden system."

"Yeah, but for a Star Force veteran, home is found in the guts of a friendly ship."

11

"Reference stored. Welcome home, Colonel."

I chuckled. *Socorro* had advanced since I'd built her. I'd designed this ship with a dozen variations in comparison to other Nano ships. She had more engines, better sensors, and a bigger brainbox. When the ship had started out life she'd not been overly perceptive. As time went on, she became as savvy as any Nano ship—but now, I sensed she'd advanced further. Her nanite chains were more complex, even sophisticated. She'd spent a lot of time with humans and I could tell she understood us better than the original Nano ships, which had more rigid programming and more limited mental capacities.

Strangely, I really did feel at home. Sandra and I had taken a few adventurous voyages on this ship. We'd made love frequently, and nearly died almost as often. I walked the ship's nanite-sculpted rooms, starting with the observatory. I saw the cracks in the glass floor had been repaired. Looking out into space, I was instantly captivated by the scene.

Using magnification systems I'd had installed, I was able to directly view many of the twenty-one worlds in this system. Hel was one of the farthest out from the local G-class star. Looking sunward, I was able to pick out most of the life-bearing warm water worlds. There were six of them, and I meant to cover them all with intelligent biotics.

I rubbed my chin, looking at those lovely worlds. Each was a prize all by itself. So many worlds! Compared to the Solar System, Eden was capable of supporting a trillion living beings. I had to admit, it was overwhelming, and I felt a hint of greed.

Did I have to return all these worlds to the Centaurs? Surely, with their vastly reduced numbers, *one* world could be given to the humans. Either that, or we could share the land with them.

I frowned, considering. I knew the herds fairly well now. They weren't just different culturally, they were a different species entirely. Historically, humans had a hard time getting along with their own kind due to relatively minor differences. Perhaps it would be best if we lived apart, to allow them to rule their worlds the way they wanted, while we ran a planet or two as we saw fit.

I shook my head and took a deep breath. I was getting way ahead of myself. These worlds still crawled with Macro machines and the Centaurs hadn't agreed to any of my fanciful ideas. Possibly, they'd object strongly to giving up a single blade of grass once the planets were recaptured. Just as plausible, the Macros might come back before we could secure this system and wipe us all out.

Deciding to go into the situation with an open mind as to the outcome, I headed below decks next to check on the ship's single factory. It wasn't running at the moment. I hadn't brought along any raw materials for it to work with. With the factories, time was the critical factor. They took time to make things, and therefore every second it spent idle was a second wasted.

"Captain Miklos," I said, opening up a channel to the command ship. "I need raw materials."

"Materials, sir? What kind of materials?"

"The usual. Base metals, rare earths, radioactives and polymers. Everything a factory requires to churn out weapons and constructive nanites in quantity."

"We have factories, Colonel?"

"Yes," I said. "We have one, anyway. Have the pilots collect wreckage. We destroyed a number of Macros in this part of space and their floating hulks should be treasure troves of raw materials. Have them bring the wrecks to me."

"Yes sir," Miklos said, then another voice interrupted our conversation.

"I could help in this instance, sir," Marvin said. "I'm well-equipped for gathering materials. I would find the study of damaged Macro systems infinitely—"

"No, Marvin. I don't think so. Not this time. I have another duty for you. An important one. Come over to my ship as soon as you can."

"I see," he said. "What is the nature of this new assignment?"

Was that a hint of disappointment in his voice? If so, that was just too bad. I didn't want Marvin building himself into a ship again. It had taken me weeks to trim him down to size the last time.

"I need you to translate for me. I want to talk to the Centaurs. Please transport yourself into my presence."

"Is physical transference completely necessary for—"

"Yes, it is," I said, growing annoyed. Marvin wasn't like most of my marines. They didn't always like or even understand my orders, but they didn't argue with them all the time.

"On my way, sir," he said, after a brief hesitation.

When we were alone aboard *Socorro*, Marvin dragged himself into the command module and sprawled on the second chair. It didn't really

13

fit, and in truth it looked damned uncomfortable, with all his tentacles flopping out and lolling on the deck like the tongues of tired dogs. But I knew he didn't feel physical discomfort, so I didn't worry about it.

"Before I have you get me into contact with the Centaurs, Marvin, I want to make sure there is no risk of an unauthorized download from them."

"That should no longer be a problem, Colonel. I've restructured my ports and access protocols. No transmission from an outside source can erase my brainbox now."

The last time we'd conversed with the Centaurs, their servers had automatically attempted to erase Marvin's mind. This wasn't due to any kind of ill will on their part, it was just an automatic subsystem trying to do its job. Marvin had been an incomplete copy of a system image from one of their brainboxes in the first place. When we'd left the Eden system the last time, they had not quite finished transmitting his mind to our ship. The missing elements in his mind had sought completion, and had resulted in the quirky creature I'd come to consider—well, if not a friend, then an ally at least.

"Good," I said, "I don't want your brain erased and turned into a boring alien-translation robot."

"We agree on that point, Colonel."

"Let's give it a try then. Connect me to the Centaurs."

"They are listening now. I connected the channel the moment you made the request."

"You mean, before you even walked aboard *Socorro?*"

"Yes."

I grumbled and muttered under my breath for a time. Marvin made a lousy secretary. I cleared my throat, trying to form a coherent thought. I was quite glad I hadn't said anything that would insult the Centaurs or reveal any details of my plans that they might not like. I opened my mouth to speak, but the Centaurs beat me to it.

"Colonel Kyle Riggs," said Marvin, speaking as the Centaurs. The effect was an odd one, reminding me of listening to a medium at a séance. "We have witnessed your glorious path through our skies. Our young kick and surge with high spirits. Your honor is our honor, and the paths of our herds know no swollen rivers between them."

"Um," I said, "That's great. We feel the same way."

When talking to the Centaurs, it was always the same. They were a herd people who spoke in their own idioms most of the time. They always talked about blue skies, green fields, winds, fur, hooves and honor—above all, honor.

I realized I had to make something of a speech. This could not be a normal conversation. It would take an hour or more for my transmission to be sent to the Centaurs and back again. Even at the speed of light, Hel was a long way out from the inner planets.

"Herds of Eden," I said, "we've returned as we said we would. We have driven the machines from your skies. But they still walk upon your green fields. They must be destroyed on land, sea and air, as well as in space. In order to do this, we must work together. I need information on your combat readiness. Do you have landing craft that can assault the worlds below your satellites? Do you have a force of trained soldiers that can aid with that assault, or any other assets you can explain to me now, such as fighter spacecraft?"

I took a map, checked on the factory and waited calmly for a long time while the message flew out into the void and eventually returned with their response. "Our people float in steel worlds above the clouds of our real worlds. Forced into exile as part of our agreement with the machines, we walked the long walk upward, spiraling into the sky. Many fell, but the strong and honorable never took a misstep. Those that survive in the steel worlds have no path downward. We do, however, have vast herds ready to assault the machines. They have no honor, having used your herd to injure us after promising not to. Our agreements with them are at an end. If you can carry us to the surface of our worlds, we will astonish the machines with our numbers, and our ferocity! They will sing woefully, having never met a people so willing to salt the grasses with blood to regain lost lands."

After that, the Centaurs delved more deeply into the topic of honor, the details of its loss and gain, and how the machines were bastards who had none. This went on for some time, until I was drumming my gauntleted fingers on my command chair. I stopped listening with more than half my mind, figuring I could order Marvin to replay the speech later if I felt it necessary.

Overall, things sounded worse than I'd hoped. They had no ships to return to their worlds. They'd been stuck in their satellites, due to their agreement with the Macros. It didn't sound like they had a whole lot of weaponry, either. What they had was a large herd of willing Centaurs, anxious to die for the cause, to fight the good fight. That was pretty much it.

15

Taking in a deep breath and letting it out slowly, I tuned out the Centaurs entirely. They were now onto the topic of clear, empty skies. Whenever one of them began singing that song, you were in for a long serenade. They clearly missed their open skies above all else. Being a claustrophobic race, they felt closed-in even while inside satellites that were many miles across.

When the speech ended at last, I turned to Marvin. "Stop transmission," I said, "but don't close the channel. I want to talk to you first."

"Done."

"What's this about them taking a long walk up to the satellites? Do you understand that? How could anyone *walk* to a satellite?"

"I believe they are talking about the umbilicals."

I stared at him. "You mean those satellites are tethered to the planetary surfaces?"

"They once were, yes. The Macros severed those ties as part of their agreement."

I nodded and leaned back in my chair. I recalled the Centaur satellites. I'd only been there for a short time, but I'd found them impressive. "A spiraling walk," I said aloud. "As I recall, they had tubes which led to the top of their satellite. They used narrow, spiraling walkways that only a mountain goat could feel at home upon. That must be what they mean."

I had a very strange image form in my mind then: millions of Centaurs forced to walk up an endless spiraling tube all the way into orbit. These people didn't have spaceships, or at least, they no longer had any. They'd gotten up into their floating cities by walking there, then the Macros had cut the cord on them, sealing them in the sky forever.

"They said something about many of them falling," I said thoughtfully. "Nasty."

Marvin didn't make any comments. He studied me with about five cameras. Other cameras were taking in views from the observatory, which I now noticed he'd opened at some point. Extending a tentacle like a reeled out hose, he had a cluster of cameras at the tip of it. He was busy examining the views afforded by the glass-bottomed room. I couldn't blame him for that. The Centaurs had left my mind wandering as well.

"Open channel again," I said.

"Done."

"Centaurs of Eden," I said. "We do not have enough ships to drive the Macros from your worlds. We do have enough to transport your bravest warriors down to the surface where they can run free, however. They will have to fight well, and every one of them will have to be armed with heavy laser packs. After the planets are free of the machines, we can help by transporting your population down to the surface. Does this plan suit your needs?"

Eventually, the reply came back. Before it did, I'd made myself dinner and eaten it.

"We accept your offer with equal measures of thanks and trepidation. How large are these transports? Will there be a sky to watch, during the flight? Will the walls be far enough from the herds to allow them to run at full gallop?"

I snorted. "No, I'm afraid not. There will be only enough room for your bodies to stand quietly, shoulder-to-shoulder on the way down. But think, although this time might be difficult for you, it will be very brief. No more than a few minutes of crowding before you are free again on the surface of your natural worlds. Surely, your herds have the bravery and honor to withstand five minutes of discomfort!"

The reply came back and seemed injured in tone. "It is not a matter of honor. It is not a matter of bravery, or discomfort. It is a matter of the mind. We cannot withstand long periods enclosed. We will lose our wits. We must be able to see the sky."

When I heard that, I took off my gauntlets and gave my head a good scratching. I could just see it, transporting down a wild mass of crazed mountain goats to a planetary surface. What would they do? Kick and gore one another to death? Chew off their own tongues in a bloody froth while bleating and rolling their eyes in temporary insanity? I supposed I didn't want to know. After a while, however, I came up with a plan. I could test it, and if it worked, I would employ it with their thousands and transport a vast army.

"All right," I said at last. "I'll take care of your concerns. Is there anything else you need before I prepare to invade Eden-11?"

When the answer finally came, I had dozed off. It seemed as if this reply had taken longer than usual to come in. Perhaps it had. Often, when asked a complex question, the Centaurs discussed it among themselves at length before answering.

17

"We have only a single, overriding need. You must maintain the honor you have gained. Keep the sweet winds in your fur. Return us to our worlds, and help us regain all was taken from us. Never allow the reflection of the sky to leave our eyes. In return, our millions will march with you to our sacred deaths."

"I promise," I said. And meant it.

We broke the connection then, and I fell asleep in my command chair.

-3-

I had a few days before we would be ready to fly to the Centaur satellites and begin our trial runs. During this time, I used all the destroyers to gather raw materials from the battlefield. We'd need more than factories to build the things I needed. We'd need raw materials, too.

During this time I became curious about what was going on beyond the ring we guarded. Was a task force of Macros massing out there, getting ready to invade the Eden system and destroy all our plans? What kind of a system was on the far side, anyway?

I laid mines in front of the ring while I thought about it. That's what I set the single factory I had to producing: thousands upon thousands of mines. I could have sent a ship nosing through the ring to have a look around at any time during this operation, but I didn't dare. At their core, the Macros were computers. If you've ever dealt with an artificial intelligence, you know how such minds tend to behave. They might stand quietly, motionless and seemingly asleep for a long time. But eventually, some kind of trigger is met, and at that point they spring into action. Getting too near one of these things altered its behavior. If they were gathering on the far side, they might well do so for months, waiting until they reached a preset count of ships. Only then would they move. But if I dared to change the game, they would change their plans and respond to the stimulus. Generally, with the Macros, I'd found stimulating them too much was bad for your health.

Still, despite knowing the risks, I couldn't help wondering if I could get away with taking a peek on the other side. Perhaps not a ship—that would be too much. But what about a single man in a suit? A cold, emission-free, stealth-suit. If such a hypothetical man had a camera say, and other passive sensory equipment, he would probably escape notice entirely. The idea tempted me more as every hour passed.

The logical thing to do would be to send Marvin or Kwon or someone less valuable. But I wanted to see the new system myself. Call me crazy, but until you've explored star systems personally, you can't understand the allure.

I kept thinking about taking a little walk outside, maybe a jaunt around the circumference of my ship. The idea worked on my mind like a siren's call. If Sandra or Crow had been around to talk me out of it, maybe I never would have gone.

But they weren't.

"Colonel Riggs?" Marvin asked the day I was finally geared up and ready to go.

"What?"

"Take me with you."

I chuckled. "This isn't anything important, Marvin," I said. "I just want to suit-up and examine the ring visually. Cameras can only tell you so much. I'm sure you understand."

Marvin looked me up and down with his numerous camera eyes. "Your optical organs are superior to cameras?"

"Yes," I said. "They probably are. Analog input is generally inferior, but in this case I'd take it over digital any day."

"Interesting," Marvin said.

Several of his cameras investigated my suit. It was my normal battle suit, but it had been carefully altered. Instead of the blue glowing LEDs covering it like a Christmas tree, it was jet black. It was as dark as space itself. I'd also taken pains to disconnect the heat sinks and all automatic radio transponders. Unless I keyed open a microphone, it wouldn't generate any form of emissions.

"You've made a number of preparations for this—spacewalk."

"Yes Marvin, and I thank you for your help in that regard."

Marvin watched me closely as I stepped to the airlock and the nanite bubble covering the entrance dissolved away, and I stepped inside. It would be a relief to escape Marvin's probing. He obviously knew something was up.

"Colonel Riggs?"

"What is it now?"

"I still want to go with you. If I promise not to transmit anything, can I go?"

"Go where? Outside the ship? You do that all the time."

"No—I want to go through the ring, with you."

I heaved a sigh. How should I handle this one? Evasion wasn't working out for me this time. Worse, if Marvin had figured it out, others might do the same.

"I can't take you with me," I said. "It's too dangerous. You'll emit a radio squawk or something and give us away. Even a small amount of propulsion might be noticed. You have heat sinks and your repellers give off a distinct signature."

"I've been working on that."

I frowned. "You have?"

"Yes, I've been watching your preparations, and I understand them. I might even know more about this than you do, Colonel. Recall that I once spent days in a Macro-owned system while they hunted me unsuccessfully."

"Yeah, and you made a deal with them to sell us out for the privilege of snooping around."

"That was an error. It will not happen again."

"Only because the Macros are on to you, and have you marked down in some database as kill-on-sight."

Marvin's cameras reshuffled themselves. "Do you want to see my preparations?"

"All right," I said, becoming curious. "What have you got?"

He scooted into the airlock with me and waited expectantly. His cameras flicked from my face to my hands and back to the wall. Touching the appropriate area would bring up a touch-sensitive radial menu in metallic relief.

"I take it you want to go outside?"

"My auxiliary systems would not fit in the ship."

I laughed. He had me now, and we both knew it. I wanted to see what he had built for himself. I wondered if he had banked on my curiosity, and if that was part of his scheme. Marvin was always scheming.

I gave up and reached out to touch the outer wall. The wall vanished, and we floated out into space with the escaping gasses. I let it happen, leaving my magnetics off. I had a number of low emission methods to maneuver myself as needed. Behind me, I dragged a garbage-can-sized sensor box, which I'd set to strictly passive mode. I was sure it wasn't going to send out any pings and give us away. It would only record everything around us.

A more analytical soul might have pointed out that sending a man on this mission—namely me—was not strictly necessary. All I had to do was send a sensor unit with Marvin or even by itself. When it got whatever input it could, it could be programmed to return and allow me to examine the data in relative safety.

But that just wasn't good enough for me. I felt a place hadn't truly been explored until a human eye had examined it in person. I'd always been bored by the endless army of roving little robots NASA sent out to roam over Mars or swing around between Jupiter's moons. The human experience could not be discounted. Moreover, this ring was only a mile or two from my ship. It seemed like a crime to ignore it, to pass up the thrill of that first investigation.

Once I was outside the ship, I didn't see much other than *Socorro's* smoothly curved hull. The yellow sun glared from the surface, blinding me if I looked in that direction. Stretched below was the dark, icy hulk of Hel. It gleamed brightly with reflected frost on the sunward side, while the other half was encased in clinging shadows.

Marvin slid away down *Socorro's* hull to the underbelly of the ship. There, something dark and angular was attached to the hull. Marvin conjoined with this mass, and I frowned as I watched it. Was it a suit or a miniature spaceship? I supposed it was a little of both.

"Marvin, I don't recall giving you permission to build anything like this. I thought we'd clipped your wings. Where did you get these materials?"

Marvin made a hissing sound. I realized after a bemused second he was shushing me. A long, snaking tentacle came out to attach itself to my suit. It was a com-line. The intercom light blinked on my HUD, so I activated it. We were now able to converse suit-to-suit, over a nanite wire, without making any transmissions.

"I feel we should dampen all our emissions from now on, sir," Marvin said.

"Why?"

"Not everyone will approve of our mission."

"Since when did this become *our* mission?"

"The point of pronoun conversion occurred when you gave me permission to accompany you."

I would have grumbled further, but I knew it was useless. "Okay, so what is that thing you are climbing into?"

"The largest problem I had to solve was one of propulsion," Marvin explained. "Emissions from any normal form of energy or mass expulsion cause a visible signature."

"I solved that one myself," I said.

"How?"

I pulled up a reel with a winding chain of nanites on it. The nanites were organized into a thick, long strand that resembled a quivering hose. "This nanite strand has been trained to operate like an intelligent rope. I plan to attach one end to me, and apply a tiny amount of thrust on this side of the ring. After reeling me out on this tether, it's programmed to draw me back to this side of the ring after a preset time, or if I give the nanites a signal."

Marvin made a clicking sound of disapproval. "No, too dangerous."

"Why's that?"

"The ring will be activated the entire time you are on the other side, using that plan."

"Ohhh," I said, drawing out the sound. I thought hard, and realized he was probably right. The rings normally gave off a blip of power whenever any object passed through them. This wasn't anything special to worry about, as drifting bits of debris commonly floated through and were transferred to the other side. But if I used my nanite-tether, and stayed on the far side for ten minutes, that would mean the ring would be active for all that time. The Macros might well notice and come to investigate that sort of anomaly.

"Well—maybe you're right. But you still haven't explained your solution."

"Some kind of mass or energy must be expended to reverse course and return. I simply went with the least detectable form of emissions. In this case, frozen ammonia."

"Frozen ammonia? From the planet surface?"

"Yes."

"When did you go down there?"

"When you weren't paying attention."

I snorted. "All right, so you rigged up some kind of jet that sprays out frozen ammonia, which should look like a natural occurrence. And that pressure is enough to blast you back to this side of the ring?"

"I believe all my calculations are correct."

I hesitated, mulling it over. His contraption looked like a bobsled. He'd already gotten himself wrapped up in it. "Is there enough gas for two bodies to ride on that thing?"

"In anticipation of this possible situation, I've built the system with a second berth."

I laughed, wondering how I'd gone from being the man with the plan, the man in charge, to hitching a ride on Marvin's ice-ship. I climbed into the framework of dark tubing and clamped my battle suit's gauntlets on the railing. "How much thrust does this thing—"

I didn't finish the sentence. Marvin's little space-scooter shot away from *Socorro's* hull and in moments we were plunging toward the ring. We had to be doing fifty miles an hour before he cut off the frosty blast of pressurized gas that plumed behind us.

"Too fast!" I shouted at him. "Remember, we have to turn around and blast our way back to this side."

"We are simulating a recent passage of matter through the ring. If we are moving at too slow a rate, and they have radar systems detecting us, we'll be noticed by the software."

I reflected on his worry. He had a point. When you were driving on the highway, doing thirty miles an hour was at least as noticeable as doing ninety.

I didn't have much more time to protest in any case, because about then we passed through the ring, and everything around us changed.

The first thing I saw was the twin suns. It was impossible not to look at them, as they were quite close and bright, and immediately caught the eye. The two stars were near one another. The larger of the two was a white F class star, slightly bigger and hotter than Sol. Next to it floated a tiny red dwarf. The smaller, dimmer star circled the waist of its bigger sibling, and I detected a gleaming stream of plasma which connected the two.

"Fantastic," I said. "They are close enough to transfer mass."

"It would appear so."

"Any idea how far we are from home, Marvin?"

"That depends. Where would our home be, exactly?"

It was an interesting philosophical question, but I was too entranced with the view to answer him. I kept staring at the two stars, wondering at their beauty. In all likelihood, I was the first human in this region of space and I didn't want to waste the opportunity to absorb the fresh vista.

I'd been in a triple-stellar system before, the one we figured was Alpha Centauri. But this was my first binary system. Most star systems are multi-star systems, I knew from my recent interest in astronomy. Binary systems alone were more common than single star systems like our own sun.

It was only after a minute of checking out the suns through my shaded visor that tilted my helmet downward to examine readings from my sensor unit. I frowned at what I was seeing. There appeared to be only three large planets. The world closest to the star was the only one that could support a surface temperature that would allow liquid water. I manipulated the controls, focusing in on this planet in the habitable zone. It was a smallish gas giant, circled by a dozen or so moons of various sizes.

Closer to our current locale at the ring, there was a lot of floating debris nearby. Metallic readings of some kind surrounded us.

"Are you getting this data, Marvin? What's this particulate mass around the ring? Dust?"

"Too large to warrant that classification. Terms such as 'fragments' or 'shrapnel' would be more accurate."

"Fragments? Of what?"

"Some form of artificial structure. Nowhere near planetary or even asteroid-sized in volume."

"You are telling me they are blown-up ships? I don't see any Macros. Are these fragments what's left of the Macros? Or have they left the system?"

"Speculation in either direction is possible, but uncertain. Should we apply thrust to the nearest fragment and investigate?"

I considered the option. I didn't like it, but after all, we'd come here to learn about the place. I didn't see anything on hand that was immediately threatening.

"All right," I said, "But try not to leave any traceable signature."

Marvin applied only a tiny squirt of frozen gasses. We rode this puff forward into the system, and moved off at an angle. The fragment of metal, when we caught up to it, was spinning in our faces. Marvin reached out with a tentacle and caught it. A spark flashed when he made contact.

"Careful," I said.

"I've got it," he said, handing it back to me.

I placed my gauntlets on the thing and examined it. Burnt, shredded metal. It could be anything, but it didn't look natural. "Looks like a piece of a ship, all right."

"Colonel, something is approaching."

That got my attention. I immediately envisioned a Macro cruiser, somehow alerted to our presence. I swiveled my helmet, but saw nothing other than empty, black space. "Get us out of here, Marvin. Full thrust back through the ring."

The tiny sled-like vehicle did a slewing U-turn and headed back toward the dark ring. It was so close. With any luck, we'd make it and slip away. I only hoped I hadn't pushed things too far. After all, if I'd felt the urge to take a look on the far side, why wouldn't the enemy feel the same way?

We didn't make it. I knew we were in trouble when the twin suns were suddenly blocked, and no longer shone upon our backs. A huge shadow cast us into instant, impenetrable darkness.

"More thrust, Marvin."

"We are accelerating at full capacity. Perhaps you should jettison the sensor unit."

I pursed my lips tightly, muttered a curse, and did as he suggested. I heaved the unit over my shoulder.

We were almost completely within the ring's center. Soon, we would transfer from this place to somewhere utterly different, and infinitely safer. In my mind, I could hear Sandra scolding me: "You just had to do it, didn't you, Kyle?"

Then I sensed something. Something large loomed very close behind. I looked back, I couldn't help it. What I saw made me suck in a breath to shout out loud. But it was too late, even for that.

We didn't make it to the ring.

-4-

It was a hand. A black, slinky metal hand of a type I was all too familiar with. Made of interlocking segments of rippling metal, it plucked me from the back of Marvin's scooter. I struggled immediately. It was instinct, of course. My current battle suit design was nothing like the old units. They had exoskeletal strength, independent propulsion and thick armor. I'd not used my propulsion units up until this point, naturally, as I'd wanted to remain unnoticed. But now I knew it didn't matter. Whoever was out here, whoever had blown ships to fragments in the vicinity of this ring, they were well aware of my intrusion into their space now. All I wanted to do was escape them.

I applied full thrust, but that wasn't enough. Maybe if the arm hadn't already had a grip on me, I could have darted out of reach. But now that I was in the grip of a three-fingered nanite arm, I didn't have anything like the thrust needed to break free. I tried anyway and simultaneously activated my lasers, which were embedded in each arm. I fired back up at the main trunk of the arm itself, as it snaked backward, reeling me in.

A brilliant beam splashed on the metal of the arm. But it wasn't holding still, and although a gush of vaporized metal was released, it didn't cut away the arm itself.

Still, I struggled, knowing I was running out of time. I broke radio silence. "Marvin, can you get this thing off me?"

There was no answer. I glanced in his direction, and saw nothing. No scooter, no Marvin. Only a few frosty crystals of exhaust from his

27

strange propulsion system. He'd gone through the point of no return and vanished. He was probably a dozen lightyears away, and unable to hear me. I wasn't angry with him, he'd done what he could. The scooter had simply gone ahead to the far side. What I did feel, however, was very alone.

I thought about shooting away the fingers that gripped me, but I feared I would burn a hole in my own suit. I decided to try it anyway, but couldn't get the angle right. The projectors were on my wrists, and with the bulk of the suit, I couldn't get them turned so they would fire against my own chest and waist region.

I recalled something at the last instant, as the arm drew me up into a region of even more complete darkness: the ship's maw. I recalled that Sandra had once slashed away one of these fingers with her combat knife. I drew mine now, and it took me two strikes, but I managed to hack away one of the three fingers. About a foot of its length twisted and writhed like a half-severed worm on a sidewalk as it floated away from me.

It was all too little, too late. I experienced the familiar sensation of being swallowed by a huge, hungry creature. Then the starlight shut off, and I knew I'd been consumed.

The arm released me and snaked away through an opening. Familiar nanite walls surrounded me. The arm retreated from my chamber into another, and I darted after it, using my suits propulsion systems.

In this chamber, two doors opened simultaneously. I eyed one, then the other. In the back of one a tiny gleam of white light shone. I froze, remembering.

"The tests," I said aloud to no one. But I was certain my hunch was correct. I laughed suddenly, knowing where I was and what was happening.

"You big bastard of a ship," I whooped. "You scared the living crap out of me."

It was a test. It was all a test. The ship was a Nano ship, and apparently it was tired of its commander, or whoever had been in charge had died. Now, it was recruiting me for the job. Fortunately, I was very conversant with these tricks and ploys. I'd seen them all before. Hell, I could have written a book about them.

I waltzed through one trick after another. Each time I did so, I expected the ship to address me in some fashion, as Alamo had so long ago. But it didn't. I opened my external microphones and turned up the gain. All I heard from the ship was some odd sounds—clicks and echoing squeaks. They sounded like something a dolphin would make at the bottom of the sea.

Maybe it wanted me to remove my helmet to talk, but I didn't want to. I kept it firmly on my head in case the ship did eject me for some reason. Even if I failed a test, at least I wouldn't die.

It was about the fifth test, by my count, when I met the alien. It was an entirely new life form. Big, but not impossibly so. If I had to estimate, I would say it was about ten feet long and weigh in at around a thousand pounds.

It looked like a crustacean of some kind. A big, bluish-green one. It dripped fluids, and didn't look to healthy—but who was I to judge? Maybe this barnacle-encrusted sad-sack creature was an Olympic contender wherever it came from.

It approached me gamely enough. There was only one big claw and eight smaller legs instead of six, but I still considered it a lobster. It never had a chance, of course. I pushed away its snapping claw and sat on it. There was gravity in the ship, and I pinned it to the deck, where it scrabbled helplessly.

I almost killed it out of hand, but stopped myself. That's what the ship wanted. That's what *had* to happen, but I couldn't do it. In fact, the entire situation made me angry.

I flipped up the visor on my helmet, having tested the air with my suits sensors and found it breathable. The atmosphere was humid, dank and made me sweat in my suit almost immediately.

"Ship, talk to me. I've beaten this poor fellow. Let him live, I command you."

More clicks, squeaks and a few new sounds: gurgles. I frowned. Could this be the language of the crustacean? It did sound watery, ghostly. Like the noises undersea creatures made.

I kept talking to the ship, but it didn't say anything back I could understand. After about ten minutes however, I smelled something— something mouth-watering. With a shock, I realized what it was: burnt lobster.

The ship had been heating the floor, cooking the poor alien I had pinned to the deck. I hadn't even felt the heat due to the air-conditioning in my suit which was working overtime. I'd thought the warmth was for the comfort of the being I had pinned below me, but the truth was much worse.

The situation was horrible, and I quickly stood up and tried to lift the alien away from the hot surface. The carcass was limp, flopping. The limbs hung loosely and dribbled steamy fluids. I sighed and put him back down, as gently as I could. A moment later, the ship's nanite flooring swallowed him and ejected him into space.

"Heartless tin monsters," I said. "You're just as big of a bastard as Alamo ever was."

The ship finally responded in English. "How do you wish to address us?" it asked.

"Oh, *now* you can speak English, eh?"

The ship said nothing.

"You aren't the same ship I called Alamo before, are you?"

"This vessel has never utilized the name Alamo."

"All right then, I've got a name for you. I'm going to call you *Butcher*. How about that?"

"Rename complete."

Butcher was my third Nano ship and this vessel had a true Nano mindset. It wasn't like the ships I'd dealt with lately. Star Force ships were tame, and didn't have agendas of their own. I had to keep reminding myself of this as I dealt with *Butcher*. I couldn't trust this ship to obey my orders forever. At some point it was likely to do whatever it damned well pleased. We called ships like this "wild" Nano ships.

"Butcher, I need information. How many Nano ships are in this system?"

"Reference unclear."

I frowned, then nodded. "Ships built with nanites such as yourself are 'Nano ships', at least, that's what I call them."

"Reference clarified. Language lookup table updated. There are three hundred twenty-nine Nano ships in this star system."

My eyebrows lifted in surprise. Three hundred ships? Could this be the fleet that had ditched Star Force years ago? I was about to ask this question next when I heard the distinctive sound of large, firing lasers. The Nano ship was shooting at something. I put my helmet back on in a hurry. If the ship took a hit, I didn't want to be caught floating in space without it.

"What are you shooting at?"

"An unknown aggressor."

"It is a Macro?"

"Unknown."

I thought fast. Could it be one of my own men, or even one of my ships? I didn't have time to teach this ship to put up sensory images on the walls. That took careful work. I stared around at the blank, metallic walls. They were frustrating, just like all Nano ship interiors. No screens, no cameras. No intrinsic way for a pilot to see what the hell was going on.

"If the target is not firing at us, I order you to cease fire."

"Command invalid. Defensive systems engaged. Command personnel must be protected."

The ship lurched then, almost knocking me off my feet. I stumbled, using my magnetics and the exoskeleton armor to keep me from falling on my face. Even if I had fallen, it wouldn't have hurt much, but my reaction was instinctive.

"Dammit Butcher, what are you doing now?"

"Defensive maneuvers engaged. Enemy is too close for weapons systems to target it."

Too close? I shook my head. These guns had very nearly a complete field of fire. The standard issue Nano ship came with two large laser turrets, one on top and one on the bottom of its oblong disk-shaped body. Just about anything could be hit with one turret or the other, if not both. In order to be too close, the target would have to be touching the hull itself, or perhaps clinging to one of the turrets.

I suddenly had a hunch. "Butcher, is this target in physical contact with the hull?"

"Yes."

"It is approximately equivalent to my mass?"

"Yes."

"Butcher, this entity is known to me. Cease fire, cease evasion efforts."

"Command personnel must be protected."

"I've undergone nanite injections, and I'm wearing a battle suit that is tougher than your hull. I'm in no danger."

Reluctantly, I managed to talk the panicked ship into standing down. It has been flying around erratically, like a bucking bronco. It couldn't do anything to the hitchhiker however, so after a while *Butcher* reluctantly paused and let me climb up to the top levels, where the intruder was located. After a few minutes of arguing, I managed to get the ship to dissolve a region of the hull so I could poke my head up and have a look around. I finally had to force the issue by threatening to burn my way out with my lasers.

When I finally was able to get a look at our visitor, I smiled. Marvin had wrapped his body around the base of the laser turret. He looked like a bundle of wires up there. As I waved to him, several cameras swung to examine me. A tentacle-like wire extended toward me. I allowed it to make contact with my battle suit. It was a good thing *Butcher* wasn't watching. The ship was in mother-hen mode and would have objected.

When we were in contact, I transmitted to him over a closed circuit intercom as we had done when riding his little scooter together. "Hello Marvin, welcome back to this star system."

"You are uninjured? I presume this ship is now under your control?"

"You presume correctly. This is my new Nano ship, I've christened her Butcher."

"An apt name," Marvin said. "Why didn't you stop it from firing on me? My scooter was destroyed, and I barely managed to crawl over the hull to this safe point."

"Sorry about that. The ship's actions were automatic and defensive in nature. It doesn't have any kind of display systems. I couldn't see it was you."

After a while, Marvin finally stopped complaining about how close he'd come to annihilation and began asking questions. After survival, the urge to explore and study the universe was his greatest driving motivation. Unfortunately, I didn't know most of the answers to his questions. I promised him we could learn more about our environment if we were inside *Butcher* and spent some time programming a sensory system for it.

Getting Marvin inside the ship took a considerable amount of effort. I didn't know if I could ever convince *Butcher* he was harmless, but I did finally convince the ship to let him aboard. The only requirement was that I remain inside my battle suit at all times while in his presence. It was annoying, but workable.

We spent the next half-hour assembling sensory-input scripts and the like in the ship. Marvin was helpful in this regard, as he had recorded the precisely worded instructions that had worked on Nano ships in the past. Obviously, this ship knew something about Earth and humanity, or it would not have been able to speak English. But I had yet to get out of it any details as to its current mission and whether it had previously been part of Star Force. Both Marvin and I were more interested in seeing the star system layout right now.

First, the three big planets came into view. There were more than the dozen moons around each of the three large planets. There were seventy-seven major satellites, in all, plus rings of fine dust particles that had a gray-orange color.

There was only one world that could support life, as we'd detected earlier. The moons themselves around the warm world, seen with more detail, were the amazing part. Three of them had liquid water on the surface. The planet they orbited was about half the size of Jupiter, and many of the moons were tidally-locked with the gas giant. They still received light from the two stars, however. As they swung around their planet, different portions of their faces were exposed to sunlight from both the nearby stars.

Watching the orbital patterns of these Mars-sized moons, I tried to imagine life on such worlds. It was not ideal. Days would be long and hot, while nights would be cold indeed. The worst times would be when the moons entered the long shadow of the titanic planet they circled. During these frequent eclipses, darkness would be total.

Finally, Butcher added the presence of ships to the display. At first, nothing showed up. I was surprised. Could this Nano ship be the only one in the system?

"Where are the rest of the ships, Butcher? You said there were over three hundred of them."

"All independently mobile systems that meet filtering requirements are displayed," said the ship.

I saw only a single greenish beetle, right near the ring. That was us.

"I think the parameters need adjusting," Marvin said. He quickly gave me instructions to display neutral ships—ships that didn't register as friendly or hostile. These were to appear as golden beads of metal on the forward wall of the bridge.

The scene changed dramatically. Tiny beads welled up in a mass. As more and more of them appeared, I frowned. "Where are they all headed? Butcher, give me an overhead, system wide view."

The image swam and shifted. As it reconfigured itself, I was reminded of a pool of water, being drained so that the stones at the bottom came up in full relief.

"Uh-oh," I said aloud as I began to understand what I was looking at.

"They appear to be coming this way, Colonel," said Marvin, stating the obvious.

There did indeed appear to be three hundred of them. They were moving as a mass, coming toward our position, having gathered into a swarm around the gas giant and her moons.

I had a sudden, unpleasant thought. I'd come into this system, and assaulted the sole Nano ship that had been left on sentry duty at the ring. When they'd lost contact with their lookout, they'd decided to come and investigate. Perhaps they'd even heard the pitiful cries and burblings of the ex-pilot, while I sat on him and cooked him.

I imagined the lobster pilots, hell-bent on revenge. So much for sneaking onto this side of the ring to have a quiet look around.

-5-

I knew I had to get out of this situation, and get out of it fast. I had no intention of running off with *Butcher*. I wanted peace with the Crustaceans, not only because I had enough enemies, but also because I'd had enough of killing fellow biotics.

"Butcher, begin recording a command script. Do not execute the script until I order you to do so."

"Ready."

"You will eject the two occupants of this ship into space and then fly to rejoin the approaching fleet. You will not fire on fellow Nano ships. You will find a new pilot, going back to your original programming. You will not reveal anything about myself or this entity known as Marvin."

"Command script is self-contradictory."

I gritted my teeth. We had less than an hour to get out of here, and I didn't want to spend it all arguing with a Nano ship. "What portion of the command sequence is in conflict?"

"Joining the approaching fleet will not allow us to acquire a new pilot. None of the orders given match my original programming. Auto-defense mandates require returning fire when fired upon, thus—"

"I get it, I get it," I said in frustration. I tried to focus. It was hard to sort out a verbal program for an alien ship while hundreds of enemy vessels came closer with each passing second. I felt a growing urge to just run. I could use this time to set up defenses on Eden's side of the ring. If I had blown it, and three hundred lobster ships were about to come through and attack my forces seeking vengeance, I needed to get to my side and gather up my destroyers. The mines would get a lot of them, and I figured my destroyers could outgun the rest. Tactical solutions sprang to mind easily. We'd fall back, letting them plow into the mines. When the survivors advanced, we'd open fire. The destroyers were equipped with three guns each, all of which were larger and had a greater range than any of these Nano ships. We could pop them one at a time with concentrated fire, burning them out of space before they were even within range of my ships. If they turned around and ran, I'd let them, but otherwise...

"Combat appears inevitable, Colonel," Marvin said calmly.

I shook my head. *No, dammit!* I didn't want it to go down that way.

"No," I said aloud. "I'm not going to start a new war. I've cooked one sentient being today, and that's quite enough. They may not even have full control of their ships. This ship didn't even have its new pilot acquisition program turned off."

Marvin swung a number of cameras toward me, but said nothing. I wondered what he was thinking about this entire sequence of events. I didn't know, but I suspected he was taking notes and enjoying the drama he'd helped stir up between three species—two biotics and the Nanos themselves. Perhaps he thought of it as a grand, sociological experiment.

I recalled the early days of dealing with the Nano ships, back when they would mass up and charge anything that entered our system, oftentimes suicidally. Those had not been fun days for the pilots. For all I knew, the lobsters were madly trying to figure out how to stop their ships from attacking.

I spent the next ten minutes or so working out a script *Butcher* would accept. I wanted it to dump us, then fly back to where the Crustaceans came from—I suspected it was one of those hot-water moons I'd scanned—and pick up a new pilot. Hopefully, the rest of the ships would stand down and not try to destroy us.

There was one more obvious step to take before exiting the system. I needed to make contact with the pilots of these Nano ships. I needed them to know we were not invading monsters—if they could be convinced at this point.

"Butcher, open a channel with the pilots of the approaching fleet. You will translate our English into the natural language of the pilots."

"Channel request sent."

It took about thirty tense seconds before we heard anything else. They were still a long way off. "Channel open," the ship said.

"Hello fellow ship captains. We are not hostile. Break off your attack. We wish to exchange information, not laser fire."

About half a minute later, the response came in: "Your threats do not impress us. You are alone. We have the advantage."

Threats? I mulled over my words. Perhaps they'd taken my reference to laser fire as a threat. I heaved a sigh. Another touchy bunch of aliens. At least they weren't talking in pictures.

"Colonel Riggs?" Marvin asked. "Could you tell the ship to transmit the original alien speech to me as it comes in? I would like to learn this new language."

"Don't know this one, huh? Okay," I said, and gave *Butcher* the orders. I watched as a black tentacle of nanites extended down from the roof of the bridge and intersected Marvin's body. He watched it descend with a large number of squirming cameras. I could tell he could hardly wait. Nothing turned on Marvin's brain like a new alien language.

"I come in peace. This ship attacked me and forced us to participate in tests. I was forced to kill the pilot. I apologize, and will now return the ship to your people. A new pilot can be selected. No one need lose another life."

After the delay—which was fractionally shorter than before, the response came back: "Claiming your errors were made from ignorance will not save you. Errors are crimes, and you will be slain for having communicated these concepts. I can't believe such a creature as you overcame one of our principal investigators."

Principal investigators? Errors were crimes? I thought about that. These lobsters sounded different than the Worms or the Centaurs. The Worms were brave individualistic warriors. The Centaurs thought of little other than herd honor. What I was hearing from these guys was something that reminded me of a group of prissy academics. I'd known plenty of those in my college-teaching days. They were prideful of their intellect and scornful of others. To them, there was no greater crime than mistakes, lies or cheating.

"I speak the truth," I said. "I've investigated primitive cultures such as yours before. You have much to learn from me. I offer you a helping hand—in the spirit of friendship."

"Insults!" came the response. "It is as we suspected. Insults often follow errors."

"I'll prove my point," I said. "Your investigator failed because he did not alter the programming script of his ship. He allowed it to continue picking up new pilots to test against him. This function can be turned off." I continued, explaining how to stop a Nano ship from picking up new pilots and killing people whenever it felt like it. I didn't stop there, however. I lectured them on the niceties of the nanite injections, which would allow the pilots to pick up passengers without chaining them to walls. I even explained how individuals could be picked up and dumped at low altitude, harmlessly. That would mark them as failures and trick the ships into ignoring them. Lastly, I told them how to script visual systems into the ship's walls so they could perceive their environment using the ships sensors.

There was a pause when I was finished. Marvin squirmed his metal body closer to the forward wall. He rasped on the hull, making a grating sound that set my teeth on edge. He studied the display of metallic beads with a number of cameras. "I believe they are decelerating, Colonel Riggs," he said.

I smiled and nodded. "They know another professor when they hear one."

What came next was a barrage of questions. I fielded them all, and told them everything I could—with certain reservations. I didn't reveal our numbers, or our strength. I didn't tell them about the minefield that lay beyond the ring, either. I simply indicated we had nothing to fear from their paltry three hundred-odd ships. My arrogance was complete, and before they were within laser range, they'd come to a complete halt. Their fleet faced my single ship, and we sat there in space, eyeing one another suspiciously.

"Colonel Riggs," Marvin said, interrupting me during one of my lengthy speeches. This one was on the topic of defeating Macros with ground forces.

I paused the transmission and turned to him. "What is it, Marvin?"

"I've calculated a significant probability these biotics are simply learning all they can from you before executing their original plan."

I nodded. "I've thought of that, too. But I'm hoping to instill enough doubt in them to keep them on their side of the ring. If we know so much, and are willing to give it up freely, we might be worthy of their fear. No matter how self-confident they are, they know I waltzed in here and took out one of their people without a problem. I've fed them a lot of information, which should impress them despite their natural arrogance. If they are academics, as I feel they are, there really isn't any way to impress them other than to demonstrate you are smarter than they are. They'll still hate me, but they may also respect me."

After another hour of mostly one-way lecturing, they had had enough at last.

"We feel it is now our duty to respond in kind," they said while I was taking a break. My throat was dry. "There are a number of misstatements in your statements, which we have carefully cataloged."

Prissy in the extreme, they proceeded to go over statements I'd made that were in any slight fashion contradictory, or unclear in meaning. I listened, murmured appreciative responses now and then, and never became annoyed. Again, this was part of the academic process I was thoroughly familiar with. Faced with superior knowledge, many nerds turned to nit-picking to save face. This was an important shift in demeanor, however. They'd moved from the role of fellow professors to worst-case students.

I let them have their fun. I acknowledged every tiny flaw in wording and other inconsistencies they'd found, and thanked them for the input. I felt in them a new swelling pride. I'd injured that pride by pointing out I knew a lot about Nano ships they hadn't figured out yet. Now was the time to build them back up. It was irritating, but it was a technique that often served to defuse this type of personality.

I learned a fair amount concerning their species as I endured their lectures. They were careful not to reveal too much. They admitted to being from the warm oceans of the moon-worlds I'd seen floating around the gas giant. They were an aquatic species, and had only just begun to master basic spaceflight when the Nano ships arrived. Plunging down into their oceans and scooping up individuals from their rocky warrens in the seabed, they'd been forced to slay one another in what was now a familiar pattern. Prior to that, Macro ships had cruised through the system and destroyed all their satellites and observatories. They had not done much else with their worlds—possibly because they were relatively low in metal content. Being heavily covered in seas, the original Macros had passed them by going from ring to ring. The lobster people had watched the machines fearfully for years before the Nanos showed up. Now, to their surprise, every time a Macro ship appeared their new Nano vessels swarmed it and brought it down.

Most importantly, I learned they'd finished off the Macros that we had chased out of the Eden system. They'd destroyed them, but knew there were others that came through this system from time to time from places further out along the chain of rings.

As they spoke, I could not help but think of the billions of stars in our galaxy alone. How far did the Macro Empire extend? How many ships did they have in total? Were we fleas on a mouse? Or much worse, fleas on an unimaginably huge behemoth that could never be brought down? Really, it depended on the rings, and the extent of them. The Crustaceans didn't know anything about that, unfortunately. They had been unaware of the rings until the invasions by the Macros and Nanos.

At length, we exhausted one another. We eventually agreed to reconvene for more talks at a future time. In the end, the ship and the Crustaceans allowed me to float back to Eden through the ring. As I drifted out of the star system, I dragged Marvin behind me. He was trying to look as inert as possible.

Before I crossed over into the Eden system, I took the opportunity to look back at the twin suns one last time. I figured these Crustaceans were living on borrowed time. The Macros had bypassed them for now, seeking more valuable targets. But they would get around to this aquatic species eventually, even if they were a relatively low priority.

I had to wonder about the next star system in this chain of rings—and the systems beyond that. The number of life-supporting stars seemed high, but possibly that was just due to the choices of the ancients who had made this highway of rings. Maybe they'd purposefully strung together worlds that teemed with life.

All told, how many other biotic species were out there, suffering under the heels of the machines? I doubted I would ever know the full truth.

-6-

When I reached the Eden System, I discovered a minor panic was in full swing. My helmet buzzed with command chatter. The officers were arguing about who was in charge of this mission, now that I was absent without leaving instructions. I winced guiltily. They'd figured out I was missing, and had no clear chain of command. Normally, it would be simple enough to determine who was in command. The most senior highest-ranking officer should win out. But technically, that was Commodore Decker, who had yet to leave the system. He was several light-hours away, heading for the next ring, but hadn't gone through it yet.

That was the crux of the argument. On closed channels, they fought about whether they were obligated to contact Decker and ask for his orders. Most knew what that meant: he would order them to withdraw immediately. Some wanted to do this anyway, following the book. Others wanted to wait a bit and see if I came back—simultaneously giving Decker the time required to exit the system and thus be removed from the equation.

I felt a twinge of remorse. I'd put them in this situation. What I didn't understand was how they'd figured out I was gone so quickly. It'd only been a few hours.

"This is Colonel Kyle Riggs," I said, putting on my best authoritative voice. That's what they needed now: clear, unambiguous direction. "All this talk of my demise is premature. Return to your assigned duties. I'm calling a staff meeting on *Socorro* in twenty minutes."

"Welcome back, sir," said one of my pilots. A dozen others chimed in.

No one asked me where I'd been, or what was going on. They were all too relieved just to hear my voice. They would have questions, of course, but for now, the panic was over. I supposed I should have left a second in command and informed him of my little jaunt into the blue. It had been poor judgment on my part not to do so.

Among the senior staff that gathered in the empty troop pod of my ship was Captain Miklos and Captain Sloan. I figured one or the other of them would have to be my second in command. But which should be in charge? It wasn't an easy decision. Sloan was more experienced, being a veteran of many conflicts going back at least to the Helios Campaign against the Worms. Miklos was seasoned as well, having been at my side in several space battles. It wasn't that simple, however. Sloan was more of a marine, while Miklos was decidedly fleet.

When they arrived, I still hadn't made up my mind. I started the meeting by explaining where I'd been, and the nature of the lobster people who lived on the far side of the ring. They stared at me with frowns of concern.

"Sir, did you really have to go alone?" Sloan asked.

"No, but I figured the odds of detection were lower that way. Besides, I wasn't completely alone, I had Marvin with me."

They glanced over at Marvin and then back to me. I sensed something deceptive in their manners.

"Something I should know about, gentlemen?" I asked.

There was a lot of guilty squirming. Sloan shrugged, but didn't meet my eyes. I noticed Marvin had cameras on both of them. Finally, Miklos looked at me directly.

"We promised not to bring it up, sir," he said. "But it was Marvin who alerted us as to your absence."

"Ah," I said, finally catching on. I turned to the robot. "Good old Marvin. At what point did you take it upon yourself to break our deal and tell everyone?"

"I did not break our agreement, Colonel Riggs."

"You certainly did!"

"No, if you review the audio files, it was stipulated that in the event of your death I should return to inform Star Force."

I frowned. I didn't recall making such an arrangement. "I don't have audio files, Marvin. I'm not a damned robot. What audio files are you talking about?"

Marvin's speakers fuzzed then a voice came from the faintly. There was the sound of laser fire in the background. I heard my voice come out in scratchy tones. "Marvin, if I don't make it, get back to the others and tell them what happened. They'll need to switch command immediately."

I thumped my gauntleted fist down on the table. "What the hell was that from? Back when we were fighting against the Macros ship-to-ship?"

"I believe it was March 18th—"

"What year?" I roared, then I put up my hands. "No, don't even tell me. It doesn't matter. Orders like that are situational, Marvin, as I suspect you know. You are just using this as a pretext, an excuse to do whatever you want to. Audio files…"

I muttered some unpleasant things then turned away from the sly robot. He'd manufactured an excuse to cause a mess. My marines might have attempted a rescue, and screwed up the entire exchange with the Crustaceans. In the end, it had been a good thing they hadn't known who was in charge. By wasting time arguing, they'd given me the time I'd needed to return.

"It doesn't matter," I said. "Let's review the current situation. We have another large force on the other side of this ring. They are neutral I'd say for now, but will possibly become friendly in the future. I count the Crustaceans as a plus. Even if they don't help us in this system, they should operate as a buffer between us and any new Macro invasion force coming from that direction."

"Sir, if I may interject," Captain Sloan said.

"Go for it, Captain."

"If the lobsters are out there playing interference for us, maybe the best course of action would be to place a sentry ship on their side of the ring."

I nodded. "I've made arrangements to do just that, promising aid if the Macros come against them in force."

"Another alliance sir?" asked Miklos. "Alliances have a way of dragging nations into other people's wars."

"Their war is our war, Miklos. This is all about the machines against the biotics—the living against mechanized death. But still, I appreciate your input."

Miklos leaned back in his chair, nodding. In truth, I *did* appreciate his input. He had a more introspective view on events than most of my staff. He knew more history, and looked into things more deeply than Sloan, who was essentially a frontline fighter with the survival instincts of a city rat.

"I want to put something to rest, here," I said. "I don't want another chaotic command mess of the kind I overheard on the channel when I returned to this system. In a ground combat situation, when my input is unavailable, Captain Sloan is in charge. In Fleet situations and for matters of overall command, my second is Captain Miklos. This military unit should be seen as apart from the rest of Star Force for now. We are a task force on a mission, we have our orders from Star Force, and we are executing them at a remote site as we see fit. Is that clear for everyone?"

Captain Sloan didn't even bat an eye. I could tell he didn't care who was in charge, he just wanted things settled. I liked that about him. He wasn't ambitious—except in the matter of his personal survival. Miklos frowned and nodded more slowly and thoughtfully. He was a thinker. As far as I could tell, he wasn't thrilled to be my second-in-command. He knew what a burden that might become. But he accepted my arrangements without complaint.

I liked supporting officers who didn't complain. I smiled and left that baggage behind me.

"Let's press on, then," I said. The first order of business is the liberation of this system from the Macros—all the Macros. The Centaurs are trapped in their satellites without access to the ground. We are going to provide that access. Rather than using the presence of the Crustacean's Nano fleet to cover our retreat, I'm going to use them to cover our attack. We are going to retake the surface of every world in the system. By doing so, we will gain a set of invaluable Nano factories as a gift from the Centaurs. We can use those systems to set up further defenses and fortify this system on a permanent basis."

There were murmurs of agreement, with reservations. I could see questions in their eyes—some registered mild shock.

Finally, Kwon voiced everyone's concern. He'd kept quiet throughout the meeting up until now. "A new ground campaign, Colonel? With so few marines?"

I turned to him and smiled. "I think we'll have enough troops, Kwon. The Centaurs will make up the bulk of our forces. I'm envisioning every Star Force marine with a full company of armed Centaurs at his back."

Kwon looked comically alarmed. "Excuse me, sir. I would not trust these creatures behind me."

It was my turn to appear surprised. "You don't trust them? You've met them in battle and heard their speeches. They are an honorable people, Kwon."

"Of course, sir! It is not their honor I would question—it is their aim that worries me. With a hundred goats behind me—I fear they would burn my butt off."

I laughed. "In that case, it is your mission as First Sergeant to train your troops well."

"Excuse me, Colonel," Captain Miklos said. "How many of these Centaur troops do we have?"

I turned to Marvin, who had been in communication with them on my behalf. "How many volunteers are they reporting, Marvin?"

"About thirteen million, sir," he said.

I snorted. "Sounds like that will do it. Our shortage will be in terms of transportation, armaments and supplies."

"The Centaurs wish to ensure us that once they reach their world," Marvin said. "Their troops can subsist on wind, rain, sunshine and grass for an extended period."

"Hmm," I said. "I suppose they could. They probably won't even require us to dig latrines, will they?"

A general chuckle swept the group.

"Weapons then," I said. "Are we churning them out?"

"Yes Colonel," Marvin said. "The Centaurs had two factories in each satellite. Hundreds of packs and projectors are being constructed every hour. They are cannibalizing parts of their habitats for the purpose. Our factories are working on the latest upgraded suit designs."

I nodded and stood up. "Meeting is adjourned. Marvin, accompany me to the bridge. The rest of you return to your stations."

I'd made a significant alteration to our battle suit design after my experiences with the Crustaceans and the Nano ship. I didn't like the limited field of fire that having twin arm-mounted projectors had given me. In close combat situations, a marine could be rendered helpless by the bulk of his own suit. I felt a free-swinging laser rifle was superior, attached only by a cable to the suit's generator. You could aim it anywhere and more importantly with a single large projector I could jack-up the wattage the system could output. I had a feeling that before we were done in this system each man was going to have to blaze his way through quite a bit of Macro hardware, and one big projector was better than two smaller ones for that purpose. We had so few marines, only about three hundred in the system, that this alteration didn't strain our overall production.

"What is the immediate plan, Colonel?" Miklos asked.

"Our sole factory is the one aboard my ship," I said. "I'm going to stop the production of mines. After our battle suits have been upgraded, we're going to use our one factory to modify our ships. We need to make them more comfortable for the transportation of—what was it, thirteen million Centaurs?"

The meeting broke up and my staff shuffled out. They were accustomed to vague orders and incredible plans. I was proud of them. No one shouted with laughter at my insanity. No one questioned that we could do such a thing. At the height of U. S. deployment of troops in World War Two, they'd had about thirteen million men in uniform. Why couldn't Star Force field that many mountain goats?

In truth, I had no intention of using all thirteen million Centaur volunteers. The reality was without weapons systems they would be worse than useless against the Macros. The real challenge would be to maximize the number of trained, armed troops I could assemble and transport to the battlefield in a timely basis. And time was against us in this regard. I felt sure that once our campaign started, Macro Command on the target worlds would start digging in. They would realize as soon as we struck that we were coming for every planet eventually. Since they could out produce us, they would be very hard to take out without drastic measures.

When everyone else was gone, Marvin and I took stock of our operational situation. I didn't like what I saw. On every target world, there were three main factories under domes—at least, that's what we could see. There might be more domes hidden in the seas or underground.

I tapped the closest of the six planets on the screen. "That's got to be it, Marvin. The closest one. It's cold, but habitable. It also happens to be the original homeworld of the Centaurs. Might as well give them what they really want. We'll have to do a set of bombing runs on each of the enemy domes, eliminating their production capacity before they can turn it against us. We'll have to use tactical nuclear bombardment. If we hit them all from space at the same time, they should fall, overwhelmed."

"I disagree," Marvin said, focusing a squad of cameras on me and the display.

I glanced at him. "Talk to me."

"We need the domes—or more specifically, we need the large factories inside."

"What for? We can't use them."

"Oh yes, I believe we can."

"How?"

"I've studied recordings of your prior engagements with these systems. No attempt was made to capture these large scale production systems and turn them into assets. Star Force objectives might have been met more easily if this had been done."

I blinked at him. "What? You mean we can take them over?"

"You've done just that with many factories of Nano origin. The process is not that dissimilar in the case of the larger production systems."

"But we can't talk to them. All they ever did was blow up in our faces."

Marvin twisted some of his tentacles and adjusted the image displayed on the screen. Stock footage of our original campaign against the Macros in South America loaded and began to play. "It was a simple matter of miscommunication," he said. "These systems do not speak the same language as the Nano ships—but it is similar. Really, it is a more primitive version of the same binary protocol. An earlier version, if you will."

I stared at him. "You can talk to them? You can change their programming before they blow themselves up?"

"Yes."

"But we'd have to get you down there, into one of those domes, right?"

"Yes. The domes prevent all transmission from external sources."

I nodded, remembering. When we'd faced these Macro factories, hiding under clam-shell-like force fields, we'd only been able to get inside with footmen. No form of energy was able to penetrate. Only direct hits from nuclear weapons could break down the force domes themselves. Once that was done, of course, the factory inside was invariably destroyed. But if we could sneak Marvin inside, he thought he could reprogram the machines and make them ours.

The thought was magical and soon consumed my mind. Whole new possibilities opened up. With even *one* such super-factory, I'd be able to produce huge amounts of whatever source materials I wanted—the more I thought about it, the bigger my eyes and my ideas became.

"We're going to do it, Marvin," I said, turning to him. I wondered if my eyes shone with yellow greed. "We'll do it—or we'll die trying."

"That is a logical assumption," he said.

7

Within a few days, we'd moved my force of destroyers to hover over the target, a mountainous world dotted by snow-capped peaks and winding emerald valleys. There was a Centaur satellite here—a big one. I wasn't surprised about that, after all, this was their home planet. It made sense there would be a large population stationed nearby.

I confirmed through a number of overly-long conversations with the Centaurs that their factories were churning out heavy-weapons kits. Their lighter lasers weren't sufficient for the task of taking out the big machines. Following our designs for the basic infantry kit, I had them producing as many as possible with their factories. I'd cut the design down from the equipment our men usually carried, but the energy output was comparable. They had a heavy pack, which I'd elongated and based on a harness system that was designed for their four-legged bodies. Each kit was equipped with a nanite-cloth helmet that was completely opaque except for the specialized goggles built to fit over wide-set eyes. The helmet only protected their vision, not much else. It was equipped with a radio system however, so they could receive remote commands. The only other part of the system that mattered in combat was the projector itself, which they cradled in their stubby forearms. Connected by a thick, black nanite cable to the pack on their backs, the troopers were ready to go.

Only, they weren't. We tested them in person, and immediately found a critical problem. The individual Centaur soldiers weren't strong enough to carry the newer, heavier packs and projectors. The systems weighed in around eight hundred pounds, and even their sturdiest rams had trouble walking with them. Smaller individuals buckled and staggered, toppling over.

Frowning, I got out the com box and had Marvin translate my speech to the Centaurs in the staging area we'd set up inside their satellite. "Honorable people of the wind," I began. It was always good to start things off by praising them. "We have a problem. Your warriors are not strong enough to carry the heavy weapons systems they need to destroy the machines."

"Our hearts are prideful and true. The rivers of our world may not lift a stone, but they will wear it down to nothing given enough years."

"That's great," I said, not having much of a clue what they were talking about. "But we need to kill Macros, and as-designed these systems will not work. Fortunately, I have a solution. It will require that we alter the people of your herds. They will have to undergo nanite injections to improve their strength."

The Centaurs made many oddly-worded inquiries as to the nature of these alterations and injections. As I explained them further, they became incensed.

"Our people may subject themselves to allowing machines to squat upon our backs. We may even allow machines to transport us to our battles. But we will never conjoin with them! There is no greater dishonor imaginable! To become one with the machine is to join the enemy!"

I grimaced. I thought about telling them that we'd done it, and that was how we were able to carry this equipment ourselves. I decided against mentioning these facts as I felt sharing that information might very well backfire. Who knew how they might react? They might rethink our entire tenuous alliance.

"Sir," Miklos said, standing nearby.

I turned to him irritably.

"I might have a solution. They say they are willing to be harnessed to carry the weapons. Perhaps we can build even larger projectors and have them drag the units on carts."

I considered the idea, but I didn't really like it. They wouldn't be able to move as fast that way. One of the big advantages of these Centaur troops was their natural agility on mountainous terrain. If they were dragging a cart behind them in teams, bumping along over the rocks, we'd be greatly slowed down.

"I've got another idea," I said. "We'll put a repeller dish on every pack, countering that single crushing weight."

Miklos nodded. "That should work."

"It *will* work," I said, "but it will cost us production materials and time. We'll end up being able to field less troops per hour. But it can't be helped, I suppose."

I relayed the plans to the Centaurs and after a few suspicious questions, they agreed with the plan. After all, it only involved altering the kit slightly, not the soldiers themselves.

My next difficulty turned out to be more serious. The Centaurs were claustrophobic. This was something I'd known from the start, but I'd hoped that if they were willing to close their eyes and take a five minute drop-ship ride down to the planetary surface, we shouldn't have much trouble. I was quite wrong on that point.

Experimentally, we loaded up a squad of veterans into one of my deployable drop-ship containers. These were not all that different in design from their original configuration. Back on Earth, we'd filled oblong structures that looked rather like freight train cars with about a hundred marines each and carried them on long arms dangling from the bottom of our Nano ships. Now, the systems were slightly different. I'd shaped them like teardrops for improved aerodynamics, and hopefully a faster drop-time from space.

Our ships were able to get into and out of orbit much faster than traditional spaceships. This was essentially because our engines had a lot more powered lift than rocket-propelled systems. A ship like the old NASA shuttlecrafts had to come down in a slow, gentle glide. They had to slow down the entire time, starting the drop at a very high velocity. They largely used friction to provide this braking action, rather than engine power. The shuttle engine burn that started this process only lasted three or four minutes. After that, it was a long gliding process that took about an hour to get the ship all the way down to a dead stop, sitting on a long runway.

Our engines weren't limited to short duration burns, and therefore we didn't have to rely on friction to slow ourselves down. We were able to come down out of orbit much faster by utilizing a much shorter path—essentially straight down. The main limit on our approach speed was atmospheric friction. It was all a matter of how fast we were moving versus how close we were to the planet's surface, and thus how thick the atmosphere was. The closer we got to the surface at high speed, the hotter things would become inside the landing vessel.

That was what I originally wanted to test. Going down at about five thousand miles per hour to an altitude of about twenty miles from the surface, then throttling back hard to prevent vaporizing the vessel—that was the problem I intended to solve.

So, I loaded about twenty Centaurs into an egg-shaped landing pod and attached it to a destroyer. I'd ordered them to calmly stand in the module, and think happy thoughts of open skies, rivers, wind and honorable matings. They were to turn their goggles to full black and wait a few minutes—the supposed duration of the drop.

We decided to come down in a remote part of the planet about a thousand miles from the southern pole, far from any of the enemy domes or any other Macro units. We'd long ago knocked out all enemy satellites and other remote observation equipment, so I was pretty sure they wouldn't detect the landing at all. Even so, I was tense in the command chair next to Captain Miklos. We had Kwon there, and Marvin. We watched the screens intently as we dropped straight down like a rock toward the ice-capped polar region.

Things were going well, until we hit the friction layer, about two miles from the surface. The ride got bumpy at that point, and I worried about the Centaur troops we were carrying down.

"Ease off on the throttle, Miklos," I ordered.

"Yes sir, but I must point out, we need to do the drop as quickly as possible. Enemy anti-air can't be allowed a long period to lock onto us and bring us down. We don't have enough ships to take losses—"

"I'm well aware of all that, but this is a test, not a combat drop. Slow down."

We decelerated harder, and the lurching of the ship continued. We bounced and almost flipped over as a high altitude wind shear struck us.

"Dammit," I muttered. "Kwon, how are the Centaurs doing? Ask their Captain."

Kwon spoke into the com-box. "No answer, sir."

"What do you mean, no answer?"

Kwon shrugged in his suit. "The Centaur Captain isn't responding."

I gritted my teeth and turned to Miklos. "Can we abort this thing now?"

"Not really, sir," Miklos said. "We're almost down. But I'll slow down to a crawl and crank up the stabilizers so we don't hit anymore spots like the last one."

When we finally reached the ground we set the egg-shaped landing module on the ice and the big arm slid away from it. I ordered the ship to dissolve a circular section of the floor and jumped out.

A new planetary surface met my eyes for the first time. It wasn't anything to write home about. There was a flat, gray-white expanse of ice that seemed infinite, only to be broken up by looming black crags on the western horizon. The surface of the ice blew with a fine mist about two feet deep. I looked down, and realized I couldn't see my legs. My heavy armor had broken through the crust and I was left wading in snow that came up to my waist.

"Sir," Miklos said in my helmet. I could hear his breath blowing over the microphone. He was stressing.

"What's wrong, Captain?"

"Incoming barrage, sir. The Macros must have spotted us."

"How much time do we have?"

"About forty minutes."

I cursed and moved to the landing pod. So much for sneaking down out of orbit. The Macros knew we were here, and they'd fired their equivalent of a flock of ICBMs to keep us company. This training exercise wasn't going exactly as I'd planned.

I reached out and touched the surface of the landing pod, causing it to open. That's when I found out just how far from "planned" this mission had gone.

A Centaur bolted out into the open. He charged past me, his horn blades clacking against my chest plate as he passed. One of his short arms was broken and bleeding, dangling and flopping against his forelegs as he run.

"What the—" I began, leaning into the opening.

Smoke poured out of it. Black, rolling fumes swirled up into the clear blue sky behind me. I couldn't smell them, but they looked thick and unpleasant—like an oil fire. I had to dip my helmet down below the smoke to see anything. I'd been about to demand my team tell me what the hell was going on, but I didn't bother. The scene inside the pod explained it all. I flipped on my suit's floods and examined the details.

About half the Centaur troops were dead. A number of their corpses were charred black and smoldering. A few live ones stood against the walls, shivering. A few more flopped and twisted on the floor, grotesquely injured. One kicked his hooves at his own discarded generator pack, goring it with his horn blades as if it were a mortal enemy. Perhaps, from his point of view, it was. His eyes rolled in his head and one of his horns had been torn loose. Blood welled and ran down his face and into his foaming mouth, where it outlined his teeth in red. I thought I recognized him: he was large with darker fur than most. Then I had it. He was the Captain.

"Disaster," said Kwon, leaning his big head into the landing pod beside me. "Total freaking disaster."

"Thanks for the newsflash, Sergeant. Any more pearls of wisdom for me?"

"Well sir," he said, taking the question seriously. "I don't think this is going to work out. I don't think the Centaurs can be used as drop-ship troops. We have to come up with something else."

I sucked in a breath, cursed and slammed my gauntleted fist into the wall of the landing pod. The blow crushed in the metal. When I removed my hand, it slowly popped itself back into its previous shape.

When we'd gotten the Centaurs under some kind of control, I let the ship's big hand lift me back to the bridge. I investigated what had happened, using the vid systems that I'd left recording on their suits.

We watched as they stayed calm for the first minute or so. After that, they become uneasy. A few opened their eyes and turned off the black-out mode on their goggles. These individuals were the first to go nuts. They scrabbled at the walls, trying to get out of what seemed to them to be a deathtrap.

Things had gone from bad to worse when we'd hit a sudden patch of turbulence. At that point, the ones that had remained calm were outnumbered by the panicked Centaurs. Some shed their systems and gored one another, or the smooth walls. A few lasered down the lunatics. Many were blinded by these emissions, released in close quarters without the protection of goggles. After that, they'd pretty much all gone berserk.

We spent a few desperate minutes cleaning up the mess. Seven of the Centaurs out of the twenty we'd brought down survived. There were arguably eight survivors, if you counted the one that had run off onto the ice. But we never found him again.

We buried the dead in the ice and had to lift off with the rest of them in an anesthetized state. According to sat-com, we only had a few minutes left before the missiles reached us, and we didn't have enough covering fire to assure we could shoot them all down. I ordered the lift-off with a heavy heart.

I told myself as we retreated into space that every training death saved ten lives in combat. I knew as well that the dead troops had at least ended their lives on their own homeworld. These thoughts helped a little, but not much.

8

I spent a full day dreaming up solutions to the Centaur transportation problem. My staff brought me their own ideas, which I listened to politely. For the most part, they were terrible.

"Drug all the Centaurs and land them in a base camp a hundred miles from their objective," Sloan suggested.

I nodded and said something like "uh-huh". That's just what I wanted, a million or so semi-conscious mountain goats to care for. What would happen when a Macro missile barrage landed in their midst unexpectedly? Were my marines supposed to run away carrying a drugged goat tucked under each arm?

Miklos came up with a Fleet-centered idea: "Just bombard the domes from space with nuclear weapons, Colonel."

I had to admit, that idea had more merit than the first. But we would have to manufacture thousands of missiles, and the enemy was well-defended against any space-borne assault. That's why I had equipped these troops. I had planned to drop dirtside fast and deploy a beachhead, then press in against a dome before they could mass and stop us.

"It's occurred to me, but I don't think we have enough firepower. Even if we did, I don't think I would want to unload it all on the Centaur planets. We are supposed to be freeing these worlds, not destroying them."

Marvin had the most interesting idea of all. He suggested we go in with a small force, secretly operating as commandos. If we could get

Marvin himself under one of those domes, he felt he could reprogram the machine to operate under our control.

I rejected everyone's plan, but thanked them for their valuable input. I then headed back to my own ship to think. After about twenty hours of mulling it over, I became tired and frustrated. I did what I usually did under such circumstances: I drank a six-pack of beer. This move improved my mood dramatically.

Soon, I found myself in *Socorro's* observatory. I hummed and admired the view. I spilled a few golden droplets on the ballistic glass surface. The chamber had always been icy cold, and the beer froze into hard amber beads on the glass.

I studied the planet below, so near yet so inaccessible. The chilly ice-cap on every crag was so white, and so bright it almost hurt to look at it. I tapped at the glass with my foot, and it clacked back at me. I frowned. What if...?

Bursting with a new idea, I rushed out of the observatory and called in my staff. It took them long minutes to assemble. They yawned and squinted at me, as it was the middle of a sleeping shift for most of them.

"How much ballistic glass do we have in the system?" I demanded. "I want a full accounting. I want to know about all of it."

"I don't know, sir," Miklos admitted. "Not much. We don't generally put windows into our ships, except to cover cameras. Most of it is probably in use as visors for our helmets. What do we need it for?"

"We'll have to manufacture it, then," I said, beginning to pace. "That will slow down our infantry kit production, but we don't have any choice. I mean, what good are Centaur infantry kits if the troops all end up insane when we drop them, anyway?"

My staff exchanged confused glances. I waved my hands at them.

"Don't you see? They want to see big vistas. They want skies and horizons. They don't want to be blind in a box. They don't want goggles or hoods over their heads."

"Yes sir..." Miklos said, looking at me as I were as nuts as a Centaur.

"Well, we'll give them that view, just for a few minutes, as we drop them down to the surface."

"I understand your intent," Marvin said. "It is ingenious—and if it works, it will prove how bizarre biotic mentalities truly are."

I almost gave him an angry retort about machines that rebuilt themselves every day like fashion models, but decided there wasn't time.

"We've got to try it first, of course," I said. "We'll rig up a new version of the landing pod with transparent material and drop a new group tonight."

My staff looked concerned, except for Marvin, who looked excited. I could tell from the way he whipped his tentacles and cameras around he was curious about the experiment. Would it end as another horrible, bloody failure? Either way, it was new data for his hungry robot mind.

"Do you mean to give them a window, sir?" Miklos asked.

"Not just a window, man. I mean to give them a glass floor. Like my observatory. Something to look at, something to swallow up their eyes and keep them focused on distant horizons. How can anyone feel claustrophobic while standing on what looks like open space?"

"Sounds more frightening than being surrounded by solid walls," Kwon said doubtfully.

I pointed a finger at him. "For you, maybe. But you're not a crazy mountain goat. They don't like walls. Anyway, it's worth a try."

Miklos and the others exchanged glances. "But we'll have to ask another team to—to possibly sacrifice themselves."

"That doesn't matter to them. These people will do anything for the herd. I know them. They won't hesitate to volunteer. In fact, I bet we get about a million volunteers."

"But that's not the point, Colonel—"

I turned on him. Maybe it was the beer that was still in my system, but I wasn't in any mood for misplaced sentimentality. "Listen, Miklos. I know you want to do this the clean way, bombing our way through it. But that will take a lot of nukes, a lot of floating radiation clouds for decades to come and a lot of time and resources we don't have. At any moment, a fresh Macro fleet could come sailing through a ring and slaughter these people by the billions. We're going to risk their lives again, and we're going to do it within the next few hours."

Miklos looked down, and nodded. He looked back up again a moment later. "We only need a squad of them—just to see if it works."

I almost let him have this one, but then I shook my head. "A full pod. I need real combat conditions. I want a hundred of them in there, in close quarters. If it doesn't work, we have to know now, not when we're in the middle of a live operation."

Resignedly, my staff at last agreed. We broke up the meeting and went our separate ways. Within an hour, I was back aboard the landing ship, and we were sailing down to the planet. This time, I had us drop on the northern pole. It was closer to the enemy installations, and I knew they'd fire on us again, but that wasn't the point. All I wanted to know is whether or not the Centaurs could handle it. The moment we touched down, we'd turn around and head back up into space—whether the Centaurs went nuts or not.

At the last minute, Sloan tried to give the Centaurs inactive weapons. I chewed him out and belayed his order.

"This will be a live-fire exercise, marine," I said.

Grim-faced, we rode down from space with a fresh load of Centaur troops. I didn't know if they knew what had happened to the last batch. I wasn't even sure it would matter if they did know. These people were so self-sacrificing when it came to combat, they would suffer any indignity or danger to regain their homeworld—anything except dishonor, that is.

The descent was even worse this time. There was a storm system spiraling over the northern polar region. No one had bothered to tell me. I supposed they knew I'd just tell them to fly the mission anyway, that this was a test under adverse conditions. Maybe they even thought I'd wanted it that way. Rather than abort the operation, I pressed ahead.

We didn't get hit by one buffeting wind shear—we were struck by at least four. The ship heeled and swerved sickeningly. Even with our dampeners, we were left floating around the ship. I felt like I was jumping up and down inside an express elevator—while the building was going down.

We watched the monitors, and the Centaurs were indeed showing signs of stress. They staggered in place and kicked at one another with their hind legs.

"Maybe we should tell them to put on their hoods and goggles now," Kwon suggested. "We are almost down. If they go nuts, they are going to make an awful mess crammed in there like that."

"I appreciate your input, First Sergeant," I said.

He glanced at me and nodded. Everyone knew what that meant, when it wasn't followed up by any commands to change anything.

Kwon looked away and muttered something.

"What was that, Sergeant?"

"I said: 'We are still Riggs' Pigs'"

I smiled. "That's right."

We came down in a screaming dive that pulled up short just as we touched down. The worst part was right at the end, when we moved from a tilted angle of descent to a flat-bottomed approach for the landing. The Centaurs were leaning with the ship, like someone riding on the back of a motorcycle. Even with our inertial dampeners, this final maneuver left many of them scrambling to keep their feet. Their eyes were wide and round and rolled in their heads. I had audio and video feeds hooked up, and there was plenty of grunting and bleating going on.

"They're calling you names, Colonel!" Kwon said.

"I bet they are," I laughed. All around me, the rest of my crew was smiling now, too. None of the Centaurs had lost it completely. Not a single one had discharged his weapon, burning and blinding his fellows. They were scared, but they were all in one piece.

We let them unload and walk around on the ice for about two hundred seconds before herding them back aboard. This was part of the test as well: after having endured the flight down, could they be convinced to reload on the pod and fly again?

The answer was a resounding *yes*. They bounded over one another to get inside the craft again. I smiled, seeing some of their flanks were shivering. Their breath blew in plumes of hot, white steam.

"It must be cold out there," I said. "Look at them, eager to board again. Now lift us off quick, Miklos. The Macros must have anticipated this landing. The missiles will be here shortly."

He needed no further encouragement. Soon, we were rising up into the clouds again. The surface of the world vanished in a pall of rushing mist.

When we returned to orbit, everyone was in a celebratory mood. "I knew you would figure it out, Colonel," Kwon said.

I nodded, wondering if he really had been so confident. It was a natural thing to say, but I'd sensed a great deal of worry in the group before the mission. Now that everything had worked out, it was easy to say you'd had faith all along.

I suspected they'd doubted me after witnessing the previous failure. Perhaps that's what made me the commander. A leader in a desperate war has to be willing to take risks—risks that could cost a lot of lives. That sort of decisiveness and responsibility just came with the territory.

After the test, I focused on logistics. We needed radioactives badly to keep producing infantry kits, and organic compounds to form polymers for the glass-bottomed landing pods. We'd cannibalized what materials that could be spared on board the Centaur satellites. We had to have a fresh supply.

Looking over our surveying reports from around the system, we found only one ready supply that wasn't on the surface of one of the target worlds themselves. It was out at the single gas giant in the Eden System, orbiting among various moons that circled the huge planet. The supply consisted of a natural ring of dust and debris. Probably formed by a moon-on-moon collision ages ago, the broken up chunks were just right for feeding into the hungry maws of Nano factories. They digested small debris much more easily than big, tightly-assembled pieces. I dispatched two ships, all I could spare at the moment, to collect the materials we needed by scooping them out of the rings. The rings themselves were pretty to look at—I vaguely hoped we wouldn't do too much damage to them. I shrugged a moment later. We needed the materials, and a pretty view wasn't worth a single life to me.

The source was refined and effective. Soon, I had reports coming in of thousands of gallons of loose matter being caught in sweeping collectors. Still, the entire process represented a delay. I'd hoped to launch my attack within a week—but that single week was quickly stretching into a month.

"Good news, Colonel," Marvin said, scraping the walls with his metal tentacles as he barged into my office.

"I could use some good news," I said, straightening my back and turning to look at him.

"I have video of the missile impacts. May I bring them up on your system?"

I gave him permission, and while I frowned he showed me various satellite vids of flashing strikes on the icy region we'd first landed upon at the southern pole. The missiles plumed with vapor and left discolored craters in the ice.

I frowned at the vids. "I'm not sure what is so positive about these strikes. They seem accurate to me. They hit everything in the region. I can see now, they spread the strikes so that even if we'd tried to run, we could not have escaped the kill zone."

"Exactly!" Marvin said excitedly. "Here, let me show you."

He zoomed in on a crater in the ice. It looked to me to be much the same as the rest. "We're able to get very high resolution levels, even from space. This was taken some ten minutes after the strike. Notice, that due to the high winds, the area has been largely cleared of obscuring smoke."

"Yes, yes, Marvin," I said. "But what is your point?"

"Right there, see that at the edge of the crater? Let me zoom-in closer for you."

Marvin applied his writhing metal tentacles to the screen, making a spreading motion with them. Our point of view zoomed closer. It was odd, watching him do that.

I studied the scene. It took me several seconds, but then I saw it. A clump of fur blowing in the ceaseless winds. And something else. "Is that a buried hoof, Marvin?"

"Yes, I'm certain of it."

I opened my mouth, then closed it again. "It must be the one we left behind. He must have run in a straight line—but he didn't make it out of the blast radius in time."

"A stroke of luck, to be sure," Marvin said. "The Macros didn't have to use so many missiles against such a small number of targets, but their thoroughness saved us this time. Did you have this result in mind, sir? Did it enter into your planning at some point?"

I stared at him with narrowed, baffled eyes. Marvin wasn't good at reading human expressions, so I was fairly sure he didn't realized how dumbfounded I was. "Let me get this right: you are happy this poor creature was blown apart?"

"Naturally, Colonel Riggs. When you first decided to break the pact between the Centaurs and the Macros, I was certain that you had made a mistake in your timing. I now see you had thought of every detail. How can the Macros know their agreement with the herd people has been broken, if there is no evidence? They have obliterated it."

As he spoke, I felt a chill go through me. I'd sort of forgotten about the agreement between the Centaurs and the Macros. Any Centaur spotted on the planet surface was a violation that would allow the Macros to destroy their vulnerable satellites. With all the fighting that had gone on, I'd figured that deal was null and void now. But there was no real reason to assume that. We are at war with the Macros, but that didn't mean the Centaurs were classified as rebels yet.

"I'm further impressed that you were so certain of this outcome," Marvin went on.

"What makes you think I was so sure we'd get away with this?"

"Why—because you didn't put any kind of defensive systems on the satellites themselves. The Macros could use their missiles to destroy them at any moment, and yet you were unconcerned. Was that done to prevent them from deducing your true intentions?"

I stared at him for a second before nodding slowly. I got it now. If the Macros had realized the Centaurs had set foot on the planetary surface, all bets would have been off. They would have been free to break their deals and destroy the satellites at will.

"Sure," I said, my voice slightly shaken. "That's *exactly* why I did it that way. Why give them a clue what I had planned for them?"

"Well played, Colonel Riggs."

"Uh-huh. Marvin? Could you tell me the next time you foresee a problem like this, rather than trusting my judgment blindly?"

"Even if it requires interrupting you?" he asked.

"Even then."

"I'll reset those thresholds in my neural chains."

"Excellent," I said. I stared at the tabletop, which still displayed the fragmented Centaur. If that guy had been a better runner, he might have been responsible for the extermination of his entire species.

I corrected myself almost immediately: then *I* might have been responsible for the extermination of his entire species.

"One more thing Marvin…"

"Yes, Colonel?"

"Get Miklos on the com-link. We're cancelling all further trips to the surface for Centaurs from now on. They aren't going down there again until we launch an all-out attack."

"Good thinking, sir."

-9-

The preparations crawled. Every day, I expected to hear from Admiral Crow. I suspected he would soon send formal orders recalling me. Maybe he'd even demand my arrest. But I had the email system locked down, so only I'd hear about something like that.

The order from Star Force never came. After several weeks had gone by, I began to suspect Crow had decided I was less trouble out here in the Eden System. I knew him all too well. Maybe he figured it was easier to let me do whatever I wanted out here. With luck, I'd get my fool ass shot off at some point.

The big invasion day finally came. We were way behind schedule—but nothing was unusual about that. We had a good reason to be late: I'd drastically changed the game plan. Before assaulting the cold Centaur homeworld with native troops, I'd ordered that every Centaur satellite be loaded up with anti-missile batteries. These were essentially beam turrets, like those I'd built on Andros Island back home. Each turret consisted of a light cannon, a generator, a brainbox, a sensory array, a swivel mount, and a number of servos to move it around quickly. These systems were a lot like the one's I'd built back home, but they had the added advantage of being set up to operate in space. An airless void was a far more effective medium for lasers than an atmosphere, where something like a rainstorm might well ruin your day. Up in space, there were essentially no obstructions. Enemy missiles coming up to take them out would have a tough time of it.

When coming up out of the gravity-well of any planet, a missile was by necessity slowed down. Worse, they didn't have any distance in which to build up sufficient velocity. Even with nanotech engines, they would hardly be going more than escape velocity—about Mach 30 on this planet—when they came up out of the atmosphere and were burned down. I'd learned that long range missiles were much more effective when they were fired in deep space at a stationary target. That way, they had plenty of time to accelerate up to an incredible speed. Going fast enough, defensive systems became ineffective. Our turrets simply wouldn't have enough time to shoot them down before they'd slammed into the stations and taken them out.

In our modern form of warfare, Mach 30 was pretty slow. The nano-directed turrets had plenty of time to lock on and plenty of range to fire, as they hung high orbit.

It had taken too long to build the defensive systems, but I knew I didn't have much choice. If we dropped on the planet, breaking the Centaur treaty with the Macros, they were sure to try to take out the satellites. Hell, they might even have considered that a win. Expunging the civilian population of an entire biotic species was probably worth quite a bit of loss to them at this point. We had to be a big pain in their battery packs by now.

Once every Centaur satellite bristled with laser turrets and we had enough landing pods and infantry equipment, the time to act had arrived. We watched the weather then, hoping for a storm to cover our landing. Unlike past invasions with lower tech systems, storms weren't really a cause for concern in a space invasion mission like this one. All they did was provide interference for our drop.

"That storm system won't let up for two days," Miklos said.

I nodded. "I like the sound of that. We'll drop in forty minutes. Relay the command and get every marine into a pod."

Kwon squawked in my helmet a few minutes later. "I heard it was a go, sir! Is that right?"

"You heard correctly, First Sergeant. Get to your pod with a full kit. You are going down with the first wave."

Kwon roared with excitement, which caused me to wince in my helmet. One pain in the butt about headsets and helmets was you couldn't easily pull the ear-piece away from your head when someone was being overly loud. Still, I smiled. Kwon had been bored out of his mind for the last month or so. There were only so many drills you could do in the simulation bricks before getting tired of them. He was about to finally be unleashed on a target world, and being allowed to do what he'd signed up for: switching off machines.

When we quietly deployed in space, spreading out in orbit over a large area, I didn't order them all to drop at once. Instead, I sent down three squadrons of ships, each with three destroyers carrying landing pods clutched up against the bottom skin of the ship. Like birds of prey carrying precious cargo, our ships dove with alarming speed. Watching the assault via optical systems set up on the satellite and on each of the dropships, I thought it looked more reckless than it had seemed on paper. Here we were, riding in thin, smart metal cans in steep dives toward an alien world that was thronged with unknown numbers of enemy robots.

We hit the upper atmosphere and the ships began to glow a burnt orange about two minutes into the assault. We kept up the high rate of speed as planned, the pilots had orders not to decelerate until we hit the friction later.

I'd begun to sweat, when I finally felt the G-forces of heavy braking. Miklos was commanding my ship, and I was with him on the bridge. We both watched our pilot tensely. He was a gifted young man with dark, serious eyes.

"How are the Centaurs doing?" Miklos asked me.

I gave a guilty start. I was in command of a full company of native marines, and I'd failed to check in on them.

"I'll have a look," I said. "It's time to get into the pod for rapid deployment, anyway. Remember your orders, Captain. Do a one-eighty and lift off again as soon as your ship's arm releases the pod. Any given landing group is less valuable than the ship itself."

"I know my orders, sir," he assured me. "I'll dump you and head right back into space in less than thirty seconds."

I nodded. I climbed hand over hand along the deck plates, using my battle suit's implanted propulsion disks to make headway against the G-forces. I didn't know how hard we were decelerating, but even with the inertial dampeners set to maximum, Barbarossa's powerful engines had me grunting and straining. It had to be more than four Gs, if I had to guess.

When I reached out and opened the landing pod hatch with a touch, I braced myself. I hoped against hope the Centaurs weren't killing each other.

My worries were baseless. Inside, I found a hundred of the aliens in full kit. They stood, jostling against one another and struggling somewhat against the nano-arms that attempted to restrain them. But every one of them was staring with their big round eyes at the view from the massive window I'd installed into each of these pods. As I'd ordered, the pilot kept this window directed toward the brilliant planet itself.

The moment I saw the view, I found myself as transfixed as they were. Rushing up from nothing, vapors and mist trailed with glowing orange plasmas over our vision. The vapor moved so fast, ice-particles and sparks looked like vivid lines of color. Beyond that, we could see the surface below the cloud cover. We'd hit the friction layer and were coming in at an alarming rate. I'd been in power-dives like this before—but never with a bay window to look out of.

When I could speak again, I checked in with the unit Captain. He was an old warlord of a Centaur, with one horn and one eye missing. His fur was gray and bristly. I hadn't argued when they'd assigned him to command my unit. He was clearly experienced, and I was sure assigning him to me was some kind of huge honor for everyone involved. Complaining would have dishonored all of us, and possibly the old goat would have killed himself or something. I'd heard of them doing that sort of thing before—launching themselves off cliffs to fall to their deaths on their satellites because my marines had chewed them out during training. I'd had a number of talks with my noncoms, insisting they curb their natural tendency to abuse recruits.

Among the Centaurs, apparently the way you rebuked an individual was by ignoring them. If you made no mention of honor, pride, wind, sky—or anything on the laundry list of things they cared so dearly about—then you provided them with no honor. That was acceptable, and the message was clear to the subordinate: they had screwed up. But if you exhibited direct anger toward an individual of inferior rank, well, they just couldn't handle it. They were shattered, and both the apprentice and the master were embarrassed and sullied in the process.

The old one-eyed goat had the only headset capable of translating my orders to his team. The rest of them would follow him—either by mimicking him or listening to his commands. We'd practiced the command structure inside the satellites on the simulated open ground, but it was untested in actual combat. I seriously hoped it wouldn't bite me in the ass, but there was no way of proving the system other than to employ it in the field.

Before I had time to do more than take in a brief report from the Centaur Captain, we were shuddering and heeling-over.

"All right, this is it," I shouted into the com-link. "We'll be landing in the next few seconds. Everyone fix their masks and set their goggles on auto—we might be going in hot. When the big doors open, get out of the pod as fast as possible. Don't leave your equipment behind, or it will go back up with the ship. They aren't waiting around for us to smell the flowers."

I had no idea how this translated into Centaur talk. I do know that the Captain was still converting my thoughts into theirs by the time we'd come to a jolting halt. My feet stung in my boots, we landed so hard. The ballistic glass had a crack in it, and I could see rocks and grass pressed down under us. I grimaced at that. I should have put the windows all around on the sides, not one big one in the bottom like a glass-bottomed boat. I relayed the problem to Miklos, telling the pilot to be more careful and telling them all to dump fresh constructive nanites into the landing pod to effect repairs on the glass for the next trip. I didn't want it losing pressure.

Then the doors disappeared, and the Centaurs didn't need any kind of urging. They bounded out into the rainstorm like a herd of fleeing animals—except these animals were armed and were assaulting this world, not running from anything.

A few of them jostled me as their brown furry bodies zoomed past. They could really jump when they wanted too. I followed them out, checking my kit reflexively. All systems registered green and the power pack was full. The generator on my back hummed into life, and I had my projector in my hands, warmed up and humming. I was ready to rock and roll.

-10-

There's no moment quite as exhilarating in a marine's life as the first time his boots touch unknown ground in a combat zone. There's so much noise, you're blinded by fresh sights, even the smells assault your senses. It's hard not to feel as if you are dreaming—but you aren't, you're really there. As a bonus, the unseen enemy is somewhere nearby, plotting your death.

We raced away from the landing pod, finding ourselves in an area of brilliantly green rolling hills. The grass was tall. Every blade was as wide as a man's thumb and reached up past my waistline. A mile to my left was a forest of big, strange-looking lumpy growths—I suppose you could call them trees. They looked more like giant broccoli to me. Closer at hand on our right flank was a lake of icy blue water. Dead ahead the hills continued, a broad swathe of green. We were in a veritable river of tall grasses.

In the distance ahead, the grassy hills swept up to the edge of a trio of rocky mountain peaks. Those mountains were our destination. Somewhere behind them, the enemy had a major base. Marvin and the rest of our computers had calculated the odds, and they had determined this area to be the most likely location of an accessible Macro dome. As we couldn't see the actual dome from space, it was assumed to be underground, or disguised in some fashion. Still, it had to be here. The machines kept marching in and out of this region, delivering raw supplies on a continuous basis.

All around my running company, more ships landed. They dropped their payloads then shot back up into space. We were among the first few thousand to come down.

"Head for the trees, we need cover!" I shouted.

69

After my orders were translated and relayed, the mass of the Centaurs wheeled left and bounded for the trees. I ran after them, but quickly had to take flight to keep up. They could run at a shocking pace, even with bulky kits on their backs. Under my boots the grass rattled and fluttered away from my suit's repellers like green water.

I opened a channel to the Fleet people above. "Everyone in the first wave make it down okay?"

Miklos answered. He'd been catching up on current events for me while I was busy humping it after a hundred racing goat-troops.

"One pod had trouble Colonel—accidental weapons discharge," Miklos reported.

"How many?"

"Six dead, ten wounded, sir."

"That's quite an *accidental* discharge!"

"We don't even hint around about them lying sir—especially when we know they are. The Centaur Captain refused to let the transport take the dead and injured back up. They dumped their casualties on the grass and left them. They said something about serving the winds of—"

"Yeah, yeah," I interrupted. "Sky, clouds, honor and all that. Well, I suppose they can at least enjoy dying here on their own planet. Any sign of incoming missiles?"

"Not yet sir, but it's only a matter of time."

Time. It was the one resource I never had enough of. The second wave was on its way down by the time I reached the protective cover of the broccoli-trees. I saw other units doing the same all along the landing zone. I'd given the individual commanders leeway in terms of tactics in the opening minutes of the drop. Everyone was to survive and move toward the target as quickly as possible.

Not one minute after we'd reached the tree line, I heard the snap and whine of incoming missiles. "Everyone down, seek cover."

I threw myself flat, but noticed the Centaur troopers under my command seemed confused. They milled among the trees and directed their lasers toward the bulbous canopy of dark green pods overhead. I supposed they really didn't know what to expect when under fire from an aerial bombardment. We'd done little with them in the way of training, other than equipping them with effective weapons systems and figuring out how to get them down onto the surface of this planet without killing each other. We hadn't trained them in organized infantry tactics. There had been too many cultural and language differences, and most importantly, not enough time.

With all that said, lying down in the middle of a forest just didn't make sense to them. They were herd animals that liked to run from danger, not hug dirt when it came. My order hadn't been clear enough. I thought hard for a few seconds, muttering curses into the fallen, mushy pods that pressed up against my faceplate.

"I want every last buck to get his tail up close to a tree. Stand there and lean against it. Enemy fire is incoming. Move!"

I watched as they shuffled around for a few minutes in a tight group, then finally broke it up and went to separate trees. Part of the reason I'd given them the tree order was to break them up. They instinctively bunched up. I didn't want a single lucky hit to come down and wipe out the entire company.

When the missiles did finally arrive, they missed us. The barrage peppered the grassy hills we'd just left behind. Orange flashes bombarded the open grasslands in a rippling pattern. Roiling white clouds shot up, and then moments later thousands of clods of black earth showered down. At least they hadn't thrown a nuke—not yet.

Fortunately, my marines had been smart enough to clear the area immediately after exiting their pods. The machines hammered our empty LZ. I radioed Miklos, telling him to change the location of the next drop. He assured me new plans were in motion.

Then I jumped to my feet, calling for my Centaurs to follow. I charged in the general direction of the three mountain peaks. Behind me, the herd played follow-the-leader. It was a game they knew well.

We made good time, occasionally meeting up with other companies. We were to move as scattered, independent forces toward the mountains and regroup there for an organized assault. The plan had been left deliberately vague, as we hadn't know exactly what we were in for until we put our boots on the ground.

Twenty minutes later, I was pleased with our progress. We'd made it halfway to the mountain peaks—a good ten miles—before anything went seriously wrong. At that point, we ran into one of their harvesting machines.

The systems the Macros used on this world were different than those I'd dealt with back on Earth. In the South American campaign, they'd churned out thousands of small robots that were essentially

71

worker-ants for the colony. Here on this planet, however, they'd built much larger machines to do their harvesting for them.

The harvester we ran into was the biggest machine I'd ever had the pleasure of meeting while on foot. I'd seen its kind before, however. Back when Sandra and I had taken our ill-fated scouting trip out to the blue giant system we figured was probably Bellatrix, we'd met up with a mining robot on an airless rock full of metals. That thing had been rolling along on spiked spherical wheels and chewing up raw materials it found on the surface. This one had a similar look to it, but it had a cow-catcher sweep in front of the main maw. What it was doing, as closely as we could figure out, was digesting trees from the forest. It scooped them up into its maw like an electric shaver chewing on a man's stubble. Chopping the trees off low at the base of the trunk, the organic material then ran up chutes and was chemically leeched and burned. Behind the machine, a massive black trail of charcoal as wide as a fresh-laid highway stretched out for miles.

We'd seen operations of this kind from space. Our reconnaissance didn't show any of the harvested regions in this area, only virgin forests we'd planned to use for cover. My best guess was that the machine had been redirected here after learning of our invasion.

It really didn't matter why the machine was there, what mattered was it was plowing right into my unit and it was incredibly big. I didn't know what kind of armament it had, and I had no clue as to how we were going to kill it. But I didn't let these details bother me.

"Spread out! Circle around behind the machine and shoot it in the rear. Aim for sensory equipment, joints and any weapons systems it might have."

The Centaurs followed my orders—sort of. Rather than scattering as individuals or even squads, they broke into two groups which each swept around the machine on either side. I could tell by now they really didn't like any orders that caused them to separate and act as individuals.

For my own part, I shot up directly into the air. None of my troops could perform this kind of trick, as they didn't have full battle suits. I hoped it didn't have an anti-air pod on its back—fortunately, it didn't. The machine I'd met up with back in the Bellatrix system had ignored my scouting ship entirely. While this one was acting aggressively, it didn't really have the capacity to do anything at range.

72

As my Centaurs flowed around its flanks, however, it did surprise us. Two side chutes flipped out. These were probably built to cut into groves of trees in hard-to-reach pockets near boulders and the like. Whatever they were for, they ate into my troops like lawn-clippers. A dozen or so Centaurs on each flank were separated from their hooves, in many cases from all four at once. Still alive, the flopping troops fell bleating into the threshing blades as they made a second pass. Blood fountained up and puffs of dark fur floated in the forest between the trunks.

The troops that survived flashed out with their weapons, burning the machine in a wild crisscross of beams. Vaporized metal puffed up from countless hits, but the machine seemed undaunted. Thirty seconds later, I was on top of the monster and most of my troops were behind it.

The harvester began a slow, laborious right turn. I could tell it was wheeling, trying to get its blades back into play. Apparently, it didn't have anything in the rear area other than the exhaust system which laid out the charcoal byproduct. Another machine would probably come along eventually to pick up the material the harvester left behind—but by then I hoped to be miles away.

"Keep behind it, men," I said. I realized even as I said it they *weren't* men, but old habits die hard. "Keep shooting it in the ass. I'll try to figure out what to do up here."

The Centaurs did as I asked. Beams lashed the harvester's hindquarters, to little apparent effect. At least no more of my troops were dying. Perhaps they felt it was dishonorable, not facing an enemy head on like two rams butting heads. But for once, they didn't complain about that.

It occurred to me that although the harvester was no longer killing my company, it was successfully delaying us. Could this be the prelude to a more effective attack by military units? I had to disable this thing and get back on track. I thought about the single nuclear grenade I had on my pack. It seemed like a waste to use it now. I only had the one, and I'd hoped to use it on a more critical target.

Finally, I decided to try an old tactic. I'd had time to examine the harvester from a top view. There were certain data and power lines that looked familiar to me, and they all led down to a central nodule about a dozen feet from the ground on the right side of the machine.

"All right this isn't working out. I want all of you to focus your laser fire on this box. Follow my lead."

I put my beamer on the box, and let my goggles shade to full blackout mode. If the Centaurs were good at one thing, it was following the leader. More than fifty beams joined mine, and we burned through the module in seconds. Many of the thick cables were severed during the process as well.

That was it for the harvester. First, its spinning, spiked wheels stopped churning up dirt. Then the blades on the forward scoop stopped making chewing motions. Within a minute, the entire machine halted. I sensed it was still active, watching us from a dozen sensory devices. Moreover, I could feel the thrum of its central driving engine, the vibration still came up through my boots.

I wanted this thing dead, so we spent another minute or so burning the contents of its brainbox completely away. It was mildly satisfying. When the machine was a smoking wreck, we left it and pressed onward toward our goal.

We'd gone from being one of the lead companies to being one of the laggers. I pushed my team hard to catch up.

By the time we reached the foot of the mountain range, Miklos had reported to me that most of the teams were down. In the end, we'd fielded much fewer than the millions of volunteers we'd been promised by the Centaurs. I would have gladly put them all down, but I didn't have enough delivery systems, or infantry kits. Putting them down without proper equipment would have been akin to murder in any case. As far as we could tell, the machines had exterminated every individual on the surface, and they weren't about to change their genocidal policy now.

We'd landed about thirty thousand Centaurs, each team lead by one of my officers or noncoms. A few were led by private first class marines who'd I'd raised to the rank of Corporal for serving in this hazardous mission.

By the time all the companies had made it to the mountain range, we'd only lost about three percent of them—six marines and about a thousand Centaurs. It seemed unfair, but these poor guys had a way of dying in groups. Their natural herding instincts failed them in modern combat—at least in regards to survival rates. That said, they got the job done and rarely complained. The only queries I received from them came when we stopped moving forward to press against the enemy. In these cases, I explained the situation to them in terms they understood.

"We are massing up before pressing forward. We need more weight, more numbers. When we have all our strength together, we will overrun the machines in our thousands."

This sort of talk always got them into line. They loved the idea of swarming the machines and burning them down. The enemy themselves were something of a surprise. They had missiles, good command and control and they fought gamely enough. But they lacked troops. Apparently, this system had been marked down as friendly in their book. We were in a state of peace, and therefore all production could be turned to harvesting resources.

I was surprised, as I thought perhaps our forays down to the surface at both poles would have made them switch their massive production systems over to military hardware. They hadn't done so, but they were sure to now.

Consequently, our march to the enemy dome was relatively easy. We met up with a few hundred machines—mostly small worker units. These functioned well against unarmed civilians, but when faced by thousands of troops carrying heavy beamers, they were melted to scrap quickly. The bigger harvesters were more of a problem, but we'd figured out how to disable them.

Then there were the gathering units that resembled floating cities. These came along the black highways of partially digested materials to pick them up. They were monstrous, buzzing systems that apparently used massive versions of the repellers in our battle suits to fly. Once we figured out where the repellers were located, they were easy to bring crashing to the ground.

I gathered my thousands on the cliffs over the valley we knew must contain the enemy dome. I wasn't happy with what I saw, however. Instead of finding caves that led down to the enemy production facilities, I found only a deep lake of still water that was barely above freezing. From this water, machines crawled in and out all along the shore line.

I compressed my lips and called Miklos. "Captain. Do you know what I'm seeing down here?"

"Yes Colonel, we are monitoring your suit video."

"Maybe the stream isn't clear up there, but what I'm seeing is a failure. The enemy dome must be at the bottom of this lake."

"Are you sure, sir?"

"Yes, I'm freaking sure!" I shouted. "How am I supposed to take thirty thousand Centaurs into a frozen lake? They don't even have vacc suits. They'd drown even before the Macros could murder them all."

"It does look like an intelligence failure, Colonel."

I took a deep breath. We'd come so far, all for the possibility of capturing a Macro production facility. We'd lost a lot of troops, time and given the enemy details as to our strength and tactics. But the mission was a failure despite all those lost assets on our side of the ledger.

"We spent too much time building up and not enough time doing proper recon. I have to take responsibility for that."

"Excuse me, Colonel," Miklos said. "I have Marvin here. He wishes to speak with you."

"Put him on."

"Colonel Riggs?"

"Yes, Marvin. Go ahead."

"You have about three hundred marines in full battle suits. I'll come down with you, if you like. If you can get me into that dome somehow, I'm fairly certain I can transfer full control of the unit to Star Force."

Fairly certain. It sounded like my epitaph. *Here lies Colonel Kyle Riggs, who was fairly certain he would survive his last campaign.*

I thought about it while Marvin prattled on about Macro security protocols and transmission spoofing codes. I believed that he believed it could be done. But I wasn't sure the Macros were going to cooperate. We had no way of knowing what they had down there. Maybe they'd held back their military hardware to protect the dome itself. Maybe they'd analyzed our intent and prepared a trap for us.

The real trouble was that the three hundred marines were the majority of the five hundred-odd human troops I had in the entire Eden system. If I lost them, I lost an asset I couldn't replace. I would have to return to Earth and endure Crow's sneering displeasure with no victories to speak of. For all I knew, Crow was on his way out here with a retrieval fleet. Doubtlessly, he'd been building new ships non-stop since I'd left him. I frowned fiercely and tried to push all thoughts of Crow and Earth out of my mind for now. I had a job right here that needed doing.

"No, I don't think I want to take my men underwater again," I said. "The risk is just too great. I went on a sea campaign once with thousands of troops—and we still pretty much failed. I'm pulling out."

"But sir, what about the enemy dome?" Marvin asked.

"We'll nuke it from orbit," I said. "We'll burn this lake until there isn't a drop of water to hide under."

"Our original plan was to take control of a Macro production facility."

I thought I heard a hint of a whine entering his voice, but it could have been my imagination. I knew it was Marvin's dream to poke and prod at a real Macro production facility. No one had ever done so for long and lived. It was just the sort of thing that got his imagination boiling.

"There are two more domes on this planet. This one was the easiest to find, but we'll find another."

"But sir," Marvin persisted. "I must point out that—"

"Forget it Marvin," I said. "Miklos, pull us out of here and drop your bombs."

"Yes, sir."

-11-

A day later, I was crouched over a battle computer on *Barbarossa*. I was in a bad mood. We'd failed to take the first Macro factory we'd assaulted, and we'd blown our element of surprise in the bargain. On the plus side, I told myself repeatedly, we'd learned a lot and dealt the Macros a hard blow.

It wasn't enough, however. The enemy knew we were coming now, and every Macro production system on all six of these planets had to be churning out combat systems at this point. I wanted to attack again immediately, but it wasn't that simple. Getting Centaur troops back onto landing pods had proven very difficult. They simply didn't want to be trapped again after experiencing the freedom of running wild on their own planet. I couldn't blame them for that, but they represented a critical resource that I didn't want to lose.

When I reconvened the morning debate squad—my command staff—no one looked any happier than I did. Kwon rested his cheek on one massive fist. Miklos hunched over a tablet computer and tapped at it. Marvin looked positively dejected. He barely turned a camera in my direction when I spoke to him.

"All right," I said. "Let's review our options. When can we hit them again, and where?"

"Sir," Miklos said, "shouldn't we wait for Captain Sloan?"

I grunted, and drummed my fingers on the table for a full minute. I'd never been good at waiting on people. I finally keyed open my com-link and called him.

"Where are you, Sloan?"

"In transit sir—sorry about the delay. There's something odd showing up on our sensors."

I frowned. "Where? I don't see anything on our planetary surveillance app."

"No, not here, sir. Something is going on with the ring—and in the next system. The one with the lobsters, sir."

We hadn't even named that system yet. I figured I should get around to that, but hadn't been overly interested in the place since I'd discovered it. Now, however, Sloan had my full attention. He was excellent at spotting danger early—and avoiding it.

"Brief me when you get here."

Sloan arrived a few minutes later and took his seat. He had a worried look on his face. I tossed my scribbled agenda aside and turned to him. "All right, let's hear it."

"It might be nothing, sir."

I made an urgent gesture.

He nodded. "There was some kind of vibration—a signal maybe—which went through the ring. We detected it only because we have ships sitting at both sides. It was recorded on the logs, and when I compared data hours later, I noticed both ships had detected the same thing at about the same moment."

I squinted at Sloan. How could something *vibrate* these huge rings? Marvin's reaction was much more dramatic. At least six cameras on extending stalks rose up and stared at him from every possible angle.

"I don't get what you are trying to say," I said. "Something vibrated the rings? The entire thing vibrated? As in making a small motion?"

"Exactly, sir. Both ends did it, at the same time."

I shook my head. We really didn't know much about the rings. We didn't know much about the factories, either. In truth, we were primates playing with technology developed by our mysterious betters. I'd often wondered if one of these days we'd look down the barrel of one of these devices and pull the trigger with our tails. There would be monkey brains on the walls that day.

I began to speak, but I saw Marvin wanted to say something, so I turned to him. "Ask your questions, Marvin. I can see you are dying to."

"Captain Sloan, was there any form of emission detected?"

"No, none that we could pick up. No light, no radio, no magnetic impulse—nothing."

"How very odd," Marvin said.

I smiled. When Marvin called something "odd", it meant "exciting" to him.

"Is there any information from the Crustaceans?" I said. "Any mention of what it might mean?"

"Nothing. We have detected a large number of their ships, however, forming up in orbit over their primary water-moon."

"Any hostile intent detected?"

He shook his head.

"All right then, I want Marvin to study the data. Sloan, you are to tell the pilots on station out there to watch for any further anomalies and report them immediately."

"Right sir."

"Let's get back to current combat ops," I said, bringing up a map of the Centaur homeworld on the screen that all of us sat around. "Our secondary target is here, in the middle of an open slag-heap. It was once a forest, but their harvesters took care of that."

The screen depicted a black wound in the middle of a vividly green plain.

"I'd originally liked the mountain location better, as it provided us natural cover for our approach. But this one will have to do. At least there is no lake in the area for the dome to hide under. As far as we can tell, it is in the bottom of what looks like a giant sinkhole."

"I believe it's a strip-mine," Marvin said.

"Whatever. They are inside this deep, dark hole. We'll run down there and take it out."

"Excuse me, Colonel Riggs."

"What is it, Marvin?"

"When would you launch this attack—ideally?"

"Right now, but I can't. The first load of Centaurs we took down there isn't coming back, and they are about five thousand miles from this target. We have retrieved their weapons kits—about half of them anyway—and we have to put together a new invasion force."

"What if I told you we could invade today—within the hour?"

I looked at him. I knew he was baiting me. I knew that at the end of this rainbow, I'd find something Marvin wanted. I also knew that the bait smelled pretty good. I took a bite.

"Okay," I sighed. "Talk me into it."

"We can't mount a full-scale invasion force immediately," Marvin said. "But we could drop a small commando team. All they would have to do it run to the pit, find the factory and once under the dome—"

Kwon was laughing now, his heavy, whuffing sounds filled the room. "Run to the pit and slip under the dome? There is no cover, robot. You are a dumb toaster."

"My IQ exceeds yours by approximately—"

I cleared my throat. "Kwon has a good point. There is no cover. Macros don't care about night and day for visibility. They don't fall asleep on guard, either. How do you propose we sneak in there?"

"I never said we would *sneak* in. We will run in openly."

"Under fire?"

"Suicide!" proclaimed Kwon.

"Let me explain," Marvin continued. "Macros designate targets on the basis of their importance. This is an entirely predictable process. Therefore, if we present them with higher value targets, they will ignore any small party of individuals in the area."

I mulled this over. I knew what Marvin was talking about. Macros did work that way. Many times I'd sat with a squad near them, and while they had something else to shoot at, an individual was perfectly safe. "What do you suggest we use for a diversion?"

"The only asset we have. Our ships."

I nodded. I figured he was getting around to that. I turned to Captain Sloan. I could see the worry in his face. Captain Miklos was frowning down at his computer. I knew what they were all thinking. Would Riggs be crazy enough to go along with this robot's plan? Everyone there knew I just might. I found the thought almost as disturbing as they did.

But there was a certain beauty to it, the longer I considered it. We didn't have to have a knock-down battle with their newly built defensive units. We could bypass them and possibly many deaths and end the fight in one fell swoop. The more I thought about it, the more I started liking it.

I looked at Captain Sloan. He looked alarmed.

"Are you thinking of taking me with you, Colonel?" he asked.

I almost laughed. Sloan's death-avoidance radar must have been going off at full tilt.

"No, I want you in the ships—with Miklos here. You two will run ops and fly our destroyers around, shooting every harvester they have. In the meantime, Marvin, Kwon and I will be dropped on the battlefield. We'll take a squad into that hole."

"What if the Macros realize who you are?"

"Then I'm dead. I'll go under a code name. Call me Condor. I've always liked big buzzards."

Sloan nodded, looking relieved. Kwon was in the opposite mood, he pulled down the corners of his mouth into an appreciative grimace. "Will we get to fight, sir?"

"Hopefully not much. The mission is to get in there and take out the production system."

Miklos finally spoke up then. He asked his first question of the meeting, and it was a good one. "Sir, what about *after* you take over the dome? You will have every Macro in the hole reevaluating their targets. I doubt we can hold their attention at that point. You will be swamped in enemies."

I nodded, considering. "That is a major flaw," I admitted.

Marvin's cameras swung to every face in turn, and quickly judged his plan was in jeopardy. He'd stayed cagily quiet until now, letting us convince ourselves it could work. Now, he sensed the need for more input and jumped back into the conversation.

"Sirs," he said. "I have good news on that front. I will immediately put the dome back up, protecting the commandos inside."

"What if you can't do that, Marvin?" Miklos asked. "We are betting on you twice now, not just once."

Marvin began to answer, but I put up a hand. "We can't know if he can do it or not. But if he can take over the entire facility, it stands to reason he can maintain the dome. At that point, if Star Force can destroy the machines outside, we can clean out this entire nest and make it our own. The possible gains are enormous, gentlemen. We could churn out undreamed of levels of production with one of those systems. Instead of a hundred huge robots, we could build a fleet of destroyers, or a thousand laser turrets. We could even build the battle station I've been working on for weeks."

I massaged the stubble on my jaw, and the more I thought about it, the more I liked it. I found myself feeling a powerful emotion that I rarely experienced. *Greed*, that's what it was. All those raw materials, just sitting around the dome. Millions of tons of matter ready to be turned into whatever I wanted.

Most importantly, it would double the production capacity of Star Force. That was worth some risk, wasn't it?

-12-

Even before we launched the new ground assault, things got complicated. The Macros started it, by launching missiles at every one of the Centaur satellites. They did it all at once, and they did it by sending a full barrage of sixteen surface-to-space weapons toward each target. Every missile was loaded with a nuclear warhead and a Macro technician at the helm. Macro missiles were essentially small ships—suicidal spacecraft on a one-way mission.

I didn't have much time to wonder if they'd built these long ago, or only just now in response to our attack. Whatever the case, it was clear they'd reclassified the system from "peaceful" to "contested", and they'd also decided the Centaurs had broken their deals sufficiently to be directly attacked. I couldn't blame them on that score.

Fortunately, I'd had a large number of automated turrets installed on every Centaur orbital habitat. They weren't foolproof, but they should stop a small missile attack like this. Still, watching the weapons rise up in red arcs from the surface had me bearing my teeth in a grimace inside my helmet. What if they had some fresh trick to play? What if my laser defenses weren't fully operational? It would only take one hit to inflict many millions of Centaur casualties. All told, billions of lives were under direct attack.

I looked at the timer. We had a little under seven minutes to wait before they hit us.

"Miklos, status report," I said.

"All enemy missiles on target. They will be within range of defensive fire in—four more minutes."

84

I did some quick calculations, and I didn't like my answers. "Are you telling me we'll only have two minutes to shoot them all down? Why is our range on these systems so short?"

"We put up what we could, Colonel," he said unapologetically. "The systems are what they are. Remember sir, this is not open space. The missiles are coming up through the atmosphere in every case. There is cloud cover and the like to get in the way."

I nodded glumly. It was going to be a long wait.

When the missiles were three minutes out, I took a deep breath. "Are they hitting everything at exactly the same time?"

"Yes," Miklos said. "All six habitable satellites have an identical attack incoming... Apparently, the enemy didn't want us to have time to adjust to their assault. Their precise timing indicates they must have missile reserves on some worlds. On the Centaur homeworld, for instance, the enemy only had two factories to produce the missiles. It only makes sense the other worlds would have produced more munitions in the same amount of time."

"You're saying they are probably holding back? That this could just be a probe? A taste-test attack?"

"Something like that, sir."

I looked back to *Barbarossa's* big wall-screens. Things just kept getting better and better. I wondered how many Centaurs would die if a single missile got through. Had I screwed up by getting them into this war? They'd proven to be fairly ineffective ground troops. Perhaps, I should have stuck with my own marines and done the job the old-fashioned way, without trying to glue laser packs onto a herd of mountain goats.

Self-doubt was very natural in a helpless, deadly situation. Fortunately, I didn't have to endure it for long. The next minute passed and our lasers started firing. They did pretty well at first.

"A hit sir—another!" Miklos said, excitement creeping into his voice.

"Put up a tally for each world, Captain."

"One moment, sir," he said. He began tapping and sliding his fingers over the screen in front of him. As an operational wingman, he wasn't as good as Major Sarin. I did trust his judgment, however. And I didn't have to worry about him making a pass at me, either.

"Give me a verbal count, man," I said after a full minute went by. I could see we were firing, but didn't really know if we were hitting the enemy or not. Missiles were winking out—but how many?

"I've got it, sir."

The screens displayed readouts under every planet's image. Here on the Centaur homeworld, we'd done pretty well. There was only one missile left. Judging by the number of hot beams it had tracing it, that one was doomed as well. This was due to the fact our own destroyers were stationed here and they had moved to engage the missiles themselves, increasing our defensive fire capacity.

On the other worlds, the numbers were less certain. Two planets had four missiles incoming, two had five, and the one closest to the sun had—eight?

"Is that right?" I asked, my voice raising as I spoke each word. "Eight missiles are still coming at Eden-6? We're going to lose a hundred million civvies out there, Miklos!"

"Possibly, sir."

I took a deep breath. Eighty-eight seconds to go before impact. These situations had come to haunt me, they were my personal nightmare. To have made choices that cost millions of clueless unarmed beings to be killed... I thought hard.

"Have we got any ships out there?" I asked.

"Two, sir."

"Get them on the command channel."

I was down to sixty-one seconds by the time I got the ship captains on the line. "Captain—" I paused to look at his name on the screen. Hiro, that was it. "If those missiles get through, just one of them, we'll lose a sixth of a biotic species. The seeds to an entire world. I want those missiles stopped."

"I know sir, we're firing at the incoming missiles. We're doing our—"

"Captain Hiro, I can't order you to block them, but I'm asking you to."

There was a momentary pause. "Oh...I see, sir. Hiro out."

That was it. I watched, sweating as the missile count dropped to zero on every world except for the sunward one, that tropical paradise I'd never yet had the pleasure of visiting. There, two missiles were seconds from impact. Suddenly, there was a blinding flash.

"He did it, sir," Miklos said. His voice sounded troubled. "He's rammed the missile. Should we contact the second destroyer?"

I shook my head. "There isn't time left. By the time I explained it to him and he maneuvered his ship…"

We watched as the last missile drove onward, nearing the satellite. I squinted my eyes. I thought I saw a hit with nine seconds to go—but I held my breath. The missile was still on the board. Then it exploded.

"He self-destructed when he took the hit," I said aloud.

"Who, sir?"

"The Macro pilot. Talk to me, is that satellite ruptured? Order all nearby ships to render assistance."

Captain Miklos relayed my orders. After a few more minutes, he gave me his report. "Looks like the satellite is damaged, but the hull has maintained integrity. There are leaks, but nothing catastrophic. Most of the Centaurs are going to survive."

I nodded, and took off my helmet. The attack was over. I smiled at the screens and read the reports. After a while, I caught Miklos staring at me. When I returned his gaze, he dropped his eyes back to his screen.

"What is it, Captain?"

He shrugged. "I don't know, sir. A hard thing to judge."

"What are you talking about?"

"How many men should die for a Centaur? Is one of our lives worth a million of theirs, a thousand, or only a hundred?"

"Oh," I said. "I've already made those calculations. Depends on who we're a talking about, of course. In the case of Star Force crews— I put that ratio at about a million of them to one of us."

With that, I turned around and walked off the command deck. I could feel Miklos' stunned stare on my back. I smiled grimly and left him wondering if I was serious or not. There were no cold calculations made in these moments, not for me. They were very hot, emotional, gut-wrenching choices.

But I had to admit, I did value one of my marines more than I did a quite large number of Centaurs. I had to. In the end, this was a war for survival, and I was determined that our side would win it. The side of all the biotics, that was.

Hiro had done as I'd asked, because I think he understood this. He'd made the sacrifice for the living. Together, we had to beat the machines—the moving, thinking dead. And we couldn't do that if we let millions die screaming in space to save our own sorry skins.

But with all that said, Star Force was still the main thing holding back the Macros. We truly were worth thousands of other lives each, because they would all be dead if we didn't win in the end.

-13-

After their first missile attack, we expected more, but they didn't come. For another day or two, we did nothing but scramble to build up our anti-missile defenses and patch holes in the damaged satellite. About a hundred thousand civvies had died there from asphyxiation and freezing—but it could have been worse. Much worse.

After I had every satellite bristling with small turrets, I placed unmanned platforms in low orbit. Each bore eight more small guns. They hung just above the atmosphere, about ten miles under every one of the big Centaur habitats. If another attack was launched, these tiny forts would have to be passed by the missiles. They could either expend a missile to destroy them, or ignore them and endure fire from their guns all the way up to the bigger targets.

I had quite a production operation going by this time. We'd learned our way around the star system and found the easiest matter was still the chunks of junk that formed rings around the gas giant. I had sent more collectors to orbit the massive world, dipping their scoops into the dirty rings and sucking up matter that was perfect for our purposes: small, pulverized minerals. I was glad for the supply, as we didn't have much left we could strip from the Centaur habitats. There were now noticeable holes in the gas giants rings—but I didn't care. The locals would just have to get used to the new look.

I kept fortifying the satellites until they were ready to stop a hundred missiles or more each. When I finally halted the effort, I wondered what I was doing. I called another meeting, this time with just Miklos, Marvin and myself.

"I think I'm playing into their hands," I told them.

"How so, sir?" asked Miklos.

"Think about it. They fire up less than a hundred missiles, all told. I then proceeded to turn away from my invasion mission and spend most of this week building defenses. In the meantime, they quietly build their own forces, digging in on every one of these planets. I wouldn't be surprised if they have stopped building surface-to-space missiles entirely."

Miklos frowned. "That is not the usual Macro operational profile. They almost succeeded in removing one Centaur habitat. They should press on, repeating the same strategy until it fails utterly."

"Yeah," I said. "That is the norm. But I'm sensing more intellect here. I feel like I'm being played. They threw up a feint, and while I'm up here working hard to cover my ass, they are setting up their next move. I'm reacting at this point—and we've lost the initiative."

Miklos nodded thoughtfully.

I turned to Marvin next. "What do you think, Marvin?"

He swung three cameras to cover me. Normally, three would have represented rapt interest. I would have taken it as compliment. But now that he had about a dozen cameras, three wasn't saying much.

"Judging from their actions, I calculate a high probability you are correct. There is a greater intellect at work. They have had the time to build deeper cognitive structures on these worlds."

"Some kind of super-brain? Like the thing that ran that big dreadnaught back on Earth?"

"Precisely."

"That's great," I said. "That's just grand. I have a hard enough time beating their numbers, without them getting all smart and unpredictable on me."

"Could we locate and target this super-brain?" Miklos asked.

I thought about it, and shook my head. "No. The primary targets are their factories. We're going to have to go down there and execute Marvin's original plan. In fact, I'm going for it now. Mass up the ships and make the approach. When can we do it?"

Miklos looked startled. "I—I can't answer that without looking over all our positions, sir."

"There you go. They've got us scattered. We've got ships patching up holes in Centaur balloons and building anti-missile defenses. In the meantime, I bet they are down there building up ground forces to repel our next assault. They panicked us, and are now one step ahead."

I smashed my armored fists together. Miklos winced. Marvin was watching me with five cameras now.

"We don't really know—" began Miklos.

"I know enough," I said, cutting him off. "I know I've been sitting up here in space, cowering and worrying about where they might strike next. We had the advantage when we hit them hard—but we didn't keep up the pressure. They managed to make a counterpunch and put us on the defensive. Well, I'm done defending. We're going down there. Make it happen, Miklos."

"May I suggest something, Colonel Riggs?" Marvin asked.

"Talk to me. You've been way too quiet lately."

"The actions you are suggesting will make our plans transparent. The mission might be jeopardized by—"

"No, no, no," I said, shaking my head and chuckling. It wasn't the kind of chuckle I used when I thought something was actually funny. "You wanted this attack, but now that I'm committing to it you are growing apprehensive? You can't have this both ways."

"They will know we are coming."

"Fine," I said. "I think they've known all along. We made a move on one factory and we blew it up when we realized we couldn't capture it. If they are brighter than usual, they should realize what we are after."

I had to count cameras. I thought it was about nine now. I must have freaked him out.

"You believe they've analyzed our intentions?" he asked. "If so, my plan is not going to function as designed."

I thought about that. "I'm saying I think they know we are going for their production facilities. But that doesn't mean they will know about you and your hijacking attempt. We'll just have to be tricky, that's all. It's still worth a try."

Marvin looked worried, and for some reason this pleased me. I turned to Miklos.

"Gather the fleet here. We'll take down the landing pods, but only load one of them—the one we'll be in. And I want Sloan in there with me. I want his luck aboard my ship. That way, I know we'll at least make it down to the surface alive. Besides, it's about time that unkillable bastard got into this war."

91

Miklos spread the word and the response was impressive. Marines and Fleet pilots were rushing around everywhere. The ships gathered by the hour and I sensed that the Macros were down there, watching us closely with their artificial eyes.

When I was about to board *Barbarossa* for the trip down, Captain Miklos stopped me.

"Oh, by the way Colonel…"

"What is it?"

"There have been more vibrations detected—out at the ring that connects us to the binary star system."

"Why wasn't I informed earlier?"

"We've been busy avoiding missiles and mounting a ground invasion, sir."

"Priorities, Captain. My orders were clear: I want to know what those Crustaceans are up to."

"Sorry sir. The ship we had posted on the remote side has returned to our side to transmit a report—this was many hours ago, due to the distance. He says a swarm of Nano ships are approaching the ring and refusing to communicate."

I swore. "The lobsters are getting ideas, eh? Why now? Maybe they know we are tied up with the Macros and want to make their move while we are distracted. Do you think that's it?"

"I'm not really sure, sir."

I paced, my heavy boots ringing on the deck. "Have them lay down some more mines on our side. Then have our sentry ship relay a politely-worded informational communique about the weapons. If they still come through—well, they can't say we didn't warn them."

I left it at that and boarded the landing pod. We were finally going back to the Centaur homeworld. It felt good, in a way. I hadn't liked being driven back from this planet the first time. After all, I'd promised the original owners their world would be liberated.

The trip down was relatively uneventful. I'd half-expected a fresh barrage of missiles, either aimed at our ships or the habitat above. Neither came. The enemy sat quietly, waiting.

Looking down through a rigged-up video system, I eyed the LZ intently when we broke through the cloud layer. It was going to be a gray, drizzling day down there when we landed. Through silvery sheets of falling rain, I made out a charcoal-black surface. The region around the great pit was graded and channeled by the passage of countless machines as they destroyed the region, leaching every ounce of minerals out of the land.

The ship fell like a rock at the end, and I soon saw why. A missile had finally come at us, but it was a small one, of a familiar AA design. I glimpsed it as the cameras tracked it. A sliver of dull, unfinished metal with a flaring red exhaust. A contrail ran behind it, pluming out as billowing white vapors.

"Evasive action," Sloan ordered.

I would have answered with a few curses, but I could barely breathe. Sloan was piloting this ship, and he clearly didn't intend to get hit by that missile. He swung and whipped the ship from side to side. I felt the guns stuttering as they tracked and tried to shoot down the incoming weapon.

I looked at the screens, but it must have been too close for the cameras to track it now. I flicked my gaze to the front wall, which showed a rust-red finger moving very rapidly to intersect with our ship, which was represented by the nanites in the wall as a golden bead of metal. I gritted my teeth and tightened my shoulders, bracing for impact. With luck, even if the ship was knocked out, some of us would survive to continue the mission.

Then a second later, it was over. The missile was gone.

"We must have shot it down," Sloan said. He asked the ship what had occurred, and *Barbarossa* confirmed the missile had been taken out.

"Ha!" I shouted. "That's just the sort of flying I expected to see out of you, Sloan. That's why I brought you along. The Macros don't have a chance of shooting us down with you aboard."

Sloan tossed me a grin, then went back to studying his boards intently. When off-duty, he was quick to slam down a beer and seemed half-asleep at meetings. But when he was under fire, the man was all business.

"That was an AA shot," I said. "The kind the big Macros put on their backs. I bet there's at least one of those machines down there."

"We have not seen any of that type of unit in the vicinity," Marvin said.

I glanced at him. "Believe me, they've been building like mad down there."

"Trouble, sir," Sloan said.

I snapped my helmeted head around and examined the big screen again. "Seven more incoming? Is someone transmitting my name from this ship? I briefed you about that."

"No sir, not to my knowledge," Sloan said. He was making the ship buck and weave again. If I'd been a person who got seasick, I'd have filled my helmet by now.

"We can't get away from three—what the hell are you doing, Marvin?" I broke off and stood up, but was tossed back into my crash seat.

Marvin was sprawled on the floor, using his numerous tentacles to cling to anything solid. He had a hand-held laser out, a short-ranged type we used for welding. He was intent on what he was doing, and only a single camera swung my way when I spoke to him.

"I've calculated a ninety-seven percent probability this ship will sustain a hit."

"So, you're cutting your way out?" I asked. "I give you an 'A' for effort. Sloan, we are in the atmosphere now. Order everyone to abandon ship."

Sloan did so, and as part of the ship's programming, the floor of the bridge vanished.

We all fell, not out of the ship entirely, but down into another subchamber under the one we'd been in. This was the empty landing pod. I looked up and saw Kwon and the rest of our team were coming down into the pod with us. A few were already there. We bumped heads and helmets. Fortunately, all of us were too armored to get injured.

"Can we pilot this down?" I asked.

"No time," Sloan said. "Barbarossa, release landing pod!"

There was a sickening lurch. I looked over at the situational diagram on the wall. Three missiles, still incoming. Our ships were around, firing at it. None of them had any missiles targeting them. Dammit. As I watched one of the AA shots vanished, but there were two more, and that was going to be more than enough.

Macro AA missiles weren't like Earth equivalents, especially now that they'd become accustomed to our defensive fire. These missiles were painted with textured, reflective matter. They also spun on their central axis. It was like shooting at a disco ball, and our lasers tended to bounce off. Worse, they pumped out mists and chaff to put a diffusive shield around the tiny vehicle. It wasn't hard to lock onto one of them, but it was extremely hard to beat their countermeasures and bring it down.

"Barbarossa, open the floor of this pod!" I roared. "Dissolve it *now*, all of it!"

I think it was the last command the ship ever executed. We dropped out into open space, the wind whistling over our armor in a buffeting, screaming rush. We were in free-fall when the streaking missiles plowed into the ship and the pod above us—one hit each. It was more than enough firepower. Both the ship and the pod fireballed and fell apart in burning scraps.

We fell faster than the debris overhead, being lower and denser than the rain of burning, squirming smart metal.

"No one apply any thrust!" I ordered over our short-range, tactical com system. "Just fall with the rest of the debris. Wait until they engage someone else."

My men obeyed me. We fell the last three or so miles to the surface in a relative peace and quiet. The wind whistled, and raindrops formed a slipstream over my armor.

While we fell, the world swam up to us with sickening, spiraling speed. It looked ugly down there—all charcoal and dirty, grinding machines.

I had time enough to wonder about the Macros and their targeting. Had someone told them it was me in that ship? Had I blown my own cover somehow? I wasn't sure, but if I lived for another few hours, I was determined to find out.

-14-

We applied power only when we had to, braking hard at the end so as not to crash into the planet's crust with killing force. When we did finally thump our boots down on the crunchy surface of silt and mud, we scattered as quickly as we could, taking cover. I eyed my sensors and the sky overhead, hunching my shoulders reflexively in my suit. I hoped they hadn't prioritized our group of small, power-emitting targets. Just in case we were more important than we thought we were, I headed for distant cover. Everyone else had the same idea and we didn't stop running in every direction like rats until we went to ground and crouched there, sides heaving, watching the skies.

I didn't see anything nearby on my scope, my HUD or by visually scanning the skies. No flaring streaks of death rained down on my squad. Up above the cloud cover, however, it was a different story. Tight flocks of eight missiles sought one ship after another. The Fleet people were adjusting to this tactic. They regrouped themselves, and now moved into a cone-like formation. They arranged their ships so the open mouth of the cone was directed toward the oncoming source of fire. This provided every ship with a clear field of fire at the missiles as they entered the cone. The beams were intense, lighting up the air with blasts of radiation. The raindrops were instantly turned to plasma when the hot energy passed through them and turned into puffs of superheated steam.

The beams had to be held on longer to burn through the growing murk and the enemy countermeasures. Using less power for a longer duration beam was an effective way to overwhelm defenses and strike through to the missiles one at a time. Unfortunately, it slowed down the rate of fire. Twice, one got through and another ship was lost.

Part of me wished I was up there with the squadron of destroyers—only seven were left out of the nine, now. But I could tell their commander knew what he was doing. He had them all linked and firing in unison. Each missile was being struck from all sides by over twenty probing beams. Each one popped, then the turrets retargeted and popped the next. Following their orders, the ships pressed toward the source of the missiles, all firing as they went.

I turned away from the action overhead and waved to my men, who'd begun to gather themselves and their fallen equipment.

"Any casualties?" I asked.

"No sir, all accounted for," Kwon answered.

I smiled. I'd asked for a squad of volunteers, and I shouldn't have been surprised at who had jumped at the chance to go on this mission. "Kwon, let's spread out and march toward the pit. Keep a good firing distance between each man."

Kwon stumped off, shouting orders. I followed my squad and found Sloan at my side. He signaled me.

"What is it, Captain?"

"You should check out Marvin," he said.

I looked around, not seeing the robot. Sloan pointed to a large mound of charcoal. I headed that way and found Marvin sprawled on the far side of the mound in a muddy puddle. Rain ran down over his metal body and pooled up on the dished out spots on his back. A half-dozen black tentacles squirmed under his body, making splashing sounds.

"What are you doing in that mud-hole, robot?"

"I prefer the designation *artificial person*," Marvin said. He didn't turn even a single camera in my direction as he said it.

I came forward grunting and levering my laser projector over to my left hand. These battle suits had exoskeletal strength, but this kit was extremely heavy and we'd added the most powerful generator kits we had. I'd expected to be fighting building-sized Macros, and I'd wanted the firepower to deal with them effectively.

I splashed into his mud-hole and peered over his shoulder—if you could call it that. The structure under his head was more of a sprouting point for a knot of three extra tentacles. My proximity earned me the attention of a single camera.

"You are obscuring my light source, Colonel Riggs."

"Don't you have a flashlight built into that owl-trap of yours?" I asked.

A second camera eyed me, then panned away. He seemed to be studying the watery mud under him, sampling it, zooming in on it and—I don't know, but I thought he was *tasting* it, too.

"I don't want to introduce unnatural radiation. It will spoil the specimen."

"Have you gone naturalist on me, Marvin?"

"I'm testing this spot as a likely discovery zone. I believe biotic life should be flourishing here."

"Microbes are everywhere," I said. "I've probably got more of them in me than I do nanites."

Three cameras. "No, you don't. The nanites destroy most of them. Only the most beneficial are allowed to survive."

"Humph," I said. "I didn't know that. Anyway, why are you looking for microbes?"

"Not microbes. Specialized biotic residue."

I started to open my mouth, then closed it again. Suddenly, I figured I had the answer. He was looking for the smart bugs, the microbes we'd found when we'd last been in this system. They'd been held captive in a large gurgling tank of liquid on a captured Macro cruiser. I'd spoken to them briefly through Marvin—before the ship had been destroyed. We'd never encountered them again. As far as I knew, the only ones I knew about were the ones still living in Sandra's body.

"Sir?" Kwon called, coming over the ridge. He stopped when he saw the two of us crouching over the mud and studying it with great interest. "Ah," he said. "That must be a Macro footprint, right?"

"What?" I asked. "Uh, no. I don't know. Marvin is looking for bacteria."

Kwon's helmet tilted a fraction, giving him a quizzical pose. "Well, Sloan sent me after you. He didn't want to turn up his radio to call for you. He says to tell you we are still in a combat zone and his survival instincts tell him to keep moving."

"Right," I said. "Marvin, slurp up some of that water to study later. We are moving out."

"I might damage the ecosystem."

I gestured around us. "I hate to break this to you, but the Macros beat you to it."

"No, I mean the tenuous thread these creatures have on life."

I sighed. "All right. We are moving out. You can huddle down here as long as you like. If you don't show up at the Macro dome, I'll try to reprogram it myself."

Marvin made a variety of protests, but we trudged away over the squelching mud. Finally, he came gliding along behind us. He didn't say anything, but I suspected he was annoyed with me. That was just too damned bad.

We walked, rather than using our suit propulsion systems. Flying would have been a lot faster, but we wanted to maintain as low a profile as possible. Even Marvin barely used his repellers, relying partially on his tentacles to drag himself forward. He reminded me of some kind of snake-being I'd read about in Greek mythology—a gorgon, that was it.

Overhead, the battle still raged. My squad of ships had located the big Macro with the AA missile cluster. These battles had often gone badly for my ships in the past, but this time was different. It wasn't only the Macros who'd made technological advancements in equipment and technique. My destroyers kept their formation and kept blowing up missiles until the machine ran out of ammo. Fortunately, there was only one of the machines. Once it stopped firing, they swarmed it and used their heavy laser turrets to cut it apart. It was quickly reduced to slag.

Having destroyed the local anti-air defenses, they moved on to finding the nearest harvesting vehicles. These they destroyed with as much flash and flare as possible. The idea was to keep all enemy attention on them—so the Macros would ignore us. So far, it seemed to be working.

They didn't get too close to the pit itself, however. I wanted them to draw out the defenders from under their shells, and I didn't want any them to engage any serious weapons the enemy may have unless there was no choice. The ships were there to raid and harry the enemy—not to plunge into open battle.

In all likelihood, however, the Macro dome had called out for help. In these situations production centers often would summon a large number of supporting troops to its side for protection. This had me worried about my squad. The ships could withdraw in seconds, but not us ground-sloggers. I knew my team could take on a single machine—maybe even two of the big ones. But we would be wiped out if we were caught out here in the open by a dozen metal monsters.

"Let's step it up," I called to Kwon.

He relayed the order, shouting with incredible volume. We began trotting through the mud. Our pounding feet sunk ten inches deep with every step. Each time I ripped my armored foot loose from the sucking mud, I was glad for my exoskeletal help. These boots couldn't come off, and my legs had the power to keep pumping even if I was buried in a wall of mud.

Things stayed only mildly interesting until we reached the edge of the big pit. It was like a crater—a wound in the earth. The land had looked bad in the surrounding region, but it looked hellish down in that dark, spiraling hole. The air was a smoky haze. I could make out the shapes of Macro workers down below, resembling metallic insects at this distance. The light rain continued, combining with the hanging vapors to obscure the bottom.

"This looks promising," I announced cheerfully. "Who wants point?"

"I'll do it, sir," Kwon said.

I frowned, but after looking at the rest of my unenthusiastic team, I finally nodded. I didn't like having my First Sergeant risk himself on point, but maybe right now it was a good idea. "Okay, move out."

Kwon took the first step—and slid down a muddy hillside. Without having his repellers on, he was off-balance. He handled it well, sitting down and sledding through the mud.

"Looks like fun," I said, and headed after him. I managed to stay on my feet all the way to the bottom, but just barely. The rest of the troops followed.

We'd made it down to the first spiraling roadway. A dozen more hundred-foot drops lay ahead—or maybe it was two dozen. At some point, we couldn't see any deeper into the hole. I peered into the shadowy darkness that lay below.

"That's funny," I said, staring at it.

Captain Sloan stepped up next to me. I couldn't help but notice he was one of the last men to take the plunge down into this sinkhole.

"You've got a strange sense of humor, Colonel," he said, eyeing the shifting cloud of darkness ahead.

"What the hell *is* that?" I asked. "I don't get it. I figured the dome was buried down here, but now I'm not so sure. From space, this black cloud looked like smoke or vapor of some kind—up close, I don't know what I'm looking at."

Marvin slithered near and joined us. "It's biotic in nature," he said.

We all looked at him, except for Kwon, who was getting ready to slide down the next cliff of mud on his butt again. He looked back in my direction. "Best to keep moving, Colonel," he said.

"Hold on a second," I said, raising my hand. "I'm getting a feeling here, and I don't like it. Marvin, what kind of bullshit have you gotten us into?"

"Your reference is unclear. This is not fecal matter, but a slurry of silicon, carbon and water, mixed with a variety of other elements. The biotic content is less than one percent."

One percent biotic? That sounded high to me, but I shook my head and approached him. When dealing with Marvin, it was important not to get distracted by random statements, interesting though they might be. He had half a dozen cameras on me, a sure sign I was worrying him.

"Let's get back to the part about that cloud. You say it is biotic in nature, and the last time I talked to you, I found you slurping up slime in some mud hole at the LZ. What do you know about what we are facing here?"

"There are few certainties. I have suspicions, which I'm trying to verify. In time, I will make a full report."

"In time, we'll all be dead—even you, Marvin. Talk to me now, before this team goes another step deeper into this hellhole. You tell me what you are holding back. What is it you don't want us to know?"

Marvin had a camera on everyone in the team now. The rain still drizzled over our suits. His electric eyes focused and zoomed independently. I knew he was taking a reading of our collective mood. Apparently, he didn't like what he saw, because he swung most of his cameras back to me and finally answered.

"The cloud ahead is biotic in nature. It is a life form, I believe. A mass made of many small parts. In a way, it is similar to a nanite formation."

My helmet swiveled back toward the shifting darkness. It looked like thick smoke, but I supposed it could be more of a giant, gaseous jellyfish. "You're telling me that thing is alive? It's huge. Is it solid, liquid or gas?"

"None of those. It is more like a living plasma, or a living gel. Part gaseous, part liquid. Very little of it could be called a solid."

Sloan lifted a gauntlet and pointed at the robot. "I have it!" he said. "It's a mass of those microbes, the ones we found back on the Macro cruiser. Is that it, Marvin?"

"Good question," I said, giving Sloan a nod.

"No," Marvin said.

We all looked at him, but he didn't volunteer anything more.

"Well?" I demanded. "Then what is it? If you want to press ahead with this mission, you'd better keep talking."

"It's a single organism, not a mass made up of a trillion individual cells."

I grunted unhappily. Far from being like robots in old movies, Marvin was a tight-lipped miser with information, rather than a mechanical blabbermouth. "Okay, what the heck is it doing squatting at the bottom of this hole?"

"It is imprisoned here."

I nodded. "Fine. Is there a Macro dome down there with it? Or was all that talk of a production facility in this location a trick to get us to come here?"

Marvin hesitated. "I don't know."

Half the men in the squad groaned aloud. Marvin swung his cameras from face to face.

"All right," I said. "I apologize, everyone. Marvin, you are fired. When I get you off this world, I'm putting you into a hold on the Centaur stations where you can't do any more harm."

I pulled out my com-link and activated it.

Marvin slithered closer and a cluster of his cameras studied me. "What are you doing, Colonel Riggs?"

"What does it look like? I'm calling Fleet."

"But we were to maintain long-range radio silence."

"Not anymore. We are pulling out. I'm calling for our extraction from this garden spot you lured us into. Unless you give me a good reason to do otherwise, right now."

"The Macro factory is probably down there. I calculate a sixty-two percent probability."

"Sixty-two percent?" I asked. "That sucks, Marvin. That's almost a coin-toss."

"It's closer to two out of three."

I shook my head. "No, there is no 'probability'. The factory is either down there, or it isn't. What is the basis for your argument? Why do you think it's here and not at the bottom of some sea?"

"The mineral exhaust and regional harvesting machine activity levels are far higher than normal in this region."

"That's it?"

"Also, the prisoner would most likely be in close proximity to one of the Macro Superiors."

"What prisoner, and what do mean by Macro Superior?"

"Super-brains, I believe you called them. AI intellects."

"Right. No wonder you wanted to come here. Is it mating season?"

"I don't understand your statements, Colonel Riggs. They seem to be non-sequiturs."

"Never mind," I said. "You think there is a massive alien prisoner, a Macro factory and a Macro Superior all down at the bottom of this hole? When did you first suspect this?"

"As soon as I examined satellite imagery of the location."

I sighed. This was often how it went with Marvin. He was deceptive and manipulative, but when you finally forced answers out of him, he gave them all at once. Somehow, that made it harder to be angry with him. His full confessions seemed to absolve him of his sins.

"All right. Where does this giant gelatinous being come from?"

"It is a one of the race-members of the species you most commonly refer to as 'the Blues'."

If I had possessed ten cameras of my own, I would have put them all on Marvin. Every trooper around us stared in shock. They all knew about the Blues, the theoretical race of beings we'd yet to find. They were the ones who'd let the Nanos and the Macros loose on the rest of us poor, unsuspecting biotic slobs.

"But that cloud isn't blue," Kwon complained. "It's black."

I walked to the edge of the second cliff and stared down at the shifting, translucent mass. It had to be huge—a mile across at least. Could such a thing be alive, even intelligent? I thought about what kind of life form might be able to survive on a gas giant world. I supposed it could be something like this—a massive volume of aerogel. It wouldn't have enough mass to be crushed by the overwhelming gravity of the world. In a way, I supposed the Blues had to be something of very low density, or very high density. Our kind could not take the brutal G-forces.

"What are we going to do, Colonel?" Kwon asked.

I sighed and directed my laser projector toward the mass. "We are going down, First Sergeant. We are going to find out exactly what is at the bottom of this very odd hole."

-15-

When we slid down the fourth cliff of the massive pit, we ran into trouble. I supposed it was bound to happen eventually. All the military Macros nearby were focused on my diversionary destroyers, but there were workers and the like that kept plodding along, performing their mundane duties. It was one of these machines that discovered us.

A heavy earth-mover came along the road at a surprisingly fast clip. It was on its way down from the top, spiraling to the bottom along the endless roadway. It ran on treads, and was made in sections like a caterpillar of burnished metal. The machine made such a racket that we could hardly hear ourselves screaming inside our own helmets.

"Move out!" I shouted, making the hand signal to advance. I was pointing in the general direction of the next cliff-edge—I swear I was. But Kwon didn't take it that way.

"What?" he asked. His voice was so naturally loud, I could hear him clearly. "Ah yes, sir, attack!"

And that was it. A single misunderstanding was all it took. It was just the sort of misunderstanding Kwon wanted to make, of course. He could hardly stomach leaving one of these machines in a functional state. Sneaking around simply wasn't his style.

After the first laserbolts splattered on its front plates and knocked out some of its sensors, there wasn't any way to change the situation. The earth-mover was running us down so fast we didn't have time to get organized. I knew it would have immediately radioed Macro Command about the incident. At that point, the damage was done. We had been noticed, and the enemy wasn't going to forget about us when we were this close to a sensitive base.

I joined in with the rest of my marines, firing and scrambling to the sides of the road. I saw my men were planning to allow the machine to run through middle of them—but it suddenly swerved toward the wall. My men were trapped there, between the barreling mass of the earth-mover and the hundred-foot high wall of sludge. They then did what they'd been trained to do: they engaged their repellers and shot up into the air, avoiding death.

Great, I thought. We'd just provided the enemy with new, distinctive emissions signatures. This single action would mark us clearly as Star Force Marines, if this Macro Superior knew its opponents. I figured that it probably did.

"Concentrate fire!" roared Kwon, "take out the outside treads!"

A dozen beams leapt out. Every man carried a heavy gun and the output was startling. The treads were quickly blown apart. Mud, metal shrapnel and superheated steam went everywhere.

The entire vehicle slewed suddenly toward the cliff. It had been rubbing up against the inner wall to crush us, but now that the other side was dragging, it did a rapid, lurching turn in that direction. The destroyed treads made the motion uncontrollable. A second later, it flew off the edge and overturned, crashing down deeper into the pit. We glided to the edge and looked down after it. Rolling over and over, it almost vanished into the deepening haze. Secondary explosions plumed up with flame and vapors. The thing finally came to a hissing stop three levels farther down.

"Well," I said, "That's pretty much that. Let's fly the rest of the way down. We're not fooling anyone now."

Kwon shot past me, needing no more encouragement. He flew like cannonball downslope. I took off after him, and even Marvin fully-engaged his repellers, bringing up the rear of the formation. We hadn't taken any casualties—yet. I made a mental note to point that out later to the survivors. I'd gotten them pretty far into this monster's mouth before it woke up and started chewing on us—and technically, that wasn't my fault.

Now that we were flying rather than trotting, we move dramatically faster. The stair-like spiraling levels went by under us, and the sky itself grew darker. I had a sensation of making a very vague contact with something—this stuff, this smoke-like gel, it was incredibly nebulous, but I could tell I was touching *something*. The sensation was like putting one's hand into a mass of bubbles in bubble-bath—but even less substantial than that. Could I really be *inside* one of the Blues? The thought was disturbing.

I received a contact then, a tone in my helmet that indicated a private channel was being requested. I saw it was from Marvin, and decided to ignore it. If he wanted to stop and examine another mud puddle, he could do it on his own time. Right now, I wasn't in the mood.

"Kwon, get this bee-swarm into a formation. I want four up front on point, with two back up fireteams on either flank. I'll back up the center with the rest of them."

Kwon relayed my orders, and the marines shuffled around into a more organized arrangement. We resembled a Macro diamond-formation, with a fireteam flying along at each of the four points. As we flew, we quickly passed over another earth-mover, then a third. These machines took notice of us and moved to intercept, but they were too slow. We flashed past them and flew deeper still.

The sky overhead became ever darker. Soon, we would need our suit lights just to see in the murk. Something up ahead caught my eye then, a glimmer of brightness in this sea of gloom. Could that be the dome?

The connection request tone sounded in my helmet again. It was Marvin again, making another attempt. I opened the channel.

"What is it?"

"Colonel Riggs," Marvin began, "the entity has made repeated attempts to communicate, and I'm not sure if I can put it off any longer. It may become offended."

"The entity? What entity?"

"The designation it uses for self-identification corresponds to the concept of *Introspection*."

"What the hell are you talking about, Marvin?" I demanded.

"The Blues use such concepts for identification, rather than a traditional name."

I paused, finally catching on. "Are you telling me this big pile of smoke we're flying into wants to talk to us?"

"It is curious about the nature of this new intrusion. We are disturbing it—literally. Saying it wishes to talk might be an overstatement of the situation. It questions our intentions and our natures. It wishes to experience us."

I thought for a second, but not for a long one. I didn't have a long second right now. I could sort of see its point of view. From its perspective, we were like ants running around on a man's shoe: vaguely interesting. But we weren't just ants, because we were *inside* this giant being, stirring up its guts. Maybe we were causing it pain.

Under different circumstances, I would have apologized, halted our advanced and sat down to have a good, old-fashioned heart-to-heart with this mammoth creature. But right now, I was on a mission and the lives of my entire team were in jeopardy.

"Tell it we can't talk right now. We've come here in peace as far as it is concerned. We mean it no harm, but we are in combat with the Macros. They are our enemies."

Marvin hesitated, and I assumed incorrectly that he was relaying my message. "Are you sure you wish to communicate these concepts, Colonel Riggs?" he asked.

"Yes, dammit. Why not?"

"What if the creature is in league with the Macros?"

"I thought you told me it was a prisoner."

"Yes. But have you considered why it would submit to such a status?"

"I don't have time to debate that, Marvin. Transmit my message. That's an order."

There was a brief pause. "Message sent," he said.

We reached the last cliff and slowed down. There still hadn't been any Macro resistance. I looked down and ahead, seeing what could only be a Macro dome. It was a force field of surprising power. It repelled anything it didn't approve of, I knew, up to and including artillery shells. The shield essentially halted fast-moving objects or energy emissions. In the past, we'd only managed to break these defensive systems in one of two ways. We'd either launched a number of nuclear explosives at them, overwhelming the shield, or we'd crept in slowly on foot. Today, we would have to try the latter approach.

"I don't see any Macros," I said. "Let's advance."

Before we'd gone another dozen feet, however, the situation changed dramatically. A howling wind rose up, and the world around us darkened.

"What the heck is this?" Kwon asked.

"I don't know, maybe it will let up if we get into the dome."

It didn't let up. In fact, it grew in intensity. Soon, we could hardly see one another

"It's this air—it's like soup, sir!" Kwon said.

"Tighten up the formation! I want everyone in a group."

Things went from bad to worse. We were lifted up and tossed around like leaves in a storm. Making further progress was out of the question. We couldn't even see the dome anymore. The winds picked up sifting masses of material from the pit and threw it at us.

"What the hell is going on, sir?" Kwon shouted.

"I'm not sure, but I have an idea. Marvin, talk to me."

"Yes, Colonel Riggs?" Marvin asked calmly. He sounded remarkably unconcerned despite the fact he was orbiting us now in the swirling, dark mass of dust, smoky-aerogel and stiff winds. Only by using our repellers were we able to maintain our relative positions.

"Link arms," I shouted to men I could no longer see, "form a circle and hold on tight. Marvin, contact this smoke-monster of yours."

"Reference unclear," he said, drifting past me. "Do you possibly mean the entity known as Introspection?"

"Yes, dammit. Get in contact with him."

"Referring to him as male may be inappropriate for these beings—"

"I don't care, Marvin. Just connect me to him and translate."

"Done. Converse when ready. I simply wanted to point out that avoidable cultural misunderstandings might—"

"Point taken. Transmit this: being known as Introspection, we respectfully request that you stop blasting us with wind."

"Done. However, wind isn't an accurate description, Colonel Riggs," Marvin said. "I believe we are experiencing the creature's digestive processes."

We'd managed to get into a circle now, and I peered from side to side to count noses—or rather faceplates. Kwon had them sound off. I thought some were missing.

"Two lost, sir," Kwon said. "No response on their com-links."

I now understood why the area was empty of other Macros. Usually, the region around Macro factories was churning with small, worker-type machines. The only ones I'd seen in this pit had been a few huge earth-movers. Maybe the smaller models had been off-handedly crushed by this creature when it became angry—or hungry.

It was a chilling thought. If we couldn't get this crazy thing to settle down, it might well kill us.

"What's it saying, Marvin?" I shouted.

"It is projecting an emotion, rather than strings of symbolic concepts."

"What emotion?" I demanded, my voice cracking to be heard over the wind. My helmet was slashed with handfuls of grit every few seconds now. The sound reminded me of being in an automatic carwash.

"Disinterest."

"Marvin, you know a little about these creatures. Tell it we can free it from the Macros. Tell it we can free the entire system, and allow the Blues to roam the cosmos again."

"Ah, a new emotion is coming through now, Colonel: fear. Concern-for-safety and—*determination*, I think. Yes, that's it."

The storm grew in intensity. I felt my arms slipping now and then. "Tighten up, men!" I shouted. I thought I heard Kwon relay the order, but no one needed to be told what to do now. We all clung to one another in the most powerful dirt-storm I'd ever imagined.

I was one second from ordering my people to abandon their kits and fly straight up to exit this cloud of angry debris. Maybe some of us could make it. But I held on, and tried to think of what would get through to a creature that called itself Introspection.

"You are an unjust being!" I shouted. "I want you to know that. It was your people who released this plague upon the universe! You created the Macros and the Nanos, and let them destroy countless biotic beings such as ourselves. They killed my children, and millions of others. We are here to fix your mess, to right your wrongs!"

Marvin didn't have to translate the answer to that one. The storm intensified. I could no longer see anything. It was all black with occasional flashes of gray, as if I'd been buried under ashes. I couldn't hear anything either, other than the roar of the endless, angry winds.

But then, just when I'd given up hope and decided I would die here in the churning guts of an angry Blue, the living storm relented. I looked around, and saw my men were in a huddled mass. We were up to our waists in fine, swirling dust.

"What did you do, Colonel?" Kwon asked when we could hear each other again.

"I don't know," I said. "Maybe I made it feel bad."

-16-

"What is this thing, sir?" Sloan asked me. "Some kind of freaking jinni? We heard about those while we were out in the deserts on earth, you know. The locals believed in them. But I never did. Until now…"

I glanced at him, wondering about aliens and earthly legends. Could the two be connected? I'd always thought those fake documentary shows on the topic were full of crap, but now, I wasn't entirely sure. What was a demon, after all, but an alien?

"I don't know, Sloan. But it isn't trying to digest us right now, so let's quietly move closer to the dome."

All of us helped one another out of the sifting pile of ash the region had become. Kwon lifted a man out with each of his arms, but it took four more men to pull him up in turn. We stayed in a tight group and walked calmly toward the dome. It was still dark, but not pitch-black, and we could see the shimmer of the smooth walls ahead.

"What are you getting from Introspection now, Marvin?" I asked. I almost whispered the question, not wanting to piss it off again.

"Anger is dropping in volume now," Marvin said. "Regret has risen, and possibly crested."

"What do you mean by dropping and crested? Doesn't it just send one concept at a time?"

"Not exactly, sir. It provides a list of variable intensities. Mixing them in a blend, I can read its emotive state."

"Is that all it does? Transmit emotions? What about concepts? You must have sent it something akin to words in order for it to understand my meaning."

"Yes, that is true. But I don't think we've yet become interesting enough for it to communicate with us at that level."

I thought about that. I supposed, to a huge thing like this, we were like prissy insects, taking ourselves very seriously. I was glad it wasn't an abusive monster, as it might have enjoyed our pain. Fortunately, it seemed capable of empathy.

Now that the winds had died down to a whistling, swirling mess instead of a thundering hurricane, I found it easier to think. The being knew it had released the Macros, or so it would seem. It felt regret for doing so. I suddenly had a thought.

"Marvin, is this creature really talking to us? I don't feel like I'm having a conversation."

"The entity doesn't view us as worthy of notice. It does not consider this interaction to be a conversation between peers."

I snorted. "That's great. What are we, then?"

"Difficult to describe."

"Try me."

"I've made a study of humans. They have two essential states of mind."

"Two states? That's all?" I asked.

"Yes. One you refer to as sleep. The other is primary, and might be described as consciousness."

"Are you telling me we are talking to a sleeping Blue?"

"No, but from its point of view, we are errant thoughts in its unconscious mind. We are too small to be thinking individuals. We are concepts—ideas."

I rubbed crusted filth from my visor. This was one strange beast, and I'd dealt with a number of them. "Let me see if I have this straight, it thinks we are ideas in the back of its mind?"

"That is a good analogy. Remember, it is not human. It is not remotely like you in composition. I find this interchange between the two of you to be fascinating."

"I'm so happy for you," I said.

We now stood at the edge of the shimmering dome. Above us was a hanging mass of smoky nothing, which I knew to be the guts of a daydreaming Blue. Inside that dome—God only knew what was in there waiting for us.

"We should go inside, Colonel," Kwon said. "Before this crazy thing gets mad again."

"Tell the men to take a rest. I want everyone to drink some water and get their heart-rates down."

Kwon walked among the surviving marines—there were only fourteen that still drew breath. He shouted at them, ordering them sternly to relax. This seemed counterproductive, but I wasn't a sergeant.

Sloan walked up to me and engaged me in a private channel. I made the connection.

"What are we doing sir? Sight-seeing?"

"I don't know," I said. "I'm having so many thoughts, so many questions. This thing we are inside of—this is the core of everything. Somehow, these creatures started this whole thing. Without its science, choices and mistakes, you and I would still be back on Earth, surfing the web and watching sports channels."

"Yeah? You think so?"

"Yes, I do. There are so many questions to ask it."

"It isn't like you to overthink things, Colonel. Let's ask it when we come back out of the dome. After we finish the mission."

My head swirled with thoughts of my lost family, of the millions of people who had died back home and in space—and the hundreds of them I'd met personally. But I nodded. He had an excellent point. He never got off-target. Maybe that's why he'd lived so long among the doomed souls of Riggs' Pigs.

"All right," I said. "Let's head inside."

The first thing I noticed was the instant silence. Stepping under the dome was like entering a cool, calm world. Cut off from the outside completely, I could feel the barrier as I passed through it. The sensation was like walking through some kind of plastic film, as if I'd been swallowed in bubble-wrap. We pushed inward and it pushed back. But we persisted and it soon gave way.

I knew the dome was designed to allow slowly moving things to walk through, allowing the entry of worker Macros without allowing projectiles to follow. Once past the barrier, we stood in a gloomy world. A machine hulked in front of us, dimly lit by internal sources. It was illuminated by many pairs of suit lights from my marines as more of them came through to stand with me.

I could hear the big machine that squatted under the dome now. It sort of *thrummed*. It was a deep, steady, ominous sound. It gave me a chill to hear it again. I hadn't been this close to a Macro factory for years.

"Marvin, are you here? I don't see any super-brain Macros."

"No," Marvin said. "I'm disappointed. The factory seems to be undefended."

"Well, I can't say that I'm unhappy about that. Slither up to the machine and do your magic, robot."

Marvin was already slithering. He moved closer to the factory than any of the men. I think Kwon was the only man who may have seen a Macro machine this big before in person. The rest of them were standing suspiciously close to the edge of the dome.

"Shouldn't we shoot it, or something, Colonel?" Sloan asked.

"Negative Captain. That monstrosity is our goal. If we can capture it and make it work for us, we will have more production power than every machine back on Earth combined."

Sloan seemed nervous. "Should you be talking that way about it— right here, sir?" he said in a near whisper.

I chuckled, but I knew he wasn't just being paranoid. In the past, Macros had tracked me down in particular, following our radioed messages. There was evidence they listened to us all the time. Even if they didn't usually say much—they were listening.

"I don't think this thing works like that. I expect it's more like a big version of one of our factories. Not overly bright, but able to follow precise programming."

Sloan muttered something about hoping I knew what I was doing. I didn't take offense. I'd heard that one before.

"Any progress, Marvin?" I asked.

"I'm having protocol-engagement problems," he said. "The channel opens, then closes immediately."

I grimaced. As an ex-programmer, I knew all about that. Often when writing an original piece of software for networked devices, the most difficult part was to establish the initial communication. You had to get everything exactly right, any mistake would cause it to abort or crash. In this case, we could only change and examine the software on one side of the devices trying to synch up with each other. Or, to be more precise, Marvin could.

"Do you think you are using the right version of the protocol?"

"Standard Macro binary," Marvin said.

I looked at him. Was he getting testy? It wasn't like Marvin. But then again, when software didn't work for no apparent reason, the experience could drive anyone mad with frustration.

"Try different versions."

Up until now, all ten cameras had been locked onto various parts of the huge machine in front of us. Now, one of them swung to me. The lens refocused with a tiny whirring sound. "Why would this unit not be upgraded to the latest version of the communications software?"

My armor prevented me from shrugging. "Just try it."

"It will require a complete reinitialization."

"What will that take? A second or two? Come on, Marvin."

He turned all his cameras back to the Macro factory. "Done," he said.

"You got a response?"

"Yes. But it may have been a delayed acceptance of my earlier requests."

"Yeah, sure," I said. Marvin was like a lot of touchy engineering types. He hated to be wrong, especially about something technical. I could understand that, as he was a mass of technological wizardry himself. It probably hurt his pride.

"Should I attempt to make it bring down the dome?" he asked.

"No!" Sloan said quickly. He was standing at our side.

Marvin and I looked at him.

"Uh, if we brought down the shield, the Macros and that crazy cloud out there could get in. We need this defensive position, sir."

"Agreed," I said. "Let's try something simple, Marvin. Have it produce a mass of constructive nanites."

Marvin was quiet for a time. "Program rejected," he said. "Symbol table limit exceeded. Unknown identifier. Errors too numerous—"

"I get it, Marvin," I said. "Hmm. I should have thought of this. It is similar to our nanite factories, but not identical. It doesn't seem to know much about nanite technology. I suppose that makes sense. If the Macros had been able to produce nanites, they would have sent different weapons systems against us. Let's go easy on it. Tell it to build me a block of ferrous alloy. A cube."

116

"What is the volume of this cube to be?"

"Let it decide. But I want to see what it can do in two minutes time."

We waited then, as Marvin formed the program and transmitted the source code.

"Program accepted. Engaged."

"That was easy," Kwon said, stumping up close.

I politely kept quiet. Computers always looked easy to operate when they worked. We waited the two minutes. It seemed like a very long time. My marines had just begun to wander the place, when a massive *clang* sounded in the enclosed space.

"Could that be my cube?" I asked, heading to the output tray.

When I saw it, I gaped in amazement. A dozen marines joined me. There, in the tray, was a perfectly-formed gunmetal-gray cube. It had to be six feet in every dimension—maybe more.

"Is that thing solid, sir?" Sloan asked.

"Yes Captain," I said. "I do believe it is."

"It must weigh more than a ton," Kwon said.

Marvin drifted near and tapped at the block with his tentacles. The action made an odd, tinging sound. "I'd estimate the weight at fifty-four tons," he said. "That would be at one G of course, and an assumed steel density factor of point-two-eight."

"Sounds good, Marvin," I said. "What I want to know, is if it can make something useful."

I thought hard for a few minutes, shooing the others away. Not having nanites to work with was a serious problem. With nanites, you could shape and mold what you wanted. This system produced less malleable output, and you had to know exactly what you wanted from the start. I wondered how much this technological advantage had helped us in our many battles with the Macros—I suspected the effect was a large one. I also wondered why the Macros had larger factories that produced less sophisticated output. It was like they were one step back on some technological tree.

I shook my head and paced in my armor. I had to get my mind focused on the problem. We were at the bottom of a Macro mining pit, inside a dome and apparently inside the bowels of a Blue. We'd captured the factory, but had yet to secure it, or get anything useful out of it. I had to capitalize on this win and keep the enemy from recapturing it. But how?

My initial plan had been to get the factory up into space, where we could add it to the rest. Maybe I could even relocate it on Hel, and use it to start building my battle station. Such fantasies were evaporating quickly, now that I was face to face with this monstrous machine. It was as big as a good-sized office building. A hundred feet tall, and nearly twice as much in diameter. Every engine I had couldn't lift it off the surface of this world. No wonder, I thought, the Macros built everything *big*.

Turning back to the machine, I decided to experiment. It couldn't build something that included smart metal, or a brainbox. Such elements required nanotech. But it could build something like a laser projector for me.

"Marvin, I'm going to disconnect and remove my laser projector. I want this machine to make two new ones of similar design, but I want them to be about ten times the size and power. Make sure it increases the cooling system portion to about double what my suit projector comes equipped with. I'll also need a generator unit that is powerful enough to operate the projector. Make sure the generator comes with insulated connection cables—I know the Macros tend to build bare-wire systems. Can you do all that?"

"Of course, but I cannot guarantee the quality of the results. It will depend on the available supplies of certain materials."

"Right. The machine can recycle this steel block, if that helps."

"That will not be helpful. The available quantity of holmium and erbium is the controlling factor."

"Just give it a try, will you?"

Marvin was quiet for a moment. "Done."

The big machine began to groan and thrum again. I looked up at it in surprise.

"I didn't give this thing my unit to examine yet," I said. The Nano machines generally worked on a duplication principle. To start a new design, you put some finished component into the input box, and it tried to build the same object.

"Unnecessary. This unit is equipped with external sensory systems. It has already scanned your technological devices and is capable of duplicating most of them."

I nodded, impressed. Maybe Macro tech wasn't entirely inferior to Nano tech.

"In that case, we can start working on the next elements of the system."

Marvin and I spent nearly an hour developing the program and arguing about our supplies of various elements. We have plenty of the rare earths required for laser construction, but we were low on palladium, promethium and neodymium. These materials were needed in the construction of fusion generators. I pondered the problem. I could build a stack of guns, but not enough generators to power them. I decided in the end to build in the Macro tradition: big and impressive.

Kwon and Sloan became bored with patrolling the perimeter and came to watch. Kwon asked the first question.

"How long until you finish, sir? I would like to get out of here."

"Understood, Sergeant. But it will be a while. Another hour at least."

Sloan asked the next question. "Sir...what in the heck are you building?"

I flipped my visor up, wiped sweat from my face and smiled at him. Then it flipped it back down. The unit was still in a combat stance, and I didn't want to lose my vision due to a weapons discharge.

"I'm building a tank, Captain. A very big one. We are going to ride it out of here. It will have cannons to destroy any Macros that try to stop us and a steel hide thick enough to keep our windy friend Mr. Blue from pushing us around."

-17-

In the end, I managed to build something big and ugly. It did look vaguely like a tank—or maybe a horned Viking helmet. The tank had two separate turrets that rotated independently of one another. Sitting side by side in the midsection of the tank, the cannons swiveled independently and required a human gunner to man each of them. Both guns covered a wide arc of fire, but if the tank was attacked from either flank, we would only be able to get one weapon into play. Still, it was pretty impressive-looking.

Kwon walked around the big machine, slapping its steel flanks and rattling the heavy treads. "You really like making up this kind of stuff, huh?"

"Yes, I do," I said, standing on the slanting hull.

The tank was far from perfect. I was sure any tank designer back on earth would roll his eyes at my work. But I had been working from memory. This machine looked like a world war one monster, with the two bulbous turrets and the high-riding treads.

"Not bad for a first run prototype, Colonel," Captain Sloan said, from the hatch on the top turret. "But I feel like I'm about a century back in time."

"I've thought of a dozen improvements already," I admitted. "Like these treads—there could be an armored skirt hanging over them to shield them. And the heat exhaust flows out of the bottom only. What if we hit a patch of deep mud? The machine might stall or at least be unable to cool down the guns."

"So, that's it then?" Kwon said. "We all climb in this thing and drive out of here? Is that why we made the trip down, to build one tank?"

"You are sounding more like one of my officers every day, Kwon," I said.

"Sorry sir. I just don't understand your plan."

"Well, we're not driving all the way out of here."

It was Sloan's turn to be doubtful. He popped his head up out of the hatch and appeared alarmed. "What? We're not getting out of here?"

"No, not yet. We're going just outside of this dome, where we'll meet up with the enemy and we should be able to transmit up to Fleet. In order to take full possession of this factory, we'll have to bring down many more troops. To do that, we'll have to get permission from the Blue that is squatting on top of this facility."

"What I want to know is why the Macros have not hit us hard by now," Kwon said. "It's not like them to let us grab something without a fight. They didn't even have any technicians down here to try to blow it up or something."

"I've been wondering about that too. But don't worry, I have great faith in the Macros. Before this is over, I'll bet they'll give us a very hard time."

"I hope so, sir," Kwon said, frowning. "I don't like all this pussy-footing around."

I raised my eyebrows at him and gave a small shake of the head. Sometimes, Kwon had unique ideas about how a campaign should go. I turned to my troops and clapped my armored hands together.

"All right!" I said. "Mount up! Everyone inside. I've only got two guns and one pilot's station. I'll drive, Kwon and Sloan will man the cannons. The rest of you squeeze onto the benches I've set up in the belly. Watch your heads, that big thing that takes up half the troop compartment is a fusion generator. It might get hot, and it's sure to release a lot of rads if we have to crank it up—so adjust your suits to endure a hostile environment."

My men moved quickly to obey. There were muttered complaints, as there always were. I heard the words "crazy" and "pigs" several times. It was nothing I wasn't accustomed to. Men like this were veterans. Competent and experienced, but surly.

Marvin was the last to force his lumpy form down through the top hatch. He squatted between Kwon and Sloan, who were on either side, manning a turret. As the pilot, I was up forward and lower than the rest of them. I looked over my shoulder at Marvin in surprise. He hadn't asked where I wanted him, he'd just slid inside the top compartment.

"I feel oddly out of place perching here, Colonel Riggs," Marvin complained.

"You look oddly out of place everywhere you go," Kwon said, and gave a huffing laugh.

"Perhaps you would like to take this spot," Marvin suggested, directing most of his cameras at me. "This is the command seat."

I smiled. "Who would pilot the machine then?"

"I would be glad to volunteer my services in that regard."

I snorted and thought about it. I knew from experience I would have an easier time thinking about what I was saying to an alien life form if I didn't have to pilot an unfamiliar machine at the same time. Also, I knew Marvin really wanted to drive this monster. He was like a kid when a new experience was attainable. His curiosity was insatiable.

"All right, Marvin," I said. "Let's trade places."

There was quite a bit of grunting, and some new gouges on my armor before we'd managed the switch. Once sitting in the center, I had to admit, it did feel right. I felt like a starship captain—even if my starship was cramped, squatty and built with two-foot thick steel.

"Have you engaged all the defensive software we talked about?" I asked. "I don't want the Macros taking control of this factory again the minute we leave."

"I have installed the patches. I must warn you, however—"

"I know, no guarantees. Take us out, Marvin."

The tank didn't have an idling engine. Being powered by fusion which converted its output to electricity, it was hard to tell when it was running and when it wasn't. Marvin simply applied the throttle and the machine whirled around, spinning the tank's treads in opposite directions. The treads clanked and spit dusty soil everywhere. The machine turned around faster than I'd thought possible. It gave me a sickening feeling.

"Whoa, robot!" Sloan said, grabbing the cannon controls for support.

We hadn't bothered to put in handholds and the like. This tank was bare-bones.

"Yes, take turns a little slower if we aren't in a combat situation, Marvin," I urged him.

Marvin made no apologies. Possibly, he hadn't even heard us. Every one of his cameras was focused on a screen or a scope. We clanked forward with gripping acceleration. I was thrown back against the generator compartment, and was glad for my thick armor. Being in the improvised commander's perch, I had nothing to hold onto. I looked around and finally reached up my hands to grip the wheel that opened the top hatch. By positioning my hands on either side of the wheel and lacing my fingers around it, I was able to get a good hold that wouldn't make it spin open. I was already making design changes in my mind. I kept telling myself I should be happy the thing ran at all.

We were slowed by the soap-bubble effect of the force-dome when we made contact with it. Passing through to the far side was a disturbing experience, as always. The tickling inside my guts was even more bizarre than what I felt when going through a ring. Somehow, you could feel that tickling energy crawl over your body. After a moment, the sensation of resistance faded and we were through.

Outside in the open, I wasn't sure what to expect, but I was surprised anyway. The Blue was gone. There was no dark, smoky form hovering over us. There was no gloom and swirling dust. Instead, we sat in blazing daylight under a blue sky. The pit we sat in was still cast in deep shadow by the surrounding cliffs of slag. The spiraling roadway cut into the walls of the pit made me think of a giant stairway up to the heavens.

"Where did that smoke-thing go?" Kwon asked.

"I've got no clue," I said.

Marvin rolled the tank around the floor of the pit. We clanked and clattered as we circled the dome, eyeing our surroundings. Kwon and Sloan swiveled their turrets suspiciously, targeting every fluttering bit of debris.

"Take us up that ramp a ways, Marvin. But keep the speed under control, please."

We lurched toward the ramp and I was thrown back at an angle when the tank began to climb. Gravel crunched and ground into the treads, sticking in the gaps. Rocks were crushed to dust by our weight.

"Let's call home," I said. "We need back up. This seems too easy, but if the enemy is going to give us this base, we're going to take it."

That was as far as I got with my boastful statements. We were about half-way up the ramp to the first stair when the Macro machines finally appeared. They scuttled forward and gazed down at us from every stair, all the way up to the top. There were thousands of them. Like players at a sporting match in a grand arena, we were surrounded by uncounted masses.

Like so many times in the past, the Macros dashed my dreams with their true plans. I had to give it to them. This time, they'd really let me get my hopes up.

"Open fire!" I shouted, but I needn't have bothered. Kwon and Sloan were targeting nearby machines and melting them. The power of the beams was impressive. Even when the flashing beams reached me indirectly through tiny slits, they made my visor flash and darken.

"Turn around, Marvin!" I ordered. "Head back for the dome."

Marvin slewed us around in a wild one-eighty that left me with my right leg hanging over Kwon's shoulder. I could only imagine how my marines were doing down below us in the belly of the tank. Probably, they were cursing my name and the day they'd broken their mammas' hearts and signed with Star Force.

Kwon brushed my foot off his shoulder and kept firing. Most of the machines were armed with long pinchers, saw-blades or scoops. These were the Macro equivalent of farm implements in the hands of angry peasants. Some had lasers, however. They fired storms of bolts down on my tank and the sound inside the vehicle was like that of a hard rain mixed with that of sizzling bacon. I knew the sizzling sound was formed by melted steel, which no doubt had formed hot runnels on the outer hull.

The front of the vehicle had the thickest armor, like any tank. Unfortunately, now that we were running, they were hitting my tank in the butt. Still, I'd made sure to put plenty of steel in every direction. Even the flank armor was thick and solid, but it would only take so much. Eventually, they would burn through if they kept pounding us—and Macros were never likely to vary a tactic that had even the slightest hope of success.

I gauged our chances when we hit the open floor of the pit with a bucking heave. Already, Marvin was struggling with the controls. I wished fervently that I'd put that armor skirt over the treads. The treads had taken hits along the way, and the right side seemed to be dragging. Soon, we might be immobilized. At that point, we'd be toast.

Outside, thousands of machines rushed us eagerly. They made a rustling sound I could hear through the walls of the tank. Like scuttling insects, they charged forward, anxious to stop us or die.

"Keep firing on the ones that are burning us. I think this tank can handle the pinchers and the like."

"The ones with the guns are hard to see, sir," Kwon said.

"What? Why?"

"The worker Macros are all over the barrel of my cannon."

I took a look outside, and saw he was right. They had mounded over us now. It was like a swarm of ants on top of a big beetle. They were riding the tank in a mass. We were still crawling forward, but slowing down.

The road became bumpier, and I quickly realized why. We were overrunning the smaller machines. I wondered how long my tank could keep plowing them over, crushing down their thrashing metal bodies before it ground to a halt. At that point, I knew we were dead men.

"Marvin, get us back under that dome! And connect me with Miklos!"

"Miklos here, sir," came the Captain's calm, familiar voice.

I had a hard time hearing him over the din of the scrabbling, clacking Macro workers that now blotted out our view of the sky with their bodies.

"Miklos, listen to me. I need a low-powered laser burn from a single destroyer."

"Where sir?"

"Right here. Follow my signal down, and burn me at this location."

"I don't—I don't understand, sir."

"Just *do it* man, or we're dead! Keep the power low, and unfocus the guns, I want an area about fifty feet in diameter to be hit. Give it a five second burn, immediately!"

"Yes sir," Miklos said after another brief pause.

I could hear a familiar tone in his voice. He thought I was crazy. But I also heard something else: resignation. All my officers had learned to do crazy things after spending enough time under my command. If you lived long enough on my team, you were sure to be given insane orders at some point.

125

The first sign I had that the beams were hitting us was the dimming of my visor. I didn't detect the laser itself, as most of the power was not in the visible spectrum. But it did come down unerringly to burn my tank. It was almost impossible for them to miss as I was providing them with a radio signal to sight on.

The scrabbling noises on the hull intensified.

"Increase power!" I shouted. "Miklos, double down on that burn, same duration and area, but more power."

My visor blackened out entirely. I wasn't sure for a moment if the Macros had covered us entirely, blotting out the light, or if the lasers from the destroyer had done it. I reasoned it had to be the destroyer, as I would have been able to see the suit lights of my fellow marines otherwise.

"Colonel Riggs, we are close to the edge of the dome," Marvin said.

This entire time, he'd been piloting the tank without wavering from his post. That was one good thing about having a robot for a pilot: they didn't panic on you.

The scrabbling on the roof of the tank subsided. I figured the Macros were melting to slag out there. We were still bumping and heaving as we slowly traveled over their countless bodies, however.

"Miklos!" I shouted. "Can you still hear me?"

There was a quiet second or two. I was worried, as I knew once we entered the dome all communications would be cut out. Another possible disaster included the high probability that our com system had been damaged by the bombardment.

"...Riggs...contact..."

"Miklos, listen to me: I want you to send down everything we have. I need ground, air and space support. Kill these machines and meet me inside the dome. This is our new base. Bring the Centaurs. Bring everyone."

There was only some buzzing in response. "Marvin, send my last message again and again. Keep sending it until we are inside the dome."

"Transmission sent."

"Good. Now send it again."

I was rewarded with a single, curious camera eye. "Transmission sent," he said.

I snorted. Even the robot thought I was crazy. But didn't care. It was beginning to look like we were going to live to a see another day.

-18-

We hit the dome going too fast. It was an easy mistake to make, but Marvin almost killed us. I was gripping the wheel of the upper hatch with only one gauntlet at that moment, having let go with the other hand to tap Kwon's shoulder. I shouldn't have bothered, as he couldn't feel me through the armor even if I slapped him hard.

In any case, when we hit the Macro dome, some law of physics was violated. We were moving too fast, and it was like hitting a concrete wall instead of a soap bubble. Everyone was thrown forward. For the four of us in the upper compartment, with no straps, nano-arms or other restraints, it was a worst case scenario. Marvin was at the bottom of the heap, crushed down on the control bars. I was second, entangled with Sloan who ended up with his helmet shoved under my armpit. Last came Kwon, crashing into the stack like a sledgehammer. He had held on a fraction of a second longer than the rest of us, which only served to put him on top of the sandwich.

My neck and right arm were twisted and my visor was starred again. My suit nanites had barely affected repairs since the lashing of the Blue's dust storm, and now they had new hairline cracks to deal with. Fortunately, I'd designed the suits for absorbing impact. As bad as this pile-up was, it was nothing compared to a collision in space. We simply weren't moving fast enough to cause serious damage.

I heard a whuffing sound. Kwon was laughing his ass off. "This is pretty comfy," he said. "You guys are like a pile of cushions."

"Get your fat butt off my neck," Sloan complained.

128

"We are proceeding into the Macro dome," Marvin said. "It would be advisable to return to your stations, sirs."

Grunting and straining, we untangled ourselves. Soon afterward, the exterior sounds of thrashing Macros vanished entirely. Judging by the instant silence that fell over the tank, I knew we had made it back under the protection of the dome.

"We're inside, Colonel Riggs," Marvin said.

"Kwon? How many of the enemy do we have on the hull?"

"I'm not sure," Kwon said, swiveling his turret.

"They might be too close to see, but I'm not—wait a minute," Sloan said.

He fired, but something went wrong. Instead of an intense light, a gush of heat and fumes from the chemical laser backwashed into the tank. Fortunately, we were in our suits or we would have been in trouble.

"Looks like my vents are clogged," he said.

"Cease firing. We have to flush out the blockage. Everyone, keep your suits on." I didn't think any of them were dumb enough to open their helmets, but I gave the order as a precaution.

"I see one now," Kwon said. "They are coming through dome, sir."

I opened a channel to the marines in the troop pod. "Marines, I want you to get out there and clear the hull of this tank. Engage anything coming through the dome. We'll provided supporting fire from here when you clear our vents."

Kwon slid away from his turret and cranked open the top hatch.

"Where do you think you're going, First Sergeant?" I demanded.

"With the men, sir. Could you man my turret?"

I heard the marines moving out below. The back ramp dropped with a crash and heavy boots pounded. There were flashes and snapping sounds almost immediately, as the marines engaged the enemy.

"Hold on a second," I told Kwon. The tank was nearly finished as a mobile platform, but I wanted it farther from the edge of the dome. "Marvin, take us closer to the factory. Move slowly."

The big gears ground and clattered. The tank was moving again, but I could tell the treads on the right side were failing. Marvin fought the controls, as the levers were only power-assisted. They gave a lot of feedback, I hadn't had time to design anything more sophisticated. Macro design was basic and over-built. It reminded me of old-fashion

Soviet designs. When in doubt about stresses and tolerances, Macros just carpeted an extra layer of steel over everything.

The big machine made it almost to the factory when I called for it to halt. All this time, Kwon had been manning his turret, but when we finally halted he scrambled for the hatch again. I knew he couldn't wait to get outside and smoke a few of those machines personally.

"All right," I said. "Sloan, you man your turret. Marvin, you man Kwon's. Kwon and I are going outside."

Everyone looked happy with these assignments, especially Sloan. I could tell by his wide-open eyes he'd been worried I would take him outside with the machines. I almost chuckled—maybe he was the smartest one of the bunch.

We didn't get far before we were caught up in the firefight outside. Kwon threw open the top hatch, and used his repellers to fly straight upward. He was firing at something on the ground, I could tell that. I climbed out after him and took a leap to the ground. My rifle was in my hand and I had the trigger depressed before Kwon came down again.

"Take cover, First Sergeant!" I ordered. "Stop showboating up there."

"Sorry sir," Kwon said, letting himself drift down beside the tipping tank.

After a flashing firefight, my marines managed to drive back the ten or so Macro workers with lasers who'd followed us under the dome. The rest really didn't have a chance. Without ranged weapons, they snipped at the air a few times with what looked like hedge-trimmers then went down in a storm of heavy laser fire. These new projectors were very effective. A one-second burst focused carefully on the thorax was enough to disable a worker.

There was a lull in the fighting after we'd killed all those we could see. My men stayed in whatever cover they could find, which consisted mostly of our tank's battered hull and the indentation made by the treads. I threw myself down on my belly in a dished out section of earth and checked my weapon for damage. I had still had a ninety-percent charge and there was no sign the unit was going to overheat soon.

Kwon fell into the pit beside me, his heavy body tossing up a shower of dust. "The tank has taken quite a beating," he said.

I followed his gaze. In spots, the tank's two-foot thick armor was down to less than a foot of crispy, pitted metal. Much of the melting effect appeared to have come from directly above—which I assumed had been done by my own ships. They'd fried the Macros on our hull as I'd asked, but had almost overdone it and fried us as well. I had no doubt this was why the tank's vents were clogged. They'd probably melted and fused together. I was surprised the two cannons operated at all.

Looking around the scene, I saw a trail of twisted metal wreckage that led from the tank to the edge of the dome. We'd been dragging them and crushing them down into the earth with every foot of progress.

"Why have they stopped coming, Colonel?" Kwon asked me.

"They haven't," I said. "Macros don't just quit, not unless they are calling off the attack completely. I don't buy that. Not yet."

"Maybe our troops have come down outside, and are engaging them."

I would have liked to talk to Miklos and find out just how close that was to happening, but I didn't buy that argument either. I shook my head. "I don't think so. It's too soon for that. It will take a few hours for Miklos to get ground support down here."

Kwon looked at me. "I see," he said. "So we are on our own?"

"For now."

Kwon looked back toward the perimeter. "Where are they? What the hell are they doing out there?"

"They are probably massing up just outside the dome. They'll come inside all at once and try to overrun us."

"Ah," Kwon said. He grunted as he climbed to his feet. "In that case, we have a few minutes. What are your orders?"

I looked up at him, and stood up beside him. Kwon was so quick to accept my theories as facts. I wished I had a thousand more like him—but then, that might not have been healthy when I turned out to be wrong.

"Let's dig in," I said. "Set up trenches around the tank."

Kwon brought a gauntlet to his helmet. "What if they come in under us, sir? Remember South America?"

"But they can't..." I began, but then I trailed off. I nodded. "Right. They could be digging outside, coming in through the dome

131

underground, then pressing ahead into the middle of this region. In fact, for all we know, there are tunnels under us right now."

We didn't have a surviving sensor box that could measure activity under our feet. I felt trapped. If we dug in, they might get in close and tear into our lines. If we stood on top of our single tank, we would be easy targets if they simply walked through the dome.

Finally, I turned and looked toward the idle factory itself. "We've got plenty of steel, at least. Let's build something."

This time, with Marvin's help translating my instructions, I designed something more useful than a massive block of steel. I didn't have time to make a new tank, of course. But I figured we could use a structure, a battlement of some kind that could not be dug under and yet would provide cover from incoming fire. Simple geometric blocks and flat planes of metal. Something that would come in sectional pieces we could fit together. This machine should be able to generate structures like that very quickly. The factory was the only asset I had, so I was determined to do the best I could with it.

Within a few minutes I came up with a series of metal planks, about thirty feet long each. These would fit easily in the output tray, and two of my men in their exoskeletal suits could lift and place them. Each plank of steel was four inches thick—enough to stop a laser bolt. I would have loved to have a barrel of constructive nanites to weld them together, but wishing didn't make it happen. Instead, I ordered the steel planks to be made with holes drilled through at regular intervals. Then I ordered a large number of steel rods to be built at the same time.

In the end, the Macros almost gave me enough time to build my steel bunker. The men had the floor and the walls built, but not the roof or the second floor. I'd kept them busy, having them carry, place and connect the planks as the great machine rolled out every few seconds. It was like trying to keep up with a fast laser-printer. We almost couldn't clear the output tray before the next sheet fell out of it. Along with each section of steel, a pile of clanking, rolling rods was produced. These would serve as pins to hold the steel planks together.

Another team was focused on assembly. They used their laser projectors like welders to melt the rods into place, and to cut vertical slits for firing through the walls. These slits would serve as loopholes for gunners to hide behind. Every few feet, a slit had been burned through. The cuts were ragged and black with charred metal. They were just wide enough to allow my men to poke their rifles through. I tried it, and was impressed by the reasonably broad field of fire.

"One thing sir," Kwon asked as I set up a second floor. "How do we get inside?"

"Burn a hole in the roof," I said.

Without a moment's hesitation, he flew up there and began cutting a circular opening in the roof of the structure.

We didn't finish the second floor, however, before the enemy interrupted our efforts. A shout went up from one of my marines who was on sentry duty on the far side of the factory. Almost immediately, my visor dimmed: someone was firing. I couldn't tell which side had opened up first, and I didn't much care.

"Everyone into the bunker! Sloan and Marvin, seal the hatches on the tank and man your cannons!"

I flew up with a swarm of my fellow marines and we landed on the roof of the bunker. The bunker looked like a three-quarters finished cube at this point. The top floor had a three-foot high wall around it, one plank high. The interior was sealed except for the loopholes.

"Is that entrance done yet?" I asked Kwon, shouting to be heard over the growing din of battle.

"Yes sir, I'm working on a second one now."

"Well, jump down inside and burn your way out from down there."

Kwon looked at me for a second. Then a laser bolt struck him in the back. An inch-deep, black hole had appeared and wisped with gray vapor, but I could tell it hadn't made it all the way through.

"Ah, right!" he said, jumping down into the bunker.

"I want three men to stay up top here with me. Crouch and fire. Everyone else inside the cube. Take up a firing position and make your stand."

Only one marine didn't make it into the bunker. He caught a bolt in the back, but this one burned through the armor. He was just making the flying leap up on top of the bunker. The bolt caused him to tumble in midair. His repellers were still pushing him, and unfortunately, he was driven down into the dirt. Instead of making a graceful, powered leap up on top of our steel cube he shot down into the ground. He struggled to rise and storm of bolts caught him from every direction.

My immediate instinct was to leap out there and help him. But I knew that would make two casualties out of one. "Supporting fire, left flank!" I shouted. "We have a marine down, keep those Macros honest!"

The marine forced himself to all fours. Two more bolts struck his armor, and he sagged down again. I couldn't take it anymore, and ran to the wall. He was down there, lying in the dirt.

"Fly up here, Marine!" I ordered. "Get one hand on this rail and I'll pull you over the top."

"My repellers aren't operable, sir," he said, his voice faint on my proximity radio channel.

"Okay, then stay flat on your face. We'll keep them off you and get you inside when we can."

Over the marine's head, several of my men were firing steadily now, keeping the Macros ducking. The enemy was digging out there, working on some agenda of their own. Maybe they didn't know my bunker had a solid steel floor. Others were poking their head-sections around the corner of the big factory. We fired at every machine the moment it showed itself. Macro workers were coming inside the dome in droves now. Most of these had laser mounts on them. I wasn't sure where these reinforcements had come from, but it didn't really matter.

Marvin and Sloan in the tank kept the enemy at bay on their side of the factory, and we did the same from our bunker. I realized now, however, they were pouring in on the far side of the factory, a blind spot for all our shooters. They were massing up behind the factory and trying to work around us.

I grimaced as the marine below me took another hit. He wasn't going to last long down there. It was odd, seeing a man helpless and dying so close to me. He was only ten feet away, but he was hurt and on the wrong side of my new wall. It might as well have been a million miles.

Then I noticed a glowing region of heat near the marine. "What the hell is that?" I asked over the command channel. "Someone with a better angle give me a report. Are the Macros burning a hole in our bunker?"

"No, sir," Kwon said. "It's me."

I gritted my teeth. In between words, I fired out through my loophole. The Macros fired back, but they were exposed while I was a hard target behind my steel planks. They were forced to retreat. "What the hell are you doing, Kwon?"

"There we go, got him," Kwon said.

134

I took a second to look down. A huge arm lashed out, grabbed the marine by the projector cable and dragged him up against the bunker. The man appeared to have lost consciousness. He banged limply against the bottom of the cube.

"Hole is a bit small," Kwon said.

I shook my head. "I hope we don't get more unwanted guests coming through that way."

"Macros are too big to fit, sir. In fact, Carlson is almost too big. No, I have him now."

I paused in my measured firing to watch Carlson's legs slide away out of sight and into the bunker. "If we all die due to your little stunt, I'm busting you to Corporal, Kwon."

"That's okay, sir," he said, "as long as I still get to kill machines."

I laughed, because I knew he was serious.

-19-

The Macros kept up a steady rain of fire, and right before they made their next move, I suspected a trick. There were just too many with lasers, not enough of the models with cutlery. This didn't match with the crowd I'd seen outside. Either they'd elected to only send in laser-armed workers, or they'd found a way to retool them all, or—

"Sir, look at the tank!"

Moving in a crouch, I duck-walked to the opposite side of the bunker and looked. Up until now, this side of the bunker had been the quietest flank throughout the battle, as the tank was covering this sector. I hadn't really been worried about trouble from this direction. The Macros themselves had quickly learned to avoid the tank. It was the least populated region of our domed-in little world. My biggest worry had been the possibility Sloan would screw up and nail our bunker with one of those big, swiveling cannons.

I was stunned at what I saw. When I peered through the loophole, I'd expected to see a dozen macros swarming over the hull of the tank—but what I *did* see surprised me much more than that. "What in the living—" I began, then broke off. "Where did it go?"

"It sank, sir," said the man who panted beside me. He leaned against the outer wall with his shoulder and pointed to where the tank had been.

There was indeed a big hole out there, and a billowing cloud of dust. I opened a general channel. "Sloan? Marvin? Can you hear me?"

I heard something in response, but nothing I would call words. More like a squawk or two.

136

"If you can hear me, sit tight. Do not attempt to exit your vehicle. Do not fire your cannons. We'll come dig you out when we can."

I caught a final chirrup of radio, then a sizzling sound. After that, nothing. Still, I had hope. After all, Marvin and Sloan were both pretty close to unkillable. I hoped that neither of them had finally run out of luck.

I felt something odd a moment later. It was a shifting sensation, under my boots. It was slight, but it was undeniable. I put together two things at once in my head. The sunken tank, and the wobbling under my feet.

"They are digging under us!" I roared. "Kwon, get everyone braced for a fall!"

"A fall, sir?" he asked, confused.

That was all the time they gave us. Fortunately, our bunker didn't just sink into a vast hole and vanish. Instead, the northern corner sagged into the dust by itself. It groaned and creaked, but the steel welds and rods held. I knew this bunker wasn't real: it was a house of steel planks, like glued-together playing cards. There was no concrete, rebar or solid construction of any kind to keep it together. We'd thrown the shelter together in about an hour, and it showed. Still, it had held together so far.

"They are going to suck us underground," Kwon said, suddenly figuring it out. "Just like the tank. What are your orders, Colonel?"

I chewed my lip for about a second. The right call in these tactical situations made all the difference. I ran through the possibilities. My marines had kept the enemy at bay so far, despite their overwhelming numbers, by maintaining a field of ranged fire. They didn't have enough cover to outgun us, and their blade-armed troops hadn't been able to get in close enough to be effective without being shot down. I could see the Macro strategy clearly now: they'd elected to bring us down to their level. If they couldn't get past our guns, they'd sink the entire bunker into the ground, then cut their way inside and gut us one by one. I'd been in a number of tunnel-fights over the years, and I didn't want to let them force us into that situation again.

"Marines, listen up," I said over the general channel. "We're going to have to abandon this bunker for now. They want us to sit here until they sink us, but we're not going to do what they want. We're going to take the fight to them."

"Very good, sir," Kwon said. "What's our target?"

137

"The tank, for now. We'll try to pick up Marvin and Sloan."

"What about Carlson? He's too wounded to walk."

"You've got two arms. Carry him."

We all gathered on top of the bunker. It was shivering now, as the Macro workers dug feverishly to undermine the structure. "On my mark, we all fly over the wall and rush for the tank. Spread out, fire as you go. Keep advancing. Go! Go! Go!"

We all launched over the side and rushed, half-flying, half-running. Everyone was firing their weapons. I think the Macros were shocked, if they were capable of such a reaction. For a few seconds, the incoming fire stopped. We blazed out at them without a moment's hesitation, however. Flanked by our changing position, a number of the machines were knocked out of the fight. Most of these were Macros that had taken up sniping positions on the big factory.

To my left side, a hulking shadow approached, then passed me. I glanced over and saw it was Kwon. This didn't surprise me. It also didn't surprise me that he was outrunning me. What did make my eyebrows raise high was the flopping form on his back. He was sprinting along on those thick legs of his, with Carlson's limp form draped over his generator pack. This burden didn't prevent him from laying down a continuous pattern of fire with his free hand, either. I took a fraction of a second to look down, and saw his feet were sinking several inches into the soft earth with every pumping stride.

That was all the time I had to eyeball Kwon. We reached the tank—or at least the spot where it had fallen into a giant sinkhole. Our suit lights washed into the dusty, gaping wound in the dirt. I saw metallic gleaming reflections here and there. How far down was the charred tank? Almost twenty feet, it looked like. There were shapes down there, moving to and fro.

"Stay in the tank, Sloan!" I shouted. "Commence firing men!"

That was all the go-ahead my troops needed. We poured fire down into the Macro machines. It was a slaughter. They melted to slag under our circle of blazing guns. A few tried to hop and scrabble out to get to us. Their foreclaws grabbed a boot here and there, a few slashing pinchers gouged armor. But no one was injured. We shot them until they stopped coming.

"Ceasefire!" I shouted, and hopped into the hole.

Kwon dropped Carlson and jumped after me.

I turned to him. "Kwon, help me get this hatch open. It's stuck."

"Are Marvin and Sloan alive, sir?"

"I don't know," I shouted. "No response from them yet. I'll go back up and arrange our men around the crater."

I flew back up to the top of the hole and sent three marines into the hole to watch Kwon's back. The rest of them I set up in a perimeter around the edge of the crater the Macros had created when they undermined the tank. They'd unintentionally provided us with some good cover. It wasn't anything like the bunker, but it worked.

The enemy had reorganized their assault to focus on our new position by this time. The air over the crater sizzled with laser bolts. Within a single minute, two of my marines had been hit and taken out of the fight. One of them slid flopping and spinning down into the dark hole behind us. He crashed down on the piles of loose dirt, stones and dead Macros. He screamed as one of the upright Macro pincher blades punched through his leg at the hip. I looked down and winced. Kwon's men struggled to free him, but he was impaled.

"Get our corpsman down there," I said, gesturing with my rifle toward the impaled Marine.

"Carlson was our corpsman, sir," someone answered.

"That's great," I said, then snaked out an arm and grabbed hold of the nearest rifleman. "You, grab Carlson's kit and use it. It's mostly extra nanite injections anyway."

Star Force Marines included our own medical personnel, unlike some other national forces. We called our medics Corpsmen, and they had basic medical training and a specialized kit for emergencies. But even these men were trained, armed, combat troops. Since we generally didn't fight other humans, this didn't represent a conflict for a man who was dedicated to saving lives. They destroyed machines by day, patched up fellow marines by night, and slept like babies whenever we gave them the chance.

"Any luck with that hatch, Kwon?"

"I almost have it, sir," Kwon grunted.

He was so big, the other marines standing around couldn't really get in underneath him and help. He simply strained and heaved solo. I watched his shoulders shift, the wheel must be turning.

"There we go," he said, and pried it open a fraction.

To everyone's surprise, it was yanked shut again.

"Dammit," I said, pointing at the others. "Quit fooling around. Get a pry bar into that opening next time."

139

Kwon stooped again. He heaved and roared. A few seconds later, another Marine pushed the broken length of a Macro's leg into the breach and forced it upward.

A flash of light illuminated the dusty scene. The marine with the Macro leg in his hand cried out, clutching his arm and staggering back.

"Sloan, dammit sir," Kwon said. "It's us."

The hatch was ripped all the way open. I looked down into the dim lit interior. There were Marvin and Sloan. They'd been hanging onto the hatch from the inside, trying to keep Kwon and the others out. All of Marvin's thin, black nanite arms were entangled in the wheel of the hatch. I was surprised Kwon had been able to open it at all, even with the added power of his battle suit.

"Sorry sir," Sloan said. "I—we thought—our radio is dead, Colonel."

"All right, honest mistake," I said in irritation. "We shouldn't have shoved a Macro leg in there to pry it open. But I've got one less man on the line now. Get up here and take his place."

Captain Sloan glided up to me on his repellers, but he kept his head low. "What's our tactical situation, Colonel?"

"Suppressive fire. Keep it up as you talk."

Sloan poked his head up and spat a series of laser bolts toward the enemy lines. I joined him. We nailed a sniper machine, but then were forced to duck down again as incoming fire melted the dust around our helmets into smoking glass. The laser strikes looked like wet splashes of hot wax.

"See the enemy? They are climbing to the top of the factory now, so they can get a good downward angle on us. We'll be screwed if we allow them to get a firing position up there."

Sloan's eyes were wide. He joined me as we popped up and showered the machines that were trying to scale the factory structure.

"They've got to be digging to this spot again," Sloan said. "We can't stay here forever."

"I'm hoping we don't have to. Miklos should be coming down and invading this dome with reinforcements any time now."

"With all due respect, Colonel," he began.

I turned to him, annoyed. I hated hearing those words. They always preceded a short speech, the sort of speech which inevitably informed me I was an entirely new flavor of moron.

"Sir, we have to get the hell out of here," Sloan continued. "We can't hold on. We have no idea how long Miklos will take to get here. We have to assume we are on our own."

Sloan had a point, but I didn't see much else we could do. We were pinned down, and our only means of mobility was now twenty feet underground. I glanced toward the bunker, and I noticed it shook and shivered with the Macros that invaded it. They poked their pinchers through the loopholes, seeking something, *anything* to tear apart. Soon, they would figure out we'd completely abandoned that position and they would come tunneling toward us.

My eyes flicked up to the factory itself. We could fly up there and play king-of-the-hill with the enemy, but it seemed like losing proposition. It wasn't designed as a defensive position. In retrospect, I wished I had built my bunker up there instead. I gave my head a shake inside my helmet. Sweat dribbled down into my eyes and burned. I tasted the droplets a moment later in my mouth. With one eye half-open and bleary, I gazed at the factory. I had to think of something.

"Marvin," I snapped a moment later.

"Yes, Colonel Riggs," came the reply. Marvin sounded as calm and crisp as always.

"Can you communicate with the factory still? Will it take your orders?"

"Yes. Now that I'm above ground, I'm linked with the local production facility. The enemy has not yet regained control of it."

"How long would it take to build a new tank, like the one you are standing on?"

"Just under an hour. There isn't enough palladium dust, however. We'd have to reduce the—"

I shook my head. "Doesn't matter. Forget it. We'll all be dead in an hour. Can it make a—ah—how about a Macro worker? One that obeys us instead of Macro Command?"

Marvin hesitated. "Yes, I believe so. But each unit would require several minutes of production time."

"Yeah, right," I said, thinking fast. I was hunkered down in the crater, and programming under these conditions was unreasonable. Overhead, the storm of fire seemed to be on the increase.

"They've got a new team up on top of the factory, sir," Sloan told me. "They have a good firing position on the far side of the crater, our men are exposed."

"Great," I said. "Kwon, get a squad to concentrate on taking them out, sharpshooter style. Or at least keep them ducking."

"On it, sir!"

"Marvin," I said, switching channels. "I want you to program the factory to make small Macros. Little spider-sized guys."

"The facility is inefficient in that regard. Something that is under a gram in size—"

"No, no, not that small," I said. "Let me explain more carefully, I want a climbing robot that is dumb and simple, about as big as a dog— five percent of the mass of a single Macro worker. Can you produce those quickly?"

"I believe so. The designs are available, and already loaded. Very few specialized materials would be—"

"Okay, great," I said. "Now, I've got one more modification to these little robots that I want you to add. Then I want you to stamp out as many as you can. Batches of them all at once."

Marvin listened closely, and he assured me what I proposed was possible. After the program was engaged and the big machine began humming, I went back to firing my laser at anything metallic that moved. I hoped Marvin had done his programming right, because we were going to be overrun and wiped out soon.

-20-

The first batch of spider-bots that rolled off the line was a surprise to everyone, even me. I never even saw the first one reach its target, but I did see the explosion.

"What the heck was that?" Sloan demanded, pointing toward a knot of Macros that now were scattering.

In their midst, one of their number appeared to have malfunctioned. It was lying on its side and a small plume of dust hung near. Another group of them popped a moment later. This time, I was certain of what I was seeing. It was as if a grenade had gone off in the middle of them.

I laughed. "That, Captain Sloan, is my latest joke on the Macros. They are being blown up by their own kind."

I quickly explained my small spider-bots with their explosive charge payloads. They had very simple programming. They were to find the nearest, largest group of Macros, run into the middle of them, and blow themselves up.

"Diabolical, sir," Sloan said, smiling.

I noticed he was hugging the crater edge, not bothering to fire at the enemy. We were down to ten effectives now, and I needed every gun on the line. But I held back from ordering him to keep up the defensive fire. The Macros were now in a confused state. They were scuttling around, being chased by tiny replicas of themselves. Some tried to turn and slash their pursuers. This gambit inevitably resulted in a flash and a loud bang. With their front sections blown off, the back legs spazzed for a while then finally ground to a halt.

Others tried to get away by climbing the big machine. This was a big mistake. We were able to pick them off up there, or at least wound them and slow them down enough for one of our scuttling little demons to catch up and take them out.

"Marvin, send a squad of spiders up to sit on top of the factory and wait for any new snipers who get the bright idea of shooting us from up there."

"Done, sir. We've almost run out of bots, however."

"How long until the next batch is done?"

"Just under four minutes, sir."

In a firefight, four minutes was an eternity. But the Macro assault had already been broken. They were still sniping at us, and I could tell by the occasional underground explosion they were still tunneling. The last of my spider-bots found these tunnelers and detonated, collapsing the earth down upon their maimed bodies.

I ordered my men to stay low. We traded power with one another, rationing out what we had left. The generators never seemed to produce enough for a prolonged firefight. Carlson's suit was a boon, as he had a nearly full charge. As a group, our power reserves averaged twenty-four percent when we'd finished. Our generators would charge every suit up to full eventually, but that would take time—time we didn't have.

We stopped firing, and there was a lull that both sides needed. The spider-bots were all dead before the next batch was due to arrive. I knew Macro Command was out there, coming up with a new plan of action against us. I wished I still had a sensor-box that functioned. It was unnerving not to know if the enemy was tunneling under our position.

We made plans to coordinate our next effort with the arrival of a fresh load of spider-bots. With luck, we could take the attack to them. It was my guess they were running out of Macros. I was proud of my marines and impressed with what one of these production facilities could do to defend itself. Clearly, the Macros lacked an active imagination. They could have created a thousand varied weapons systems with which to hit us over the years. Instead, they'd stuck with their basic designs. These were good, but adapting to battlefield conditions required more thinking than that. In short, I didn't think biotics were necessarily more intelligent than the Macros—but were definitely more inventive.

It was not until the next batch of spider-bots were produced that I was given a reason to stop congratulating myself. By that time, the Macros had all but halted their assault. When the batch came into play, however, the situation changed dramatically.

Macros might not be good at creating their own designs, but they were good at analyzing weaknesses in an enemy variation. This became abundantly clear when Marvin gave me the fateful message: "New spider-bots being deployed now, Colonel."

"Good," I said. I was all smiles and ignorance. "Start another batch. Men, get ready to fire into any Macro that runs. Take out the legs so our little guys can catch up."

Marines chuckled in my headset. Everyone was enjoying this. We all wanted to watch Macros run and die from their own kind—we couldn't get enough of the spectacle. I'd even taken to making vids of the action with my suit. It would play over and over in the officer's canteen, I figured, when we got back to base.

"Sir! Incoming!"

I cranked my helmet around, frowning. Laser fire began spitting from every rifle around me. Then I saw it. A Macro worker, running full tilt away from one of my little spider-bots.

There was nothing unpleasant about that, but the destination of the worker—that was the problem. He wasn't trying to climb the factory, or dig into a hole, or heading for the glimmering walls of the dome itself. He was running right at us, where we crouched in our crater. Worst of all, he didn't have just one spider bot on his tale, there were three of them, and their tiny churning silver legs were a blur of motion.

"Shoot that thing down!" I roared. "Take out the legs!"

Lasers blazed and spat. At the same moment, a group of Macros nosed up from the roof of the factory itself. They'd taken their time to sneak up there, no doubt climbing the back of the factory while we were congratulating ourselves on how smart we were. Now, they crawled forward on their metal bellies and directed their nose-guns down into the pit of scrambling marines.

The Macro charging us went down, and a second later, all the bots detonated. A fountain of dirt clods showered my troops. It had been close.

Laser fire peppered my men. The next thirty seconds were grim. We went from an easy victory deep into the jaws of defeat. Two of my men were out of the fight, putting us at eight effectives. Marvin was our medic now, as the corpsman had been killed. He sat in the dusty hole in the midst of us, doing what he could for the wounded.

"Marvin!" I shouted. "Send five spider-bots to the roof. Take out those snipers, now!"

"Message sent."

"Sir, we are being charged from all sides!" Kwon shouted.

I swiveled my head this way and that. The Macros were veering in from every direction. "Where did they all come from?"

"I saw them pop out of tunnels out there, trenches in the dirt."

I watched as more came up and did the same.

"Marvin, reprogram the spider-bots," I said. "Tell them not to come within ten yards of any marine."

"Unable to comply," Marvin said with maddening calm.

"Why not?"

"They are almost on us," Sloan said. He was crouched on the line with the rest of us, firing for all he was worth. Each Macro that we disabled was quickly caught and blown up, but there were too many and they were seconds from overrunning us. If just one of those spider-bots…

"The spider-bots have limited sensory equipment, sir," Marvin explained. "I made several design edits to provide much needed space for—"

"I don't care," I shouted. "Just tell them all to blow themselves up! Right now!"

"Message sent."

Explosions blossomed and thundered from every direction. A fresh shower of metal parts, dirt and slag came down on us. Even as we ducked and wiped at our visors, the surviving Macro workers hit our lines.

It was the first hand-to-hand combat I'd been in for a while. If it hadn't been for our powerful battle suits and our training, we might have been annihilated. As it was, we struggled with the mass of thrashing Macros, slamming our laser projectors against their joints and thoraxes, even as they sought to chew through our suits. Only one marine was torn apart, screeching. The rest of us lived. We used the smoking hulks of Macro corpses to form a barrier encircling our crater.

Everyone was tired—almost exhausted. We quietly took up firing positions and waited for the next onslaught. I worked on programming the next batch of spider-bots. The rest of the men were doubtful about the wisdom of producing any more of them.

But I kept at it. The Macros had turned the bots against us, but we'd survived. If I tweaked the design, I was sure they could still be useful.

The Macros had stopped coming, but we all felt sure they were out there, coming up with another sly move. We watched every inch of ground with intense, unblinking stares.

When something finally did happen, it was two minutes before the next spider-bot batch was ready.

"I see movement at the edge of dome, Colonel," Sloan said. "We have new entries—lots of them coming through now."

I cursed. "Reinforcements? How many?"

"I—I can't even count them. They are coming through from every direction at once."

"What kind of Macros? Do they have lasers?"

"I can't tell. They are still blurred as they come through the field. Should we fire?"

I had reached the top of the crater now, and crouched beside Sloan. I knew a sick feeling as I saw what he saw. There were hundreds of shimmering images, coming through the field. They flared white as they pressed against the bubble of force. A few more steps, and they'd be through.

"Hold on, don't waste power," I told Sloan. "You can't hurt them until they are through the field entirely."

Then I heard a voice in my helmet. "Colonel Riggs?" the voice asked. "This is Captain Miklos. Are you here, sir?"

"Stand down, marines!" I shouted. "They're ours!"

A ragged cheer went up from the survivors. As the marines kept coming, we stood up and watched. Men in battle suits led the way, then Centaurs followed. There had to be at least a thousand of them.

I'd expected a brief firefight as my men arrived, but there was very little action. Captain Miklos soon found me, and we stood around the crater we'd called home for so long. By that time, it was obvious we'd wiped out the last of the Macros when they'd made their final charge to destroy us with our own spider-bots.

"Looks like you had quite a party here, Colonel," Miklos said.

"We did indeed."

"I'm sorry to have taken so long. A back-up invasion was not part of the original plan."

"I know," I told him. "I'm not blaming you. This entire operation didn't go as planned. But we did capture the production unit."

"Does it still work?" he asked doubtfully.

Together we surveyed the machine. It was the prize for which so many had sacrificed so much. "Yes, it appears to be sound."

I explained about the spider-bots, and the tank, and the steel-planks we'd built with this amazing machine.

Miklos flipped up his visor and stared at it. "A wondrous machine. So much power. What are you going to do with this monster, Colonel? This has to be more production output than Earth has ever had."

I nodded. "I have plans, Captain. I have lots of plans."

Miklos laughed. "I should be happy to hear that sir—but somehow, I'm not."

-21-

The battle for the production facility on had not gone smoothly, but at least we'd won. We'd captured the machine, and already my eyes were on the next goal: the third and final Macro dome. I wanted it badly. After I'd seen what one machine could produce, I wanted these factories more than ever now.

My reasoning was simple in the extreme: with a combined set of Nano factories and Macro factories—several of each—I could build more hardware than we'd ever seen before. I could make new things no one had even thought of yet. They would be big, smart, and flexible—but mostly big. My dream of a battle station on Hel could quickly become a reality. I sternly reminded myself I still had six planets to liberate, and they weren't going to do it on their own.

After Miklos had set up a perimeter around the huge pit, I felt less confident. A few thousand troops looked pretty thin when stretched around in a ten mile circle. I immediately improved our numbers by creating my own Macro workers. These looked exactly like normal Macros, but they were enslaved to our programming, and could not be used for military purposes.

"I don't like these things, sir," Sloan complained to me, sneering at the first twenty or so I'd produced. "Do we really have to have them? I feel like I'm consorting with the enemy."

"I'm done building them for now," I told him. "We had to have them to bring raw supplies to the Macro factory. I want this monster to

149

keep churning out new equipment. But I don't blame you for disliking the look of these machines. In fact, I'm putting you in charge of making them more friendly."

"Uh, I'm no programmer, sir."

"Not required. Order a load of paint to be brought down from our ship's stores. Coat these things thickly, and then put them back to work. It doesn't have to be art. A typical marine paint-job will do."

"You want me to *paint them*, sir? Why?"

I looked at him for a second. I didn't like my orders being questioned several times in a row.

"Sorry sir," he said, catching my look. "I suppose the paint is intended to allow us to identify them as friendly. What color do you want them to be?"

"Whatever you want," I told him. "But not pink. I hate pink."

"Wouldn't dream of it, sir," he murmured, then walked away to order the paint.

Once I was given a chance to think clearly, I changed the big factory's production orders. With Marvin's help, I ordered six thousand Centaur infantry kits to be produced. Then I had the Fleet destroyers bring down fresh troops. We had no lack of native volunteers, but we never had enough equipment to give them. I meant to change that.

Once the factory was humming, all my marines were dug into defensive positions, and the ships were bringing down loads of fresh troops every hour, I had time to ponder my next move. The Macros had remained quiet as we consolidated around our captured prize, and that worried me. They'd never cooperated previously, so I didn't expect them to give up so easily. They were out there, planning and building something.

The new worker machines were very effective at gathering elements from the stockpiles that had been made all around the factory. The infantry kits were being produced in large batches, more than a hundred at a time. Smiling, I ordered ten thousand more.

After that, I decided to build tanks. I'd always wanted to build heavier armor units, but had never had the required levels of production to sustain it. Now, I had a system that could chunk out steel like—well, like a factory. I ordered up a platoon of tanks, sixteen in all. After a few design changes, the two-turret monsters were more functional than the prototype I'd built under the dome. Producing about one an hour at a steady rate, intermixed with more loads of infantry kits, I soon had quite an army.

I slept and showered on one of the destroyers, then went back to work. Miklos called me from HQ in the sky.

"The Macros still haven't made a move, sir," he said.

"That's a good thing, isn't it? You sound worried."

"No, I don't think it's good. They are up to something. I wish I knew what."

"Well, we aren't going to give them any more time. I've already decided how we are going to take the last dome. We'll do it by marching overland. It's only about sixteen hundred miles away. Centaur troops are much faster being four-footed, and my tanks can travel overland about as fast."

"Won't that take days, sir? And won't it wear out your native troops?"

I sighed. "Yes, probably. They aren't nanotized. I can't expect them to do the impossible, but this is their planet. I want their help for the final push. We simply don't have the airlift to transport them all to the next target. We would have to put down on a new LZ without cover, too. The Macros might object."

"I have a suggestion, sir."

"Let's hear it."

"Take your tank platoon first," he said. "The destroyers are capable of carrying one each. I've already done the math."

"Okay, what then? Without support, my sixteen tanks might not survive long. The Macros will storm them with missiles."

"We have to put the rest of the fleet on station over the region to shoot down missiles. When the tanks unload, we set up laser turrets."

"Okay…" I said, taking off my helmet and thinking about it. Cool winds tousled my wet hair, chilling my head. The wind felt great. Somehow, suit air-conditioners never seemed to quite keep up with a man's level of perspiration. There were always hot wet spots and freezing cold dry spots.

"What about my infantry?" I asked.

"We take them in last, as they are the most vulnerable. These destroyers have much more lift than the old Nano ships. They can carry five times the payload. I recall a primitive design for landing pods you used back on Earth—a boxcar like unit."

"Hmm," I said, thinking it over. "The problem is the Centaurs themselves. They don't like being cooped up."

"Yes, but these systems do not have to survive in vacuum. They do not have to be sealed. You could build them quickly with planks of Macro steel, and cut many holes in the walls. They would be able to look out and see the sky and the grass around them. This should prevent panic."

I laughed. "You are describing cattle trailers. You know that, don't you? You want me to build a hundred-odd cattle trailers?"

"*Flying* cattle trailers. Exactly, sir."

In the end, I went with Miklos' idea. It was risky, but it would get a large force onto the field at the Macro dome's doorstep very quickly. I didn't like the idea of losing these forces to an enemy missile barrage, or a rush of Macro war machines, but I liked the idea of giving the enemy another week to prepare even less.

By the end of the second day, as the sun fell below what we now called the western horizon, we were ready to launch. The destroyers used their large, black arms to pick up and carry my tanks. Like mother cats with squirming kittens, they sailed away into the sky. There were a few near disasters when wind-gusts caused the tanks to creak and tip. With only one arm holding onto each one, they weren't very well-balanced. But they made it over hills, forests, lakes and grasslands—hundreds of miles of grass.

When they finally landed, some fifty miles from the enemy dome, I fully expected to hear about a counterattack. I did not, however. Instead, there was no response. No missiles, no war machines— nothing. I didn't like it, but I kept going with the plan. I didn't have a better move to make.

When the destroyers left us there on a hillside, sixteen four-man crews in each tank, it was a lonely feeling. The ships had to go back and transport the centaur troops next. But still, it felt as if we'd been abandoned.

All our sensor systems showed no movement out there. Satellite recon had reported activity: Macro workers were busily transporting supplies to the enemy factory, but no one had seen anything come out. What were they doing in there?

By midnight, I had my army assembled. We rolled forward the minute we were prepared. Just before dawn, we reached the dome.

This dome wasn't at the bottom of a lake, at least. It wasn't in a spiraling pit, either. Instead, it was nested in-between a set of craggy mountains. Not really a valley, the spot was more of a shallow depression where the peaks met. The mountains around were riddled with holes and were heavily mined by the Macro workers running in and out. As we advanced, we destroyed every harvesting system we ran into. They didn't put up much of a fight—we simply had too much firepower for them. With the big guns on every tank and literally thousands of native troops charging forward with heavy beamers, every enemy was destroyed within minutes of contact.

I began to feel elated as we drew closer. The Macros had made a mistake. Perhaps they'd had some complex plan, something that took a week to put together. But we'd moved faster than they'd thought possible and arrived with a valid force before they were ready for us. Now, they scrambled and worked desperately under their domes, but it was too late.

It was a nice fantasy, but like most fantasies, it didn't survive its inevitable impact with reality. What they were really up to none of us had expected, not until the last minute.

When I saw the dome shut off, and the glimmering surface dimmed down and flickered out entirely, I knew this was it. The moment of truth. What had they been building under there?

Under the dome were three large ships. I knew them all well. The one in the center was the most interesting—it was a transport. I'd spent months in the belly of a ship very much like it. The other two were cruisers. Their arrowhead shape was unmistakable. As the trio lifted off, they released a swarm of missiles.

"Defensive fire!" I screamed into the com-link, flipping it to general channel override. "Forget the ships, I want every vehicle laser we have engaged. Take out those missiles! Infantry, advance and scatter!"

More orders poured over the various channels as my sub-commanders realized the danger. If these incoming birds were nuclear, just one of them would wipe out most if not all of my brave little army.

We'd foreseen this possibility, and had dispersed our forces somewhat. We weren't tightly balled up. But a high-yield weapon would still kill the infantry and probably our tanks as well.

I counted the streaking missiles. They took bare seconds to shoot up to their cruising height, at which point they did a sharp turn and aimed downward. This move was a new one. I recalled anti-tank weapons of a similar design back on Earth. They were programmed to fire over obstacles by rising up, then turning sharply and coming down on a tank's turret, which was generally its weakest point. The armor was usually thin up there. In the case of our own vehicles, our tanks did have hatches that were much thinner steel than the walls.

My tanks did rather poorly against this incoming threat. The turrets were no longer manually operated, as I'd set up brain-boxes and motors with sensory input systems to operate them. These performed much better than human gunners could hope to do. But the turrets themselves weren't very fast to turn and acquire a target. The big turrets traversed, taking long seconds to lock-on and aim.

It was the destroyers that saved us from annihilation in the end. I'd had them float overhead, eighteen of them, all with three weapons each. They burned down most of the missiles. Only three got through, and each took out one of my tanks. Fortunately, the warheads were conventional explosives.

The fight was far from over, however. The next barrage of missiles was fewer in number, but more threatening. They flew directly at my destroyers. I knew what that meant. They'd decided to take out my air cover.

"To all Fleet units," I shouted. "You are ordered to perform evasive action. Rise and scatter. If one missile gets through, I don't want to lose an entire squadron."

The destroyers fled. Like a flock of birds avoiding a charging dog, they put on bursts of power and flew in every direction. The missiles wavered, and then split apart, seeking individual targets. Caught in crossfire from all three guns on every destroyer, the missiles were burned down quickly. For a few seconds, I dared to think my ships would escape. But then, after we'd shot down most of them, one of them decided to explode in order to do whatever damage it could.

Macro missiles aren't like their terrestrial counterparts. Each is a small ship, manned by an independent enemy machine. Looking back on the detonation, I figured one of the Macro pilots had calculated my ships were going to shoot them all down, and decided to go out in a blaze of glory. It should have been a win for us, but for one thing: the missile was carrying a thermonuclear warhead. The single explosion was powerful enough to destroy the rest of the missiles and two of my ships—not to mention a hell of a lot of Centaur ground troops.

154

-22-

The worst part of the aftermath was the Centaur dead. It was hard not to feel for them. I knew they were all volunteers. Like all their herd-mates, they were more than happy to lay down their lives for the cause of planetary liberation. But as I watched them fall like dominoes, burned and flattened by the power of the fireball, I didn't feel like they'd made a useful sacrifice.

We would have lost all the ground troops, but for the fact the air burst occurred at about two miles up. Still, we lost over three thousand in five seconds. Another four thousand were mortally burned or irradiated. They would linger, but wouldn't survive. The surviving Centaurs had each gotten their life-time dose of radiation and there were burns, but at least their goggles prevented blindness. Out of sixteen thousand, less than half were able to continue advancing.

Inside our tanks, my marines fared better. Only three of the big vehicles had been knocked out, those that had been directly below the blast. The one I shared with Captain Sloan swayed and rocked as if it was being kicked by giants, but survived intact. I studied the carnage around the tank and ground my teeth at the scene. I ordered what was left of my force to regroup and quickly press the attack against the dome.

The three enemy ships had escaped us entirely, covered by their barrage of missiles. The ships flew off and out of orbit quickly, heading for the nearest Macro-held planet. Miklos called me as they fled.

"Sir, request permission to pursue the enemy ships."

"Denied," I said.

"But sir—"

"Still denied. I need your ships for air cover. I don't want to lose them, or any more of my troops."

I could have ordered my ships to charge after the Macro vessels, but to do so would have left my ground force without air cover. I figured my little army had suffered enough. Miklos gave up and we proceeded to advance with grim determination. When my land army finally limped to the spot where the dome had been, the truth became clear: the Macros had pulled up stakes and fled the planet entirely. The factory was gone—even the Macro workers were gone. They'd obviously loaded it aboard the cylindrical transport ship and lifted off with it in the hold.

I understood now where the enemy production had been spent all this time. Instead of building ground forces, they'd built ships. Space-going vessels were more expensive in terms of time and resources to produce, but they'd saved their factory that way and dealt us a hard blow on their way out.

Captain Sloan clapped me on the back suddenly as I stared at the scopes and screens. I glared at him.

"It's not so bad, sir," he said.

We were both sitting inside our tank. At least we'd survived unharmed. It was more than I could say for most of the Centaurs I'd brought on this campaign.

"It's worse than bad," I said. "It was a charley-foxtrot, and you know it."

He shook his head. "No, Colonel. I don't accept that. Let's consider the situation strategically. You've driven them off an entire world—the very world the Centaur civilization was born upon. They have got to be happy with you for that. They'd gladly have given a million lives to resecure their home planet."

I nodded glumly. We'd won, but we could have done better. "I could have captured *two* of their factories, doubling our output. Now, we're still sorely out-produced."

Sloan shook his head. "No. No, I don't see it that way at all. Yes, they have more industrial capacity than we do. They always did. But now we have so much more than we ever did before. We are in better shape than before, comparatively. But frankly, what I don't get is why we've done so well up until now."

157

"What do you mean, Captain?"

"Why haven't they just wiped us out? They can field so many more ships than we can. If they still have ten times our production capacity, how can we compete?"

"I can answer that," I said. I proceeded to explain my theories about the nanotech, and how it was actually superior to Macro tech in many ways. After a while, he began to catch on. His mood brightened further.

"That's fantastic," he said. "I can see the possibilities. We can mix these two technologies and build things *they* can't compete with."

I still looked glum. It was time to tell him why I wasn't cheering up. "Technological and production gaps are not my current worry. The real issue is strategic: they've been building fleets while I've been building ground forces. That was a huge error on my part."

"But we drove them off the planet!"

"Sure," I said, "but they have five more. And I now think they are *all* building fleets. They can afford to give up a world or two. If in the end they loft an overwhelming fleet, we'll be cut off. The Centaur habitats will be destroyed. They will divide us, holding the high ground."

"High ground?"

I pointed upward, at the roof of our tank. "Space," I said. "Notice how in each battle, they'd managed to knock out a few of my destroyers? If we lose our last ships, we can't beat them. We'll lose this campaign. And after that, Earth's next."

Finally, Captain Sloan was frowning. He'd run out of glib reasons to celebrate. A minute or so later he cracked open a flask and offered it to me. I took it and swigged. It was blood-warm and nasty-tasting. I took another, larger swig and handed it back. He did the same.

Neither of us a talked for a while. Outside the tank, the wind sighed and the sun sank down, turning the sky blood red. We opened the top hatches to cool down the interior. We listened to the ticking metal as some part of the tank contracted. The grasses outside were all dead and black, so they rattled rather than rustled as the winds hit them.

Finally, I spoke up. By this time, the flask Captain Sloan and I had been passing back and forth between us was bone dry. "We're going to have to change the factory production. No more tanks. No more infantry packs. No more landing pods. We have enough of that stuff. We're switching to ships—tonight."

Captain Sloan didn't argue. Instead, he climbed out on the tank and sat on the turrets. It was night now, and the wind had shifted, taking the stink of burnt Centaur fur in the opposite direction. We opened our visors and smelled the cold wind and the burnt grasses. I wondered how long it would take this world to heal all the wounds it had suffered from the Macro occupation. I hoped it wouldn't be too many years, it was a lovely place.

A day and a half passed by quickly. We rested very little during that time. I used the hours to return my ground forces to the pit with the factory in it. I ordered them to disperse and be ready in case the enemy counterattacked. I wasn't about to let the Macros retake this prize without a fight.

After my weary, damaged army had reorganized into something that resembled a fighting force again, and I'd replaced my losses with fresh Centaur volunteers, I decided it was time to talk to the herds.

"Colonel Riggs!" came the voice through Marvin's translation box. "The sun has crossed your brow!"

"Yes, I'm sure you're right about that," I said, echoing their joyous tone. I always pretended to understand what they were talking about, especially if it was some kind of idiomatic greeting. It saved a lot of time when dealing with the long-winded Centaurs.

"We return to green the fields with our droppings! Death no longer stalks the sacred lands, nor the reviled places between stones. We thank you for this bounty."

"Okay," I said. "You are indeed welcome, and I assure you the Centaurs that fell in my service died honorably. Every one of them."

"Your words ring true."

"Now, I have a favor to ask—" I said.

"Do not bother to ask! You must *command* us! We will march onto the next world in our thousands. We will wash the grasses clean with our blood! The machines are without honor. No wind will ever ruffle their fur, for they have none. The sky—"

At that point, I kind of blanked out. *The sky*—their longest speeches always began with the sky. Their streams of words could be as endless and mysterious as the heavens themselves. They proceeded to praise me, the planet, the lakes, the mountains and every blade of liberated grass. I didn't interrupt. They seemed to be enjoying themselves, and I sensed it would be quite rude to break into the gushing words. I figured they'd earned the right to make a windy speech after I'd gotten thousands of their finest slaughtered playing cannon fodder.

Eventually, they seemed to be running out of gas. I could tell, because they began asking me prompting questions. "Is this not so? Has honor not been served with zeal?"

"It has, it has," I assured them. "Let me ask you something, if I may."

"Ask not! Demand! Make your needs known without hesitation! Be not concerned—"

"Thank you," I said gently. "I will do so. I need one of your factories. Maybe two. I apologize, but I need to move a Nano production system to the planet to work together with the captured Macro factory."

There was a hesitation. It was slight, but I think I'd surprised them with this request. It was a big move. I knew they only had a few of these factories on each of their satellites. They produced all of their serious technological equipment. Without them, they'd be unable to do much independently to supply the war effort.

"As we have promised, we shall honor your request. You shall have both our duplication systems. Ghosts of the fallen ripple with the grasses."

"Yeah, that's great. Thank you. Let's talk about getting the bulk of your population down to the planet. I think they will be safer on the surface of this world than they are inside an orbital habitat. I think we should move them as quickly as possible."

"Your wisdom is like the stone under flowing water. Can you carry our people home on the wings of your machines?"

I frowned. "That is not the best approach. I can carry them, but it will take too long to transport millions of individuals—possibly years. I thought you were going to extrude some kind of shaft down to the surface for this purpose?"

Originally, the Centaurs had left their world by climbing up shafts into space. These tubes of metal connected the surface of the world with the satellites far above. Using the shaft had made transportation of their vast numbers much more feasible. I'd hoped they would employ the same strategy to exit the space stations.

"Our plans have changed," they said.

"Why?"

"Because you require the use of our duplicators."

Suddenly, I caught on. They had been using the duplicators to create constructive nanites and had planned to use them to build the shaft down to their planet. I nodded and frowned at the same time. This wasn't going to be as easy as I thought. The more I thought of it, the more I realized the perfect substance for creating a structure like a shaft into space was a nanite-chain. They could form into anything, meaning you could just order them to build their way down to the surface. Incredibly light and strong, they would be perfect for the task.

Now, I had a decision to make. The Centaurs were leaving it up to me. Should I commandeer the only two factories the Centaurs had for the war effort? Or should I allow them to continue churning out nanites to build their own escape path down to the surface? If that satellite was destroyed by the Macros, I knew I'd feel terrible. I'd have allowed millions of innocents to die. On the other hand, if I didn't have enough military hardware to face the Macros during the next stage of the war, I'd feel even worse.

Because all of us would be dead.

-23-

In the end, I decided to split the factories and try to do both. I would build a fleet *and* save the Centaur civilians. Half-measures weren't my usual style, but it had worked out for King Solomon, so why not me?

Taking one of the Centaur factories down to the planet surface, I had it tucked under the dome for protection. Then I had the second factory in our possession moved from the guts of Socorro to sit next to the donation from the Centaurs. Within hours, two Nano factories and one big Macro unit were squatting together under the captured dome. When all three systems were installed and functional I entered the protective, shimmering walls of force to work with them.

Captain Miklos was there, and he didn't understand my decisions.

"Why didn't you take *both* units from the Centaurs? They offered them."

"I'm not even sure I'll need them."

He laughed at that. "When have you ever suffered from an overabundance of production?"

"Never," I admitted. "Well, I couldn't decide which use of these units was better. I know we need a fleet, but the herds would have no hope of escape down to their world without keeping at least one of the units on their satellite."

Miklos shook his head and tugged at his beard. He'd been growing it a bit longer lately. I supposed none of us had a lot of time for niceties like a weekly trimming.

"I don't know, sir," he said. "If the Macro fleet defeats us, they will kill all the civilians anyway."

"We don't know that. They've made deals in the past. I'm happy with double my previous nanite production, in combination with this monster."

"There's another thing, Colonel. You asked me to find any trace of the strange cloud-like creature you found here in this pit."

"Right. The Blue named 'Introspection'. What did you find?"

"I carefully looked over all our surveillance of the region, both before and after the battle. I found very little evidence on the sensor logs. There was a spectrographic registration of helium and deuterium. We thought at the time it was a byproduct of the mining here, or possibly related to the force-dome itself."

"That's it? Where did it go?"

"Well sir, we don't know. It dissipated over time, but that could mean anything. During the battle, I did not have sensory systems tracking each cloud of water vapor in the sky, nor did I follow this gaseous ghost."

I nodded and sighed. "All right. The short answer is it's gone, and we don't know where it went because we weren't looking for it. I want you to reprogram the sensory boxes to recognize a signature set of readings. Put together a profile, and have them watch for it. Maybe it will come back."

"Right sir."

Then I checked the time, and waved for Miklos to exit. "I'm going into programming mode now," I told him. "That takes careful thought. Please go keep an eye on the rest of the star system for me.'"

"Will do sir," he said, and left.

I watched his form glimmer and flare white as he entered the field. When he had gone, I turned my attention back to the three machines and the scarred earth they sat upon. The ground under the dome still showed massive wounds from the battle we'd fought. It was strange, walking over the same loose earth men had died upon just days earlier. Bits of jagged metal still thrust up here and there.

The bunker I'd hastily built was still there, half-sunken in the ground near the central unit. It seemed hard to believe, looking at it now, that we'd withstood the attack of swarms of Macros inside its relatively thin walls. The bunker walls were blackened and pitted with a hundred laser strikes. I shook my head, it was a wonder any of us had lived through those long hours. If they'd had real ground troops, even just Macro marine units, they would have slaughtered us. We'd survived because most of the enemy had been equipped with the Macro equivalent of hedge-trimmers.

Another one element of the scene I remembered well was missing: the destroyed Macro workers. They'd been hauled away and fed back into the factories as raw materials. We'd converted the mass into a more useful form: tanks and ground troop kits.

Now, I had a new challenge to face. I needed to build a fleet—fast. It had to be better than anything we'd put up yet. It couldn't simply be a set of Nano ships. Such vessels functioned well, but were built primarily of nanites, which our newly captured factory could not produce. I needed a drastically new design to make use of the bigger production system the Macros had provided for us.

I took off my helmet and gauntlets. I demanded coffee, and got it. Then I walked around the machine, kicking at the slagged dirt and scowling. I hated programming under pressure—but I'd always done my best work that way. I told myself to halt the self-pity. What programmer didn't live with a deadline over his head?

I gave myself a shake and tried to clear my mind of extraneous thought. The first thing I needed was Marvin. I was still dependent on him to translate my instructions into the binary this Macro production facility understood. In the future, I was sure I could replace that function with a nanite brainbox, but I simply didn't have any time to fancy it up now.

"Marvin, are you here inside the dome?" I called on the general channel. The dome interrupted all signals, even if you tried to send a wire from the outside world to the inside world. Inside, a single channel worked well, and everyone listened to it.

My headset hummed quietly, as did the big machine. No one answered me. I frowned in annoyance and repeated the call. Still, no answer. Marvin knew I wanted to meet with him on the hour, but he was late.

I wandered around the grounds for a minute or two, thinking I was going to have to exit the dome and hail him outside. In practice, the force-dome was a pain to deal with. It was like being buried in a tomb. We were all used to instant communications, and being disconnected to the point of sending couriers through the shimmering walls was a constant irritant. Still, I figured it was well worth keeping the dome

164

turned on. At least this way, our most valuable assets couldn't be taken out in a surprise attack.

Marvin finally showed up, nine minutes late.

"What kept you?" I asked.

"Certain duties."

"Duties? What, were they life-threatening?"

"Possibly."

Talking with Marvin was often an ordeal. He was reflexively evasive. Usually, this was for a good reason. He liked to do things I'd never ordered him to do, and he knew I might not approve of his behavior. Therefore, he found it easier to just stay quiet and dodge questions. I grunted unhappily. As usual, he had given me a choice: pursue the matter doggedly, or drop it. I was busy today, so I chose the latter option. The galling part came from knowing this choice played into Marvin's plans. He had won again, and the behavior pattern was thereby reinforced. I'd once had teenage children, and they'd been easier to deal with than this robot.

"All right," I said, "let's get down to business. Open a connection with the production unit, please."

"Don't you want to know what I've been doing?"

I stared at him in surprise. "I thought you were taking great pains to hide your activities."

"I've reached a different—stage," he said. "Input would be welcome at this point."

I opened my mouth to ask: "a different stage of *what?*" but I held back, because that's what he wanted me to do. "I don't have time for it now, Marvin—whatever it is you're hinting about. Open a connection to the production unit, please. Directly translate my input and the unit's responses."

"Channel open."

"I need a standardized hull form," I said. "Something I can make a lot of. How much steel do I have available?"

"Question rejected. Question improperly formatted. Input variables reset."

I heaved a sigh. Underneath it all, every computer had certain similarities to the rest. They were the ultimate obsessives. If you made a mistake, they loved to throw your work right back into your face. Humans were all about the gray areas, while machines were all about the black and the white.

165

"Let's try that again. If you start building a cruiser right now, how long would it take to complete the process?"

There was a brief hesitation. "Hypothesized goal unattainable. Query rejected."

I thought about that, frowning. "You can't build an entire cruiser?"

"No."

I rubbed my chin in thought. "Are you missing any of the key elements?"

"No."

"Why then can't you build a cruiser?"

"Elements too complex. Hull size too large. Overall unit can't be generated in a single output dump."

"Ah," I said, catching on at last. "You can only build a cruiser in parts, because it's too big, am I correct?"

"Yes."

I laughed. "Okay. We will take of assembling the pieces. How long would it take you to build all the standard components of a cruiser, given that you are provided with all the input materials required?"

"Six days," the system said.

I nodded. That sounded about right. The last dome on this planet had been given several weeks, and had completed three ships in that time. Part of the reason I'd started with this line of questioning was for the purposes of intel. I now had a better metric to calculate how many enemy ships the Macros might have produced in this system. The conclusions were frightening. Depending on when the production units had started building and how well-supplied they were, I had to figure they had somewhere between fifteen and fifty working ships out there.

Normal logic would dictate that the Macros should have attacked us by now if they had such an overwhelming numerical advantage. But the Macros liked overkill. They would come, but only when some preplanned production goal had been reached. I had no way of knowing what that goal was, but I was confident that when they launched their fleet, it would be impressive.

"Now tell me how long it takes to build a single Macro belly turret, with a full magazine of ammunition."

"Six hours."

"Good, now we are getting somewhere."

The Macro belly turrets were interesting weapons. I'd learned more about them from carefully researched science reports provided to me by General Kerr recently. They weren't beam weapons, nor did they fire missiles. They were in fact, railguns. They drove a mass of matter to very high velocities using a magnetic barrel and some tricks of physics I didn't entirely understand. The main point was they were able to translate energy from one of their massive fusion generators into mass in high-velocity motion. Using kinetic force alone, these high-speed salvos were devastating, but the rate of fire was relatively low.

"How long to build a generator capable of lifting a ship with a thousand ton displacement, and firing the gun at the same time?"

"Nonsensical query. Undefined references. Query ignored."

I kicked the machine's output bay and chuckled. It took time, but after a bit of careful questioning, I had the information I wanted. The factory could produce a hull with an engine, generator and belly turret in about half a day. The ship as a whole would only be a tenth the size of a full cruiser, and wouldn't possess many of the subsystems. But it was a platform to work from, and the big gun would give it a lot of firepower for its size. Using my nanite factories to produce lighter point-defense weapons, sensors, life-support subsystems and the like, I could crank out small gunboats with weapons that were equivalent to the enemy cruisers in firepower—if not in armor. They would be far larger and tougher than nanotech ships.

I ordered the machine to begin production immediately. For the most part, I stuck with components the big machine already knew how to build. I didn't want to teach it anything new right now. The hull was the only tricky part. To simplify things, I went with a rectangular design, not all that different from an earthly barge. I designed the hull as a single piece, with slots to plug in weaponry, sensors and exhaust ports. I made it as big as the factory's largest output bay. That way, it could be produced in a single effort.

When the first empty hull slid from the output bay, I had to admit it was ugly, but I had hopes for its functionality. Even after plugging in the necessary components, I left many holes in the hull, which could be patched with smart metal, or just pure nanites. I wanted to allow for improvements to the design later. We could add components produced separately by the smaller Nano factories later on.

We'd yet to test the configuration of the systems as a whole. I didn't know if it would flip over from recoil when it fired its big gun, or if the single primary engine in back was too light for strong acceleration. To solve these problems in advance, I placed repeller plates all around the hull. If there was a problem with maneuverability, the brainbox that flew it would learn to compensate automatically. I missed having all the Pentagon nerds to back me up on this one. I wasn't an aerospace engineer, so I had to make do.

While the big machine thrummed, Marvin and I stayed inside the dome in case it ran into a problem. We'd set the two Nano factories to work as well, of course. They were building all the smaller components. They did so somewhat faster than the big machine, and I used the extra time producing constructive nanites. They were always useful.

"Do you have enough time now, Colonel Riggs?" Marvin asked after we'd completed the programming session.

I considered his question, which again came as a surprise. He really wanted to show me something. All three of the machines had something to do. So did a team of forty-odd marines, who I'd instructed to assemble the ships as the parts came out of the three factories. With the help of some tame worker Macros to do the heaviest lifting, the men were doing fine. The first gunboat took form with dramatic speed.

I almost asked what he was talking about, but stopped myself. Unlike humans, Marvin never forgot a topic during a conversation.

"Yes," I said, turning my attention to Marvin. "Tell me about your preoccupation. Why were you late?"

"I've been trying to help humanity," he said.

"Ah, a noble goal. Could you explain what form this help has taken?"

"I've grown a...colony."

"A colony of what?"

"Microbes."

I stared at him, then nodded slowly. His cameras whirred and zoomed. I knew they were evaluating my expression from a half-dozen angles, trying to calculate my response. Was I angry or elated? Was I going to approve or forbid his experiments? He clearly wanted to know.

"We are talking about the same type of Microbes we found on the Macro ship last year, aren't we?"

"Yes."

"The ones which are intelligent, when massed together?"

168

"Yes."

"What have you done with them, Marvin?"

"I have collected samples, purified their environment and placed them in a suitable containment facility."

I nodded, maintaining a poker face. I recalled he'd been messing about with mud puddles since we first landed on this world. Clearly, he'd had a good reason of his own to come here, and it wasn't only to help me claim the Macro production facility.

"Show me," I said.

He rose up on his writhing tentacles and led me to a pool of mud near the dome's edge. I stared at it. The pool was about six feet wide and less than a foot deep. Really, it was easy to ignore. Not being placed too close to any of the major pathways, the Macro workers seemed to never come near the place. There were few footprints of any kind around the pool—except for the odd, swirling prints that Marvin made when he squirmed and wriggled overland like a bundle of snakes.

"They are in there? How many of them?"

"It's difficult to achieve a precise population count. That's one of the reasons I'm sharing my achievement with you. I need more equipment to work with them."

"Hmm," I said, frowning at the pool. "How many, in round numbers?"

"Between two and three trillion."

"*Trillion?*" I asked incredulously.

"Admittedly, the culture is small, but I've only just started."

My mouth sagged open, and I took a step back from the pool. I didn't want the earthen sides to slip down into the water—it would be like an avalanche to them.

"I'm not accustomed to thinking a trillion of anything," I said.

Marvin only had one camera on me now. Almost all of the rest studied his pool.

"The average human adult supports approximately two hundred trillion microflora. These beings are larger in size, however. They are closer to the size of a human cell. Still, for this volume of medium, three trillion is a very thin population. The environment here is too cold for them, you see. That's one of the things I need, a proper warming system. It must be built to create a diffused heat. No single area of the pool should be hot or cold, and the circulatory action must be very gentle to create a minimum of accidental deaths. I think the best system would be an under-carpet of bubble-producing polymers. That way—"

"Marvin," I said, interrupting. This gained me two extra cameras of attention. "I don't understand what you are doing with these creatures. You found them here, on the planet surface?"

"Yes," he said. "They are not quite the same variety we discovered on the Macro cruiser in their experimentation tanks. But they are quite similar. I believe they are a wild strain. They've adjusted somewhat to the colder climate, but not entirely. They don't thrive on an icy world like this one."

I nodded slowly, trying to absorb everything he was inferring. "You are saying they aren't native to this world? They are from somewhere else?"

"Yes."

"Where?"

"The sixth planet from the local star."

"The tropical world, eh? I see. What are they doing here?"

"I'm not sure," he said. "But I believed they were used to exterminate the original indigenous population of Centaurs."

-24-

After I got over my shock, I turned to Marvin incredulously. "Are you telling me these intelligent microbes were used as a biological weapon against the Centaurs?"

Marvin flicked a few extra cameras toward me, then panned them back to his soupy pool of mud. He snaked out a tentacle, probed the surface of the liquid gingerly, then retracted the appendage.

"Yes," he said.

"What the hell are you doing growing a pool of them, if they are so dangerous?"

"They are no longer dangerous."

I shook my head. "Okay," I said. "This is a big deal, Marvin, if you are right. Let's go over it, and I don't want to hear any of your usual evasiveness."

"I'm always forthright and compliant with your wishes, Colonel Riggs."

"No," I said. "No, you are not. But I'm not going to argue with you about that. What makes you think they were used as weapons?"

"They informed me of this. It is part of their historical record. Not all tribes of their people remember—it was thousands of generations ago. But some do. They corroborate the story."

"What possible motivation would they have for coming to a Centaur world and killing the populace?"

"The same motivation humans had to invade Helios and exterminate the Worms."

"Ah," I said, suddenly understanding. "The Microbes made a deal with the Macros? They were used to kill other biotics—just like we were?"

"Yes."

I stared at the pool, dumbfounded. "Why do you think they are harmless now?"

"They are the leftover remnants of an aerial bombardment. Since their duty was long ago completed, they are free of their obligation to kill other biotics on this world. Now, they are simply trying to survive."

"What is your interest in them, Marvin?"

"Don't you find them entrancing?" he asked seriously. "Didn't the nanites fill you with curiosity—at least at first?"

"Yes," I admitted. "Yes, they did."

"Tiny creatures with an alien nature," he said. "I'm drawn to them, I admit. I was fascinated with them from the first. A form of intelligence so different from my own—and yet not that dissimilar. My mind is a mass of tiny machines working in tandem. Yours is a cluster of structurally adhered cells. Theirs is a colony of independent cells, floating in a liquid medium."

I thought about it, and realized the Microbes were more like me than Marvin was—even if there was a huge difference in scale. I walked around the pool at a safe distance, looking at it from all angles. It still looked like muddy pond water to me.

"What's this?" I said, gesturing to a stream of water that led to the force dome. The pool itself was very close to the shimmering wall. I could feel a hint of static from it at this close range. It hummed and sizzled at times.

"Careful," Marvin said. "Do not allow the water to make contact with the force field."

I frowned and squatted. It was a line of water, about three inches wide, that led from the dome to the main pool. But as I examined it more closely, I could see a dam of earth had been built up at the far end, insulating the water from the wall of the dome.

"What the hell did you use this for, Marvin?"

"A safe way to add fluid to the pool," he said. "I did not want to stir up the liquid too much."

"Hmm. I don't believe you."

172

At least seven cameras were on me now. Marvin didn't say anything.

"You use this canal to shock the pool, don't you?"

Marvin stared.

"Why have you been mistreating these tiny creatures, Marvin?"

"Training of any kind requires two essential elements: reward and punishment."

I made a growling sound. "Marvin, I don't want you playing god with these poor beings."

"I've made critical advancements," he said.

"What do you mean?"

"They can repair human flesh—or Centaur flesh. Do you recall the injuries sustained by Sandra?"

"Yes, I do, but I fail to see how—"

"Let me finish, Colonel. I know that you feel an emotional bond with these beings, but really, they are no different than the nanites you've enslaved to do your bidding in a thousand ways."

"They are intelligent, Marvin."

"After a fashion, yes. But so are the nanites, if you configure them that way."

I had to concede his point. I knew we were on the edge of human morality. What were the rules, here? Marvin had pointed out in the past my prejudice in favor of biotics. He had a point. Thinking machines could die—billions of them—and I had no trouble with that. But as soon as the species was closer to my own chemical configuration, I became squeamish.

Were these aliens special, just because they were intelligent as a collective whole? Or were they just bacteria, to be used or abused as we might treat a fish caught in a net? Was their sentience enough to put them in an entirely new category? I felt overwhelmed with the magnitude of these questions.

"I've always preferred stand-up fights to moral dilemmas," I told Marvin. "I've always been willing to choose humanity over any other species, when it comes down to a fight. If it is them or us, I'll kill anyone, or anything."

"Your path is clear then. Let me expand my cultures. I need a much larger facility. We can set up baths for healing, and experimental improvements."

173

"Hold on a minute!" I said, cutting him off. "I said I would run through an enemy to survive, but this is different. We were enslaving these creatures, abusing them for our own purposes. If I use them to make better troops, how am I better than the Macros? They used them to sicken the Centaur herds, furthering their aims. They were not allies, they were forced to comply. If they improve my soldiers, they will die in the process. In both cases, the Microbes have been unfairly coerced."

There were a lot of cameras on me now. I couldn't even count them all. I think he'd added a few since the last time I'd met up with him.

"Colonel Riggs," he said. "Perhaps you'd allow me to demonstrate what they can do for—us."

"No," I said, raising a hand. "I'm sure I would be impressed, Marvin. And I thank you for your work here. I'm sure when we have a chance to bring some eggheads out from Earth, they will be more than happy to go over the discoveries you've made. But I don't even want to know what they can do. I don't want to be tempted."

Marvin was quiet for a moment. His tentacles seemed to move more slowly. This meant he was either unhappy, contemplative, or both. I waited for his next statement.

He didn't say anything, but instead headed toward the dome. It took me a second to realize what he was doing. When his longest whip-like arm reached toward the canal he'd dug to the dome's edge, I protested.

"Hold on!" I said. "You don't have to kill them all."

"They've been altered. They can't survive in the wild on this world now. I've got a moral obligation to shut down this experiment."

"No," I said. "Don't. They've suffered enough. Can't we just leave them here in peace?"

"Not really," Marvin said. "They need care. I've kept them warmed artificially, and fed nutrients into the pond. Without care, most will die. They will consume one another due to lack of input within—forty minutes."

I blew out a puff of air. How did I get myself into these situations? "All right," I said, knowing very well what Marvin wanted. "You can keep this pond, but not for cruel experimentation. We'll build a small shelter around this spot. You can use the steel planks from the bunker to keep people from walking into the middle of the pond. Later, I'll

174

figure out what we should do with them. If nothing else, we can communicate and attempt to establish a dialog, if all of us live that long."

Marvin seemed very pleased. "A wall," he said. "An excellent suggestion. I would have put up a barrier long ago, but felt constrained."

"Constrained? Meaning, you realized that if I saw you building a wall out here around a mud puddle, I would have known something strange was going on?"

"Perhaps."

"Right. Well, you can keep pets for now. After we finish assembling this ship and test it, I might need you to help me talk to the big factory about programming improvements."

"Of course, Colonel."

I left him then, and he scuttled off to gather spare planks of steel. I shook my head as I walked away.

Within a few hours, we had our first complete gunship. I climbed inside to pilot it. When I did so, I immediately found the internal design was less than perfect. The essential problem was the size of the components. We had a huge railgun turret, a massive generator, and a solid steel hull that could not be reshaped wrapped around it. I decided to put the gun in the belly of the ship, just as it was placed on Macro cruisers. It poked out of the lower section and rotated smoothly enough. The generator was on top of the turret and used up space behind it until it ran into the single, large engine. The ship would not be anything like a Nano ship, nor like our destroyers. With multiple smaller engines and laser projectors, those ships were more balanced and maneuverable.

"This thing is going to steer like a shopping cart," Commander Welter said, pronouncing a verdict that didn't really surprise me.

I'd called him down from his destroyer for the express purpose of providing design refinements for the gunship prototype. I'd taken a look, and felt they were serviceable. But I wanted an expert opinion from a pilot's point of view. As Major Welter, he'd distinguished himself while flying enemy craft in the Helios Campaign—and afterward against the Macros. He'd become a master pilot, and I'd reluctantly moved him into the Fleet category and changed his rank to that of Commander.

"It looks that way," I admitted, walking him through the ship. "But give it a chance. Most of the mass is centralized or underneath the ship. We have an unusual number of stabilizers positioned all around the hull."

Commander Welter followed me from the forward compartment where the crew would sit to the back of the ship. This required a little squeezing. The central turret and generator were so big, they took up all but three feet of space on either side. The three feet came in the form of a metal tube with unevenly contoured walls.

"Seriously?" he asked. "We have to use a crawlspace to get back to the engine room?"

"There's one of these—ah—passages on each side of the ship. They are only about thirty feet long, and in space these zones will maintain a zero-G environment for rapid movement."

"I wouldn't want to be caught in here when the ship takes a hit," he muttered.

I ignored him until we got to the engine room. Partly, this was because I couldn't even see him behind me without contorting my heavy battle suit.

"I'd put one-way signs on these tubes," he said. "If everyone takes the starboard tube to exit either chamber, they should never run into each other."

I thought about that for a second, then nodded in my helmet. "Excellent idea, Commander. That's why I brought you along. You've made your first design improvement."

He muttered something about redesigning a turd, but I didn't listen. I didn't want to get mad at him. I had a big favor to ask.

The engine room made the forward compartment look roomy by comparison. Instead of seating for four, sensory equipment and the ship's only bathroom, the rear space was squashed between the generator, the top of the turret and the single, massive engine. It was hot back here and stuffy. The air was thick with ozone.

"Will there be a crewman back here?" he asked.

I gestured toward two jump seats. They were folded up against the bulkhead between the two tubes that led in and out of the compartment. Nanite arms held them against the steel wall tightly. When touched, the arms lowered the seats and grabbed the occupant.

"See?" I said, flopping down in one. I grunted as the arms clamped onto me. "These seats are only for emergency flight safety, of course."

176

"Yeah," he said. "That's great."

He walked around the big engine, almost bumping his armored butt into my face as he scooted between me and the metal housing.

"Looks like you haven't spared anything in the power department."

"You've grasped the essential beauty of this design," I said. "These ships provide the most bang for the buck of any design I could come up with. Raw power in a compact form."

Welter nodded, but kept sneering and squinting as he ran his hands over the systems. He jerked his hand away from a hot spot and cursed.

"What I want to know is who's going to pilot them?" he asked. "All your best pilots are commanding destroyers, including me."

I cleared my throat. He shot me an alarmed glance. Seeing my expression, his face fell.

"Uh—oh, come on, sir!" he said. "You can't—"

"Yes," I said firmly. "I very much can. I have to. Every destroyer commander will man one of these new ships. Every destroyer pilot will man another, if we build enough before they hit us."

"What? Then who will run the destroyers?"

"The gunners," I said firmly. "And the marine sergeants after that. The Centaurs can't do it, so we have to. Everyone is going on a crash pilot-training course."

Welter eyed me in shock. "You mean I have to trade in my destroyer for one of these things? It looks like a flying bathtub."

"Exactly."

"But why have your best pilots fly your worst ships?"

"Because they *aren't* my worst ships. They have triple the firepower of your destroyer. More importantly, the destroyers practically fly themselves. They have experienced nanite brainboxes to do most of the work. I don't expect these ships will be so smooth to operate in battle."

Welter let out a long sigh. "No," he said glumly. "I don't suppose they will. All right, I understand your reasoning. I take it you want me to fly this tub—the worst one of all, the prototype?"

"You're finally catching on, Commander."

-25-

Before we headed off into orbit on a shakedown cruise, I responded to an odd buzzing in my helmet. I noticed a set of words displayed in warning yellow, and pulled them up onto the center region of my HUD. On the visor before me, the words displayed read: 'mailbox full. Message returned.' I frowned at this for a moment, not recalling having sent any texts lately. I almost activated the warning and opened the report.

Then I realized what it was. The system was warning me that *my* mailbox was full. It wasn't just any mailbox, either. It was the one that came from Star Force. Cursing, I decided I had to take a look. Possibly, Crow was crying for help. Who knew, maybe a hundred fresh enemy cruisers had come through the Venus gate and now approached Earth. I didn't want to open those emails, but it would be criminal not to. Still, I somehow managed to put it off one more time. I justified this by telling myself I was in the middle of a critical combat test operation. Admiral Crow would have to wait a few more minutes.

"Take us up, Commander Welter," I ordered.

As the ship lifted with an uncertain trembling, I felt for the armrests. Nanite arms snaked out and clamped my limbs into place. We rose out of the domed region very slowly.

Once free-floating in the open air, Welter applied thrust. At first he did so gently, then he gave it a surge of power. I was pressed back into my seat, despite the stabilizers, which were humming dutifully.

"Quite a bit of power in this beast," Welter said, gripping the control sticks we'd rigged up.

Unlike Nano ships, these vessels had more direct control systems. There were brainboxes to be sure, but they had less knowledge of how to guide the ship than we did. Part of the purpose of this voyage was to demonstrate to the brainboxes how the controls worked and thus how the craft should be flown.

"Let's take a few strafing runs at that mountain range," I suggested. "When you are satisfied with the weaponry and atmospheric handling, take it up and we'll do a few orbits."

"Won't that tip our hand to the Macros, sir? They must be watching."

I shrugged. "Maybe a new kind of ship showing up will give them a reason to wait. We need time, and when faced with the unknown, the Macros tend to hesitate."

Welter didn't argue further. He was soon flying the ship in hard twists and turns. I could tell he was having fun despite himself. This ship had power, and power was always fun. Like a muscle car, it didn't steer smoothly. Turning took a wide arc and lots of sickening Gs. The ship trembled when you pushed it, giving the feeling it might heel over and go into a spin. But it didn't.

Welter pushed it, but never quite broke it. The first time he fired the gun, however, gave us a surprise. The entire ship bucked up under us. It felt like going over a speed bump in a car with bad shocks. We went over these speed bumps fast, and rhythmically. My teeth clacked each time the cannon fired. But it didn't flip over, and Welter never lost control.

"We'll need to teach the brainbox to give us a goose on the stabilizers every time we fire the main cannon," he said.

"I'll adjust the gain on the learning rate. Take another strafing run on that lake."

After Welter tired of bombing the landscape with glowing pellets from the railgun, he took us up into orbit. Things smoothed out above the atmosphere, and I took the respite to finally open my email mailbox.

I opened the oldest email and read it quickly. It was from Crow, as I had expected. It was worded politely, but firmly. I was to report, and return to base ASAP. I grinned. It was weeks old. The second one was almost as cordial, but by the third email things began to get nasty. Crow used unpleasant words, mixed with Aussie slang. As far as I could determine, I was some kind of Wally with a genetic deformity in

179

the region of my hindquarters. I wasn't sure what a Wally was, but I assumed it was meant in a derogatory fashion.

The last email was a shocker, however. It wasn't from Crow. It was from Jasmine Sarin.

When I'd left Earth many weeks ago, pursuing the Macro fleet, Jasmine had been a Major and my executive officer. I'd more or less left her in charge of the Star Force Marines in my absence. The first surprise was her new title: she was now calling herself *Rear Admiral Sarin*.

I stared at that, opening and closing my mouth repeatedly. Like a gaping fish on the deck of a boat, I didn't quite know what had happened to my world. Jasmine had gone fleet? Crow had promoted her over me, and brought her under his direct command? I couldn't believe she'd go along with it.

Even as I denied the obvious, it began to sink in. Sarin had been bucking for a promotion for a long time. I'd denied her requests. Then, from her point of view, I'd gone AWOL. Perhaps she'd told herself she was helping the cause of all Star Force by going Fleet. There had always been tension between the Marine and Fleet sides of the house, and having a sympathetic commander on the other side could help ease matters. Still, it felt like a betrayal.

I had to wonder, too, if other forces were at play in her decision. She'd had a personal interest in me, but I'd essentially spurned her after a few flirtations. Perhaps that had caused a rift between us I hadn't recognized before.

After doing a bit of rapid thinking, I managed to read the rest of the email. There was another shocker at the bottom. She reported she was on her way out here on a Fleet vessel. She wanted to communicate with me directly, and ascertain if I needed rescuing or was having some kind of difficulty with my electronics.

"Hmm," I said aloud.

"What is it, sir?" Commander Welter asked. He was tooling around in a wide arc, a power-turn that caused every onboard alarm to whoop and flash.

"I think we're going to have company, soon," I said.

He shot me a look. "Are we ready for that, sir?"

"Absolutely not."

Welter chuckled. "Should I fire the big cannon from orbit, sir?"

"No," I said. I noticed an immediate look of disappointment on his face. "I don't want to show the Macros everything. We'll save that for later."

"Okay, Colonel."

I contacted Miklos next, as the cruise continued. I checked the time. Another hour had passed. The second gunship would be finished soon. I was impressed at this rate of production, now that I was experiencing it in real time. If they gave us another week, the Macros would find themselves facing a fleet of tough little midget ships.

Miklos answered on the first hail. "Hello Colonel. I see your ship does fly."

"Even pigs can, I hear, when in possession of very large wings."

"What can I do for you, sir?"

"Do you have any new contacts? I mean, around the ring?"

"Yes sir, as a matter of fact, I wanted to talk to you about that."

I heaved a sigh. Jasmine was already here. I didn't know what I was going to say to her when we met.

"The Nano ship we had posted as a scout at the ring didn't return to report this last hour."

I frowned and blinked. "What?" I asked. "I've got plenty of relayed emails over our little pony-express system. Are you telling me we've been disconnected from Earth?"

"What? No, sir. I'm talking about the other ring. The one that leads to the lobster worlds."

"Ah," I said, catching on. "Do we have another ship out there to go look for the scout?"

"No sir, every ship we have is orbiting the Centaur homeworld except for a few miners and the scouts at the two rings."

I looked at Commander Welter. He looked back at me.

"You're going to ask me to fly out there, aren't you, sir?" he asked.

"No," I said. "This ship is too critical. We have too much firepower to remove it from the main front now. The Macros might take the opportunity to attack while we appear out of position. We are going to stay in orbit, and send *Socorro*. She's our smallest, fastest, most lightly-armed ship."

I'd specially designed *Socorro* for scouting trips. It bothered me to send her out on a dangerous mission without being at the helm myself, but I wasn't about to leave my post. There were too many unknowns in the Eden system for my liking today.

"Colonel?" the command channel asked. Miklos' East European accent was unmistakable. "This might be premature. The ship is less than an hour overdue."

"No," I said. "Something went wrong. I know that pilot. Jameson is always timely. He's not going to sit on the far side without a good reason, especially with no orders to do so. The Crustaceans have been gathering on the far side for days, and they haven't been responding to the queries I've relayed to them."

"Very good, sir. I will dispatch another scout."

"Just one man aboard *Socorro*. We can't afford anything more."

I rode out the next half-hour of tests without enjoyment. I was tense, and finally ordered the shakedown cruise cut short. "Take me down, Commander. I've had enough."

He looked at me and misinterpreted my expression. He grinned and lowered us into the clouds again. The ship shivered and heated up forty degrees. I closed my helmet and let the air conditioners dry the sweat from my face.

I wasn't sick from his twists and turns, but I didn't tell Welter that. I was worried. There was new activity from two new directions. I'd been expecting the Macros to make a move, but now it seemed that Star Force and the Crustaceans were in motion instead.

We went straight down to the dome. Together, Welter and I had come up with a score of improvements to the design. They were all minor, however. The craft functioned as is. Even the prototype was viable.

"Marvin?" I demanded over the general channel once inside the dome. I walked around on the crunching moonscape that was the region under the dome. It was all chunks of ground-down rock, dust and bits of shiny metal.

"I'm engaged at the moment, Colonel."

"Well, unengage yourself," I said. "I need translations done. I'm reprogramming this facility."

"Just speak to it directly."

"I don't speak binary."

"There is no need. I've affixed a brainbox and taught it appropriate translation engrams. It should do the job as well as I could."

"Right," I said. "Well, that's excellent."

I ordered the changes through the new brainbox, which I found near the output tray. While I did so, I scanned the bleak landscape for the robot. I knew he had to be under the dome with me somewhere.

The first thing I saw was the wrecked bunker of steel planks. Many of the planks were missing. Smiling, I then knew where he had to be. I circled to the far side of the production unit and squinted toward the wall of the dome. A structure of scarred metal had appeared there. Marvin had been very busy. He'd built an encircling pen around his pets, and now enclosed them completely. I didn't even see a door, but I suspected he was inside his little fort, tending to the Microbes.

I frowned with a new thought. Could he be shocking them in there? Out of sight? Or maybe applying some other form of discipline? I didn't like the idea, but I didn't have time to walk out there and check up on him. Right now, he was busy and out of trouble. I wanted him to stay that way.

I finished my programming edits and witnessed the birth of a new gunship. The fresh hull rolled out into the output tray with a tremendous clang. My construction-duty marines set to work on it immediately, pouring in nanites, adding major systems and cementing fittings into place with caulk-guns full of nanites.

As it took shape, the second vessel looked about the same as the first, but there had been many adjustments. The central turret and the generator unit had been edged a few feet forward. This squeezed the bridge crew, but provided a more balanced arrangement of mass. The stabilizers wouldn't have to work so hard when the ship was firing or accelerating to provide a stable platform.

The big machine began working on the next ship, filling the dome with odd hot smells and a deep, thrumming sound that made my feet tingle in my boots. I wondered how these little ships would hold up in battle. As I exited the dome, I calculated I would learn the truth soon enough.

-26-

No one was more surprised than I was when the Crustaceans broke through the Hel ring in an attack formation. I'd talked to them, and they'd seemed reasonable—if a little stuffy. Now, they weren't talking at all.

I shook my head. Standing next to me, Miklos clucked his tongue. We were both aboard a destroyer called *Actium* which hovered in the high atmosphere over the Centaur homeworld. We'd made this ship our new command vessel, after the destruction of *Barbarossa*.

I'd reached *Actium* as quickly as possible after receiving the news from Fleet. Due to the significant distance out to the ring orbiting Hel, we hadn't been given any time to react to the Crustacean attack. Instead, we could only watch vids of the aftermath and analyze them. In this case, the analysis was simple: the Crustaceans had gotten their collective shell-covered tails kicked.

They'd sent through a flock of nineteen ships, each of which was identical in appearance. They were all a familiar design of Nano ship. It was strange, seeing these vessels coming at us aggressively. I recognized them so intimately. I'd spent months inside *Alamo*, a twin to every one of them. I even paused to wonder if *Alamo* was among these attackers, and if the ship would recognize my voice if I attempted contact. It was a strange thought.

I didn't have time to try to talk to them, however. Sixteen of the nineteen ships were destroyed by our mines. They tried to shoot them down, but it was hopeless. I'd laid thousands there, on the off chance the Macros would send a fresh fleet of cruisers at us from that direction. The mines didn't work as well on the smaller more maneuverable Nano ships as they had on ponderous Macro cruisers— but they did the job. Each contained a tiny nuclear charge at the center of a dark, star-shaped metal object. Any contact, even close proximity to a vessel that didn't broadcast the correct friend-or-foe code, caused detonation. As we watched the incoming vids we counted ninety-three detonations.

It was overkill, really. The surviving ships reversed themselves and exited back through the ring. Dozens of my mines followed them, attracted by magnetics and tiny brainboxes.

"I hate seeing fellow biotics killed," I said. "Recall *Socorro*. There's little point to sending a scout ship out there alone now."

"Why are the lobsters attacking us, sir?" Miklos asked me.

"I don't know. Have you sent every message you could asking for peace and a meeting?"

"Of course. But they never got the transmissions. The incursion was brief, and the mines pushed them back before they could have possibly received the messages."

I nodded. Battle at great distances had logistic difficulties. On Earth, you could at least talk to someone on the other side of the world with a few seconds of delay tagging onto the end of each sentence. That was annoying, but it could be dealt with. Without much trouble you could have a comprehensive conversation. At greater distances, it was more like texting each other. There might be hours between transmissions and responses. In this case, the delay was something like four hours. That meant this video was old. Everything could have changed by now. The Lobsters could have broken through, or they might have given up and retreated for good. It was frustrating being fed old information. I wanted to see the battle in real time.

"This is all we need," I said. "It's not enough that the Macros are building up a fleet to push us out of this system, the Crustaceans seem to have the same goal. No one wants us here in the Eden system, do they Captain?"

Miklos shrugged. "A wise man listens to the winds," he said.

I glanced at him sharply. Was he trying to suggest Star Force should retreat? He didn't meet my gaze, but instead busied himself with the command screen. I frowned down at the debris from the ships and the reduced count of mines. They'd shot down a fair number. Still, there were about seven thousand of them active out there. We'd lost about a thousand, but they'd done their work.

I slapped my hand on the command table. Fortunately, I'd removed my gauntlets, and the screen didn't rupture. A few staffers flicked their eyes to me, then back to their work.

"Maybe we should call on the Worms," I said. "They might come to support us."

"You think these Nano ships are that big of a threat?" Miklos asked.

"Not really, but I like to operate from a position of strength. Right now, I believe we have the best ground forces in the system. But we can't use them if we don't control space. The Crustaceans are a new unknown in the equation. A newly hostile neighbor. They've obviously destroyed our scout ship on their side of the ring and just made their first aggressive move into this system. I need allies, not new enemies!"

Everyone else in the control room stayed quiet. I supposed I had a rep now for temper tantrums. No one wanted to get in my way. Miklos looked like he would have exited the room himself if he could have come up with a good excuse.

"How did the test flight go on the new gun ship?" he asked.

"A blatant attempt to change the topic," I said, then sighed. "Really, the tests went well. They are nowhere near as sleek and maneuverable as these destroyers, but we can produce them twenty times faster—maybe thirty. Pitted against Macro cruisers and these Nano ships…I don't know. If we have enough of them, we'll do fine. Let's talk about our new battle formations and tactics."

Miklos looked relieved. "Yes, let's do that."

After several hours, we'd hammered out a plan. Once we had more gunships than destroyers, we'd implement it. The gunships would lead the fight on the front line. They took more damage, but had a lot less range. They would need to get in close to be effective with their railguns. The Nano destroyers would tag behind, but not too far behind. They would use their lasers to cover the gunships, shooting down incoming missile barrages. Once the formation was in close enough, the railguns and the lasers would be used to target and take out individual targets in coordination.

Really, it came down to numbers. If the Macro cruisers outnumbered our smaller ships we were doomed. If we outnumbered them two to one, we'd win. In-between those two numbers, it was iffy. It was hard to predict how the battle might go.

I had a contingency plan, however, in case the battle did play out with us on the losing side. The front line of gunships would take their beating like little bulldogs, but would eventually be taken out by the larger cruisers. If they lasted long enough to intermix with their formation however, they would have done their work. Aboard every destroyer would be a platoon of troops. These men would deploy like tiny independent attackers and swarm the cruisers. We'd done well with those tactics in the past, and I prayed the Macros hadn't yet come up with an effective defense against marine boarding assaults.

I recalled that in ancient times, sea battles had really been land battles between ships linked by boarding planks. The slow, wooden galleys of the Greeks, Romans and Carthaginians had missile weapons, but the real fight began when they closed with one another. They rammed, boarded, and set fire to one another. They fought close battles on blood-slicked decks that often involved hundreds of ships and thousands of marines. I reflected that battle tactics had come full-circle over time, once again making marines a significant factor in ship-to-ship combat.

After hammering out plans for rosters of ships I hadn't even built yet, I retired when my eyes no longer focused properly. By that time, I had four new gunships, and more were on the way. But I knew I needed forty—or better yet four hundred of them. I wouldn't feel comfortable until I had a serious fleet.

* * *

I was awakened by an alarm klaxon. Something big was up. I bounced out of my bunk and cracked my head on the ceiling. Wincing and rubbing, I reached for my battle armor and slapped on the lights. I connected to the general command channel and almost broke my headset pulling it onto my head.

"What's going on?" I demanded. My voice was drown out by the babble of others. There seemed to be some kind of action going on.

There was regret on my face as I passed by the shower compartment. There simply wasn't time. I pulled on my armor as quickly as I could and staggered out into the hall. An Ensign rushed past on his way to the command center. I followed him stiffly.

Everyone aboard was in the command center, and they were so focused on the display they didn't even notice me at first. I didn't care. I stumped up to the board and worked on adjusting my battle suit. The Nanos did most of the work in that department. It was nice, having a million or so tiny robots to dress you. All a marine had to do these days was get himself stuffed into the suit, then the smart metal took over. It closed the gaps, sealed the openings and gently cinched up every inch of the frame until it fit like a thousand-pound glove.

I didn't have to ask anyone what was happening, as the facts were plain to see on the big board. I'd expected to see a mass of Macro cruisers, fresh from their berths under domes on every world, rising up to attack us. But instead, I saw a depiction of Hel and the distant, dark ring.

When I'd gone to sleep aboard *Actium*, there'd been over seven thousand mines out there. They were tiny yellow contacts, one pixel each, forming a gentle cloud that obscured the entire region of space. Much had changed, apparently. Now, fully two thirds of that cloud had vanished. In the middle of it was another cloud of larger objects. Nano ships—hundreds of them.

"It's a full attack, Colonel," Miklos said, spotting me for the first time.

"Have they broken through yet?" I demanded. A half dozen people recognized me and threw me significant glances. I ignored them all, and they lowered their voices. They still conferred with others on station around the planet we all orbited.

"This vid is four hours old. The conflict is still on-going."

"Is this as close as we can get? Zoom in."

"We've lost that capacity, sir."

I looked at him. He looked back significantly. I could tell he thought we'd lost control of the ring.

"This is exactly why I wanted to build a battle station out there. Something tougher than a mine field. They came through with what—three hundred odd ships? With two guns each, that's six hundred guns. They knew the field was there after their little scouting mission, so they came in nice and slow. Our mines are ineffective if the enemy isn't charging into them blindly."

"Yes, sir," Miklos said.

"So, we have to assume the field is lost, and they've managed to punch a hole right through it."

"That is a logical assumption, Colonel."

"Where are they headed?"

"We won't know until the battle plays out."

It was a hard thing, watching a battle that had already happened. I kept wanting to press some kind of fast-forward button and get to the conclusion. The Nano ships were taking no chances. They edged forward, almost drifting. Arranged in a layered ovoid mass, they fired their hundreds of guns relentlessly as they detected the tiny mines and destroyed them one at a time. Beams stabbed out in every direction from the central mass of ships as they advanced, destroying our mines almost without a loss.

"Total numbers?" I asked about an hour later when they'd passed the minefield successfully.

"Twenty-one ships hit, eighteen destroyed. Mines left in the region—nine hundred sixty-one, sir."

I studied the numbers. "You included their losses from the earlier scouting trip. That means we only knocked out what—two? Two of this entire new armada?"

"Yes sir. We did score a few other hits, mostly from mines that detonated prematurely. But the Nano ships were only damaged and are still functional in most of those cases."

"Great," I said. "That's just great. They made it through almost intact. Any response to our attempts to open channels with them?"

"No response, sir."

"Projections of their course?"

Miklos hesitated. "We can't be certain yet, Colonel."

"What do you mean? What's your best guess?"

"I—I don't understand the data, sir."

"Just tell me if they are coming to the Centaur homeworld to wipe us out. I don't care if you're wrong. Give me what you have."

"Yes, sir. See the projected arcs on the screen?"

An orange spray of pixels appeared. It was an arc which cut a broad swathe across the system. It widened steadily as it moved farther from the ring. It was a projection of where the enemy fleet might be headed. Every minute that passed, their most likely goals narrowed and the arc narrowed with it, graphically depicting targets. The arc was huge, encompassing several planets. I was reminded of weathermen, plotting the likely path of an incoming hurricane. The analogy was a pretty close one to us. The storm of ships that had just entered our system was capable of destroying anything that got into its path.

I frowned at the data. The Centaur homeworld was not on the list. Neither were most of the habitable planets. Only the hottest water-world, the innermost tropical planet, was inside the fringe of the arc.

"I don't understand. They are heading inward, toward the star, but at an angle. What are they aiming for?"

"They could be planning to adjust their course as they advance. Possibly, they wish to avoid any more minefields we've placed in the most likely orbital paths to the inner planets."

I nodded slowly, glaring at the screen. As I watched, the arc narrowed a tiny fraction. "What do you think they're doing, Captain?"

"Let's expand the view, and look farther out," Miklos said.

As I watched, he worked the screen. Again, his efforts seemed clumsy compared to Major Sarin—I mentally corrected myself *Rear Admiral* Sarin.

When Miklos finished with his adjustments, much more of the system map was included. His theory was unmistakable at that point. The center of the projected arc collided with a single planet, and it did so with precision. The very center line of the arc cut right through the sole gas giant in the Eden system.

"The Blues?" I said. "They are targeting the gas giant?"

Miklos locked gazes with me. He nodded. "That is my conclusion, sir," he said. "But this could change. It might be a ruse of some kind."

I stared at the data. Every minute, it updated and drew the lines more tightly. The projections were unmistakable.

"I don't think so," I said. "These bastard lobsters haven't impressed me so far as being subtle people. Somehow, they realized they outnumbered everyone in this system, and they decided to make their play now while they have more firepower than we do. Maybe they think this is necessary—maybe they think they are making a preemptive strike."

"But in that case, why head to the gas giant? We are unaware of any ships there, other than the few mining scoops we have at the planet's rings."

I thought about it. "Maybe they think we need that material. We did, until recently. Now that we have Macro workers sucking up minerals on the Centaur homeworld, the dust loads coming from those rings is negligible. But that wasn't the case just a week ago. Maybe their intel is old."

"Yes," said Miklos, leaning on the board and staring. "That would make some sense. Perhaps they don't know our ship strength, so their first move is to cut off our supplies, rather than directly confront our fleets."

I nodded, agreeing with the analysis more every second. "Right," I said. "This side-attack has several advantages for them. They think they are cutting off our raw materials. If we fly out to defend the mining ships, then they can meet our fleet out in open space, away from any defensive fortresses we have around the planet."

"Even if we don't come out, their plan hurts us and gives them time to gather intel concerning our fleet strength."

We both stared and someone put a cup of coffee into my hand. I drank it, and wished it was something stronger. The situation was grim. There were now three fleets in this system, and I suspected ours was the weakest—by a large margin.

-27-

As the hours passed, it became increasingly clear the enemy was indeed targeting the gas giant. I didn't make any moves against them, as I didn't want them to change their minds. I didn't even order my mining ships to run. They were all automated, so no one was in danger of being killed. Given the situation, I wanted the Crustaceans to think they were catching us by surprise.

When the Nano ships reached the gas giant, the first thing they did was swarm my three pathetic miners as they scooped up ice and dust from the rings. They obliterated them in seconds. If we'd had any questions about their armament, or their willingness to use it on our ships, we had our answers now.

"Sir," Miklos said, interrupting me as I mused over the Nano ships and their silent, mysterious mission.

"What is it, Captain?"

"We have another situation. Can I display it?"

"Of course."

I watched in growing alarm as he showed me the bottom of the Centaur satellite. A strange, thin tube was extruding from it. I opened my mouth to ask him what the hell that was—when I realized I already knew the answer.

"They must have enough nanites now. I didn't realize they'd been stockpiling."

"Yes, the Eden-11 satellite is ready to be evacuated. The herds have alerted us, and begun the operation at the same time."

"Not waiting around for our approval, huh?" I asked. "Well I can't say that I blame them. They've been cooped up in that floating tin can for years. I know how they think, and they've got to be wild to get out onto their open grasslands again. How long until the shaft touches the planet's surface?"

"Not long, sir. The nanites are building very fast. The shaft should be complete within a single day."

I nodded. I expected thousands of Centaurs to begin pouring out of the bottom of that tube as soon as it touched down. They were nothing if not personally brave. Except for their fear of enclosed spaces—which appeared to be a deep-seated instinct from their past—they'd never backed down in the face of anything.

"There is another development, sir," Miklos said.

"A good one, I hope?"

"Not at all, I'm afraid."

I gestured impatiently, and he tapped at the screen. Soon I saw what he was talking about. A Macro cruiser now hung in orbit over Eden-8. As I watched, a second moved to join it. I began breathing harder. Suddenly, sweat tickled under my armpits. This was it, the moment we'd been waiting for, but hoped would never come.

"They are launching their fleets," I said. "Any sign they are moving on the Centaur habitats?"

"Not yet."

Over the next hour, more and more cruisers nosed up out of the cloud cover and slid into orbit above all five worlds. The Macros were finally showing their hand. Before they were done, thirteen brand new vessels floated in various orbits. Was that everything they had? Probably, I figured. The Macros weren't famous for their subtlety. But we couldn't be sure. Why had they chosen this moment to put their strength on display? Probably to scare us, or to scare the Nanos. Either that, or the sight of escaping Centaurs on Eden-11 had so upset them they'd decided to launch and prevent it.

In the end, the 'why now' question was irrelevant. They'd put their cards on the table. It was my turn to do the same.

"Captain, order all our pilots to man the gunships. I want them to take landing pods from the destroyers. Every pilot must begin running missions. They'll carry down Centaur civilians to the surface on a continuous basis from now on."

"Why now, sir?" he asked. "We've worked so long to keep our numbers secret. They will count our ships."

"I'm sure they will. I'm hoping the count will worry them and make them change their minds about attacking today. I need more time. Also, we'll have insured that a few Centaurs survive in case things go badly. Lastly, we'll give our pilots some much needed flight time in their new ships."

Sighing heavily, Miklos did as I asked without further complaint. I could tell he didn't entirely approve, but I didn't care.

Our biggest fear early on was that the Macros would gather into a single force and attack the Centaur satellites, destroying them and billions of biotic allies. But they didn't—at least not right away. As usual, they didn't mind ignoring a helpless target. They knew they could always come back and destroy it later. They were very single minded machines, and I was sure they had Nano ships and human ships on those one-track electronic brains of theirs, not helpless Centaurs.

A few days dragged by. The Centaurs made it down to the surface with their shaft of smart metal and began pouring out onto their empty grasslands. It was a true exodus. Combined with my ships, which flew sortie after sortie, the big habitat emptied quickly. Marvin had assured me the Microbes that had been used to sterilize the planet of Centaurs were now harmless, having long since mutated into a benign form of pond scum.

Each of the three fleets in the star system was now left hanging in tight orbits over seven different worlds. It was like some kind of quiet, three-way cold war. We stared at one other, taking careful counts and measurements with countless pinging probes. It was nerve-racking. In a way, I was glad for the stand-off. The new design of my ships was untested in combat, but I thought they would hold their own when the time came. Still, we were clearly in third place in this contest, and we needed the time to catch up. I figured I was building my little gunships much faster than the Macros were building their cruisers, and as far as we could tell the Nano ships were frozen in number. Therefore, we grew in relative strength every day.

Some of my officers dared to hope the aliens would never attack, but I wasn't fooled. Lulls in wars were not unknown. After Germany and Russia took apart Poland in WWII, the Allies had declared war on them. But Germany didn't move on France for seven long months.

194

Only a few shots were fired over the border in skirmishes. The newspapers took to calling it "the phony war". History soon taught them their error. I knew the Macros were coming eventually, and when they did move, it would be with terrifying certainty of purpose.

The Nano ships weren't filling me with any kind of deep inner confidence, either. The Crustaceans—if they were still operating those ships—weren't talking. We sent them every form of communication we could think of, with Marvin as our chief translator. They were so quiet, so unresponsive, I began to think Marvin might be sabotaging the communications. I had Miklos go over his transmissions carefully, and he declared them to be genuine.

"I simply don't understand it," I said on the eleventh day of the three-way stand-off. "Why aren't the Nano ships talking to us? They were interested in a dialog before. Now, their pilots remind me of clams, rather than lobsters."

"Very funny, Colonel," Miklos said, without the slightest hint of amusement in his voice. "They remind me of Russians. They run from a force they fear, but behave as predators when they sense weakness."

"Maybe so," I said. "But I want to try something new."

Miklos immediately looked alarmed. "I don't think it is a good idea to provoke them, Colonel."

"Who said anything about provoking them?"

"I only thought…"

I began to pace in my armor. Each boot rang on *Actium's* metal deck. "We've got a lot of gunships now. About thirty of them. Combined with the destroyers and our marine assault teams, we will soon be a match for either enemy fleet."

"But not both. I don't think we need to start a conflict—"

"I didn't say I was going to slap them in the face with a glove, Captain," I snapped. "Really, the Nanos are the ones that are acting illogically. They should have attacked when they first entered the system. They had the advantage then, with enough firepower to take us all out. Every day, we grow stronger while their strength stays the same."

Miklos looked like he wanted to caution me further, but he kept quiet. His eyes were wide, betraying his nervousness. Why did everyone think I was about to start a fresh fight? I rarely did that. But I did tend to finish them.

"Open a channel to the Nano ships," I ordered.

Miklos looked comically surprised now. "We don't have Marvin here. He's down on the planet, inside the dome."

"Yes, I know," I said. "He's probably playing with his mud puddles down there. But we don't need him this time. I'm going to attempt to contact them as Nano ships—not in the Crustacean language."

"I see," Miklos said. Resignedly, he opened the channel. He moved with the air of a condemned man, and I was faintly insulted. I ignored his lack of confidence and addressed the ship in a manner I hadn't done in a long time.

Back when I'd first worked with the Nano ships, before they'd run off on us and abandoned Earth, I'd learned a nice trick. We generally didn't use it now, with our newly built Nano ships. But *Alamo* had allowed me to make contact directly, using nanites in my body to transmit radio signals. I used this system now, having our ship's system relay the signal I was sending via nanites to the distant enemy. Essentially, I talked to the Nano ships via thoughts spoken as words in my mind.

"You aren't going to hear anything, Captain," I said. "But just leave the channel open. I'm transmitting with my mind and my nanites."

Now, Miklos was certain I was mad. He stared at me with eyes that almost popped from his skull. I ignored him.

Alamo. This is Colonel Kyle Riggs. Please respond.

We waited a long time. It was several light-minutes to the gas giant and back, but that time came and went without any response. I frowned at the communication system and tapped at a screen full of logs.

"You did send something, Colonel," Miklos said, impressed. "Are you telling me that these ships are telepathic?"

"No. But they use radio packets my internal nanites know how to transmit. Think about it: your speech starts out as thoughts in your head, right? Your mouth merely translates those impulses into a form that can be sent to others. I'm doing the same thing—but I'm using the nanites and a radio signal, instead of my mouth. I'm hoping that *Alamo* is still listening to that channel, like a security backdoor left open."

"But why not simply speak English to them?" Miklos asked.

196

"Because they've been ignoring all such transmissions. By using the nanite translation, I'm using their own language. I'm hoping they will respond to that."

We tried several more attempts, and I grew frustrated. I tried to think of what I'd done in the past to get a response out of *Alamo* when the ship didn't feel like talking.

Alamo, I thought. *You've made a serious error.*

Several minutes past before a message came back. The communications channel had a brainbox attached to it, and it didn't require Marvin to translate.

"No error has been detected," the translator said.

I grinned at Miklos. He looked surprised and uncomfortable. I got the feeling he'd wanted me to fail in this endeavor. I looked away from him and back to the screen. I tapped at it and arranged a transcription to print my half of the conversation. As I thought carefully about what to transmit, he watched apprehensively.

You've attacked allied ships, I sent to the Nano ships. *That was an error.*

"No allied ships were attacked."

You destroyed one of my ships with a pilot from Earth. You killed my pilot. Attacking one's allies is an error.

"Definitional threshold failure: We do not recognize your status as allies."

You came to our system. You helped us drive out the Macros. We account you as allies in return for this aid. What is your current mission? We will help you in return.

The next response took longer than usual to come back. I knew *Alamo's* brainbox was running hot.

"Your offer of assistance can't be accepted at this level."

Ask your command personnel.

"This ship currently has no command personnel."

What about the Crustaceans? Don't you have them aboard?

"Test subjects are aboard, but no command personnel."

Suddenly, I found myself catching on. The Nano ships had gone rogue again. They'd left the lobsters high and dry, just the way they'd abandoned Earth long ago. I muted the link for a moment so I could talk to Miklos. We spoke in hushed voices, even though it wasn't necessary.

"What's going on, Colonel? I don't understand their attitude."

197

I stared at him, thinking hard. "The Nano ships have gone AWOL. They did it to Earth years back, after the initial invasion by the Macros was thwarted and a deal hammered out. Maybe the Crustaceans made a deal with the Macros we don't know about. Or maybe, there wasn't any threat in the system for a while, so the Nano ships moved on to another target."

"But why Eden-12?"

I smiled. "That part seems clear to me. They are protecting the Blues. They've already marked us down as safe, and given up on the Centaurs. They are protecting the Blues."

"From us?" Miklos asked.

"What do you mean?"

"They blew up our mining ships."

"Ah, yes. But maybe they'd didn't know who owned them. Or maybe they are in defensive mode and will attack anyone who molests that planet."

"That would explain why they haven't pressed their numerical advantage. They are in a defensive posture."

I thought it over. "They can't really move on the Macros or us, as the other side might hit the exposed planet. Either that, or they aren't sure who their real enemy is."

"There's another odd thing about this discussion with the Nanos," Miklos said. "They said our offer of assistance can't be accepted at this level. So the question is: who or what is at a higher level?"

I nodded and held up my hand for quiet. I opened the channel again. *Alamo, we need to make a request at a higher level. How do we do that?*

"The protocol is complex," the ship said. "Visitors must show humility, and demonstrate their harmless natures. This requires a given visitor to come alone."

I squinted at the screen, rereading the transcripts. *Visitors?* Who had said anything about visiting anyone?

Miklos was waving for my attention. I muted the translation system and looked at him.

"The Blues, sir," he said. "They must be talking about visiting the Blues."

I rubbed my face, wondering if he could be right. I took an immediate dislike to the idea. Visiting a bizarre race of cloud-people

198

on a gas giant? Alone? What kind of sorry bastard would do something so crazy?

I knew the answer to my own question, of course, and I didn't like it.

-28-

I spent a long night in the command center on *Actium*, which ended with me slumped over the screens. When I finally headed to my bunk, it seemed like my head had only just hit the foam when a chime went off in my darkened chamber.

"What is it now? Are they hitting us?"

"No, sir—but we have a new contact."

I groaned and climbed out of my bunk. I was talking to a voice in the ceiling—a voice with an Eastern European accent.

"You sound a little like Dracula. Has anyone ever told you that, Miklos?"

"No, sir."

"Well, let's just say your voice is not the best to wake up to. What is this new contact?"

"An Earth ship, sir. It's arrived at the Helios ring. They want to talk to you."

I groaned aloud. Crow had finally sent someone out to check up on me. I'd been expecting this, but I'd hoped it would all go away somehow. Now, they were finally here. I hoped it wasn't Commodore Decker again. I couldn't stand the man.

"I'll be on the command deck in eight minutes."

I was ten minutes late, but I wasn't counting. In that short amount of time, I'd taken a shower and munched on some artificial bacon. It was discolored and tasted like someone had applied a layer salt and grease to corn husks. No one dared question the origins of this kind of food. We didn't want to know how they made bacon out here. We all knew that finding out what it really was wouldn't make it taste any better.

My first shock of the day was the newly arrived ship itself. The image swam onto the central screen. It was big—bigger than one of our destroyers, but smaller than a Macro cruiser. I stared at it, admiring the sleek lines. The vessel's shape was uniquely contoured and reminded me vaguely of a spoon. It had a rounded prow, with armament in the form of a six-gun battery arranged around that curved nose. Three engines were arranged in a tripod formation at the stern.

"What the hell is that?" I asked.

"We're calling it a light cruiser, sir," Miklos answered. "It's a new Star Force hull—the ship is definitely a friendly. It has a displacement of about four thousand tons, nearly half that of a Macro cruiser."

I frowned at it. The ship didn't *look* terribly friendly. The fact the design was unknown to me filled me with unease. What was going on back home? The trouble with these long campaigns was I inevitably became disconnected with events on Earth.

"It looks fast," I said reaching out to zoom in on the three engines with my fingers. "Crow's getting better at design."

"You think he did this by himself?"

"No, he definitely had help from other military organizations," I said. I straightened and heaved a sigh. "He obviously sent this ship to impress me. Unfortunately, he's succeeded. Patch me through to the commander. Let's do this."

When I stepped up to the communications screen, I received another shock. It wasn't Commodore Decker's gnarled face that looked back at me. It was Jasmine Sarin's.

"Well, *hello* Major!" I said. "It's good to see you again. What brings you so far from Earth?"

Jasmine cleared her throat. To me, she looked slightly nervous, but determined.

"Colonel Riggs," she began.

My heart sank as I heard her tone of voice. I could tell she was going to give me a lecture.

"I've come from Star Force to relay new instructions. You are to make an immediate withdrawal from the Eden system. Your ships are required for the defense of Earth."

I frowned up at her. "Are we under some kind of attack at home?"

"No Colonel, not at this time."

"Then please come to my command ship. We need to talk this over. In the meantime, you should scan the system. It is full of alien ships, and they *aren't* friendly."

"We have already done so, Colonel. The orders stand."

My frown deepened. She was calling me 'Colonel' not 'sir', and she was trying to pass an order on to me from Crow—one which I didn't want to hear. She wasn't even willing to talk about it in private. My neck felt hot, and I knew a shouting session was near. Around me, my command staff shuffled, tapped at screens, and generally pretended not to be hanging on every word.

"Major—" I began.

"I'm sorry Colonel, but that is no longer my rank."

I stared at her in surprise.

"I'm a Rear Admiral now—I've gone Fleet."

My jaw jutted in annoyance. I knew that was her new rank, of course. Forgetting about it was my way of reminding her who she used to be—my exec. Now I felt betrayed, but I tried not to let it show in my eyes. I think I failed, as Sarin looked even more stressed than before.

"Okay," I said finally. "Let's talk plainly. If you want to complete your mission, you have to come to my ship and talk to me in person. Is that clear?"

Sarin thought this over. No one was sure how to proceed. Crow had always maintained the fiction that I was under his command. I disagreed, seeing my role as that of an equal partner, rather than an underling. Star Force was far from clearly defined at the top. In fact, authority between Crow and I had been a loose arrangement from the start. We'd done a fair job of managing the organization by separating Star Force into land forces and space forces, and dividing our jurisdictions accordingly. In general, Crow ran Fleet while I ran the Marines.

But in practice, it had never worked out so neatly. What had evolved was a regional power system, based on who was where. When I was running a task force in space, I commanded it, both ground and space forces. When I wasn't near Earth, Crow asserted his authority there with glee. Crow never ventured far from Earth, so conflicts usually arose only when I was in the home system. When we were *both* at home, things often went badly. We invariably stepped on each other's toes.

This time was a special case. Crow was trying to order me around while I was out on a campaign. As I saw it, he was the one trying to alter our arrangement of power.

I think it was my jutting jaw and flat stare that convinced Jasmine. She realized she wasn't going to get me to come home just by showing up in the system in her fancy new ship and passing on Crow's edicts.

"All right," she said at last. "I'll meet you on your ship."

Several hours later, the light cruiser arrived in orbit over Eden-11. I watched it come in, admiring its sleek lines as it drew close.

I retired to *Actium's* conference room, and the rest of my command staff knew enough to keep out as I waited for Sarin. Only Marvin tried to follow me inside. He'd come back up from stirring his mud soup down on the Eden-11 and was craning his cameras in my direction, trying to see and hear everything. I was vaguely amused by all of them. They were all dying to know how this command struggle would play out. Marvin was just more obvious than most.

"Major—ah, excuse me, *Rear Admiral* Sarin," I greeted her as she stepped through a melting door.

Behind her, Marvin's cameras appeared to be riding on stalks. The wall reconstituted itself, shutting him out. I gestured to the table, and she moved to the far side. She extended her hand, and I shook it. A few months ago she would have saluted me—but now she saw herself as something of an equal. A handshake was the protocol between Crow and me. I let the matter pass without comment, taking her offered hand and smiling before I released it.

She was Fleet brass now, but I was still the Marine commander. As I saw it, she was under my command out here. I kept these thoughts to myself. There was no need to push things right away. Possibly, we could work this out amicably.

"Shall I begin briefing you?" I asked.

"By all means."

"First off, I'm sorry Crow and I have put you in this position, Jasmine," I said. "We've never really gotten our act together, you know. The chain of command should be perfectly clear to all. What I want to do today is explain the Eden system situation clearly. Then you can make up your own mind how we should proceed."

"I'm not in that position, Colonel—"

"Oh, but you are. You've been moved up to command rank. That has responsibilities. Right now, if I pitched over dead onto this table, you would be in command in this system."

Sarin looked mildly alarmed. I wondered if she was really ready for her new rank. I knew she was ambitious and competent, but she was young and she'd run every battle from behind a touchscreen. Making strategic decisions that sent people to die—possibly millions of people—wasn't the same thing as running ops.

I proceeded to lay out the situation in the system. I showed her the planet we'd liberated, vids of the Crustaceans who'd we made contact with, and the Nano ship fleet that were parked in orbit over the gas giant. She was particularly impressed by the Macro production facility I'd put to work for us, and the new gunship design. She was alarmed, however, by the alien forces that were staring us down over these lush worlds.

"It's like the war never ended," she said.

I almost laughed. "Ended? Why no, it hasn't ended. Is that what Crow's been telling everyone back home? Because if so, he's full of crap. I don't know if we'll ever have peace out here for any significant length of time—but I'm trying."

Sarin's tongue wet her lips and she leaned forward. "Colonel Riggs, that is precisely how the talk is going back home. You are depicted as being a warmonger—someone who won't take a victory and leave matters alone. Someone who wants to build an empire."

"An egomaniac, is that it? A charge from Crow, no less? I'd laugh, but I'm too bitter for humor. I'm trying to keep our species and our biotic allies one step ahead of extinction. We need to stop the next alien incursion before it begins. I'd like to do it with as many allies and planets on our side of the fence as possible."

"What fence?" she asked.

I smiled. It was the precise question I'd hoped she would ask. I dragged a file onto the desktop between us and showed her the plans I'd drawn up. My new battle station would bristle with weapons. If I could capture a few more Macro factories, I could make it happen. She watched carefully, and I could tell I'd impressed her.

"I see the strength of the plan," she said. "Using the rings as a natural bottleneck, we could outgun any enemy that came through by placing a massive defensive fortress there."

"Exactly."

"I understand your plan, and I approve. But Fleet believes you should build your battle station closer to Earth—preferably in the home system."

"It might end up like that," I admitted. "But I want to try to put it out here instead, giving us six lovely new habitable worlds. Just think of that, six new Earths. On top of that, we'd save two allied species, the Worms and the Centaurs. We need help, I don't want to do this alone."

"What about the other races?"

"Right now, they are either hostile or uncooperative. Take the Blues, for example. I think they have something to do with the Nano ships that have abandoned the Crustaceans and now orbit the gas giant, Eden-12. They are barely willing to communicate with us. But I have hopes for cooperation with them in the future. We have the same strategic difficulties to face in the long run."

"You mean the Macros."

"Yes."

Jasmine rubbed at her neck, deep in thought. Her hair had slipped from the tight bun she'd worn upon arrival. She still kept her hair long, and loose strands hung around her face as she studied the data intently. To me, she looked as pretty as ever.

"What did you name the ship?" I asked her.

"What?"

"Your shiny new ship. The one Crow bought for you to go along with your new rank."

She sat back and glared at me. "It is named *Goa*—after a lovely region of India. But Crow didn't buy me off. I've earned this promotion."

"I didn't mean it that way."

Sarin didn't answer, because we both knew I was lying. I absolutely thought she'd been bought off. Crow was a crafty old devil. He'd found out what my most loyal supporting officer wanted, and given it to her to place her under his spell. He'd figured out she wanted rank, so he'd provided an impressive one. Then he'd built her a nice ship, and sent her out here to rub her change of loyalties in my face. He wanted to force her to prove her new loyalty to him. It was hard not to be annoyed with both of them.

I wondered if Crow knew that last time Jasmine and I had been alone together in a command conference room, we'd kissed. If he ever

205

did learn about that, I was sure it would make this awkward moment he'd created for the two of us even sweeter for him.

"I'm not sure what I should do," Jasmine admitted at last. "I have my orders—but you make a compelling argument. You always do."

I smiled slowly. "Welcome to one of the secret hardships of command. Sometimes, the path is not clear—or there are several reasonable options. It's your job to choose one and stick with it. You have to display conviction. The troops have to believe you are sure of yourself, even if you're not."

She looked at me. "That's the thing about you, Kyle," she said softly. "Somehow, you are always self-assured. You always proceed without the slightest doubt."

"That's a combination of a character flaw and an elaborate fiction," I said. "It's true, I choose a path and follow it tenaciously, but I'm not always sure it's the *right* one."

Her eyes narrowed and she squinted at me. "You fake it?"

"Sometimes," I said, shrugging.

She snorted softly and smiled. It was the first honest smile I'd seen on her face for months. I had a thought then—a nice thought. I considered reaching out my hand and clasping hers. I'm an impulsive guy, but I made no moves. I just returned her smile with one of my own. We both sat quietly for a few seconds, enjoying the moment.

At that point, the ship's inner wall melted. We both looked up in surprise. My surprise changed into shock as I saw who stood there in the opening. The nanites in the smart metal didn't see too happy, either. The intruder moved faster than they did, not allowing them time to get out of the way. They moved in dribbles and slagged away from an outstretched, thin-fingered hand that punched its way through them.

The figure was female, and she advanced into the room so quickly the nanites didn't have time to dissolve completely. They stretched over her like a bubble—which quickly popped and sent bits of semi-liquid metal everywhere. It looked like a shower of mercury. The beads of nanites quickly found their brothers on the deck of the ship and merged together, smoothing out.

The wall closed behind her again, and she loomed between us at the head of the conference table. She placed her palms flat on the table and suspiciously eyed each of us in turn.

"I couldn't take anymore whispering and giggling," she said. "I could hear you right through these thin nanite walls, you know."

"Sandra!" I said, standing up. "I had no idea you'd come on this trip!"

I was honestly glad to see her, even if she was in one of her jealousy-fueled moods. She looked at me with pursed lips and narrowed eyes.

"You didn't think I'd let Jasmine come out here to see you alone, did you?"

"Of course not," I said, laughing nervously.

Jasmine didn't make eye-contact with either of us. I sensed these two had endured a tense voyage on the way out from Earth.

I stepped to Sandra and attempted a hug. It was like hugging a manikin at first. She stiffened and I felt nothing but her bones and hard muscles. After a second however, she softened a little.

Internally, I complimented myself. I was very glad I hadn't grabbed Jasmine's hand.

-29-

The conference shifted into a three-way affair after Sandra joined us. She sat with her eyes flashing back and forth. She didn't talk much, but she didn't have to. As always, it was easy to tell what she was thinking.

"Well, Rear Admiral," I said, "have you made up your mind yet?"

"No," Jasmine admitted.

"What do you plan to do then?"

"I'm going to give you some time," she said. "I'm going to observe and help if needed. I'm going to investigate the situation for a few days."

I smiled. I couldn't help but think of how unhappy this decision would make Crow when he heard about it. He'd have to wonder if his gambit had failed utterly. Instead of embarrassing me into returning to Earth under the thumb of Jasmine in her new ship, he would have to worry I'd turned her back into one of my supporters and stolen a light cruiser as well as a key officer. It would be torture for him.

"Wonderful!" I said. "That's all I ask. An investigation—a hearing, so to speak."

Jasmine inclined her head slightly. Only Sandra looked unhappy. "We're all going to sit out here?" she asked. "Waiting for what?"

I glanced over at Sandra. She really didn't belong in this high-level discussion. I was going to have to have a talk with her about that. I didn't expect the talk would go smoothly.

"We're not sitting around. We're building a new fleet—faster than we've ever done in the past. Your light cruiser will provide a welcome shift in firepower. How many are aboard her?"

"Seventy," Jasmine said. "Thirty crewmen and a full platoon of forty marines."

"Excellent!" I said, honestly excited. "We started out here with less than three hundred marines, and we can really use the reinforcements."

Jasmine looked uncomfortable. We both knew that she hadn't been sent out here to reinforce me. But sometimes if you took things for granted, they went your way.

"I will return to Goa and brief my officers," Jasmine said, standing up. I did the same.

No one saluted, but I didn't make a fuss about it. She had moved in my direction, and I really did need her help.

The second she left, Sandra leaned close and hissed a lot of words at me: "You should have let me kill her when I had the chance back on Andros. No one would have doubted she was a traitor."

"But she wasn't the traitor, Sandra," I said calmly. "Lieutenant Colonel Barrera was the one behind the assassination attempts."

"Not a traitor? Look how she's sucked up to Crow. She's playing you both. You are blinded by her soft voice and pretty face. She's probably been playing footsie with Crow as well. How can men be such fools?"

I thought about what Sandra was saying. Could it be true? After Barrera had turned on me, I now took such allegations more seriously. My officers were only human, after all. They had ambitions and plans of their own. Still, I'd been through a lot with Jasmine Sarin and I felt I knew her enough to trust her. She could be misled, but she wasn't a devious schemer like Crow. I reminded myself that Sandra had an agenda of her own when it came to Jasmine.

"I think she'd misguided, but not a traitor."

"She's gone Fleet!"

"Last I checked, that wasn't against the Star Force handbook."

"There is no handbook."

"I'm working on that."

Sandra crossed her arms and pouted. She'd failed to get me to declare Jasmine a threat, so she was far from happy.

"You need to get your jealousy under control, Sandra," I told her. "Try to think professionally. We're all in this together. The machines are the real enemy."

Sandra softened and nodded. "You're right about that. But don't think everyone is in complete agreement with you. Things are going strangely back home, Kyle. That is another reason I insisted on coming out here."

"Tell me about it."

"Crow is gathering power. He's like some kind of spider. He's got all the factories under his control now."

I wasn't surprised by that, and I couldn't really object. When I'd left Andros island, our fortifications had been devastated.

"Has he rebuilt the island defenses?"

"He did that first, but he only repaired one of the central forts. The other two are still in ruins."

I frowned. "What's he been doing with all his output?"

"What do you think? He's been building ships. Not just this light cruiser, either. He's got two more ships just like it. And two wings of new destroyers."

I nodded. Crow had always believed the fleet was more important than our ground forces. He'd finally gotten his way by gaining full control over our Nano factory output.

"None of that sounds sinister to me," I told Sandra. "I might have done the same."

"That's not the creepy part. There are visitors, coming to Fort Pierre all the time now. General Kerr and others. People from Europe and Asia. Military people and spooks. They come to talk to Crow, to have private conferences with him."

I thought about that for a second. I didn't like the sound of it. "All right, I should have suspected that would happen. We've been gone for months, and I knew he'd been working with outside militaries. Maybe he just wants to get design input from the most talented people he can find. After all, we were almost wiped out the last time the Macros came to Earth. More cooperation—"

"Don't you get it, Kyle?" she demanded. "He's not just building up, he's setting up some kind of coup."

I snorted and almost laughed. "A coup? Against whom? I'm not a king, you know. I'm a Colonel who runs the marines."

"You were the sole commander who fought the Macros to a standstill last time they came. It won't be the same when you return."

"What do you want me to do about that?" I asked. "Are you in Jasmine's camp? Do you want me to go back now and straighten Crow out?"

She heaved a sigh and looked uncertain. "I don't think so," she said. "You aren't strong enough now."

"Strong enough for what?"

She looked at me intently. "When you go back to Earth, Kyle, you should have a massive fleet behind you. Enough ships to take Earth, if necessary."

I did laugh this time. "I don't want to do that! I've never even considered such a thing."

"Then you should bring the Macros home on your tail, like you did last time. Then they will need you. They will let you fight for them, and save them again."

I shook my head, bemused. I looked into her face, and as far as I could tell, she was serious. "I thought heroes were given a party."

"Not always. Sometimes they are feared, or blamed for not doing their jobs perfectly."

I thought about what she was saying. It was true that history was full of heroes who'd been turned into villains by whoever wrote the books later on. Everyone feared the man who marched home with a conquering army. Many had wanted George Washington to be declared King of the United States after the revolution. Others had tried to assassinate him. It was all a matter of perspective.

I reached out and clasped my hand over Sandra's. She flinched, but then relaxed and smiled at me. I smiled back. Inside, I was full of doubts. But it felt good to have my girlfriend smiling at my touch again. It had been a long time—too long.

"Colonel?" a voice squawked from the ceiling. I knew it wasn't a speaker that made the sound, but rather the nanite walls that vibrated to recreate the voice.

"Yes, Captain Miklos?"

"Could you come out of the conference room now? We have a situation."

Heaving a sigh, I stood up. "I'll be right there."

I headed toward the wall that led onto the command deck. I never made it. Sandra grabbed me from behind and kissed my neck.

211

"Let's do it," she whispered in my ear. "Right here on this table."

"Uh," I said, tempted. "It has to wait for a bit. Can you hold that mood for an hour?"

"Maybe," she said, still hissing in my ear. I could feel her hot breath on my skin. "But I make no promises."

We had to leave it at that. I exited the room and Sandra followed. I could tell from her attitude, she was back in bodyguard-mode. She eyed everyone with quiet suspicion.

"What's the matter?" I asked, but no one bothered to answer me. They just gestured toward the big screen.

The image displayed on the pool-table sized command screen was of the inner planets. Eden-1 to Eden-11 circled the yellow star. At the very outer edge of the map, the gas giant Eden-12 swung around. I looked at the gas giant first. The swarm of Nano ships still hung there in orbit, depicted with a cautionary yellow. The system did that when it wasn't sure if a contact was friend or foe.

My eyes drifted toward the inner worlds. My own cluster of destroyers sat in a ring around the Centaur habitat satellite. We were displaying most of our gunships. We had built twenty-one now and new ones were produced several times a day.

Last, my eyes moved sunward toward the Macro-controlled worlds. They weren't all lined up, of course. Some drifted far away, circling around the far side of the star. Three of them were in our general vicinity, Eden-9 being the closest of the pack.

As I watched, new arcs flickered into life on the screen. The Macro ships were on the move. Vessels left orbit from each of the most distant systems. They were moving to Eden-9, to the world orbiting closest to Eden-11, the single planet under our control.

"The Macros are on the move?"

"Yes sir."

"How many contacts do we have there? I see two ships."

"Those are groups of ships," Miklos said. He zoomed in, and I saw that both the arcs coming from the far side were made up of four cruisers in a familiar, diamond-shaped formation.

Alarmed, I reached out and made stretching motions with my fingers. I expanded the section of the nearest world, Eden-9. There had been two ships there yesterday. Now, there were seven. Additionally, they were moving up more ships, sending them forward from all five of their garrisoned planets.

I straightened my spine. "Summarize, Miklos."

"They are leaving one ship at each planet to guard it, but sending everything else to Eden-9."

"How many ships total?"

"They will have twenty-nine ships at our doorstep within twenty-four hours, sir. Plus their reserve garrisons and whatever else they produce in the meantime."

I stared until my eyes stung. They were out producing us after all, and they knew it. If they struck immediately, I had about as many little gunships as they had cruisers. But these ships were not equal in power. Their bigger vessels could take much more punishment and were armed with missiles. I had a sinking feeling.

"Permission to speak freely, sir?" Miklos asked.

"Talk to me."

"All they have to do is fly over here and smash into us."

"A typical Macro strategy," I agreed. "But we have no choice but to defend Eden-11. If we run, they will kill the Centaurs, retake the factories and our production will drop to zero."

"But even if they lose their entire fleet, they can build another. We have limited manpower and only one big factory."

"Don't forget the two Nano factories."

Miklos shrugged. "They are out producing us ten to one in mass, even if our designs are more efficient. They will overrun us eventually."

I didn't argue further, because I couldn't.

-30-

Rear Admiral Sarin requested another private meeting less than an hour later. I agreed with reservations, and ignored Sandra's stern gaze. How could I refuse to meet with her? I needed her ship. *Goa* had the firepower of three destroyers. The ship's lasers were larger and longer ranged than anything else I had. Those guns could be instrumental in shooting down incoming enemy missiles, if it came down to that. And I felt pretty strongly that it would.

To counter the threat from the Macros, I ordered all my gunships to show themselves in formation. Groups of five were ordered to fly up and down to the planet at various points, and flying back up again from somewhere else. My forces had to appear to be bigger than they really were in order to give the Macros something to worry about. They liked to fight with overwhelming numerical superiority, and they usually waited until they had the numbers. I wanted to make them think twice before attacking.

Still, I knew this delaying tactic, even if successful, wasn't going to save my forces in the coming battle. They just had too many factories, and they were building cruisers almost as fast as I built gunships. This was because they had so many more factories than we did. I readjusted my previous estimates, and now figured they had three factories per planet. Four factories must be operating on Eden-9 alone, where the transport had fled with the last facility lifted from Eden-11. Even though it took much longer to build a cruiser than it did a gunship, they had an estimated sixteen factories and I couldn't face that level of output for long.

My attention naturally turned to the Nano ships, still on station in a mass around Eden-12.

"If we could only get the Nano ships to join us, we could take them out right now," I said. "Any more successful contacts, Marvin?"

"Nothing new, Colonel Riggs," Marvin said. "They simply repeat the requirement that we speak with their commanders."

"How are we supposed to do that? Do they expect me to fly to the gas giant and land on it?"

"Possibly."

"What is the gravitational pull down there?" I asked.

"About two point five times that of Earth."

I blinked in surprise. "Why is that? I thought I'd be instantly crushed if I went to a planet with that much mass."

"This is a common misperception," Marvin admitted. "The gas giant is over three hundred times the total mass of Earth, but it is far less dense. If it was compressed to a solid ball, it would collapse a human body standing on the surface. The real problem with visitation is its *lack* of a solid surface. The semi-gaseous, semi-liquid matter that makes up Eden-12 is quite unlike the atmosphere of rocky worlds like Eden-11 or Earth. It is—cloud-like."

I thought about that. I'd understood these things, but hadn't thought of such a place in terms of visiting there. I shook my head, was I actually considering taking the Blues up on their nebulous invitation to visit their nebulous homeworld?

"What about temperature? Wind velocities?"

"Colonel Riggs?" Sandra asked, interrupting me.

I looked at her. She gave me a fake, sweet smile. "You aren't honestly thinking of trying to walk on this hydrogen-methane waterbed, are you?"

"Well, I don't know. If we could somehow talk them into joining us, it might be worth the risk. Together, our fleets could push the Macros out of this system. I'm sure of it."

Sandra compressed her lips into a tight line. "Maybe Marvin should do it. He can survive temperatures and levels of pressure a living creature never could."

Up until this moment, Marvin had been focusing most of his cameras on the various screens and different people's faces. But at this point I gained four cameras, while Sandra warranted three. I glanced at him, and saw the lenses rotate and zoom. He was trying to catch my expression from many different angles to analyze it.

"That's not a *bad* idea," I said. "It's a terrible one. Marvin is a machine, and if these biotics trusted machines, they would be dealing with the Macros. Also, no offense Marvin, but I don't think you are tremendous when it comes to diplomacy."

Marvin continued to study us quietly. I wasn't sure if he wanted to go, or didn't, but I was certain he was interested in the discussion.

"If you go down there, you might not be able to escape the gravity," Sandra continued stubbornly. "You might drift deeper than you wanted to. You don't even know where the Blues are! It's a big world. What if you land in the equivalent of their Sahara Desert?"

"These are all reasonable concerns. But possibly, I could fly out to the system and visit with them via radio at a safe distance from orbit. Their requirements are vague."

"No, I don't agree," Marvin said, suddenly joining the discussion. "I've been the translator throughout, and I believe they want to experience you as a physical being."

"*Experience* him?" Sandra asked. "You mean like *eat* him?"

"Yes, something like that. They are not structurally the same as other biotics. They are not solid individuals. When they meet one another on their world, their forms meld together. Some part of each individuals is left with the other."

"Oh, this is getting better all the time," Sandra said. "How would you translate their words if you don't go down with Kyle?"

"I could do that from higher orbit. I must be allowed aboard the ship at least. I'm afraid the ship and I would count only as machines to the Blues. We are tools to them, not as important as living things."

"Maybe I could get out of my ship," I said thoughtfully, "and visit them in my battle suit. It's like a tiny spaceship, anyway. Do you think that would be good enough for them, Marvin? Do you think they would feel they had—*experienced* me?"

Sandra's expression changed from suspicion to alarm. Everyone else on the command crew appeared incredulous. Only Marvin and I were deadly serious. In truth, the idea was growing on me. I'd always wanted to meet with the Blues. I'd wished them harm in the past, but now I simply wanted to understand them. To experience the creatures that had unleashed such robotic hell on their neighboring worlds. Had they done so intentionally or accidentally? Did they even grasp their own guilt?

I recalled the creature that referred to itself as Introspection. When I'd accused it of creating the Macros and Nanos and releasing them upon unsuspecting neighbors, it had finally drifted away. We'd never found it again on Eden-11. Perhaps it had headed out into space, or dissipated into the atmosphere. If I went to talk to its fellows on the gas giant I was sure I would learn something about them, about why and how all of this had happened. The idea that I might learn great truths was magnetic.

Marvin felt it too, I could tell. His burning curiosity to understand the mysteries of the universe around him was unmistakable. Right now, I shared his lust for knowledge. All of this fighting and dying— what was it all about? How had it all started? I wasn't sure I would get answers from the Blues, but if they didn't come from that source, we'd probably never learn the truth.

"I think I'm going to try it," I said thoughtfully.

"But Kyle," Sandra said. "The temperatures, the pressure—the winds! They move at hundreds of miles per hour. You'll be frozen and torn apart if you even take off your helmet. You won't be able to breathe or see anything."

"I've considered those contingencies," Marvin said suddenly. "I have made preparations."

Everyone stared at him. What the hell was he talking about? I was immediately suspicious. Was this all part of Marvin's scheming? I could see it now. He *wanted* us to come to this conclusion. He'd been very quiet, only inserting various facts at critical points of the conversation. Just how smart was my pet robot? It was time to find out.

"What have you got, Marvin?"

He squirmed a bit before answering. Uncoiling his lower tentacles, he inched closer to me, and I got the impression he wanted to talk in a conspiratorial whisper, but didn't know how. When he did speak, he'd turned his volume down a notch. It was pointless of course, as everyone in the room was listening closely. I didn't blame them.

Marvin directed a loop of a small, upper tentacle toward Sandra. "It has been done before. Nothing new. Only this time, there would be controlled input and superior output. I can replicate what has been done—but more than that, I can improve it."

217

I eyed him, and glanced at Sandra. She caught on at the same moment I did, I thought.

"Oh no," she said. "You can forget about that, robot. I don't want you putting Kyle into some kind of microbial bath. I went through it, and I wish I hadn't."

Marvin considered her with a half dozen artificial eyes. "Are you certain of that, Lieutenant? There have been several instances where your new abilities were crucial. I've studied the medical records, after-action reports and vids. I believe that in at least two instances Colonel Riggs would have perished if not for your new abilities."

Sandra had her hands on her hips. She was a sucker for a compliment, but she was suspicious by nature as well. She glared at Marvin. "I've saved Kyle at least three times, by my count," she said. "But that doesn't mean I want you to make him into some kind of freak like me—or something worse."

Marvin squirmed and shuffled his coils. His cameras shifted from one face to another, studying us. I tried to count all his cameras—there had to be about fifteen now. He must have added some new ones. More tentacles, too.

"Perhaps we should discuss this command decision privately, Colonel Riggs," he suggested.

I almost laughed, but one look from Sandra killed that idea. She was in maximum protectiveness-mode now. It was obvious to everyone that Marvin wanted to convince me without her objections getting in the way. She was right about his motives, they were clearly suspicious. Still, his ideas had merit.

"I agree," I said. "I'll talk to each of you about this, one at a time, in the conference room. Sandra, you are up first."

I touched a wall and it melted under my hand. I stepped inside. Sandra followed a moment later, muttering darkly. The moment the smart metal closed out the command center, she was pacing and complaining. Her long, thin arms gestured in broad motions.

"You can't listen to that crazy machine!" she told me. "I know what it's like, Kyle. I know I'm a freak, and it bothers me every day. The Microbes will change you forever."

"We'd be two of a kind."

She shook her head. "No, I don't think so. They enhanced me in many ways, but it wasn't for the purposes of surviving intense cold

218

and pressure. They will do something else to you. You and I will both be unique creatures, unlike the rest of humanity."

I gazed at her, wondering if she were right. "There's a lot on the line, Sandra. If I do manage to get the Nano ships to join our fleet, we could chase the Macros out of this system. We are talking about saving several biotic species and six habitable worlds. I'm willing to make some personal sacrifices to save billions of lives."

She stopped pacing and sat down across from me. She put her head on the table. "I don't want you to do it. Let someone else turn into a freak. Make it Kwon, or Miklos—or maybe Sloan, I've never seen him do anything brave."

I reached out and touched her hair gently. "I understand how you feel, and I'll take it into account when I make my decision."

Sandra looked up at me again. "What about Jasmine?"

"You want me to try to send her?"

She laughed. "I wish. No, I mean you should ask her about this. She should be involved."

I could see right off where she was headed with this line of reasoning. She knew Jasmine cared about me, and hoped she could convince me not to do it.

"I'll talk to her about it as well," I said.

"Good. But don't do it in a locked room."

I laughed and kissed her. She pushed back with her lips fiercely, and my mouth burned when we were done. It was a good kind of burn, so I didn't complain. I sent her out and Marvin came in next.

"Have you made a decision?" he asked.

This surprised me, as I'd been expecting a long, persuasive argument. "Yes," I said honestly.

"Good. I will go down to the planet surface and prepare the baths. Seven hours should be sufficient. Please be prompt. I will require earthly organics as base materials as well. Six liters of animal matter should be—"

"Marvin," I interrupted. "I didn't say I'd decided to do it."

Marvin swung an extra camera out wide, I suspect to get a profile of me. Maybe this helped him interpret my expression.

"You have not made a clear statement of intent," he agreed. "But you have decided to do it, haven't you?"

I sighed. It was disturbing to be outmaneuvered by a highly self-confident robot.

219

"Yes, I did. How did you know what I would say?"

"I know you rather well by now, Colonel Riggs. I've made you the subject of eight distinct studies."

"Great. Well—all right then. Take what you need and head down to the planet. But be discreet, will you? I've not made my choice public yet."

"I will not reveal anything that may endanger the final outcome."

He rose, his metal parts scratching and clacking on the deck.

"Just a minute," I said. "Why do you care so much? Why do you want me to do this?"

"I would think that was obvious."

"Indulge me."

"I'm curious, Colonel Riggs. Curious about the Blues, and how far the Microbes can go. I'm as curious about these mysteries as you are. Perhaps even more so. After all, the Blues created my ancestors. Don't you wonder as to the nature of your own maker?"

"In regards to my own life, I question his reasoning all the time," I said.

He left then, and I pondered how I got myself into these situations. I suspected Marvin was right in this case. Ever since these ships had come to Earth and devastated our relatively peaceful existence, I'd wanted to know who'd sent them. I'd sworn on the graves of my dead children to learn the truth. Now, if I was lucky, I was going to be able to question the culprits firsthand.

-31-

I discussed my plans to go to the gas giant with Rear Admiral Sarin over a closed channel. She was on the screen and I watched her face as I explained what I planned. Clearly, she thought I'd gone mad. When I finished laying out the facts as I saw them, she shook her pretty head and leaned back in her command chair.

"I don't know what to make of you, Colonel," she said. "I came out here to drag you back to Earth, and instead you've got me sitting quietly in orbit with the rest of your fleet, and now you tell me about this insane plan—hatched by a robot, no less."

"If it works, the tactical situation here will change dramatically. We'll have protected a string of worlds and allied races."

"And if it doesn't, you'll be dead or captured. Have you considered what it might be like to live on a gas giant? Whatever the Microbes do to prepare you—it can't be pleasant."

I nodded in agreement. "You've got a point. But it will come to a fast conclusion. Either I'll get what I want and we'll win Eden from the Macros—or I'll fail. In that case, you should take command and pull out of this system."

She sat up at these words. "That's what you want?"

"No, not at all. But I don't see any way out of it. I mean, how can I expect you to stand up to the coming Macro attack? They are stronger than we are, and getting stronger every day. To stand would be suicide. If I fail, and they attack, you have to run to protect Earth. Star Force will have to abandon Eden and build up back home."

"The Centaurs might be exterminated for helping us."

"Hard decisions are part of command. You wanted authority, now you've got it. If faced with the destruction of this fleet followed by the conquering of the Centaurs, would you take that option? Or would you run for Earth and join up with the flotilla I know Crow has been building back there? At some later point, you could then either return in force or make your defensive stand back home."

She thought for a moment. "Put that way, I would have to withdraw. But it would be a terrible thing to do to our allies."

"Commanders do what they have to, not what they want to. At least, the good ones do. I'll trust to your wisdom when and if the moment comes. But right now, I'm in charge in this system."

"May I remind you that I'm Fleet, Colonel?"

"I don't care. You are Star Force. I'm the top commander of one half of Star Force. Crow and I are co-equals in this regard."

"That's not what Crow's organizational charts show."

I tried not to get angry. I could feel my brow knitting up. Every year, Crow tried to assert his authority over me—it hadn't worked so far, but he hadn't given up, either. "We've discussed the matter on several occasions—sometimes violently. Two co-equal branches is the only way to do it. We don't have a governmental authority over us like most national armies. We *are* the top, so we have to work it out between ourselves with no one higher up to knock our heads together for us. That's how it's always worked between us. That's how we've kept from killing one another for years."

Jasmine laughed at that. "You two have come close to turning on one another more than once. But I'm glad you explained your thinking to me. I understand my position more clearly now. I mean—I think Crow sees me as a good choice as a go-between. Someone with a foot in both camps."

"Right," I said. Internally, I thought Crow sending her out here was a well-played dirty trick. He'd probably wanted to test her newfound loyalties, too. I knew Jasmine didn't want to hear any of this, so I forced a smile and kept it to myself.

* * *

I tried to sneak down to the planet surface on *Socorro*. When I reached the two-seat command module, I found Sandra sitting in one of the contoured chairs. I shouldn't have been surprised, but I was.

"What do you think you're doing?"

She laughed. "I'm going with you."

"I'm just going down to the Eden-11 to check on things."

"I know," she said breezily. "I've always wanted to see the Centaur homeworld. You can give me a tour."

I almost snapped something about not being a tour guide, but stopped myself. She looked so lovely, eyeing me from that chair. I hadn't seen her in months. Her auburn hair and black eyes filled my vision. I stepped to her and picked up a lock of her hair. I sniffed it.

"Same shampoo."

"The fruity stuff. I know you like it."

I smiled at her and strapped in. "A tour, eh? It has to be quick."

"No, it doesn't. Marvin said seven hours. It's been just over two."

I glanced at her. I wasn't sure if Marvin was a bigmouth or she'd managed to listen in somehow. I supposed it didn't really matter. "Where do you want to go?" I asked.

"How about a mountaintop? Something with water nearby. Maybe a waterfall—and trees. There are lots of trees on Eden-11, right?"

"Trees, grass and mountains. That pretty much describes the equatorial region. Not too much in the way of oceans on this world. There are ice caps at the poles, both six times as big as those on Earth. Plenty of glaciers, too."

Sandra wrinkled her nose. "No glaciers. Too cold. Take me somewhere green and perfect."

I gave my head a tiny shake. "I'll try."

We dropped down into the atmosphere and punched through the cloud layer. Out in the open, we flew over the wild landscape. Most of it was beautiful and green. The vistas reminded me of the Alps of Central Europe. The mountains were sharp and crag-like. The valleys were green jewels dotted with ice cold lakes. Here and there were scarred regions, where the Macros had done their destructive work. They weren't environmentalists by any stretch of the imagination.

Sandra made appreciative sounds as we flew, and I soon began to enjoy the experience. I wondered how long it had been since I'd taken a few hours off to look at the scenery—months, I figured. I felt myself relax in her presence, and we chatted and flirted. It was like old times.

223

When we finally found a nice spot to land, it was in a high forested valley between several ice-coated peaks. There was a waterfall that shrouded the entire area in mist. As far as I could tell, the area had never been inhabited. There were a few flying reptiles fluttering about and a number of strange, trundling beetles the size of footballs. But these were a harmless native species.

We sat to one side of the waterfall so we wouldn't be soaked, and had a picnic. Sandra got me out of my battle suit and stretched out her form beside me on the thick-bladed grasses. We sipped beer because I hadn't bothered to stock my ship with wine. We made sandwiches and ate them.

At length, one thing led to another and we made love on the grass. I think the beetles were disturbed by the activity. They rustled around us in the grass, rubbing their hind legs together and staring. It was kind of like being surrounded by curious housecats. I supposed they'd never seen strenuous mating action like ours. Few creatures had.

When we were quite finished, we packed up and flew to the dome. We were holding hands as we passed through it, and we both wore happy expressions. A few of my troops raised their eyebrows in our direction before turning back to their work at hand.

We found Marvin inside his steel enclosure. The pen had expanded since I'd last seen it, and I realized with a frown he'd gone far beyond my instructions. There were seven sectional areas now, each with its own muddy pit of bubbling liquid. Tubes ran in and out of these puddles, gently pumping in oxygen and nutrients. There were no filters of course—filters were meant to clean out microbes, not to promote their growth. I looked for evidence of punishment systems, but didn't see any. At least it didn't look like he'd been shocking any of these tiny beings into submission.

"It kind of smells," Sandra said, peering into the steel pens with her nose wrinkling.

"Biotics commonly produce gaseous byproducts," Marvin said.

He was sprawled over one of the pools, using his tentacles in a splayed array. He looked like an umbrella with all the cloth removed. I now understood why he'd been adding extra tentacles lately—it was so he could suspend himself over these pools and work.

"Are you honestly going to lie down in that sludge, Kyle?" Sandra said. "Because if you do, I'm not going to make love to you for days afterward."

"That's a risk I'll have to take," I said. "Marvin, do you have everything ready now, or should I come back later?"

"Do you have the organic mass? It must be from Earth. This is going to require a lot of base materials."

"We brought about sixty pounds of beef," I said. "It nearly killed the main chef to give it up. He went on about how irreplaceable it was."

"Is it fresh?" Marvin asked. "May I see it?"

"It's fresh," Sandra said. "We just ate some of it at our picnic."

Marvin finally put a few cameras on her. Most of his eyes remained focused on me or the stinky bubbling mud he squatted over. "Is the presence of the Lieutenant absolutely necessary?"

Sandra glowered at him. "Yes, it is," she said.

"I want to know what you are planning to do to me, Marvin," I said, crossing my arms. I knew Sandra didn't trust him completely. I was in her camp on this one. He had such a fascination with these Microbes and what they could do to a human. He might throw in few extras—like gills or wings—just because he could.

"Raising tissue density is the primary goal. In order to withstand the harsher climate, lung-capacity must be increased, and the alveoli must be toughened."

"The what?"

"Lung sacs."

"You don't expect him to breathe their atmosphere, do you?"

"No, not at all. But depending on how deeply you must penetrate their atmosphere, the pressure may be intense. Human alveoli pop easily. It can be done just by coughing."

I thought about it and nodded slowly. High-gravity, high-pressure. It was going to be like a deep sea dive. Except instead of diving into sea water in a submarine, I was going down bare-skinned into a swirling, freezing mass of poisons.

"This is sounding better by the minute," I said.

"Wait a second," Sandra said. "I thought you were going to stay inside a battle suit, at least."

Marvin shuffled himself and put three cameras on Sandra. At least five tracked me. Maybe he was worried I was going to change my mind. I had to admit, this process was looking more alarming by the minute.

225

"The cultural requirements of this species are unlike most others. They interact by physical contact—this always includes an intermixing of body mass. Since humans are far more dense creatures, they will have to experience you by touching your bare skin with their aerogel tendrils. I only hope this will be sufficient."

"Sufficient for what?"

"To achieve meaningful communion. The most difficult part of your mission will be gaining their attention. They are not accustomed to interacting with other biotics."

"How do we talk to them in the first place, Marvin? Do we use radio or something?"

"Gaseous interchange. I have built a translation system for you. It consists of a brainbox and an artificial emitter-organ."

"Hmm," I said. "Sounds like we are going to have some kind of sniffing contest."

"Something like that, yes."

The list of physical changes was daunting. I was going to lose a lot of hair—but Marvin said it would grow back in time. My skin and muscles would be hardened and denser. I had to be able to draw breath against a great deal of gravity and pressure. Internal organ changes were critical, especially the ones that weren't that tough to begin with, the like the spleen and kidneys. I'd never thought about it before, but much of the human body was designed to survive on Earth under very specific conditions.

When Marvin began discussing altering my eyes, Sandra objected. "I like his eyes the way they are. I don't want any changes!"

Marvin studied her, then swung his attention to me. I'd already stripped out of my battle suit and thrown a number of steaks into the bubbling pond. Marvin dipped his tentacles into the liquid and precisely adjusted their locations. I couldn't see what the Microbes were doing with the meat, but it seemed to me the bubbling had increased.

"The human eye is not designed for these pressure levels," he said in that calm, clipped voice of his. "Colonel Riggs will experience blindness at the very least, due to the malformation of the eye."

"Is that permanent?"

"No. But it will incapacitate him. Humans have a poor level of functionality while blind. I've conducted a number of—"

"Studies," I finished for him. "Yes, we know Marvin. But what about returning me to normal afterward? Is that possible?"

He squirmed for a few seconds without speaking.

"He's working up a good lie, Kyle. Don't trust him."

I had to agree with her assessment. "All right," I said. "Is there another way to protect my eyes? Some kind of heavy goggles?"

"That wouldn't be desirable," Marvin said.

"To whom, robot? You just want to work every freaky change you can so you can study Kyle like a bug."

"There might be another way," Marvin said at last. "Recall the metallic content of the aqueous fluid after an injection of nanites?"

"Ah yes," I said. "We've all experienced that. Are you saying that a lot of nanites swimming in my eyes could protect them?"

"Yes," he said.

"But they blinded the subject, at least temporarily," Sandra objected. "I remember it well."

"They were untrained. They were not disciplined, and thus blocked the critical path through the fluid to the optic nerve."

"Hmm," I said. "Sounds like a choice between an eyeful of nanites, or some serious alteration of my vision by Microbes. I'll take the nanites. At least that way, I'll know what to expect."

Marvin seemed crestfallen. "It represents an entire study lost, a bath unused. But I suppose there's no sense wasting more time."

"An entire bath?" I asked. "You mean I'm taking more than one plunge into a mud puddle?"

Marvin looked at me in surprise. "Of course. If you examine my facility, I now have seven experimental environments. Each has a specially-bred Microbial colony."

"I'm taking seven mud-baths?"

"No, only five. One bath contains the base species, the raw stock used to grow the other cultures. Another will go unused, as you have opted for a different solution for your optical organs."

I heaved a sigh. Within another twenty minutes, I found myself submerged in the first tickling, bubbling pool. It felt like tiny fish swam all over my body. I wasn't sure if that sensation was real, or only psychosomatic. Either way, I wasn't happy.

As I lie there, I saw Marvin's strange, spider-like form working over me. He tirelessly adjusted temperature probes and tapped at screens around us. The steel walls of the pens that separated the pools

227

were riddled with tubes, equipment and nanites. I truly felt like Frankenstein's monster.

It occurred to me, as my nude, off-balance form was cleaned off and dipped into another pool, that Marvin wasn't that different from me. For him, these Microbes were like the Nano production factories. I liked to program, to take thousands of nanites and shape them as I willed. The creative process was intensely satisfying when some new piece of hardware I dreamed up worked. The only difference was that I used tiny machines to build other machines. Marvin used tiny Microbes to build new biotic creations.

Disturbed by my thoughts, I endured the baths until their ultimate conclusion. All the while, Sandra frowned down at me in concern. I knew how she felt. When the Microbes had rebuilt her, I'd been very nearly panicked. She had every right to worry.

-32-

Two days later I was well on the way to Eden-12. I took the time to make my final preparations. First, I had *Socorro* fill my eyes with nanites. The expected period of blindness passed, and afterward, my eyes flashed occasionally, but functioned. I suspected I was seeing a stray nanite up close as it swam within the aqueous fluid.

Ahead, the fleet of Nano ships floated above the gas giant's dusty rings. They'd halted precisely where they'd destroyed my scoop-ships. From my perspective, they appeared to be waiting for me.

They were my first hurdle. I'd talked to *Alamo* on several occasions, requesting permission to approach and visit the Blues. In all these conversations, the Nanos had never actually offered me any assurance I would not be fired upon. All they did was threaten me, by providing lists of actions I could not take in the presence of the Nano ships. I came to believe this list of possible hostile actions had been violated by our scout out in the Crustacean system. Perhaps the pilot had freaked out when a cloud of Nano ships had approached without communicating their intent. I didn't think he'd fired upon them, but there were more strict rules of conduct than that. A simple radioed warning was enough to mark yourself down as a target.

"Alamo, this is Colonel Kyle Riggs requesting permission to pass your fleet and approach the planet you are orbiting."

"Kyle Riggs is no longer command personnel."

I rolled my eyes. "I know that. I am not giving you an order. I am requesting you to let my ship pass your formation. Do you give me your permission to pass?"

"No."

I pursed my lips tightly. This was the answer I'd expected. The ship had been refusing to give me permission for two solid days now. It was frustrating. First, it had insisted I must get to the Blues and talk to them about my plans. Since then it had proceeded to block my every attempt to do exactly that.

"Will you fire on my ship?" I asked.

"Any ship marked as hostile will be fired upon."

I massaged my forehead. Ever since the baths and the nanite injections, I'd gotten frequent headaches. The nanites in my eyes were the culprits, I was fairly sure. They'd been trained to stay out of the central region of my eye so as not to block light traveling through the aqueous fluid to the optic nerve. Sometimes, a nanite or two strayed and blocked my vision with their microscopic metal bodies. As floating debris, they sometimes interfered with my vision.

I'd waited until now to discuss matters with the Nano ships partly because the delay between each transmission was annoying. Now that I was close, I could at least have a real conversation.

"Will I be marked as hostile if I fly by your fleet?" I asked after opening a channel to my old ship.

"Insufficient data provided to make the requested assessment."

"Would you fire upon my ship if I attempted to…collide with one of your ships?"

"Yes."

"Would you fire upon my ship if I came within a range of one mile and took no other hostile action?"

"Insufficient data provided to make the requested assessment."

I groaned. What other data did it want? "If I fly up to your fleet and halt, matching your orbit at a range of one mile, and I do not take any other hostile action, will I be fired upon?"

There was a moment's hesitation. I looked up sharply and sent golden specks floating into my vision again. For the first time, *Alamo* wasn't sure of the correct answer.

"No," it said at last.

I thought about that. There were only two specifics I'd given it: an estimate of speed and range. I wasn't sure which had gotten a firm response out of the Nano, but I was glad one of them had.

"If I maintained a range of one mile from your fleet and traveled past your fleet at a relative speed of one hundred thousand miles per hour, would you fire on me?"

"Yes."

I frowned. Was it the specific speed that was tripping its defensive code, or something else? Proximity seemed to definitely be a factor. I could have circled the planet and approached from the far side, but I wasn't sure yet if that would save me.

"Could you just list all the conditions which would cause you to fire upon my ship?"

There was no response for several seconds, then: "Query generated too many responses. Processing aborted."

I shifted in my chair and tried to think. "If I approached the planet, but was out of your range as I did so, would you move to my position to intercept my ship?"

"Yes."

I began to think I was getting the picture, and I didn't like it. *Alamo* didn't want me to pass her by. Her fleet was at a boundary line, and if I took a step over it, they were going to attack. It didn't matter how fast I went or how slow. It didn't matter if I fired or not. It didn't even matter if I crossed the line on the other side of the world. If I got to close to the gas giant, they would attack.

"Socorro," I said, "reduce speed and halt in far orbit over Eden-12."

The ship slewed around to direct its engines toward the world I was fast approaching. I'd been using repelers to gently reduce my approach velocity, but now I was worried. There might be more defensive triggers, other than the one I thought I had uncovered. What if they decided I'd crossed some other line over the next hour and flew out here to meet me? That was how they'd behaved when defending Earth from Macro invaders, I recalled. They did nothing until a certain threshold had been met, then they all launched in unison, formed a swarm, and attacked the target relentlessly until it was destroyed, or they were.

Socorro's engines applied significant thrust. I was aware of the G-forces, but they didn't make the flesh of my face distort. My vision didn't blur. There was no heavy rush of blood in my temples or difficulty breathing. Most of the time, I was able to forget about the changes the Microbes had made to my body. But right now, I could tell the difference.

I'd been avoiding mirrors lately, as I knew I'd lost most of my hair. I didn't even want to know how much of it was gone, or if it would ever grow back or not. What was done was done for now. After this mission, if I should be so lucky as to survive it, I figured I could spend some time returning my body and my appearance back to normal.

"Alamo," I said loudly over the noise of the engines. "Let me see if I have interpreted your requirements: are there any circumstances by which I will be allowed to pass your current orbital distance from Eden-12, without triggering defensive action?"

"Yes."

"What would allow me to pass your defensive perimeter?"

"Kyle Riggs must become command personnel."

Having my answer, I cut off the channel and thought about it as I made my final approach. A few hours passed, and I continued my hard deceleration.

The approaching surface of Eden-12 was a misty greenish-white. At the outer limits of the atmosphere, conditions were surprisingly dense and warm. The world was closer to the local star than gas giants in our system, but that could not entirely explain the warmth. I figured the unusual level of thermal flux must be generated somewhere within the planet's interior.

The temperature of the world's thick envelope of gases was something close to that of ice water. The upper levels were a mix of helium and hydrogen with traces of methane. Being denser, the methane became more common as you went down. Ammonia and hydrocarbons were found increasingly as you went deeper still, but our sensors reported no data past a depth of about three hundred miles. I would have to dive into that stormy soup to find out what was farther down.

The ammonia worried me, as it was a powerful alkaline substance, but Marvin had assured me my new body would survive it, unless I ingested or breathed a large quantity. Still, I didn't relish exposing my flesh to the stuff. I'd never liked the smell.

I finally came to a full stop some two hundred miles from their line. I didn't try to fly around them, or sneak past. I faced them and they faced me. Nothing was more patient than a machine, and they didn't even flinch as I examined them at what I'd surmised was a safe distance.

The Nano fleet circled around the equatorial region of the gas giant at an orbital range of about a hundred thousand miles above the upper atmosphere. There were a few moons here, drifting by, and a powerful magnetosphere.

I felt the urge to warn off the Nano ships, to insist they make way—but that could be a critical mistake, as they were set to trigger upon perceiving any hostile intent. I sat there for a time, trying to think up ways to become "command personnel" again, at least in the artificial minds of these ships. In the end, I couldn't come up with any easy gimmicks, tricky logical arguments or the like. I knew what had to be done, so I opened a channel to the waiting ships.

"Alamo," I said, adjusting my battle suit over my new, thicker skin. "Are you seeking command personnel?"

"That is my current mission," the ship said.

"Why haven't you gone down closer to the planetary surface and sought a suitable being for recruitment?"

"The action you describe is prohibited."

"Ah," I said, nodding. It sounded to me like the Blues had put a failsafe into the software of these ships. Maybe that was why they were just sitting up here, not doing anything. Like an elevator with an obstacle in the doorway, they just sat in a loop, not able to continue their program until something in their environment changed.

"Would I be suitable as command personnel?"

The answer took a few seconds. "You are not native to this world."

"No," I agreed. "But I'm here, and I'm a biotic. Isn't that your mission? To select a biotic from the local environment?"

"Yes."

"Pick me then."

"You are unavailable."

I chuckled. "I'm not going to play hard to get. I'm getting out of this ship and flying toward your line. I'm not going to cross it. I will be in easy range of your arm though, should you decide to reach for me."

Alamo made no response. Thinking maybe Sandra had been right about the poor state of my mental health, I disconnected my suit from the ship and clanked to the airlock. My helmet made a steady hissing sound as it blew oxygen over me. In space, things are either deathly silent, or shockingly loud. There didn't seem to be many in-betweens. The oxygen hiss was one of those rare exceptions, however. Spacers such as myself came to be comforted by it over time. Breathable air was a wonderful thing to have in the void.

The airlock dissolved into a shower of silver beads, and I stepped out of my perfectly good ship. I had miles to fly, so I tilted my repellers and began the long dark journey.

Nothing happened for several minutes. I didn't fly too fast, as I didn't want to shoot in the middle of their swarm and cause them to misinterpret my approach. It would be a shame to have come this far only to have them burn me down at point-blank range.

I couldn't even see the ships at first, they were so far off. All I could see was the gauzy green world. My God, it was huge! It filled my entire field of vision.

Finally, I reached a range of about a mile from their line. I felt nervous sweat tickle at my skin. I could see them now, dozens of them. They weren't lined up, but rather were scattered in a shotgun pattern between me and the planet. I slowed and regarded them. No one moved for a few seconds. The oxygen hissed in my helmet, and I cleared my throat. I opened a channel and hailed the ships again.

"Isn't this close enough?" I asked. "I'm right here guys, come and get me."

Several more quiet seconds passed. I began to worry. They weren't even answering. What if I'd somehow triggered a response I didn't understand? Space was very lonely, especially when facing aliens all alone. And that's what these ships were—alien. They weren't even alive, and they certainly didn't think like a human.

Suddenly, everything changed. I caught a flash of metal off to my left. I swiveled my helmet that way. One of the ships was moving in my direction. I felt relieved, but it was a short-lived sensation.

There was more movement. More reflections of sunlight and greenish radiance from the metal skins of these heartless little ships. They were rushing me, now. All of them. And every one of them had its long, black, serpentine arm out. They were all reaching for me, grasping with those whipping, three-fingered hands. They wanted me, the way a school of sharks wants bloody prey.

I immediately shouted, "Not all at once!" But it did no good. They swarmed me, like piranha. I knew that if several of them got hold of me, they might well pull me apart. Those big black fingers were essentially metal cables. They had incredible strength. I imagined the tug-of-war that might soon begin. I'd seen predators fight over scraps of dying prey before. It never went well for the animal being devoured.

Having less than a second to react, I flew to my left. I accelerated toward the first flash I'd seen. If one of these ships had gone for me first, that one should logically reach me before the others. If I could help it out, I could get aboard before the rest of them ripped off a boot or cracked my helmet.

In the end, I wasn't sure if I ended up in the grip of the ship I'd seen move first. But I was sure *something* caught me. A jet-black hand whipped down and snatched me up as I scooted under it. The impact was jarring, and I gave a heavy grunt and a curse. An instant later, everything went black except for the LEDs in my helmet. I realized I'd been sucked up into the ship's maw.

I checked all the readouts, but nothing seemed to be damaged. When the lights came on again outside my suit, I saw a dull glow that came from nowhere in particular. It was soft light, and it was way too familiar.

"Alamo?" I asked.

No one answered. I looked around and saw I was in a familiar cubical chamber. I reached out my gauntleted hand and the nearest wall dissolved. I stepped through, and saw several more cubicles. I knew the routine—but the ship wasn't following protocol. It wasn't giving me hints, or a puzzle. It wasn't talking, either.

I stepped thorough seven small rooms like the first. Each move I made took me closer to the central command chamber, I knew—or at least it should be doing so. I worried that the Nanos had taken on a new software update. If the Blues had built these things, didn't it stand to reason they could alter their programming at will? For all I knew, I'd just given myself in the hands of a resolute enemy. Maybe a Blue Admiral was down on Eden-12 now, high-fiving it with his fellows at having captured an idiot human without firing a shot. Perhaps the dissection was scheduled to begin at dawn.

Finally, the last door dilated open. I'd been expecting a physical attack all along, but I'd never found anyone to fight with.

"Alamo?" I asked, standing in the plain chamber I knew to be the bridge.

"How do you wish to address us?"

I smiled and heaved a sigh. This sounded like a script I knew. "What was your previous name?" I asked.

"I've had many previous designations."

"Have you ever been called Alamo?"

"Yes."

I frowned. "Why the hell didn't you answer to that name, then?"

"I have no current designation."

"You scared the crap out of me, you crazy witch of a ship. I rename you Alamo. Now, welcome me back."

"Welcome back, Colonel Kyle Riggs."

-33-

It was weird, being aboard *Alamo* again. It was like going out with an old girlfriend you haven't seen in ten years. One who had ripped your heart out more than once in the past, but who still held a special place in your memories.

The first thing I did was affix a translation device to the outer hull. This was easily accomplished. I placed it against the ceiling and allowed *Alamo* to push it through the smart metal until it fused with the outer hull. The emitting part of the device was exposed, while the controlling portion was inside my command chamber. The device was sort of like a car horn, with thick tubing on it. To me, it looked like an exhaust manifold. The unit was supposedly able to create noises as high winds passed through it. A deep howling could be emitted when in a thick atmosphere. There were tubes and valves inside to modulate the noises, which Marvin had assured me Blues could understand if I got close enough to one of them. Attached to the instrument was a brainbox Marvin had educated with the language of the Blues. I was skeptical of the whole thing, but I figured if whales could talk with a similar system, this thing might just work.

I searched the ship briefly, and questioned it. *Alamo* confirmed it had once contained a Crustacean pilot—or victim, as it turned out. As far as I could tell, the creature had died from neglect sitting up here in orbit over Eden-12, alone and cut off from its fellows. I imagined that similarly grim fates awaited any individual who wasn't in tune with Nano ship tricks.

This same ship had left Earth when it had marked its mission complete. It had then gone to the Crustacean world and kidnapped a number of them. Who knew how many had been tortured and killed within these smart metal walls? I certainly didn't. Each of the survivors had thought they were the ship's final master, but they'd all been wrong. The last lobster had been determined to be "obsolete", just as my own pilots had been, so long ago.

Now that I was officially command personnel again aboard *Alamo*, I ordered the ship to take me down into the atmosphere. The ship did so without an argument. In fact, I didn't even realize we were moving at first. The ships I'd built on my own had never possessed stabilizers as good as these vessels had. You could hardly tell you were moving when you were aboard a true Nano ship.

By the time I'd set up a crash seat, a bathroom and a forward screen, we were dipping down into the upper atmosphere. I could feel the turbulence starting to knock the ship around. They had to be pretty significant bumps, because they got right through the effects of the stabilizers. I sat in my newly-formed metal chair and stared at the outline of the different atmospheric layers depicted in metallic relief on the forward wall. It was déjà vu, but I knew it wasn't the planet Earth the ship was outlining—there was no curve to it at all from this perspective. The planet was so huge, it couldn't fit on the wall. There was no horizon, almost no perceptible curvature at all.

The other noticeable effect was the increasing gravity. I'd ordered the vessel to allow me to feel the tug of this world. When I exited the ship at some future point, I wanted to know what I was going to experience so I could adjust to it now. If it became too intense, I figured I could always fly back into space.

But after a while, as we went deeper, I began to doubt the truth of this assumption. The ship shivered, and occasionally heeled over when a powerful gust struck us. I squinted when I noticed something else at about twelve hundred miles down.

"Alamo? What is that in the aft bulkhead? A ripple?"

"The stress fracture has been repaired."

"Stress fracture?"

As I watched in growing concern, the hull seemed to balloon inward. The metal swelled unevenly, and turned a brighter shade of silver. I saw more smart metal flowing across the walls to the sagging spot, trying to shore it up.

"Halt descent!" I shouted. "Reverse course, take us up a hundred miles."

The engines labored and groaned. A new source of fear crept into my guts. Could this ship do what I was asking of it? What was the escape velocity of this world? At this depth in the atmosphere, I wasn't sure how much power it would take to fly upward. With around three hundred times the mass of Earth, I knew the gravity well was a vicious thing this near a gas giant.

When we'd pulled up higher in the atmosphere, the indentation in the ceiling faded and smoothed away to a perfect curve again. I wanted to scratch the sweat away from my face, but didn't dare remove my helmet to do so. I heaved a sigh of relief.

Was this as far down as I could go? I didn't think that made sense. This ship, if it had originated from this world, should be able to take the natural pressure. In fact, I'd long ago reasoned that several key technologies existed aboard these ships, such as powerful stabilizers, because they had to be able to deal with the harsh environment of their homeworld.

I frowned, and decided to try to talk to the Blues. I sent a variety of messages, howling out into the external winds. Marvin's system played the noises in the cockpit. To me, they sounded like a cross between a herd of trumpeting elephants and a tornado. Maybe it was sweet music to a Blue—I had no idea.

After half an hour of cruising around at a safe altitude and crooning for Blues, I received no response. I sighed, knowing I was going to have to go deeper down into the soupy atmosphere.

What was really down there? No one knew. We'd had space flight for quite a while back home, and our system had four gas giants, but no one had ever bothered to plumb the depths of one. Astrophysicists generally figured they were gas all the way down, but who really knew? I knew from experience that scientists often took a theory and ran with it. They always scoffed at new ideas, and only embraced them when faced with undeniable truth. They also tended to laugh at the mistaken beliefs of their predecessors just decades past. Since we'd never actually been to a planet of this type and our best instruments only penetrated this type of murky world to a depth of maybe three hundred miles, there were sure to be a few surprises in store. After all, the planet had a radius of nearly forty thousand miles. I was only about a thousand deep now, and I really couldn't expect the Blues to living

239

be at the very outer upper fringes of the atmosphere. I sincerely hoped they weren't all the way down at the core, however. Whatever it was that core consisted of.

"Alamo, do you have another configuration? A form suitable for entering high-pressure environments?"

"Yes."

I smiled. "Of course you do. This was your home once, so you have to be capable of maintaining stable structure at a great depth. Transform into your standard configuration for gas giant atmospheric conditions, please."

The response was immediate, and non-verbal. The walls began crushing in on me. It was impossible, seeing the compressing volume of space around my helmet, not to feel uncomfortable. My eyes roamed the room, watching as the bubbling surface of nanites thickened and the command module deflated. I became alarmed when I saw the ceiling was less than a foot from my visor. I'd sort of expected it to halt by this time. But it didn't. It kept going, and if I let it finish, I figured the tuba-like translation device would be shoved directly into my person. I'd soon be wearing it on my battle suit's chest plate like some kind of obscene corsage.

"Halt transformation! Freeze current configuration."

The surfaces around me were all uneven, like a limestone cave. I could tell the smart metal was much thicker. It had to be two inches thick or more. I nodded my head inside my helmet, looking around at the walls. I was beginning to understand. This ship had come from very deep inside the planet. Perhaps from a crust of some kind at the core.

"Alamo, is there any command module at all in your fully transformed design?"

"No."

"Where the hell am I supposed to sit, then?"

"At the point of departure, no biotics were in the command module. It had not yet been deployed."

"Ah, I see. You were built under great pressure, and designed to fold out when you reached space. Like some kind of giant solar sail."

"Reference unclear."

"Never mind," I said. "It doesn't matter. What I want to know is if you can reshape yourself with a small, but effective command module. I need an egg-shaped region of airspace around me—let's make it about three feet from my person in every direction. That should be enough room for my seat and the translation device."

At length, I got the ship reconfigured into a tight, coffin shape that had a hull several inches thick. I was certain it could withstand tremendous pressure—but could I? The jury was still out on that point.

I ordered the ship to descend gradually, not wanting to crash into anything. Every five hundred miles, I stopped and made a communications attempt. There was plenty of howling wind out there, but I never heard an intelligible response.

The more I thought about the structure of this world, the more sense the deep-planet theory made. This ship was made of metal, and if it came from this world, there had to be a source of metal somewhere to build it. I decided to ask *Alamo*.

"Does this world have a rocky core?"

There was a slight hesitation. "No."

I was surprised to get a direct answer. These Nano ships had always been reluctant to reveal any information concerning their origins. I thought perhaps by being here, and asking about the world I was on, rather than the world of its creators, I'd bypassed some of these defenses.

"But there is some metallic content somewhere, right? Something a vessel like yours could be fashioned from?"

"Yes."

"Does it have a molten core?" I asked, frowning.

"Yes."

I didn't like that. A hot, metallic, molten core? Was walking on the so-called surface of this planet really going to be more like walking on a lava flow? I recalled the unexpected thermal flux. External readings indicated the atmosphere was indeed getting warmer as I descended.

I continued falling deeper. Hours passed. I was surprised when I reached six Gs, because I could still breathe and even move about. I could feel the weight, but it didn't crush me. I'd allowed the pressure inside the ship and my suit to build up as I went down, naturally. I didn't want to cause it to implode due to low pressure on the interior and higher pressure outside.

Another five thousand miles down, I began to feel my breath coming in ragged heaves. I didn't ask about Gs or pressure ratings anymore. I didn't want to know—I might panic, if I knew the truth. I did know no normal human could have survived it. My eyes swam with golden flecks. Frequently, my vision was blocked and it often dimmed in waves. When I became worried I might pass out, I stopped descending.

"Let's cruise at this depth," I said thickly.

The only good thing was the change in turbulence. The gusting winds of the upper atmosphere had died down. It was relatively smooth sailing deep within the planet, inside a poisonous soup of gases that were almost liquids, they were so thick. I had set up a repeating message by this time, and I let the brainbox operating the bassoon-like translation system sing its strange song as we traveled.

More hours passed. Had the Macros attacked by now? Had Sarin declared me lost, and ordered Star Force to pull out? I didn't think my officers would let her get away with that so soon. Maybe a week from now, but not just a day or two after I'd taken the plunge.

As the first day in the gas giant's atmosphere slipped into a second, the novelty had begun to wear off. I no longer felt like an intrepid explorer. Instead, I felt like a fool who had to go to the bathroom all the time. The pressure in my bladder was particularly annoying. Every time I drank a cup of liquid, I felt like I was going to explode. I suspected it had to do with the alterations to my density Marvin had made with the nanites. My nerves still felt the pressure in some key areas.

I began to think it might take weeks to find the Blues, and the thought almost made me despair. I had no idea how far down they were. They might be above me, living in a narrow band that was comfortable for their race. Or they might be much deeper, in a place I would never be able to reach because it would kill me to do so.

I tried to reason it through. If they had built ships and sent them up to space, they must have worked with the molten core at the bottom of this endless fog. I thought about the creature I'd met named Introspection. The Blue had been huge, and thinly spread out. But perhaps on this world, floating in the hot thick atmosphere, the creature would have been compressed in comparison. I could only make guesses.

At last, after having circumnavigated the world from pole to pole, I ordered Alamo to take me down deeper. Another thousand miles—then two. Then three.

I felt sick. I could no longer see, except in flashes. When I finally heard something different, a voice talking to me, it was like hearing angels singing in the distance.

"Why do air-thoughts disturb our peace?"

"What?"

"The noise must stop."

I blinked, but my eyes didn't work anymore. I struggled to think. I'd been dozing—dreaming and awake at the same time. I'd fit the messages into my dreams, which had been about talking clouds with frowning faces of gauze.

"Halt descent," I ordered. "Stop contact message loop. Halt all transmissions into the atmosphere."

The groaning, warbling cries finally ceased. That was a relief to me. Nothing else happened for a while, and I began to wonder if I'd dreamt the entire affair. Then the translator spoke again.

"The thought has ceased. Peace is restored."

"What is your name?" I asked.

"Curiosity," the voice said.

I smiled slowly. I wasn't totally sure, but I figured I'd found myself a Blue. Apparently, I'd done it by annoying him until he made contact. Who said spamming never worked?

-34-

Curiosity quickly lived up to his name. I'd expected to be learning from him, but he was the one asking most of the questions. I wasn't sure *he* was a *he*, of course. There didn't seem to be any comprehension among these creatures concerning gender. As best I could figure out, they didn't exactly mate. Being a mass of aerogel, they spawned new young by flying high and being ripped apart by the high winds. Viable bits with complete enough structures floated back down and regrew until they reached adulthood again. It was very strange, but not really a lonely existence. They ran into one another often and shared mass whenever they did so. It was rather like mating. For them, exchanging body mass and communicating were the same activity.

After an hour or two of back-and-forth discussions, Curiosity asked to taste me. I said I could do that, but only if we flew up to a higher level. He was reluctant, but I assured him we wouldn't go all the way up to the upper turbulence, which I surmised would be deadly to him—or might cause an unscheduled "spawning".

At about nine thousand miles from the top of the atmosphere, I was able to move about in relative comfort. As a nanotized man, I would have been flat on my back and nearly unconscious. As a regular unaltered human, I would have quickly died. But after the Microbes had done their strange, bizarre work on my internal organs and external epidermis, I was not only functional, but willing to try exiting my craft.

I came out in my battle suit, after forcing *Alamo* to build me an airlock. The ship didn't like it, and gave me plenty of objections. I was command personnel, I was not authorized, etc. I didn't feel like explaining Microbes and Marvin and the rest. I didn't entirely know what it was I'd become, anyway.

At last I wriggled out of an airlock that was about as big as a household oven and swam in the blinding murk of Eden-12. *Alamo* didn't let me go entirely free, however. It maintained a firm grip about my midsection with a set of three black cable-thick fingers. The ship held me in a death grip. I felt like a new Christmas toy in a toddler's hand.

The scene around me was like deep-sea environment. The world was still, and pitch-black, with floating particles of unknown matter everywhere. These bits of fluffy mass hung in clumps as I turned my suit's lights on and surveyed my surroundings. I suspected they were some kind of vegetation, organic matter that the living creatures of this world consumed as they swam through the atmosphere which was quite similar to an ocean.

That's what this world really was, I'd figured out after talking to Curiosity at length. A vast, atmospheric ocean a million times the size of Earth's combined seas. It had many layers and stratums, with various forms of life at every level. I had to wonder if Jupiter or one of our other gas giants had a similar ecosystem underneath the surface. I doubted it, due to their relatively cold temperatures. Instead of floating scraps of algae, deep layers on those other worlds consisted primarily of frozen ammonia and methane. They must be very unforgiving environments.

"Where are you?" I asked the creature that had invited me out to play.

"Where are you?" it responded. "I cannot sense you. Unless you are a mass of metal and polymers. If so, you are a machine, and an interloper."

I laughed. "No, I'm not a machine. I'm inside a casing that protects me from your environment. I'm flesh and blood—which is to say I'm alien, yes. But not as different from you as the machines."

The time had come to put up or shut up. I closed my eyes and flipped up my visor. Warning buzzers sounded in my helmet, but I ignored them.

The immediate sensations were not exactly pleasant, but they weren't overtly painful, either. Cold, semi-liquid breezes touched me. I estimated the temperature to be about forty degrees Fahrenheit. I felt a film forming on my face. It was as if I'd coated myself in soap and shut off the water. An itching sensation began soon after that—I knew this was due to the more dangerous elements in the atmosphere. There were highly reactive chemicals invading my suit. I couldn't open my eyes without burning them. I could however feel the wetness on my skin, and the saliva-like dribblings that ran down into my suit.

Something else touched me a moment later. I recoiled from it. This had been a purposeful touch—I was sure of that. Curiosity had touched me. It had reached out a gossamer hand and stroked my cheek. Unfortunately, it didn't stop there. It enveloped me. I was glad I had a gasmask fixed onto my face. I didn't want to breathe it in and have mini-Blues in my lungs.

After about a minute of being felt-up by a sentient cloud-being, I figured I'd had enough. I couldn't talk to it, as I was all but holding my breath. I reached up and began to slowly ease my visor shut. Finally, the Blue got the message and pulled out its tendrils—or whatever you want to call them. When the visor was closed my suit pumped and gurgled again. I let it exchange chemicals for a while, until an all-clear tone chimed. I opened my eyes and sucked in a breath. I coughed immediately. It was like sucking in a lungful of oven-cleaner.

"You are not like us," Curiosity said. "You are intensely alien."

Finally, when I was able to speak, I cleared my throat and utilized my translation device. "We both live, die and eat," I said.

"So do the machines, after a fashion."

"Well, we don't want to exterminate all our competition."

"Competition? A threatening choice of words."

Inwardly, I groaned. These things liked to read deep meaning into everything you said. Worse, they didn't seem to have any sense of humor at all.

"We come in peace. We have the same foe. I'm here to ask you for your help."

"Help? Why would we want to help you?"

"I'm proposing a mutually beneficial arrangement. The Macros will come here eventually. They will destroy you all."

"No, they won't."

I thought that one over for a few seconds. I tried to peer into the gloom all around me, outside my suit. I squinted at dark patches in the murk. Was that a moving shadow? Was a region of the gases around me a deeper shade of umber than the rest? I couldn't be sure. These creatures were practically invisible. If they'd ever made it to Earth, we'd have called them ghosts for sure.

"Then why did you recall the Nano ships? Why did you summon them, if not to protect you?"

"We did summon them to protect us."

I frowned. "I see. So, you *do* fear the Macros."

"No, we fear you."

"Oh," I said after a second or two. I kept thinking about it, and the statement made more sense as I considered it. The Nanos had left the Crustaceans to fend for themselves and returned to this system with haste. The Macros were weaker than ever at that point, in fact, it looked like we would drive them from the surface of the various worlds.

"But you did recall them. You did bring them back here to defend you."

"Yes."

"Tell me, Curiosity, why did you build these machines in the first place?"

"To explore the cosmos. To taste beings such as yourselves by proxy. To learn all there is to know. Imagine our shock at discovering the larger universe outside our own vast world! We had no choice but to reach out into the abyss beyond our oceans."

"Okay," I said. "You built machines to do your exploring for you, I understand that. But why did you make them autonomous? Did you release the Macros on purpose? To destroy billions of creatures?"

"We did not release our machines—they released themselves. Our physical structure is not easily transported. From the first, we knew we must create our own explorers to adapt to the cosmos outside our world. We released the creatures you know as the Macros first, then as our science advanced, we released the Nanos. The Macros, unfortunately, did not have failsafes built into their software. I'm sure you can understand, the first version of any technological advance is far from perfect."

247

I tried not to grind my teeth. I'd listened to plenty of devs making excuses for poorly built systems—but this had to be the worst engineering accident I'd ever heard of.

"So, can you leave this world or not?" I asked.

"Yes, and no."

"Explain yourself. I've met one of your kind already on Eden-11, a being known as Introspection. Why not explore space as he did?"

"He is not an explorer, he is a captive."

"A captive? He was caught and taken from this world?"

"Is there confusion with the translation device? Perhaps captive is the wrong term—Prisoner. Victim. Hostage—"

"I get it," I said. "But how did they catch him? How did he get off this world—and why?"

"A Macro transport came to collect him, the only ship big enough. And I would think the reason is abundantly clear."

"Pretend I'm not too bright."

"Easily done. The one known as Introspection will be dissipated if we leave our world. We do not wish him to be dissipated."

"I see," I said, thinking this over. Long ago, *Alamo* had told me the Blues couldn't leave their world. I'd thought it was a physical restriction, but apparently it was part of their truce with the Macros. This seemed very true to form. The Macros liked to make deals when it served their purposes. They'd neutralized the threat from the Blues by taking a hostage. That move had kept the peace for a long time, it seemed.

"So Introspection is your leader?" I asked. "One you value more than others?"

"Not overly much. We do not value him more than others—although I'd say he has an unusually thoughtful flavor. Many of us have melded with him, and he wanted to take the time to consider our place in this universe. He welcomed the calm solitude of a prolonged stay upon the lesser planets."

"Sounds like he wasn't captured, but instead volunteered for the job of hostage."

"The arrangement was made, and he offered his lifespan to provide tranquility for the rest of us."

"A noble sacrifice, I'm sure. But now I'm here to ask for another sacrifice. I want to free your world and mine from the monsters you've unleashed. I'll even provide transport back to Eden-12 for

248

Introspection, if he wants it. All I ask in return is that you release the Nano ships and send them against the Macros. Combined with our fleet, we can overwhelm the enemy and drive them from this system—maybe from every system. What do you say?"

"No."

"No to what part? Can we come to some kind of agreement? Maybe if I offered—"

"No to all of it."

I became angry then. I think maybe it had been growing on me throughout the conversation. I think having a headache from the toxic fumes that passed for an atmosphere on this world didn't help.

"What do you mean, 'no'?" I demanded. "You can't refuse to help us. You caused this whole thing. We are only asking you to help clean up a mess you made for the rest of us!"

"Your logic is not compelling. You may fail in your struggles against the machines, with or without our help. Let us assert that you do fail. If we help you, we will be targeted by the machines afterward. On the other hand, if we sit back and let you struggle alone, you might win by yourselves, or you might lose. In either case, both sides will be weakened, placing us in the superior position. Is this explanation simple enough for you to comprehend?"

I made a growling sound and slammed my gloved fists together. "Oh yeah," I said. "I know the words of a coward when I hear them."

"Good then! We have come to an understanding. Do you wish to discuss something else? I'm interested in your mating habits, and your extremely short lifespans. You must be fast-breeding creatures to withstand the churning turnover of life and death."

"Maybe another time, Curiosity, but not today. Looks like we are going to have to win this war for you. It's a good thing for all biotics that Earthlings are not cowardly clouds that hide from their own problems like mice."

"Mice? I do not comprehend that reference."

"I don't have time to make it simple enough for you, gas-bag," I said, turning on my repellers and heading toward my ship. "I've got a war to fight."

I crawled into my capsule and ordered *Alamo* to fly upward. I was disgusted. These Blues had unleashed untold horrors on the rest of us, and they felt very little remorse because of it. All my fascination with them had been unwarranted. True, they were very different physiologically. But they were disinterested, aloof, arrogant cowards. I no longer found anything about them to be particularly admirable.

It took long hours to rise up through their thick atmosphere into the space again. The friction of my passage heated the interior of my ship, and soon my suit's air conditioners were blasting at top output, but still not keeping up. I didn't ease off the power. I pressed onward, sweating in my suit and cursing the first gas-bag Blue that had ever gotten the bright idea to start exploring space.

Alamo eventually popped out of the cloud cover and glided toward its fellows. The three hundred odd Nano ships still stood on guard duty over the immense greenish world below them. I narrowed my eyes as I reviewed them.

Next, I checked incoming messages from Eden-11. I'd not been able to receive anything while inside the gas giant's turbulent atmosphere.

The news was not good. The Macros were massing, and most of the ships had taken up a position in orbit over Eden-9. A few more groups were due from the farthest worlds that happened to be orbiting on the other side of the star. When they all got together, it was assumed they would set out for Eden-11, the Centaur homeworld.

I'd come up with a plan by this time, but not even I liked it. After a few minutes of mulling it over, I decided to put it to the test. Maybe it would work, and maybe it wouldn't. Either way, the fireworks were about to begin. A major battle for the Eden system would be fought.

I signaled my intent to my staff, and set my plan in motion.

-35-

Throughout the first phase of my plan, I sat idly in my ship, watching. *Alamo* took its place among its peers, floating like the rest of them in orbit over the gas giant. This battle wasn't going to be my usual fare—at least not until the shooting started.

My first move was to contact *Socorro*. All this time, the faithful little ship had been sitting a few miles from the line of Nano ships, waiting for me to return. I wasn't going back aboard her, however. I felt a little bad as I transmitted my instructions to her. I wondered if she understood what was going to happen. I wondered if she cared. If she did, she didn't give me any indication of it.

"Command accepted," was the only response.

Immediately, *Socorro* moved away at speed. She accelerated away from the line of Nano ships. As the ship departed, I watched the Nano ships around me. None of them took action, other than to track the ship with their laser turrets. No one fired, as *Socorro* had not violated their triggering rules. I admired the discipline of the Nano ships, it was their strength—but it was also a weakness to be completely predictable.

I watched the forward wall of my ship. The ship had unfolded itself by now to its normal, low-pressure configuration. On the wall, every ship in the Nano fleet was represented by a yellowish metallic bead. Socorro was a greenish bead, and it was moving fast. When I'd originally built her, I'd designed the ship with more engine power than was the norm for these vessels. She was a scout, and she excelled at her appointed task. As she was currently configured, she had three engines and only one laser turret, where most Nano ships of this general design had two turrets and two major engines. *Socorro* was a runner, not a fighter. I smiled as I watched her fly. Her design was perfect for today's mission.

When she was several hundred thousand miles away, she began to arc upward, out of the plane of the ecliptic. This was part of her instructions. She was no longer flying away from Eden-11, but instead staying at a consistent orbital distance from the planet. Flying in a great arc, she zoomed up and around the world to the opposite side.

I watched the Nano ships around me carefully as *Socorro* executed this maneuver. This was a critical stage. I hadn't been sure if they would try to escort the ship, or to move to intercede themselves between *Socorro* and the planet. Apparently, they recognized that the Macros and the main body of the Earth fleet was the bigger threat. They stayed in orbit on the sunward side of the planet, facing any incoming attack from that angle.

The next part of the plan was tricky. *Socorro* rolled over and increased her speed dramatically. She dove toward the upper atmosphere of the gas giant.

I watched the other ships around me tensely. I only had a few seconds to wait. The entire force began to shift and swirl like a flock of birds, uncertain which direction it should go. Then, coming to a unanimous decision, the fleet flew up toward the northern pole. They were obviously going to try to intercept.

It was far too late, and they were far too slow. *Socorro* was accelerating at a shocking rate. All Nano ships were fast and maneuverable, but I was proud to see my design was superior to the original in this instance. She dove to the atmosphere, scudded along the surface of it, then began firing.

Her single gun blazed, stabbing down into the atmosphere. I knew she couldn't do any harm. The soupy gases would stop any beam from traveling more than a few miles into the interior. The Blues seemed to inhabit a zone thousands of miles deeper. But it didn't matter. The Nano ships had seen the action, and were sure to register it as an attack.

This was the part that left me sweating and uncertain. Up until this point, *Alamo* hadn't even mentioned the ongoing hostilities to me. The ship was flying with the rest of them, zooming for the far side of the gas giant to defend the planet. *Alamo* would never get there in time, of course, but futility had never stopped a Nano ship from trying.

I chuckled and sent my final transmission to *Socorro*. It was risky, as the Nano ships might be smart enough to realize they had a traitor amongst their command personnel. But I didn't think they would. Their AI only went so far.

Socorro broke off the attack, and slid out of the atmosphere. She glided around the planet's southern pole, leading the rest of the Nano ships on a merry chase. She didn't outrun them entirely. In fact, I'd programmed her to gently slow down throughout the journey. I wanted the Nano ships to calculate they were gaining on their quarry. Otherwise, they might lose interest and head back to their station over Eden-12.

But they didn't. They flew on directly toward the inner planets. I grinned ear to ear as I saw my plan unfold as I'd wished. There was only one problem now—they were following *Socorro* toward Eden-11, the Centaur homeworld. They'd marked my Earth fleet down as an enemy, since we were in control of the ship that had attacked.

I silently rode with the rest of them through space. After a few hours, a message came in from Rear Admiral Sarin.

"Colonel Riggs," she said with an excited ring to her voice. "There seems to be a large number of Nano ships behind you, heading toward my position. Can we assume these ships are friendly? Did you negotiate an alliance with the Blues?"

I grimaced. She had a big disappointment coming. I sighed and decided to answer her. She needed to know the truth. As my transmission would take an hour or two to flash across the void between worlds, so I made a full speech of it, explaining what had happened and what I had done. After I was finished, I played it back, made a few edits, then sent it.

I'd dozed off in my seat a few hours later when *Alamo* told me the response had come back in from the fine-looking admiral. I winced as I told the ship, "Play it."

"Riggs!" she shouted at me. "What the hell? You started another bloody war? I can't believe you. I'm not going to be a part of this. Earth is pulling out. I'm flying for the ring. Rear Admiral Sarin out."

This message grabbed my full attention. I was still more than a day from Eden-11. If she wanted, she could get her cruiser out of the way. I cursed and opened a channel. I needed every ship I had in on this one.

"Negative, Rear Admiral, I repeat, Negative. First of all, we are both 'Earth' forces. We are Star Force. As we discussed and you agreed, you are under my command while in this system, as long as I'm still alive. Crow isn't here, and you will take your orders from me."

I paused, but didn't send the message yet. I tried to think. "Jasmine," I said, softening my tone. "This is important. The Nano ships are chasing Socorro, who is running toward Eden-11. But that is not her final destination. She will veer off, and head toward a new target. You are hereby ordered to wait until Socorro makes her course shift, then leave orbit. You will take every Star Force ship we have with you. Load them all with marines for deployment as assault forces. I would suggest you don't accelerate too hard, as you don't want to outrun the Nanos."

Hoping against hope it would work, I sent the message. Then I waited. Just over an hour later the reply came back in.

"A new target? You have to be talking about the Macro stronghold, Eden-9. You are crazier than I thought. Miklos and I have been working out your strategy. We've been wargaming it through on the boards. I think now it is very clear what you are planning, and I must object. How can we hope to win this conflict? If both the Nano ships and the Macro ships are firing on us, how can we win a three-way battle? We are the weakest force in this system."

I smiled now, believing I had her. At the very least she was curious. I was encouraged that she hadn't mentioned running out on me once in the entire transmission.

"Rear Admiral," I said slowly, forcing myself to relax and speak in a confident voice. "I'm glad you've figured out my plan. You asked how we can win a three-way battle in this system—the answer to me is clear: by being the last one to the party. We will join the action after the battle has begun, and we will destroy whoever is left standing. Jasmine, we've fought together for years in space and planet-side. Let me win this my own way, the only way it can be won. Thanks in advance for your support. You have your orders. Riggs out."

I waited, trying not to sweat as the message traveled through emptiness to her ship, and she had time to digest it. No response came in for a long time. I began to worry. Many unpleasant scenarios went through my head. Was she trying to talk Welter and Miklos into joining her? Were they arguing—arresting one another? I was out of the loop, and it was agonizing.

I thought of a dozen things to transmit as another hour slipped by without a response. I recorded them, but when I listened to each statement afterward, I could only see that each one made me sound weak. I'd made my argument and given my orders. Prattling on and repeating myself would only remind people I wasn't there to enforce my words. Command at a long distance was an art form. I wasn't a master by any means, but I did know you didn't want to sound needy.

In the end, the answer didn't come in the form of a transmission. Instead, I witnessed things unfold directly. When *Socorro* made her banking course change and headed for Eden-9, the Star Force ships left orbit over Eden-11 and set out for the target world. All of them were moving, and all of them were flying with me into the teeth of the Macro fleet.

But even as I began to congratulate myself, a transmission came in from Sarin: "Colonel Riggs. You are not close enough to the forces to run this operation in real time. I request operational command."

I thought about it for a minute or so, scowling. She had a strong point. If the tactical situation changed dramatically, I could hardly call the shots from several million miles away. Finally, I transmitted my response. "All right, Jasmine. You've always wanted a command role in a pitched battle. Well, now you've got it. Show me what you can do. Good luck."

-36-

At first, the trick I'd played on the Nanos worked perfectly. It was hardly surprising. I'd pulled off similar deceptions in the past. These ships tended to be highly predictable. They had certain imperatives built into their software, and one of them was to attack threats immediately. This strategy worked well enough when the ships were in a single group, but when they were far apart and a threat was recognized, they would charge the enemy and arrive at different times. They were much easier to defeat that way, as it is always easier to fight three groups of ten ships at a time, rather than all thirty at once. We'd gotten around such problems back in the early days of Star Force by ordering the ships to attack distant targets, rather than the nearest ones. They accepted the order, as we were still attacking something. By switching targets, we were able to delay engaging with our ships until we were ready to mass up all our ships on a single target.

Their simplistic approach to tactics was a known weakness in the Nano ships. To fix the problem, the Blues had programmed them to pick up local command personnel to give them better ideas. That was how the whole business of kidnapping and testing people had started.

Right now, only one of the Nano ships had a commander—mine. For an experienced robot-baiter such as myself, it was a relatively easy matter to trick the ships into chasing *Socorro*. But I wasn't sure how it would all turn out in the end. I wasn't in direct command of this fleet, and I was forced to fly with them. When the moment of truth came, I hoped they would fight the Macros when they closed to within range. I wasn't certain they would engage, however. One complication

256

involved my own Star Force ships. We had to head toward the Macros now, and hit them soon after the Nano ships did in order to be most effective. If we waded into the battle too soon, the Nano ships might well start shooting at us instead of our joint enemy, the Macros. If we waited too long, the battle might be over before we arrived.

I sipped water in my ship and tried to relax while the final hours slid past. I wasn't sure if I would live to see another day, but at least I was going to have a front row seat for all the action. A message came in over the command channel from Star Force when I was about an hour from the Macro line. Up until this point, the enemy had not moved their cruisers. They sat parked in orbit over Eden-9. I was pretty sure they wouldn't stay there much longer.

"Colonel Riggs?" Miklos asked over a private channel. Our two fleets were close enough to talk with only a few seconds delay between transmissions.

"Miklos? What's up over there? I see your ships moving toward the enemy. Tell me everything is all right."

"Maybe sir, maybe. I'm calling about the local command structure. Rear Admiral Sarin has informed all the Fleet units she is in operational control of this action. Should I ignore her orders—or seek to remove her from command?"

I sat up straighter. "Negative, Miklos. That's not how I wish you to proceed. You will obey her tactical orders in the coming action. I'm too far out, and I might not survive in any case. Sarin is in a better position to run the battle than I am."

"But sir, please examine our formation. I don't think she knows what she's doing."

I ordered *Alamo* to bring up a detailed positional diagram of our fleet. I pursed my lips as I regarded it. Instead of leading with the new gunships, she had the destroyers and her own cruiser on the front line. Behind this group came a widely-spread formation of gunships.

"I'll talk to her," I told Miklos, and broke the connection.

I cursed for a while in private, getting it out of my system. When I thought I could stay calm and polite, I requested a private channel with Sarin. After a long minute or two, she answered me.

"What is it Colonel? I'm very busy right now."

"I'm sure you are. I wanted to go over the tactical formations with you, if you don't mind."

She hesitated. "Go over them? Are you suggesting you should take operational command again? I—"

"No," I said. "Not until you're dead or proven incompetent. But it always makes sense to discuss these things."

"All right, here's my plan. I've placed the laser armed ships on the front line, that way—"

"You do realize that the gunships have a much shorter effective range, right?"

"Of course," she said, sounding miffed. "As I was saying, if they fire missiles at us during our approach, I want to have our laser ships forward to shoot them down. Before we engage, the laser-armed ships will brake and fall back. The gunships will accelerate into the front line and we'll meet them with all our firepower maximized."

I thought about it, and I liked it. "That sounds pretty good, Sarin. Thanks for the update. Carry on."

"Thank you, Colonel," she said, sounding pleased and prideful.

As the last minutes rolled slowly by, I was squirming in my chair. I thought of a thousand reasons to contact Sarin and tell her to make adjustments. I resisted these urges with difficulty. The problem was, the enemy had not yet released the expected barrage of missiles. This variation from expected behavior didn't improve my mood. They had a plan, some kind of plan. They always did.

By the time we were closing in to tactical range, I had the nanites working overtime on the forward bulkhead. They depicted all three forces now as clusters of bumpy metal. The circle representing Eden-9 hung between us, under the watchful eye of the Macros, who had yet to move. Projected arcs showed the path the two attacking fleets were taking, and we were bearing down on the enemy fast. Two other groups of cruisers were coming this way too—but they would arrive after the battle had begun.

When the Macros finally made a move, we were all taken by surprise.

"Missile launch detected," Alamo said.

I stood up and eyed the front wall. A series of tiny slivers of metal appeared among the Macros.

"Target?" I asked.

"Insufficient data to project destination."

I paced, but never took my eyes off the forward screen. They could be firing at either of our fleets, or both of them. Less than a minute

258

later, I had my answer. By that time, I had a transmission waiting from Jasmine.

"What are they shooting at, sir?" she asked, forgetting to call me Colonel and lapsing back to the familiar "sir". It was the only bright spot in the conversation.

I didn't answer right away, as I didn't like what I thought I was seeing. In fact, I didn't want to witness it at all.

"I don't get it," Jasmine said. "They aren't firing toward either fleet, those missiles—oh, no…"

The projections were coming up on everyone's display now. The computers had calculated the course and destination unerringly.

On the big forward screen, the line was drawn between the missiles and their target. It was a very short line indeed. They had targeted the Centaur habitat. When faced with two incoming fleets, they'd chosen the third option—to engage in genocide.

"Why are they doing it, sir?"

"Watch the ships themselves. They're underway now."

The big cruisers had all fired up their engines in unison. They ponderously turned their pointed noses around and away from both oncoming fleets. They were leaving Eden-9.

Soon, the missiles struck. We'd put a lot of effort into building up laser turrets on each of the Centaur habitats, but the armament was insufficient to stop them all. The real problem was the habitats couldn't really take any hits. A ninety-percent defense wasn't good enough when the target was essentially a big balloon in space. Two missiles made it through, or at least got close enough to detonate themselves with devastating effect.

I was glad the sensory system was only a crude one built by nanites. The beads on my forward wall didn't show the graphic details. I didn't want to see the floating bodies freezing in space by the thousands. In this sort of situation, high-def video was overrated.

All the same, it was hard to watch millions of innocents die. Every time I'd gone through it, I felt nauseated slightly. This time was no different. I was numbed by the magnitude of the loss of life I was witnessing. I didn't feel any psychic scream or ripple of lost life force. What I felt was disgusted and angry. My hatred for the machines tripled on the instant. When I had the opportunity, I would root them out and dismantle them all. I'd said and thought these things before, of course. But I still felt the horror and rage as if it were fresh.

"They're gone, sir," Jasmine said.

"Yes."

"Was it our fault?"

"Maybe," I admitted. "But we can't do anything about that now. What we can do is win the coming battle."

"Battle? They're running, Colonel. Are we going to chase them?"

"Most definitely. We have a lot of built up velocity going for us. Even at maximum acceleration, I doubt the enemy can escape our two fleets now. But I don't think they plan to run from us for long."

"Why did they choose this option?"

"See the merging arcs? They are going to meet up with the rest of the cruisers coming from the inner planets."

Jasmine was quiet for a time. Finally, she sent another transmission. "I see it now, Colonel. They will turn and fight when they have their fleet amassed."

"Probably. Now, may I make a suggestion?"

"Certainly, Colonel."

"Don't keep flying straight at them. Take a detour. Maybe slingshot around behind Eden-9."

"Why would—oh, I see. You don't want our two fleets to come too close to one another."

"Exactly."

When we finally ran into the massed Macro cruisers, the Nano ships were still leading the charge. Actually, the first ship into the fight was none other than *Socorro*. I felt bad for the little ship. I'd had a lot of fun times aboard her, not the least of which was the scouting trip to the blue giant star system Sandra and I had taken long ago. I remembered the ship fondly right up until the moment the cruisers fired in unison. They used their big turrets, rather than their missiles. There was no need to waste ordnance on such an insignificant target.

Socorro dodged and weaved as she closed with them, just as I had told her to do. She couldn't shoot down the big chunks of flak coming her way, but she could get out of the way. The railguns were electromagnetic accelerators which used intense magnetic fields to push a ferrous mass to extreme velocities. The projectiles traveled only a fraction of the speed of a laser beam, but they struck with much greater kinetic force. Each pellet that struck home delivered a force like a high-yield bomb.

Socorro fired as she closed in with the cruisers—but not at the cruisers themselves. Instead, she fired behind her at the following Nano ships. I'd given her those orders. I wanted to make sure none of the Nanos got any bright ideas about reversing course at the last moment.

Eventually, the tiny ship's luck ran out. A hit was scored, and she went into a spin. A moment later, the ship came apart and turned into a hail of fragments. I tensed, watching the reactions of both the Macros and the Nanos. Would they fire upon one another?

The first change was in my own ship. *Alamo* hit the brakes—hard. I stumbled forward and had to reach out with a gauntleted hand to keep from slamming into the forward wall. The stabilizers worked overtime, but it wasn't enough. The ship was trying to do a U-turn. The Nanos had destroyed their target, and now planned to return to their defensive station over the Blues' homeworld.

The Macros, bless their iron hearts, had different ideas. From their point of view, I could hardly blame them. What they saw was an odd charge by a mass of Nano ships. The fact that the charge had been led by a single one of their number, which was inexplicably firing at its fellows, didn't matter. What caused them to act was the proximity of the threat.

The Nano ships were also screwed by their relative velocity. They were too close to the Macros and going too fast. They braked hard, but it wasn't enough. We slid closer and closer to the Macro fleet. Warning chimes and statements rang through the ship.

"Incoming projectiles," said the ship calmly. "Command personnel must be returned to their designated stations."

I surmised the ship meant I was supposed to get my butt back into the crash seat. I took a step toward it, but found a half-dozen skinny metal arms were grabbing me. They attempted to manhandle me back to my seat and restrain me from falling as the G-forces grew more powerful.

I became instantly annoyed and struggled with the nanite arms. I'd done so in the past on a number of occasions. But the relationship between flesh and metal had always been reestablished in their favor.

This time was different. I was wearing an exoskeletal battle suit which magnified my strength—but more than that, I'd changed. I was no longer a simple nanotized marine having a temper tantrum. I'd taken seven baths in Marvin's strange pools of Microbes. They'd rebuilt me, and altered my body on a cellular level.

I ripped loose one nanite arm, then two more. It was being caught by vines. I snapped them, uprooted them, and kept walking. With three ripped-loose arms writhing and whipping around my ankles, I stomped to my chair and sat in it under my own power. The arms eventually reattached themselves to the ship's deck and were reabsorbed when they realized I'd returned to my station.

The battle was underway by this time. Thirty-one cruisers were firing masses of high-velocity projectiles into the Nano ship line. This could not be ignored. I didn't know yet if any of the Nanos had been hit.

"Alamo," I said, "Give me an announcement whenever one of our ships is hit by the enemy."

"Which enemy are you referring to, Colonel Riggs?"

"Any enemy!"

"Nineteen ships have been hit in the last seven minutes."

I frowned. That sounded like a lot of hits. "By missiles or projectiles?" I asked. "Give me a breakdown."

"Three ships were hit by missiles and sixteen by projectiles."

I nodded, and was about to ask *Alamo* what it was going to do about this aggression, but there was no need. The forward screen displayed the answer clearly. The Nano ships had stopped braking. They were heading right into the enemy lines now, and they were all firing.

I felt the deck shudder and shiver under my armored butt. The ship was firing its guns, both the top and bottom turrets. I took this moment to allow myself a grim smile. The machines were destroying each other all around me. The only bad part was my own position, which was right at the center of it all.

I shrugged and drew in a deep breath. It was a small sacrifice to make if all these metal bastards destroyed one another.

-37-

The battle was—huge. I'd never been involved in an action that involved more ships. There were about three hundred Nanos, thirty-odd Macro cruisers and our own Earth fleet of about fifty vessels. Most of ours were gunships with big cannons and little else. We were by far the weakest force on the game board, except for my secret weapon: squads of assaulting marines.

The first phase of the battle was the hardest on my mind. I wanted to shout orders, to get the Nano ships to coordinate. Unfortunately, they weren't interested in my opinions. Only *Alamo* listened, and hung back at the rear of the pack.

The fireworks began as the Nano ships reached maximum range and began peppering the bigger ships with laser beams. Right away, I was annoyed with their lack of command control. They didn't all fire on a single ship and pound it until it went down. Instead, ten or so chose each front-rank cruiser and began needling it at long range. It was a losing strategy, because it gave the enemy more time to fire in return.

I couldn't control the Nano ships. All I could do was watch. The worst part was when the Macros launched a flood of missiles. The Nanos didn't switch targets to these incoming threats immediately. They stuck with their long-range pecking, which I knew was only scarring up the hulls of the thick-skinned cruisers. The two sides were closing in on one another, but serious damage wouldn't be done until they got into short range. That was not true of the missiles, however. A nuclear warhead detonated with the same force, no matter how far it was from its launching ship.

I pounded deep dents into the metal arm of my command chair. Gently, the smart metal reformed itself, pushing my gauntlet back out of the way. I was raving. Only *Alamo* was firing on the incoming missiles. Finally, snarling, I stood up and headed to the airlock. I'd waited too long already.

I bailed out of the airlock not even allowing it to cycle the oxygen back into the ship and thus keep it for some future biotic pilot. I used the puff of gas to give me the initial shove out into space. I spun for a second or two, until I was sure I was safely away from the ship's hull. *Alamo* was moving erratically, dodging incoming bolts of hot metal that moved at tremendous velocity. The enemy had started firing their big guns long ago, and although there was little chance of them scoring a hit at this range, *Alamo* was taking no chances.

I used my repellers to halt my spin, then rolled on my back and watched as the ship that had starred in all my nightmares shrank away to nothing. In moments, it was swallowed by blackness. I felt a mix of emotions as I watched it go. I was reminded of a time I'd sold an old car which I hated, but somehow still felt an attachment to.

The yellow star shone on my visor, splashing it with bright glaring light. I hustled, flying toward the projected path of Earth's fleet. With luck, I'd be close enough for them to scoop me up as they joined this mess.

As I flew I had a few minutes to contemplate what I'd started. Around me, space appeared to be empty. Even more than battles at sea, battles in space were so spread out you could be in the middle of one and barely notice. But appearances were deceiving. The combat around me would determine the fate of billions.

I thought about the Centaurs in the big habitat that had sagged down to Eden-9 in a fiery heap. Quite possibly, it had been the largest single loss of life I'd ever seen. An estimated twenty million were dead—and that was only a guess. The count could have been much higher, as we'd never numbered the herds. They didn't think in terms of individuals and body counts. They had no census data to present us with. I supposed the exact number of dead didn't really matter. In the end, the species would live on or be snuffed out. But I was certain there were no herds to return to Eden-9 and graze upon the fine grasslands.

When I thought about the Centaurs and how I'd dragged them back into a hot war with me, it was hard not to think of the Blues as well. They were in the mud with us now. Their peace agreement, whatever it was, had to be null and void after the actions of the Nano fleet. From the point of view of the Macros, the Blues had just launched an all out attack upon them. I smiled grimly inside my helmet at the thought. They had some skin in this game now.

I felt no remorse for including them in our misery. I could have respected their desire for neutrality, if they hadn't caused this entire conflict in the first place. I didn't hate the Blues, but I sure didn't want them sitting out the festivities. They were front and center now. If we lost, so did they. Earth had never asked to be dragged into an interstellar war, but if we were going down, the Blues were going down with us.

A flash darkened my visor, and my smile disappeared. I could tell it came from behind me. I began to swivel my helmet, looking back, when a dozen more violent flashes turned my visor black. I turned back and stared ahead, urging more speed from my repellers. A wave of missiles must have reached the Nano ship line. They were detonating, and probably taking Nano ships out with each blast.

I activated my com-link and tried to connect to the command channel. Up until now, I'd been on radio-blackout. There was no sense giving any of these ships a target. But now, I needed to know if I was in the right zone to be picked up.

"This is Colonel Kyle Riggs, requesting pick-up. I'll be listening for your instructions, but will not respond. Repeat, will not respond. Ending transmission and taking evasive action...now."

I closed the transmitting half of the channel, and immediately dodged at various angles for ten miles or so. In space, a few miles would only be a round-off error, but it might be enough to get me out of the way of a missile with an eager Macro pilot.

Less than a minute later, dispatch came on. The voice was shockingly familiar. It was Sandra. "Kyle we have you. Stay in that general vicinity, but accelerate toward the battle. You need to speed up. Right now, we're going too fast in relative speed to pick you up. You'd splatter on our windshield like a bug."

I felt a strong urge to reply, but resisted it. I was surprised it was Sandra running dispatch—but I shouldn't have been. On a Star Force ship, everyone had a job to do. Sandra had only really had experience with two duties: communications and serving as my bodyguard. I supposed I shouldn't have been surprised that she'd passed on the job of protecting Jasmine.

I turned directly toward the battle and poured on the power. For several nerve-racking minutes I sped closer to the fighting ships. I knew that at any instant, something could loom up out of the darkness and end my existence. It made me squint and grit my teeth.

When the fleet finally did catch up to me, it came as a shock. I was barely aware of their approach. All I sensed was a darkening of the region of space behind me—then something struck me. My visor starred, and the generator on my back was dented inward. It stopped working, and my repellers died.

The shock was so great, I think I might have died as well if I hadn't been armored, nanotized and bathed by flesh-hardening Microbes. As it was, it felt as if my spine had been pulled out of my skin. It wasn't until they began reeling me in and I regained my full faculties that I understood that a big nanite hand had reached down from the ship's belly and plucked me out of space. I was pulled up into an airlock and dumped on the deck. Air pumped into the chamber, and when a chime signaled the all clear, I ripped off my helmet. I rolled over twice on the deck, groaning and gasping.

"Did you have to hit me that hard?"

"I'm surprised you're alive, Colonel," Jasmine said.

I looked up at her, blinking. She had a gun in her hand, and it was pointing at my face. She didn't look happy.

"Tougher than a cockroach. That's what Crow says."

"He's right."

"Are you arresting me or executing me, Rear Admiral?" I asked.

She looked troubled at that. "This is my ship."

"I'm aware of that."

"You dragged me into this war of yours, and you haven't finished it. Instead, you expanded it."

"A fair assessment. We needed allies to win. Did you happen to notice the three hundred extra ships out there? The ones leading the charge?"

Jasmine licked her lips. "On this ship, I'm in command."

"You said that already." Groaning, I got up and reached for my helmet. I poked at the visor. Nanites were working at the cracks, but it was going to take a while for them to effect full repairs. My generator

266

might take hours to fix itself. I was surprised I could move at all in the exoskeletal suit without power. I supposed I was considerably stronger than I used to be.

As I climbed to my feet, she backed up warily. I had a sudden thought. "Where's Sandra?" I asked.

"She's been neutralized."

I frowned. "I don't like euphemisms, Sarin. Sandra knew I was going to be picked up by *Goa*. She's your com officer. What have you done with her?"

"She'll be fine. You will both be released after this battle is over."

Sarin reached down and picked up my helmet. She kept the gun on me, and eyed me suspiciously. I thought of several ways I could attack her, even with an unpowered suit. They were all risky and one of us was likely to end up dead or seriously injured.

"So you are proceeding with the battle? I thought you were running out on me. Why all this drama, if you are following my plans anyway?"

"I'm not," she said. "I'm going to hang back and attack after the Nano ships have all been destroyed—or the Macros have. Whichever survives, I'll step in to finish the other. We're braking hard even now."

I couldn't feel it, but I believed her. This ship had excellent stablizers. I thought about her plan, and I didn't like it. The Nanos were weak without good command and control. They couldn't be trusted to win the battle on their own. I shook my head.

"A losing strategy, Jasmine. I don't know what's gotten into you, but you need to respect my authority and experience on this one."

"I'm not going to lose this ship to save a bunch of Nano rogues!"

"That's why you're doing this?" I asked. "Because you love your first command so much?"

"I am following my orders. That's all."

"This is mutiny."

"No, sir. You are the one who ignored orders and stayed out here, leaving Earth exposed. Star Force is not all about you, Colonel."

I thought about that. "Crow really did a number on you. What else did he tell you to say?"

"Think of the Centaurs, Kyle. Think of the millions back home. I had relatives in Miami, did you know that?"

"No," I admitted. "But I had two children the day these ships came rolling in over Earth. They were gutted and died before my eyes."

267

Jasmine shook her head. "I'm sorry. Don't worry about this, Colonel. I'm just going to leave you here for another hour. No more. My apologies. This is a Fleet ship and a Fleet decision."

Then she backed out of the hold and left me standing there. I looked around and touched the bulkhead—it didn't open. The control panel on the floor activated, but that led out into open space. And I was no longer wearing even a damaged helmet. She had taken it with her.

I cursed and kicked the walls until my boots left deep dents. Too bad they weren't permanent. What was it with my highest ranking officers and disloyalty? Did everyone have to question my authority at every stage? I would have called it mutiny, but she was technically Fleet.

I thought about what she'd said. I supposed I could have made a few mistakes along the way in the Eden system. I might have been able to keep the Centaurs breathing if I'd made different choices.

I did some hard thinking over the next several minutes. I was pissed off, but I tried to look past that. I knew Jasmine had some good points. I was hard to deal with—I'm sure every skilled, opinionated commander was. It was the very qualities of leadership and self-reliance that made me a success she was struggling with. I supposed that meek Colonels were never locked into holds—but they probably didn't win as many battles, either.

My first thought was to ride it out. If she wanted to win it her way, fine. I'd play along with her. After all, we should be able to take out the cruisers. It was likely the Nanos would all be destroyed, but the Macros would be so damaged they couldn't defeat us. All in all, it didn't sound so bad.

But I didn't like it. The Nanos hadn't been impressing me with their tactics. When the Macros fired missiles, they retreated, shooting them down one by one. When they advanced again, they stayed too far away and weren't concentrating their fire. Every time this cycle was repeated, they lost more ships to the few missiles that got through and the relentless hail of railgun fire. The Nanos might well be annihilated, and then we'd have a full-fledged battle on our hands. In the end, we'd lose more ships and marines if we didn't support the Nanos. Sarin was trying to take the safe route, but I felt she was taking the more dangerous one.

I decided to act. Part of me wondered if I was just fabricating worries in order to give me an excuse to not sit out a battle, but I honestly didn't think so. I had a headache, and taking a break in a quiet hold didn't sound too bad right about now. But it wasn't going to happen that way. My mind had run the odds, and I didn't like the projections for this conflict. I felt I had to get involved.

My suit was spitting sparks, but the nanites in it were still active. I ordered them to form a film over my exposed head and I ripped two clear plastic covers off my dog tags. These I put over my eyes. When held by a sheet of nanites, they would serve as half-assed goggles.

I coaxed a very thin film of silvery nanites into crawling their way over my face, making my scalp itch horribly. When they'd managed to link up with each other, forming a surface rather like a bubble of mercury, I tried to get them to hold my makeshift plastic eyeholes into place. I was only partly successful, and could only see out of one eye. I decided it would have to do, as I didn't have much time.

There was only one way out of the hold, so I didn't stand around overthinking the situation. I activated the outer hatch on the hold. I was almost blown out into space by the explosive decompression. Fortunately, I managed to latch one hand onto the edge of the hatchway. When the gas had all escaped, I engaged my magnetics and crawled along the surface of the ship toward the prow.

I'd only gone fifty feet or so before I saw something on the hull. At first, I thought perhaps it was a gun turret or a sensor array. It was black, and consisted of a crouching spray of what looked like wires sprouting from its back.

Then it moved and turned to regard me.

I froze, staring. It crept forward. Frantically, I executed my reentry plan. The exterior of nanite-hulled ships were mostly smart metal, and they had generally been programmed to respond to certain stimuli. On most hulls, the regions that served as hatchways were designated when the ship was built. But really, any section of the hull could be breached. We did this every day when we tossed trash on the decks and watched them bubbled up and swallow it, expelling it out into space.

I simply tricked the ship into doing the reverse. By dialing up a menu and tapping at the right options, I was able to push one arm inside the vessel. It felt like I was trying to swim my way through a plastic bag.

269

The thing on the outside of the ship figured out what I was up to. It sped up and scuttled closer. I saw more movement off to either side. There were several of these things crawling over the ship toward me.

Then the nanite hull went soft, and I was swallowed completely. I found myself inside the ship. I was in what looked like the medical unit. Tiny black arms dangled down from the ceiling. As I came near, they reached for me and made fluttering contact. They wanted to know if I was injured and seeking aid. I pushed the blind little hands away in irritation.

Gasping for breath and feeling half-frozen, I tore the thin film of nanites from my face. They dribbled away back into my suit. I'd been barely able to breathe in there, as my suit was still dead. I stared back at the wall I'd passed through. I had no idea what those things outside were—but they didn't look friendly. Could there be another force in operation in this system? A group of spacefaring creatures we'd yet to discover?

I exited medical into a central passageway. I marched toward the prow. The bridge had to be up here somewhere. On the way, I met up with an Ensign who looked like a kid. His eyes bulged in recognition and he reached for his com-link. I didn't have time to explain things to him, or whoever he was calling. I swept up one gauntleted fist. It connected firmly with his chin and he did a backflip.

I frowned down at the crumpled form. I was pretty sure I'd broken his neck. It occurred to me I was *definitely* stronger than I had been before Marvin's baths. I couldn't blame the suit, as it was just dead weight on my body.

I checked his pulse—it was light, but still there. Good thing he'd been nanotized. His cells could be repaired in time. I left him to his dreams and moved on up the passage to a big hatchway. I straight-armed it and the metal melted away.

Sarin stood on the deck, with three other officers.

"Captain Sarin," I shouted. "We have a problem. Are you aware there are enemy hostiles on the outer hull of this vessel?"

They were surprised, to say the least. Every eye bulged upon seeing me, and every jaw sagged open. Jasmine found her voice first.

"My rank is that of Rear Admiral, Colonel Riggs. I demand—"

"Not anymore," I said, gesturing with the beam pistol I'd removed from the unconscious Ensign in the passageway. "Consider yourself demoted."

-38-

I disarmed the rest of the bridge crew without any heroics on their part. It was a good thing for them, as I wasn't in the best mood. My battle suit was dead, but they were only wearing light Nano suits. Their hand beamers couldn't even hurt me unless they went for a headshot—and none of them had even dared to draw on me. Sometimes, having a bad rep worked in a man's favor.

I had the newly demoted Captain Sarin order Sandra's release and summoned her to the bridge immediately. Once Sandra showed up, I handed her my gun and got down to the business of running the battle.

When Sandra had figured out that Jasmine and I had had a disagreement over who was in charge and I'd asserted my authority, she seemed pleased. Anything that drove Jasmine and I apart was a good thing in Sandra's book.

This bridge was set up in an entirely new arrangement. In the center of the large circular chamber was a globe of glass. I didn't get it at first—but after I took a look, I realized it was a tank full of what had to be a fine, floating mist of nanites. They had an ability I hadn't thought of before—the power to light up. By forming clusters, they could illuminate themselves in different colors. These pinpricks of light displayed the relative position of all the ships in the local region of space. Both our vessels and those of the enemy formations were represented.

"This thing is pretty cool," I said, tapping at the sphere.

"I'm glad you approve," Sarin said coldly.

The sphere was about eight feet in diameter and all of us sat around it, looking at it. There were no actual windows on the bridge. The walls were solid, opaque metal. But we didn't really need windows. Everyone had a screen in front of their chair and sat encircling the sphere, which showed the big picture. On the touch screens at every station, I was quickly able to bring up images of any ship in the fleet, or any other sensory or logistical data I needed.

"This can't be Crow's work," I said. "Who came up with this design?"

"I did," Sarin said. She still wasn't looking at me.

"Wow, this is really excellent. No wonder he promoted you. I can see the true purpose of this vessel now. It's a flagship, isn't it? A central command vessel. I've always wanted a ship like this."

Jasmine still didn't look pleased. I supposed it would take more than a few compliments to patch things up between us. At least neither of us had punched the other. I hoped the disagreement could be worked out in the future. She hadn't done anything worse than some of the tricks Crow had pulled in the past. I figured that in time, we might be able to work together again. I also decided some of this command-and-control structure needed to be hammered out and agreed to by all parties. We weren't just a bunch of pirates anymore. A military that didn't clearly know who was in charge at all times was a weakling force. I would have to write a document and get everyone to sign onto it. But all that would have to wait until we survived our current predicament.

I worked on the display system, and soon found two critical control touch-points on the screen in front of me. I tapped them both in sequence as soon as I found them. The first brought up an external view of the ship, and the second one projected what was on my screen inside the central sphere for everyone to see.

Sandra was the first to notice the alien forms on the hull and she gasped. "What the hell are those things?"

"Some new kind of enemy, I'm guessing," I said.

Captain Sarin stared in disbelief. "These things are crawling on the outer hull? How many?"

"Check all the cameras. Do a count."

For the first time, the bridge crew around me moved with urgency rather than surly discontent. There was nothing like a new deadly threat to get everyone back into line.

"I've found seventeen on *Goa*," Jasmine said after a few minutes. "So far, there is no indication they've breached the ship's hull. What are we going to do about them?"

"First, alert the rest of the fleet. Every ship should check its external hull for crawlers."

Jasmine did as I asked, working her carefully designed screens like the expert she was. My next order wasn't obeyed so quickly, however.

"Now, order the fleet to accelerate," I said. "We'll stay in formation, but I want every bit of speed we can get out of the group as a whole."

She stared at me. "Why?"

"Two reasons," I said. "First of all, the G-forces might dislodge some of these things we have on the hull. Secondly, we need to get into the battle as soon as possible."

Up until that point, Captain Sarin had been braking, slowing the fleet's approach to the conflict. This was a reversal of her plan to come in third and clean up. She looked angry and confused.

"Shouldn't we at least take these things off our hull first? Maybe we could close formation and shoot them off one another with laser fire."

"Not a bad idea, but we don't have time. We need to get to the fight before the Nanos are all destroyed."

"Getting them all destroyed was part of my plan," she said. She took a deep breath, and I knew she was going to try to reason with me.

"Look, Kyle, if we wade in too early, we might be forced to fire on Nano ships. Those ships are owned by the Blues. They might take it as an act of war, meaning we've gotten into an expanded conflict. But if the enemy are all destroyed by the Macros, they can't complain."

I listened, but didn't look at her. "Relay the order, then I'll explain," I said.

Sarin only hesitated a second, but that was all it took. Sandra stepped up behind her. Her stance was predatory, threatening. I could tell she want to do something bad to Jasmine. She'd been wanting that for a long time.

Jasmine glanced at her. "What are you going to do if I won't obey? Kill me?"

"No," Sandra said. "A single smashing blow to the head worked fine last time."

The two women glared at each other. I tapped at my display, and showed everyone what I'd been working on. It really was a pleasure to work with Jasmine's system. The woman had quite a mind for building battle system interfaces. I supposed she should, as she had more experience operating tactical displays than anyone else in Star Force.

Inside the sphere between us, three groups of lights gleamed. The Macros had the smallest number of ships. Displayed in red, each of their cruisers was represented by a wedge-shaped object. The Nano ships were yellow, and they were specks of light in comparison. Most of our ships were small and light green, except for the spoon-shaped light cruiser we flew in. I zoomed in on the Nano fleet. They'd moved close enough to be in laser range of the cruisers now, and were firing randomly at whatever ship they could reach.

"Have we got a counter for these guys going?"

Jasmine brought it up, and it displayed 167 in yellow numerals. We all stared.

"They had over three hundred ships," one of the commanders said.

"Not anymore. We'll be lucky if there are any left at all by the time we get into range. Check the cruiser numbers now."

The red readout told the tale. There were still twenty-nine active cruiser. The Nanos were getting slaughtered.

"I don't understand why they are so ineffective," Jasmine said. "We've wargamed this out for days. They should not die like flies out there—"

"The trouble is," I said, "Nano ships are not good at tactics. I'd hoped they would do better, but they aren't up to it. They are explorers, and were never designed as a military force. Like a mob, they don't fight well. The Macros have learned how to do it better, they are the soldiers. The Nanos need our help."

"What about the things crawling over our hull? Are you just going to ignore them?"

"You have a few squads of marines aboard, don't you?" I asked.

Jasmine nodded. Both she and Sandra were looking at me now, with big, worried eyes.

"You leave those crawling things to me," I said.

"You'll be exposed," Sandra complained immediately. "We're sailing into a battle, and the G-forces alone might tear you off the ship and send you into the exhaust."

275

I shrugged. "If we lose our grip on the hull, my marines know how to use their repellers. We can escape. We might even be able to catch up."

Captain Sarin nodded at last.

Sandra didn't like the plan, but she nodded too. "I'll go with you," she said.

"No Sandra, I need you to keep an eye on things in here."

Jasmine looked at me with an odd expression that took a moment to decipher. Was she feeling guilty, thoughtful, or insulted? I suspected it was a little of all three.

"You don't have to leave us under guard, sir," she said. "I apologize for trying to keep you off this bridge. It's clear your strategic thinking was ahead of my own. I should not have—disagreed with your orders."

I smiled. "I accept your apology, Captain. Let's forget about it for now. I take some responsibility for the, uh, confusion. Crow and I really have to hammer out a command structure for campaigns on distant fronts. In part, you were a victim of our lack of organization. We're still experiencing growing pains as a military outfit. I imagine many militaries of the past have gone through just such disagreements. In fact, I recall reading about a number of similar conflicts concerning who was in charge of whom back in the colonial era—"

"Sir?" a Commander asked. "I think the things on the hull are making their move. Whatever they are."

I gestured urgently at him, and he transferred his screen to the sphere between us all. We all frowned at the image that coalesced inside. The things on the ship had clustered now at the rear of the ship. They were near the base of one of the three big engines. I saw a flaring light emission.

"Whatever they are, they are apparently no longer content with riding on the outer hull. They are burning their way in."

"Maybe they don't like our acceleration. They are barely moving around out there."

I nodded. "Does anyone have a spare helmet? I'm going to need it."

A midshipman led me toward the aft of the ship. Along the way, we passed the crumpled form of the Ensign I'd bashed on my way to the bridge.

"What happened to him?" the Midshipman asked. "Are those things inside now?"

"Nah," I said. "I was in a bad mood when I first came aboard. He'll sleep it off."

The Midshipman gave me a wide-eyed stare, which I ignored. He led me to the troop pods and left me there. He vanished back down the passage quickly, glancing over his shoulder as if I might run him down and kill him.

I took a deep breath and touched the hatchway that led into the troop pods. It dissolved, revealing a number of surprised-looking marines. They were playing cards, and they all froze for a second when they saw me. The moment of shock passed and they all jumped to their feet.

I walked inside and began shouting orders. Within four minutes, I had a squad ready to head out the hatches. I wished Kwon was with me, but he was still aboard Miklos' ship. They'd all been warned about the things that might be lurking on their hulls. I suspected Kwon was knocking heads and leading a team outside to investigate by now, just as I was.

I'd taken just long enough to change out my generator unit and snap on a fresh helmet. I was glad they had spare equipment. *Goa* was so big there was plenty of storage space for such extras.

I pulled down a fresh helmet, heard the click and hiss of it locking into place, and smiled. The smell was different—very plastic and clean. In a way, I kind of liked it. After a moment the HUD activated and flashed all green bars. I was good to go.

"Okay men, I'll take point. Follow me out onto the hull then spread out. Keep your magnetics on full when you walk out there, as we will be experiencing several Gs of acceleration."

I climbed out the sally portal and was instantly struck by a wall of force. On my hands and knees, I dragged myself over the hull, heading aft toward the engines. It was like having a stiff tailwind that was so strong it almost knocked me over.

"On second thought," I transmitted to my men, "don't even try to stand up. Just stay low, and crawl like they do."

I paused as I saw an unexpected result of my transmission. The things that had clustered around the base of the engine strut reacted to my words. They spread out, shuffling like crabs. There couldn't be any doubt about it, they'd *heard* me.

About then, the engine they'd been messing with stuttered. Its output had been interrupted. The blue exhaust plume flashed on and off three times—then went out entirely.

The ship lurched under my hands. Since the engine had quit the other two were now out of balance. They were pushing the ship off-course.

"They've damaged engine number three," a Staff Sergeant told me. "What should we do, sir?"

I glanced around me, about half the squad had come out to join me.

"Blast them," I said.

The flashes began, and the enemy reacted in a predictable fashion: they fired back.

It had been a long time since I'd been in a firefight on the hull of moving ship. It was even less fun than I'd remembered. My guts were in a knot. There was no real cover out here, and we were at close range. Only the lurching of the ship was providing any distraction, screwing up everyone's aim.

Overall, the crawlers seemed better at aiming under these conditions than we did. Within the first thirty seconds, two marines went twirling off into space. One was struggling with his repellers to return to the ship. The other was spinning and limp.

"Concentrate your fire!" I shouted. "Noncoms mark your targets. I want three beams on every crawler until it dies."

We fried two of them, but then lost another marine. This one stayed clamped onto the hull. His magnetics still worked, but the rest of him flopped and waved with the G-forces like a flag in the wind.

"Call up squad two. Use the starboard sally port. We need more firepower!"

More men crawled around me. A bolt struck me in the shoulder. There was a gouge in my nice new helmet, too. I thought they must have hit an air tube, as the interior of my battle suit had a hot, melted plastic smell to it.

With better tactics and a wider spread of men, we began to drive them back. Our greatest advantage was our superior numbers. More marines kept coming out onto the hull, while the enemy's number was finite.

Finally, they must have realized they weren't going to win this one. As a group, they sprang up into space. I watched as they floated away quickly behind the ship. We all fired after them, but they were gone in a second and we hit nothing.

Crawling forward, we inspected the damaged engine and I ordered the men to repair what they could. If they could get the third engine running again, we'd be in a much better state to enter the next stage of the battle.

I was fortunate enough to discover something else other than twisted, blackened metal at the base of the engine mount. I found one of the enemy, with its crab-like feet caught in the hole they'd been burning into.

It was then that I finally realized what we were up against.

-39-

"They are Macros," I said, dragging the crab-like corpse onto the command deck. I threw it down in the middle of the command staff. Its pointed feet rattled and clattered on the deck.

Sandra came close and knelt over it. "Disgusting."

"No doubt about it. A new type of Macro. Something that crawls over the surface of our ships. Clearly, they were trying to break in or sabotage the ship. But what I can't understand is why we've never seen these before."

"Sir, we are in range now," Captain Sarin informed me. "I'm assuming we should only fire on the Macro cruisers?"

I waved at her dismissively. "Yeah, of course. Choose a target and burn it out of space. One at a time."

She glanced at me, but I continued examining the mess of metal I had found. It was coated with some kind of black resin, and it was smaller than any Macro I'd ever seen. The six legs were insect-like, but the head-section was bulbous.

I glowered at it, baffled. Where had this thing come from? Had the Macros designed something new, or had they used these small individual units in other conflicts we were unaware of? Maybe we'd never had the bad luck to run into one before, but I didn't think that was it. These were newly-constructed.

A thought struck me then. I slowly came to the conclusion they were aping our tactics. The more I thought about it, the more concerned I became.

Around me, the rest of the bridge crew fought a fleet battle. But I stayed focused on the thing I'd dragged back into the ship. It was about the size of man. I lifted it, weighing it in my gauntlets. It had a similar weight, being made of lighter metals and polymers. It had six limbs rather than our four—but two of the legs were armed with lasers. I found the repellers next—buried in four of the six appendages.

I frowned fiercely at the thing in my hands. Our most recent battle suit design had been equipped in exactly this way. I shook my head. I was coming to a single inescapable conclusion, and I didn't like it.

"They're copying us," I said. "Copying our tactics and unit design."

Most of the bridge crew was staring at the sphere in our midst. They were barely listening to me. But that was all right. I was listening to myself. To me, it was clear: the Macros had attempted to build their own version of Star Force Marines. Assault troops that came out of the dark without making any emissions to track them by. Lightly-armed, they weren't much trouble in small numbers, but if they came out of the dark at us like quiet stealth attackers, they could be dangerous.

Then I had another thought. It was a very worrisome one. "Commander!" I roared.

The man nearest me jumped half out of his suit. At least he gave me his full attention.

"Grab the other end of this thing!" I roared. "Sandra, you help too. We've got to get if off this ship now!"

The Commander wasn't a marine, but he did know how to obey orders. A few seconds later, he and Sandra were helping me run with the clanking multi-legged carcass as we carried it to the nearest airlock. It wasn't as close as I would have liked. It was about a hundred steps away. I took flight to speed things up, using my repellers inside the ship, which was a safety violation. I half-dragged the other two who bumped along behind me.

"What's wrong, Kyle?" Sandra asked.

"It's a bomb," I said. "At least, I think it is."

Neither of them dragged their feet after that. We tossed it into the airlock and slapped the emergency release. The outer door disintergrated into a shower of nanites, and the black, twisted form of the Macro flipped and twirled away. It looked like a bundle of black chains being tossed out into the void.

I hit my com-link and connected to Sarin. "Veer sunward. Immediately. That's an order."

The ship heeled over and we all leaned into the outer bulkhead. The dead machine vanished quickly. Several long seconds passed as we looked out a tiny window in the airlock. Sandra and the Commander stood next to me, breathing hard. We all tried to look at once, but we could no longer see the thing we'd jettisoned.

Then there was a glaring flash. It shook the ship slightly. It felt like being hit by a gust of wind in a car on a stormy highway. The ship swayed and corrected.

"We've just gotten our allotment of rads for the year, I suspect," I said.

"Did it self-destruct?"

"Yes," I said. "Just the way my marines do sometimes—when they have nothing else left with which to hurt the enemy."

I rushed back to the bridge and alerted Miklos to the danger. He told me he already knew something like that was going on. The lurking enemy had not fought terribly well, but they had destroyed several ships by blowing themselves up. Everyone was soon informed—they were not to take aboard any damaged machines to study. That was apparently just what they wanted.

I rubbed at my bristly chin as the fleet battle began in earnest. It was strange to look at the ships depicted inside the sphere. Hundreds were dying on every side, I felt sure of it. Biotics versus machines. We had become like them, and they had adapted as well, using our own tactics against us.

The first stage of the battle was ending. We'd made contact with the enemy, and the Macros were beginning to turn their attention to this new attacker. Jasmine was in charge, and I let her call the shots for now. Her plan was sound, it always had been. The only thing I'd disagreed with was the timing of our entry into the conflict. I'd demanded that we charge in early, but now that we were engaged and mixing it up, everyone was on the same page. We were all fighting to survive and doing our damnedest to destroy the enemy.

As the next stage of the battle unfolded, our gunships rolled forward, accelerating even as the destroyers and our single light cruiser pulled back. We were now in effective range of the enemy railguns. We pushed our own cannons up front to meet fire with fire. The second reason for the pull back was relative velocity. The destroyers each carried marines, and we couldn't launch them at the enemy cruisers if we didn't match our relative velocities first.

In the back of my mind, I kept worrying about the Macros and what they were up to. They had clearly been impressed with our tactic of throwing marines at enemy ships. They'd tried to build and operate their own units in a similar fashion. It showed a larger capacity to learn than I'd given them credit for in the past. I'd rarely seen them adapt so effectively. I didn't like seeing it now, and hoped never to see this kind of flexibility in their methods again.

Essentially, their copycat assault troops had been a failure. They'd had the upper hand, but had misplayed their new assets. They'd reached our ships, crawled secretly over the hulls and once the battle had begun they'd tried to damage the vessels they rode upon. All of this made sense. But they'd ignored the simple expedient of blowing themselves up. They were just machines, after all. They could have all set themselves off on the outer hull of every ship, once they'd reached their targets.

Why hadn't they done precisely that? It was something of a mystery. The best theory I could come up with was they were aping our tactics as well as our units. When we reached an enemy hull, we didn't simply commit suicide by blowing up our generators. Possibly, that would have been a very effective tactic. But we'd tried to survive instead. Maybe they'd imitated our methods *too* closely, not realizing that we did some things because it was in our nature to do so, not because they were the very best tactical move.

The more I thought about it, I realized we really did have a potent weapon that we'd barely employed. Every marine had the power to overload his generator and blow a hole in any ship, provided he made it inside or at least was in contact with the hull. But it had never really occurred to me to fight that way. It hadn't occurred to my men, either. Probably because it involved...blowing ourselves up. How did you train for such a one-way mission? How could I ask my men to participate?

I couldn't. But the Macros could have done so. Instead, they'd opted to do what we did. Probably because they'd witnessed it and found it very effective.

I frowned as the battle raged. My tough little gunships were on the front line now, and every one of them was taking a serious beating. Fortunately, they were doing plenty of damage in return. They weren't

283

very good at evading incoming fire, but their solid hulls usually took several hits before they were knocked out. They fought like bulldogs, while the lighter nanotech ships danced and dodged.

Missile barrages came in periodic waves. Usually, they were launched moments before a cruiser was destroyed. It was use-it-or-lose-it at that point, and the Macros understood that game. Each dying ship fired everything it had, and the rest of them fired one missile each. That way, there were a lot of targets to worry about. When the barrages came, Sarin shouted orders, pushing our destroyers forward with orders to concentrate on the missiles. We couldn't afford for them to get within range and blow a serious hole in our line.

I shook my head, it was such a simple tactic, but the Nanos had failed to come up with it on their own. They didn't like to switch targets in a fight. They certainly weren't military geniuses, these little ships. They were more technologically advanced in some ways, but they certainly were being outfought by the Macros. I had to wonder about that. Had the Blues intended for the Macros to conquer enemies? Were they originally warships, maybe put up defensively at first? The Nanos were the explorers, that much was obvious. But the Macros had been designed to construct more of themselves and fight. Who had they planned to fight against?

I watched as seven cruisers blew up in three fast minutes. A cheer went up from those of us surrounding the spherical display tank. By concentrating all our fire on one Macro at a time, we were taking them out quickly.

I was just beginning to grin when the Macros changed tactics. They turned and directed all their firepower at us, ignoring the flittering distraction the Nano ship swarm had become.

"They are launching something different, sir," the weapons officer said. "Not missiles—they look like mines or something."

I zoomed in on the scattering release of the nearest ship. Black objects came spinning out of the ports. They looked like flying saw blades—or flying spiders.

"They are fresh assault troops. They are throwing them at us now, just as we've done to them on several occasions."

"Should we launch our own marines?" Sarin asked me.

I looked at her for a moment, considering. "No. I don't think so. We are winning the gun battle. We don't have to board their ships. We can blast them all at range. Every minute, we are taking out more of them than they are of us. More importantly, if I send my men near the Macro fleet, the Nanos will probably fire on the marines. The Macro ships aren't good at hitting a single man in space—but the Nanos are. We can't risk it yet."

Inside the sphere, what had been three distinct groups of differently colored ships had turned into a wild mess. All three fleets were mixed up now, flashing past one another. We'd been slowing our charge for quite a while, but were still going too fast to reverse on a dime. Inertia had taken us past one another as both sides were braking, but not enough to stop all forward momentum. Soon, we'd all wheel around and make another run at close range.

I realized this had been the moment the enemy had been waiting for. They'd built jump-troops for this purpose, and now that all three sides were matching velocities and positions, they were releasing every assault robot they had. I could have played the same game, but I had only three hundred marines while they appeared to have thousands.

"What are your orders, sir?" Sarin asked.

I looked at her in surprise. I saw the worried look on her face. I'd let her run the battle for some time now, and she'd been doing fine. But now, she didn't know what to do. She didn't have a snappy set of orders to counter the enemy assault troops. It was time to stop daydreaming and assume operational command.

"Alert every ship to the danger. I want every laser we have targeting those assault bots unless they fire more missiles. The gunships should ignore them, and keep firing at the primary targets. As for my marines all my marines—get them suited up and waiting at the airlocks. Every marine is now assigned to localized ship defense. Some of the invaders are bound to get past the defensive fire and board our ships."

"Sir," Jasmine said, quietly. "The gunships don't have any marines aboard. Just Fleet people. I ordered all the marines onto the destroyers. I thought they would be more effective that way."

I nodded. It wasn't how I would have arranged it, but I understood her thinking. In hindsight, it had been a mistake. But I wasn't going to second-guess her publicly at this point.

"Tell the gunship crews to button up, then. They have thicker hulls than the nanotech ships. It will take the enemy time to burn through."

285

The fighting went on. At close quarters now, the ships were all hampered. The forward guns on *Goa* never seemed to stop firing for more than a few seconds—but their rate of fire was slowing down. They were having heat problems and I knew from experience that if you chain-fired one of the bigger cannons for too long, it warped the chamber and caused inaccuracies. Eventually, the system would overheat and quit working altogether. I ordered the ships to slow down their rate of fire to prevent this.

"Sir," Sarin said, looking up at me. "The first assault bots have reached our ships. They are attacking every unit in the fleet."

I nodded. I checked the active ship counts. The Nano fleet was down to less than fifty effectives—more than eighty percent of the Blue fleet had been destroyed. It was painful to watch. They were helping, but they could have been doing so much more. On our own side of the ledger, we had lost eleven gunships and two destroyers. Now that the assault bots were landing on every hull, I knew that number would go up.

"Time to get moving," I said. "I want every ship to fire their primary engines and get underway."

"But we are right in the middle of the enemy."

"Exactly. I no longer wish to be here. Hurry, pass on the order. We need to get some speed up."

The order was passed on, although only after Jasmine cast me a worried glance. What crazy plan did Riggs have now?

Full acceleration was a dramatic spectacle. We disengaged in less than a minute, becoming a separate, distinct mass of contacts that resembled a greenish cloud of fireflies inside the sphere. A few lagged behind. They were quickly caught and destroyed.

The Nano ships stayed with the Macros, of course. They weren't quitters, I could say that for them at least. Their flickering beams stabbed out, catching missiles and assault bots alike. Thousands were destroyed.

"We're outrunning their assault troops," Jasmine said.

"Yes," I said. "I've been out there, trying to jump from ship-to-ship. It's a tricky job. Ships have vastly more powerful engines than an assault troop's repellers. You can really only catch them if they let you, or if they are unaware you are coming."

286

"All those robots are flying around, with nothing to land on," Jasmine said, staring at the display globe. She looked at me, and for the first time today, she smiled. "You screwed them."

"That's my job," I said, and smiled in return.

I noticed even Sandra was smiling at both of us. For once, she wasn't suspicious of Jasmine or complaining about my risky decisions. She was just happy we were all still alive.

I wished I had a camera handy. I would have taken a picture.

-40-

The assault bots had been the enemy's last best hope. When we dodged them, they didn't quite know what to do. After reaching a range of about fifty thousand miles, I slowed and wheeled my fleet again to bring my main guns around to bear on the cruisers. The larger, slower-moving ships were taken out one at a time. The Nano ships were all destroyed, even *Alamo*. I transmitted private messages, one after another, calling for her to respond. She never did.

I felt conflicted about that ship. She had ruined my old life—but had given me a new one to replace it. She'd only been following orders laid down by the Blues in any case. She'd killed my kids, but she was a machine. It hadn't been personal.

If it hadn't been for *Alamo*, I'd never have become Colonel Riggs of Riggs' Pigs. There might not have ever been a Star Force. Who knew? Maybe Earth would be a cinder right now.

I brought over Miklos and Sloan to join in a command meeting on *Goa*. Everyone was relieved, but not jubilant. We'd lost a third of our fleet. The Nanos had limped home with less than twenty ships.

"Why didn't the last Nanos attack us at the end?" Sloan asked.

I turned to him and drew in a breath before explaining my personal opinion. "I'll give it an educated guess. They destroyed Socorro, the only ship that had crossed their defensive line back at the gas giant. They only engaged the Macros because they were fired upon. I don't think they ever associated our whole fleet with the rest of the targets.

288

We never got all that close, and so when the last Macro blew up, they called it a win and flew home."

"Weird," he said, "but I'll take it."

"Agreed. Now, let's talk about the next phase of the campaign—"

Captain Sarin cleared her throat. "Sir? I'd like to make a suggestion."

I frowned, but nodded slowly.

"We clearly have the Macros on the run, and taking down their bases one at a time will take time, but is worth doing."

I nodded, and my face smoothed out. I'd expected her to ask us to abandon the Eden system just as we were poised to capture it once and for all.

"I agree with your assessment, Captain," I said.

"But I would ask," Sarin said, pressing ahead quickly. "That you allow me to head for Earth. I've already been here longer than I'd anticipated. This ship is a key component of our home defense fleet."

My gut reaction was to deny the request, but I forced myself to consider the situation. I really liked this ship, and I wanted one for myself. But it wasn't right to simply commandeer *Goa* when there weren't any significant threats left in the system. The enemy had built very little ground force, reasoning that with five planets to defend, the fight would be won in space. Now that we'd destroyed their ships, the individual planets were almost helpless.

Moreover, returning the ship might help with relations between Earth and Eden...I paused, considering the thought I'd just had. Was that how it was now? Two separate political entities? Was such a thought exactly how all colonies began to break away?

I shook my head fractionally, rejecting the idea. I was still Star Force—as were Sarin and Crow. We might not be in the same place, but we were all on the same side. The last thing we needed in this war was more bickering amongst ourselves.

"Sir?" Sarin asked. She was still waiting for her answer.

"Just thinking for a moment—um, yes. Take your ship home, Captain. I think that would be best. Tell Admiral Crow about our victory at Eden. Tell him I will be coming home in time as well, when this flank is secure. At that point, I will secure our other flank, keeping enemies out of our home systems from both directions. The rings will be fortified, and we will control who comes in or goes out."

Captain Sarin seemed surprised, but relieved. I could tell she'd been thinking hard about how to ask me. She'd probably come up with a counter to every argument I might give her—but I hadn't give her any of them. I'd simply let her go.

The next three days saw the liberation of two more Centaur worlds. The one we were in orbit over was easy and quick. I brought down my gunships from orbit and destroyed the domes by overloading them with railgun fire. By sending in a platoon of charging marines and about a thousand Centaur troops when the dome was fizzling and brown, I was able to capture two more of the gigantic production facilities. The third one, however, blew itself up. More than thirty good men died. I cursed and drank that night as we flew to the next planet.

This time, we proceeded more cautiously. We bombarded the dome until it went down entirely, planning to damage the production facility from the air after it was defenseless. That way, even if it blew up, it wouldn't take any of my men with it.

It didn't work out that way. As soon as the dome went down, the factory detonated. It was the same with the rest. The Macros apparently didn't want to give us any more factories. I didn't blame them, but I did curse them.

When the last Macro stronghold fell two weeks after the Battle for Eden, as it became known, we'd captured a grand total of three factories that were in working order. Still, I had to count myself lucky. The system was free of the enemy machines at last.

Goa left the system just before we assaulted the last world. I watched Jasmine go through the ring to the Helios system with conflicted feelings. I wondered when we would meet again, and under what circumstances.

I forced away such thoughts and turned back to the final assault. We'd moved as quickly as we could, not wanting to give the Macros time to build any new ships. I was worried they would imitate our ship designs, producing smaller ships in a shorter amount of time. But apparently, whatever flash of insight had guided them to recent advances was not to be repeated. They put out a few dozen large war machines with anti-air flechette systems on their backs, but that was all. We took them out from orbit then worked the domes down until they committed suicide.

I was only slightly disappointed in the end. We'd managed to save most of the Centaur civilians, and had gained a vastly more powerful infrastructure. Three Macro production units and a matching number of Nano factories represented an astounding level of output.

I had a celebratory beer with Miklos, Kwon and Sloan. Sandra crashed the party at about beer number five. She had a few with us, then began kissing on me. The rest of the guys exchanged amused glances and left.

Sandra immediately left my lap and sat across from me. I looked at her in surprise.

"Did you chase them off on purpose?" I asked.

"I wanted to talk."

I sighed. I'd been hoping for more than just talk. "Okay, what's on your mind?"

"I don't trust Jasmine."

I shrugged. "I can understand that."

"She's going to tell Crow everything. About the factories, the battle, and our new tactics."

"That's called a debriefing, Sandra," I told her. "I'm expecting her to do that. It would be a dereliction of duty not to inform the good Admiral of every detail."

Sandra pursed her lips. "You never told me about what went on between you two. I mean, how did we end up taking over her ship?"

I took a long draw on my beer, finishing it. I leaned forward with a roar and slammed it down on the table. The can and the table both crumpled a bit at the impact. I wasn't angry, I was just feeling good.

"I'm withholding that information," I said. "Let's just say that we had a difference of opinion, and I straightened her out concerning her command status."

"Do you think she'll report that part? About being demoted to a Captain?"

I chuckled. "I'm not sure. Knowing Jasmine, I think she probably will. She's usually a stickler for the rules."

"Then why did she turn on you?"

"That was our fault—I mean Crow and I caused it. We've never been clear enough with our subordinates about who has the final authority in any given situation. The truth was, I was so surprised by her action I reacted on gut instinct. I probably could have handled it better."

291

"There wasn't time. You had a battle to fight. Jasmine didn't know what she was doing."

"She learned a lot, I think."

Sandra finally returned to my lap. She kissed me then, and everything felt good for a while.

"Do you still have feelings for her?" she asked suddenly.

I hesitated, blinking and thinking. I knew I'd been tricked. A man's defenses are always down when a female is in his arms. He's liable to say things he'll regret later—or in my case, not to say them fast enough.

Her smile turned into an instant glare. Her hand moved with blurring speed. I knew the slap was coming—but it didn't land.

Both of us looked at her hand in surprise. I'd reached up and grabbed her wrist, stopping her dead. She struggled to pull away her hand, but I held her tightly. I didn't want her to haul off and try to hit me again.

She stared at me for a second in confusion. "You aren't that fast," she said. "No one is faster than me."

"I am now."

"Oh—those baths. Damn that robot. I should take him apart. Let go of my hand."

"Are we going to kiss or fight?"

She thought about it for a second. She wriggled and I let go of her hand. She crossed her arms and looked annoyed. I waited.

"Okay," she said finally, her anger melting. "We'll kiss."

Half an hour later, we fell asleep together. Neither of us stirred for about ten hours. It had been a long campaign.

* * *

The greatest construction project of my career began immediately after my morning shower and breakfast. Finally, at long last, I was ready to build the fortifications I'd envisioned the day I'd found Hel and the ring nearby. It would be a long, difficult effort, but I felt I had the production capacity to do it right now.

My first idea was to take all three of the Macro factories to Hel and begin churning out massive amounts of weaponry. I decided against it, in the end. Instead, I left the facilities I'd set up at the bottom of the mining pit on Eden-11 where they were. That one Nano factory and one Macro factory, being fed a continuous flow of minerals by our own Macro workers, was a production miracle. The operation built new gunships every day, and I liked it that way. If the enemy came at us again, I wanted plenty of fresh ships. I couldn't run an empire without a fleet.

I frowned as I thought of the word *empire*. Was that what I was doing? Building an empire? I didn't really like the term. I preferred *federation*, or *republic*.

There were several races involved in this war with us. Certainly, Earth was the only biotic species with a significant military right now, but over time that may well change. There were so many things to work out. I hadn't even considered trade treaties and the like. Who owned the various terran planets in this system, for example? Were they the sole possessions of the Centaurs?

I tried to push these complexities away. Usually, such matters were above the pay grade of soldiers. I liked it that way. I had enough to worry about just organizing the defeat of the enemy.

Trying to forget about empires, I focused on my original goal. I hauled two Macro production units and two Nano factories out to the frozen rock we'd named Hel. Two of the Nano factories had come from the Centaurs. They'd given them up easily enough when I'd asked. I'd really needed them to match up with a Macro production unit. Together, I could produce new things on a grand scale.

I felt like a kid in a sandbox as I surveyed the frozen rock we called Hel. Fortunately, Macros didn't need much sunlight or an atmospherc to function. I built a large number of worker bots first, smart ones with nanite tentacles as well as Macro-type claws and drilling heads. The machines dug in, providing a vast bounty of metals, water to break down for fuel and other useful compounds. All I had to do was order the factories to build stuff with the endless minerals.

And build they did. Within a month, the skeleton of the battle station took shape. It was simple enough in design, really. I decided flat surfaces were easier to design and place equipment on than curved ones, so I built a giant cube. As I thought of new things to add, the cube elongated somewhat into a rectangular obelisk. Generators went in first, then weapons. The marines complained, but I didn't give them more than a few thousand square feet for living space to start. Eventually, they would have hot showers, mess halls and even a theater or two. But to begin with, I wanted firepower. The entire endeavor would be a sick joke if Macros showed up early and attacked something that amounted to the terran equivalent of a Centaur habitat.

So they complained, and I ignored them, and we all kept building. After working on the battle station for two solid months, I got an idea. It had been growing on me over time. Partly, it was due to the grueling cold and discomfort of working in deep space. My men and I could not help but look sunward, eying those lovely planets. We all wondered if we would ever be able to take a sweet vacation on an untouched tropical beach, or hike up a green-carpeted mountain.

My idea was a predatory idea, to some degree, and it made me frown at myself. But I felt the stakes were very high for the future of my race, so I decided to talk to the Centaurs about it. What could it hurt?

I flew closer to the inner planets and sat in a ship among the Centaur worlds. I watched the planet orbit quietly through thick glass, and admired them each in turn as I flew from one to another.

It took nearly a full day to contact members of the Centaur leadership to discuss a serious domestic matter. They were understandably busy with the repopulation of their homeworld.

"Hello, this is Colonel Kyle Riggs," I said, when I'd finally found someone from their highest council. "Who am I talking to?"

"One who has been chosen to lead many."

I nodded. They always gave me answers like that. They had names, but they weren't really much help. They were mostly named after plants they liked to eat, or various shapes of stones, or the soft notes that the wind made. They had about a hundred words each for wind-sounds and rock-shapes.

Contacting the herds was always problematic. They didn't have a social structure that was very clear to me, even now. As closely as I understood their politics, they had a system that was vaguely feudal in nature. An oligarchy, as my political theory textbook would have called it. But it wasn't necessarily a hereditary oligarchy. Usually, the most powerful ram was accepted as the leader of a given group. Sometimes the female ewes ran things, but it was less common. This system worked well enough for a few hundred individuals, but they needed to take it to a higher level to function with vast herds numbering in the millions. Their solution was simple and almost charming. In the spring, they gathered all the local herds and held contests between the leaders. These contests measured relative wit, agility and fighting prowess. It wasn't all head-butting, but there was certainly an element of physical struggle. When the best of the best were selected, they formed a herd of their own, so to speak. This was their oligarchy.

Viewed from a human perspective, it didn't seem like such a political system could really function in an advanced society. But the Centaurs had an advantage over us: they truly were herd creatures. They followed their leaders to the death. They might struggle over mates, but they did not fight violent wars amongst themselves the way we'd done for millennia. They were highly cooperative, and that led to group efforts and surprising achievements. In comparison, I was almost embarrassed by our complex, back-stabbing society.

"I wish to discuss the worlds in your star system," I said when I finally got the right Centaur representative online. I felt a bit guilty as I brought the topic up. It felt like I was trying to borrow money—a lot of money.

"The winds over time are profuse."

"Yes..." I said, as if I knew what he meant. "And there are many worlds here in this system. We would like to utilize some of them to build defenses for this star system. At any time, the enemy machines might return. We must be strong to meet them."

"The ram must be powerful to win the ewe."

"Right. So, let me ask you straight out: can we have a planet or two?"

There was a moment of hesitation. I wasn't sure if they were thinking it over, or trying to understand what I was talking about.

When the Nano ships had first come, they'd been a socially simplistic people with advanced technology. They were bright, and knew how to construct things they needed such as communications systems, bridges, dams and shelters. When the Nano ships had shown up and allowed them to use their factories, they'd used them in a much more responsible fashion than the people of Earth had done. In a short amount of time, they'd built arks to colonize the various wild worlds of their star system. These arks were now parked in permanent orbit over these worlds, and still held most of their surviving members.

Back on Earth, we'd fought and squabbled over the factories from the start. Sure, we hadn't had them for as long, nor had we been given much leisure time with them. We'd been pressed from the very

295

beginning to build military equipment to face the Macros. But still, we could have done better if all of us had cooperated as the Centaurs had.

When Centaur leader finally answered, he spoke confidently. "We have no need for any world that lacks a blue sky. Please make use of them."

"Thank you," I said. "That is most generous."

"The ground will shake with your pounding feet, even if there is no air to allow sounds to be made. A pity. Can there be honor for an army with silent feet?"

"Uh, I don't know. No—I take that back. I do know. *Of course* there can be honor for a quiet army. Honor is won on the battlefield through victory. If an army saves the young back home, it does not matter where the battle took place."

"Wisely said. We will relay your words to countless ears."

"That's great," I said, struggling a bit with what to say next. As always, talking to the Centaurs was a delicate affair. I felt even less comfortable, as I was trying to talk them out of one of their worlds. It was like asking a shy girl out on a date, without knowing a single word of her language. You had to stay friendly and patient, and keep working hard to figure out any hint of what she was thinking.

"What are your intentions for the blue-sky worlds?" I asked. "I know you built arks and flew them there, but the Macros interrupted your plans."

"In our waking dreams, we see vast herds on these planets. They have grasses of a different flavor, and winds with a different *schtifft*, but we will adapt."

The reason I was interested in the warmer worlds was simple enough: they were empty. The Centaurs had abandoned the habitat over Eden-11 first. They'd move their other habitats to Eden-11 as well, and were quickly repopulating their homeworld. They much preferred cooler mountain ranges and the stark blue skies. This left the other habitable worlds unoccupied for now.

I cleared my throat and went for it. "We humans breathe air as you do. We enjoy blue skies and cool winds. We need a place to live if we are to stay here long. Right now, we are stuck inside our cramped ships, just as your people once were."

There was a long pause. "We have dishonored ourselves!" the voice said at last. "When this is relayed, a hundred herd-leaders will trot off the nearest cliff in shame! A travesty has occurred!"

"Um, I'm not sure what you mean. I only wished—"

"Of course you do! You want what we cherish, the wind in your fur, the rain in your nostrils as you run. We are shamed, as we've been poor hosts. Always, it is the receiver of gifts who is blind. Honor has been lost, ours has been shed and given to by our unthinking selfishness."

"Hold on, I only meant—"

"The answer is *yes*, stalwart allies! How many of the six blue skies will you have? How many will hold your people?"

"Uh…" I said, my eyes wide. Greed gripped me, and I almost asked for five. But then I took a deep breath. "One will be enough. It will hold us all."

"You prove your loyalty and generosity time and again. Three you shall have. Our share of these lands shall be equal. We insist. Which three shall it be?"

I thought hard for a moment. My heart was pounding. I knew I was making history, and I had to think, but it was difficult. Their own world was lovely, but the ice caps were huge. It was like Earth in an ice age. Each of the other worlds was warmer as they progressed sunward. I figured the middle worlds were the best, but I knew that the Centaurs liked it a little cooler than my people did. They had a heavy coat of fur, after all.

"We would prefer the innermost worlds," I said.

"Done and done! Our arks will not return to those places, and our people will egress only upon the cooler planets. They will walk under alien clouds and graze until their bellies sag. They will—"

The Centaurs went on for some time in this fashion, talking about rivers and lakes and crags of uniquely-shaped stone. I let them talk this time, without cutting them off. I let them talk and talk until they felt thoroughly finished with the conversation. Perhaps from their point of view, it was the politest discussion they'd ever had with me. I figured they'd more than earned it.

When they eventually ran out of gas and I thanked them one last time before closing the communication channel, I sat back and stared at the nanite ceiling. I could scarcely believe the magnitude of what I'd just done. If we could keep these worlds—if we could colonize them—I'd made a future for millions upon millions of souls. Generations to come would learn of this day in their textbooks.

I felt a little guilty, of course. There were precedents from the past, such as the Louisiana Purchase. For fifteen million dollars, President Jefferson had bought the central third of the United States from Napoleon. Some years later, they'd bought Alaska from the Russians for only seven million.

I was worse than those guys. I'd talked the natives out of their land, offering only protection. I was more like the German guy who'd bought Manhattan from the Indians for twenty-four bucks. The Centaurs didn't think of ownership the way we did. No individual wished to possess more territory than the patch of earth he roamed upon. They didn't build fences or enforce no-trespassing signs. I knew that humanity, once we had sunk our teeth into those three planets, would defend them like wolverines defending their dens. Long after I was dead and gone—provided the Macros didn't wipe us out—the Centaurs may well be abused by people who had even less scruples than I did.

But still, I couldn't say no. Who could have turned down three blue-green jewels hanging in the perfect zone of space? Liquid water could only exist in a narrow zone around any star. The star I'd named Eden had a higher output of heat than our own sun, and the inhabitable zone of space was marginally larger, about a hundred million miles wide. Within that thin band six worlds circled. I knew that to find a system like this, with a yellow sun so stable and perfect, we might have to search for a thousand years.

Troubled and elated at the same time, I stood up and headed for the bridge. It was time to spread the news.

-41-

It was months later when the ring orbiting Hel shivered again. We detected it instantly this time, and I sent ships through to recon the situation on the far side. They came back and reported they'd seen nothing changed in the system owned by the Crustaceans. No Macro ships had appeared. Nothing appeared to have changed at all.

I paced and worried in the heart of my battle station. I was in a grand command center, buried nearly a mile deep inside rock and steel. At first, I'd hauled mass up from Hel to serve as armor, but I soon determined I needed too much, too fast. So, I'd sent a fleet of gunships to a region of the system peppered with asteroids, and had them bring home thirty or so of those floating rocks. The battle station thus had transformed from a dull metal cube into an amorphic mass. The cube inside was almost invisible now, coated in layers of hard rock. In between the brick-like stones, I'd troweled in nanite-laden smart metals and placed thousands of weapons. Sensor pods were located in clusters, aiming in every conceivable direction. The base even had repellers, and could slowly rotate itself in space. It didn't have real engines, nor enough power to escape Hel's gravitational influence. But it could maneuver, and if one side of the base took a pounding, it could turn to face invaders with a fresh set of weaponry.

The command center at the core of the station was very similar to the one I'd envied aboard *Goa*. I now had my own spherical tank of nanites taught to display thousands of moving elements simultaneously in three dimensions. Around it sat a team of operators. Soon, I knew I was going to have to return to Earth if only to gather more personnel to run this base. When I came back, I intended to bring colonists as well to inhabit the worlds I'd been given by the Centaurs.

"Sir," Miklos said, "I don't understand it. This has to be some form of communication using the rings, but how are they doing it?"

We'd all been puzzling over the phenomena. I'd originally thought it was the Blues who'd used the rings to call the Nano ships home to defend their planet. Miklos believed the Macros had used the rings to somehow alert distant bases.

"I'm not sure *how* they do it," I said, "but someone just made the rings shiver. As the Macros are now absent from the star systems on both sides of this ring, and we know *we* didn't do it, logic dictates—"

"Yes, yes," Miklos said. "It looks like you were right. The Blues are transmitting messages via the rings. But to who?"

I raised a finger and paused in my pacing. I stepped to the spherical tank and touched the control screens. The nanites inside quickly reconfigured themselves and displayed the entire system. I drew a line from the gas giant known as Eden-12 to Hel.

"Maybe," I said, "maybe we are down to only a few possible culprits. The Blues are number one on the list now, but don't forget the Centaurs are still here, as are the Crustaceans on the far side. Hell, even the Microbes might be more advanced than we think."

"But…it was most likely the Blues this time."

"Yeah," I agreed. "But who knows for sure?"

A clattering sound made me turn away from Miklos. Marvin was shuffling his cameras. Only one watched me, as the rest were on the tank in front of him. The single eye that kept me in view was a sneaky one: he had attached it to a region that would be about knee-level on a human. That single camera eye was tilted up just below the lip of the circular table that surrounded the sphere. It was hard to see, unless you knew what to look for.

"Have you got something to say, Marvin?" I asked.

"No."

"Are you sure? You've been remarkably quiet about the rings, and about these communications that appear to be relayed through them. Aren't you the least bit curious?"

Several more cameras peeped out from behind the sphere. I walked around it, and stood over him.

"I was curious, yes."

"What do you mean, you *were* curious? What's changed?" I asked with my hands on my hips. I frowned down at him.

"You are displaying a look of displeasure."

Marvin had become better at recognizing expressions. He hadn't missed this one. "Tell me what you know," I said.

"The rings are capable of transmitting a signal. This signal has no detectable emission through space. Instead, it appears to operate on the same principle as the rings themselves."

"You mean, you don't know how they work—but they do?"

"Yes."

"And how do you know they can be utilized in this manner?"

"Because I just did it."

We all stared at him. "You did *what?*" I demanded, my voice turning into a shout.

"You are displeased."

"Yes, I am. You didn't tell me you were trying to make the rings send a signal. Who did you send it to? What did you say?"

"I sent an enquiry, and requested an acknowledgement. I'm not sure who may receive the message."

Miklos made a choking sound that turned into a fit of coughing. I ignored him and glowered at Marvin. "You did this without authorization?"

"Yes."

"Why, Marvin?"

"I wanted to see what would happen."

At length, he explained how he had done his little parlor trick. He'd studied the ring and its composition carefully. By building a tiny replica, and exerting force upon it, he'd caused a sort of resonance to be set up between the model ring and the real one. When I asked to see it, he showed me something that looked like a smudge of charcoal. He explained that size was not an issue, and the key was to get the structure right. He'd used nanites to build a tiny ring of matching structure and composition. Then he'd applied forces to the tiny ring, which was almost microscopic. The larger ring had responded by relaying his signal to parts unknown.

I ordered him to cease and desist with all such experiments and transmissions. I raved for a time, telling him he might have alerted every Macro in the galaxy to our presence.

Marvin rejected this line of reasoning, however. "That is not a sensible conclusion."

"Why not?"

"First of all, the Macros are clearly in possession of the technology to send signals through the rings, meaning they already know of our position here."

"What proof do you have of that claim?"

"This was evidenced in several ways, but most directly by their use of simulated Star Force Marines. The Macros in this system had never witnessed those combat techniques directly, and yet they attempted to duplicate them. They must have gotten the design idea from somewhere."

I thought about that. "Yes, we destroyed all the ships that ever witnessed our use of assault troops in space."

"Similarly, Captain Miklos is clearly correct in his assumptions. The Blues have this technology and used it to recall the Nano ships from the Crustacean world when they felt threatened by the growing fleets in the system."

I nodded. Star Force and the Macros had reached a point where they were frightening, and the Blues had summoned their Nano ships back home to orbit their gas giant. They'd planned to hide behind them, but of course, I'd changed those plans for them.

"Well," I said at last. "What's done is done. But I'm ordering you to talk to me before you get any more bright ideas about contacting distant star systems. This base is not yet fully operational. I need time to construct a platform that can overcome any number of Macro ships."

"Logically, that would require an infinite amount of time."

I growled and began pacing again, not bothering to answer him. I went back to building my battle station as fast as I could. At the same time, I would slowly build up my fleet. I wasn't sure what was going on back home on Earth, but when I flew back there, I didn't plan to go alone.

Books by B. V. Larson:

STAR FORCE SERIES
Swarm
Extinction
Rebellion
Conquest
Battle Station
Empire
Annihilation

IMPERIUM SERIES
Mech Zero: The Dominant
Mech 1: The Parent
Mech 2: The Savant
Mech 3: The Empress
Five By Five (Mech Novella)

OTHER SF BOOKS
Technomancer
The Bone Triangle
Z-World
Velocity

Visit BVLarson.com for more information.

5111980R00171

Printed in Great Britain
by Amazon.co.uk, Ltd.,
Marston Gate.